INCOGNITO

I0594024

MOIRA McGHEE

Published by INUFOR – Independent
Network of UFO Researchers

INCOGNITO

A novel about extraterrestrial beings who have integrated with humans and Earth society.

All characters in this publication are fictitious, and any resemblance to real persons, living or dead is purely co-incidental

Copyright © 2019 by Moira McGhee.

All rights reserved.

ISBN 978-0-9587045-7-1

Printed in Australia.

INUFOR. P.O. Box 169, Katoomba NSW 2780 AUSTRALIA

ind.net.ufo.res@bigpond.com

www.independentnetuforesearchers.com.au

INCOGNITO

MOIRA McGHEE

CHAPTER 1

Commander Aldon didn't normally dance on duty. Today was an exception, and he boogied across the room to express his joy and anticipation. At long last he was getting some companionship and assistance. It could be lonely and isolated confined on the Terrans' Main Earth Base, so far from his home planet, out there in the Galaxy.

Despite some limited contact with their agents on the surface, sometimes the crushing tedium of repetitious tasks really got him down. There were the two little grey biological robot workers, types of cybernetic organisms, Thelta and Delta. They did what they were told, and were controlled by a telepathic mastermind.

Although Aldon also had Andy, a very advanced human looking android, he was still the product of artificial intelligence. They may talk to each other, and engage in games of skill and intelligence, but it was not the same as being with another unique individual Terran like himself.

He could hear the sounds of the shuttle craft arriving in the landing bay, and rushed to the door as a familiar figure entered. "Martina!" he exclaimed in surprise.

"Why? Were you expecting another male as an assistant?" the attractive woman retorted.

"No..no," Aldon stammered, "it's just a surprise that you are here. I can see by your insignia you have been promoted to Captain."

She smiled. "I was promoted after the Xvar Wars, but it all took its toll on me, physically and psychologically. The Guardians decided it would be a good break for me to help you co-ordinate our people who are assisting on planet Earth."

Aldon went on to conduct Martina around the base which, although relatively small, was self sufficient and contained all the equipment they needed, living space and more than enough supplies. It was bright, with spacious control areas. Through the windows, which looked like part of the cliff from the exterior, she could see the blue sky outside.

"You must understand," he explained, "this is strictly a 'need to know' Base. Some humans, and also our Xvar adversaries and their allies, must realise it exists. Nobody except our own trusted Terrans can know of its location.

"We are underground, and normally only accessible by transporter or our own craft. They arrive and depart from the two concealed entrances, one in the side of the cliff, and the other under the nearby sea-bed. If all else fails, here is the one and only exit/entry to the surface. It is well camouflaged and must only be used in an emergency.

"This facility should always remain top secret. Sometimes our envoys come to meetings with various governments, but they rarely come here, and usually arrive by craft at a specific place on the surface."

Aldon started to explain her posting was not as easy as she imagined. "Because of the strict non-interference policy, everyone is working under the radar with more subtle methods. Most of our Terrans here on Earth have integrated, incognito, with the general population. While their main target is to influence various areas of concern, it is not easy due to a multitude of competing nationalities, powerful corporations and aggressive militaries. In recent years there has been the added complication of Xvar/Katon infiltration and manipulation.

"We have quite a few agents, many with respectable professions such as scientists, teachers, doctors, vets, and shop and cafe owners. One is a priest, who comes in handy when we have to hide someone, either under the church or disguised as a nun! Some of our people masquerade as inconspicuous gypsies and street people.

"It has been more difficult to create some false identities since Earth discovered computers and digital technology, but we can usually get around that."

"What about the humans we raised ourselves," Martina asked, "and all the contactees we took on our craft and implanted or genetically enhanced?"

Aldon frowned, "These people present a bit more of a problem. There are some who can be relied upon, and we meet them in the few 'Friendship Clubs' we have initiated. The rest are not 100%, and if we have to contact them it is usually telepathically or in isolated areas. Most have all the human frailties and a tendency to confide in family or other people. Sometimes they can be persuaded to 'swap sides'. Their governments and big corporations try to seek them out and use any means they can to persuade them to 'tell all'. They are not so useful if we have to block their memories.

"We must steer this planet into peaceful and more co-operative behaviour before their advanced knowledge allows them to venture out into the galaxy, where the Guardians fear they could cause havoc. We are also fearful that some of our less ethical neighbours, such as the Xvars and Katons, are also enticing these humans with gifts of dangerous technology."

Martina smiled, "I hope I'm up for the challenge. I have already been given some training and insights. I know how important it is that we retain control of all our outposts in this star system"

Aldon nodded; "But neither the Guardians nor the Council have any idea of the other problems I've got! While they are only here for a limited time, as our own Terrans assimilate with the human population they tend to adopt some of these people's less than desirable behaviour. I'm forever getting them out of all the sticky situations they should never have gotten into in the first place!"

A warning light started flashing on the monitor and Aldon commented, "You can see one of them, whom I think you already know, arriving just now. She is not exactly respectable, and can cause problems"

Andy called out - "Incoming" – and a man and woman, both very wet and naked, appeared in the teleportation dock.

The woman turned and looked at her two colleagues. "Is this the officer you wanted?"

Aldon, suddenly feeling embarrassed at Martina's presence, tried not to look directly at the couple. "Yes. You've done well. We need to find out if they know about our Base on Mars. If so, do they have any plans to attack or infiltrate us. With a bit of luck we may get some security codes. Nothing to be concerned about! Just like all the others - he won't remember a thing."

Andy leapt into action and took hold of the tubby middle-aged man, placing the metal memory transfer unit on his head, and injecting a minute implant into his bloodstream.

Martina stared at the attractive blond haired woman who was assisting Andy with her very confused male companion. "Chantelle!" she gasped in horror. "What do you think you are doing? You were banished from the Zarcon Base for seducing the boss's husband! Don't tell me you are still up to your old tricks!"

"I'll explain everything later." Chantelle replied, as she held her glassy-eyed captive. "Don't worry, he'll forget all about this!" They both re-entered the teleporter and disappeared.

Aldon glanced across at the stunned Martina. "Chantelle is one of our best agents. It was decided to utilise her seduction skills to our advantage. She set herself up as an earthling 'callgirl' – a woman men seek out and pay for sex. Because she is so good at her job many important men and military officers engage her services. Nobody suspects that we are accessing all their memories and knowledge, besides implanting biological monitoring devices."

"But she was naked," Martina protested, "they both were!" Aldon went on to explain how the shower in Chantelle's expensive apartment was in fact a transporter which humans could neither recognise nor activate.

"She gets her prey into the shower, up here, and back again without them recalling any of it. We have gathered so much valuable intelligence through her. The only problem is she has developed too much of a liking for her job, along with the presents and money. She tends to forget that her occupation is very dangerous, especially if her true identity is discovered."

Martina spent the next few days familiarising herself with the base. The equipment and protocols were similar to those on other Terran Bases. There was direct communication with their main Solar System 'Control

4

Base'. A telepathic translation unit and a direct, encrypted communication device connected with their agents on Earth. In addition to the transporter and escape tunnel, they had their own shuttle craft in the docking port. Aldon promised that shortly she would be able to go on the surface, mingle with the population, and meet some of their agents.

Aldon himself was looking forward to getting out into the fresh air. He had been going 'stir crazy' cooped up underground. There was a strict rule that the main Earth Base must be manned by a Terran at all times, and could not be left with Andy solely in control, no matter how advanced his artificial intelligence.

After a couple of days he made his first brief trip to the surface to see Victor, one of their agents, who had merged into the population as a bookshop/coffee lounge owner in a provincial city. Victor had been told he was not a Terran. Rather, he was one of the genetically enhanced humans who had been born and raised on their Solar Base. His posting was important in that he ran the 'Friendship Club', where some of their 'helpers' met under the pretext of holding 'Book Club' meetings.

The location of the shop was ideal. Nobody suspected that some of the Book Club members were in fact very trusted Terran hybrids and contactees who were assisting Victor and Aldon in their efforts. Not even the 'friends', whom they called 'protégées' knew that in Victor's upstairs flat was another tubular shower transporter. It was also available for any other agent who needed refuge or a quick get-away.

Victor tried to hide his surprise as Aldon sat down and ordered a coffee. "What are you doing here? Normally it is me who has to come and see you."

Aldon grinned, "Now I have a Terran assistant I'm free at last – free at long last!" He went on to tell of Martina's arrival, and how he would soon meet her. "But," he added, "nobody must know her true identity. These are dangerous times. You can show her around the area, but people must think she is just a relative or a casual girlfriend."

"I agree," said Victor. "We have had a couple of new customers that make me feel wary. I know the government takes an interest in

UFO/alien experiencers, and it would be a real feather in their cap if they could identify me, let alone capture one of our agents."

"That is not our only problem," Aldon sighed. "Solar Base has confirmed that the Xvars are disobeying the 'no direct interference rules' and secretly liaising with the Katons to gain a foothold on this planet. It is rumoured they have already given dangerous advance technology to these people we are trying to help evolve peacefully."

Victor gave Aldon a nervous glance. "What will that mean for us? Will we or our friends be in any further danger? Will they try to hunt us down?"

"Exactly! We could be in jeopardy from not only the customary human organisations but also the Xvars and their agents." Aldon confirmed.

"While Martina and I may risk attending the occasional get-together, none of our other people can risk being known. I hope you and the other Terrans are following the rules, and when you have to meet only arriving and leaving, as I did, through the transporter in your flat?"

"Of course," Victor assured him, "none of our agents ever go downstairs when there are meetings, so no-one, not even our 'friends', can recognise them."

Aldon finished his drink. "Best coffee I've had in a long time! Before I go I'll take a quick stroll in the town, and enjoy the fresh air and scenery. When I return, can you have a bag of those delicious pastries ready for me to take back to Base?"

Back on the Base Martina had settled into her quarters, which comprised of a bedroom and an office/lounge room. They were small but adequate. She had established good communications and understanding with Andy, and Thelta and Delta proved reliable little workers.

Martina was looking forward to meeting everybody on the surface, and getting familiar with this planet, which was supposed to be very beautiful. She was still coming to terms with Chantelle's current role. They had been good friends, especially when they were together at the military college, and later comrades in arms during the Xvar campaign. Hopefully they could spend some time with each other in the future. Martina wondered if she would even be able to show Chantelle the 'error of her ways'.

When Aldon returned with the pastries, she thought maybe Earth might be quite an enjoyable place after all. She wondered about Aldon. He seemed very serious and dedicated to his work. She had known him some years back, on another base. He was different then – a family man, very likable and full of fun. Afterwards she heard that his wife and children had been killed in a Xvar attack on their home village.

Martina had always been attracted to Aldon, and wondered what the future held now they were working together. Perhaps their superiors had, in their wisdom, posted her here to cheer him up, and coax him out of his lonely self-protective shell and isolation. They had indicated that they expected her to report back if there was anything of concern in his behaviour. They were worried that his hatred of the Xvars could cause him to take some unsanctioned action against their enemies who were also trying to influence and eventually control the planet.

A few days later Andy called out, "Victor identified and incoming." Before he arrived Aldon had explained that people with Victor's status had restrictions on their transporters, which Base scanned and monitored each time before activation.

"I thought the combined telepathic, microchip and biological recognition was enough?" Martina queried.

"Not if their identity is discovered," Aldon warned. "One of our opponents may try to use it to invade this base."

Martina turned to meet Victor as he came into the room to greet her. She remembered him vaguely from Solar Base, several years ago, when he had been much younger. Now he appeared to be middle-aged, with a light brown moustache and thinning hair.

"Martina! You haven't changed a bit!" he observed. "Not like me. Time is taking its toll on my looks!"

She was actually surprised that he was on planet Earth, as he had spent most of his life on Solar Base. Victor had always considered it to be his home and family, and had resisted previous attempts to even visit the planet of his ancestry. Aldon told her that more recently Victor had shown an interest in his own people and their future.

The only concern, which Aldon shared with the Guardians, was that he may be tempted to look into his true origins and the identity of his biological parents.

Martina was to go with Victor on a trip to his bookshop. Aldon told her that since it was her first experience on the planet, this was just a social occasion. Any further trips would require additional security measures and monitoring, which he would provide later.

"Before you go," Aldon said, "you must pack your uniform away, and change into these Earth clothes which Victor has brought for you. From now onwards you must always avoid looking conspicuous. He will take you on a shopping trip to buy you some suitable outfits."

After they beamed back into Victor's flat they agreed that she would pose as a relative, visiting from out of town. Martina couldn't wait to learn more about Earth. Even though she knew what to expect, once they got out into the street it took some time to familiarise herself with the buildings, streets and their archaic transportation system.

The shopping expedition into a local department store was a new experience for Martina. Victor was quietly at her side, suggesting a choice of suitable outfits. She had mentioned that slacks and tops would allow her the freedom to move in a hurry if the situation required. He could hear her giggling in the changing rooms as she tried on various garments. Every so often she would throw something out, and he would pass a replacement through the door.

They left with several bags of Martina's new wardrobe, and walked on to the local park. Victor explained more about the bookshop along the way.

"It is a very important asset in our work here. Several members of the Friendship Club help us individually with many covert projects, but it can be risky. We keep everything compartmentalised on a 'need to know' basis. Any instructions always come through me, as an intermediary. Except in an emergency they must never know the identity of any of our other contacts, especially our own Terrans here.

"When they meet the normal official discussion is about books and also projects and campaigns to improve the Earth, both its people and ecology. Within the group are quite a few humans we have had contact with, and are monitoring. Some are already partially Terran since we genetically enhanced their parents before they were conceived. All these protégées have their own private little 'support group'. The trusted members counsel those who are still a little confused about our intervention and what happened during our contact with them."

Martina looked up at the blue sky above and the trees and flowers around her. There were ducks on the pond, and she could hear the birds singing as she drew in a deep breath of the fresh air.

"How could these humans not look after one of the most beautiful homes in the galaxy? So full of life! Don't they realise that everything is connected and inter-dependent?"

"It's not just their environment they're destroying," Victor sighed. "They are full of greed and aggression, killing not only the wildlife but millions of their own fellow beings. You can understand why the Guardians want to contain them on their own planet until they mend their ways."

They walked back to the bookshop and Victor commented on how much he enjoyed her visit and being able to discuss their work – a subject which was taboo in the normal community. He didn't get to meet with other agents very often.

Martina paused, "Before I go back can I ask a favour?"

"Your wish is my command." Victor replied, giving a little bow.

"Can I have a cup of your delicious coffee, and some of those yummy pastries for Aldon as well? They're much nicer than the boring, healthy food at the Base"

As they sat at the table, enjoying their coffee break, a smartly dressed man came in and ordered some lunch. There was something about him that made Martina uneasy.

"Who's your friend?" he asked Victor. "Some new romantic interest you've been hiding?"

"No, she's just my cousin who popped in while passing through town on a shopping trip."

Martina noticed that in between eating his meal the fellow was continually staring at her. Victor said nothing, but she could pick up his thoughts which were advising caution. After the man left, Victor told Martina that he suspected he maybe some form of government agent, or even a Katon spy, trying to identify and hunt down the Terrans and their friends.

"There is a clandestine war going on for control of planet Earth and its people. We want the best for humans, so they can progress to joining the Galactic community, but the Xvars and Katons don't care about them. They have ambitions of their own, and only want control so they can establish their own bases here."

Martina arrived back at Earth Base a short time later, and realised how cramped and restrictive it was compared to life on the surface. No wonder Aldon was happy he now had the chance to get out and about more often.

She watched him scoffing the coffee and pastries she brought back, and thought to herself that she must do more to coax him out of the obvious depression he must have been suffering ever since the loss of his family.

CHAPTER 2

Victor pulled out the metal cash box hidden under the floorboards, and gave a worried frown as he counted the contents. He definitely needed more money to finance their activities, and would have to speak to Base.

He contacted Aldon on the communicator and explained the situation. "Martina's shopping trip really depleted the funds. All women are the same when they get the chance to go on a spending spree! Can you send me some more cash?"

"I'm in a bit of a pickle where money is concerned." Aldon grumbled. "Our banknote replicator is faulty, and I'm still waiting for a replacement part from Solar Base."

"What now? We must always have sufficient money for emergencies. Those are the rules – your rules." Victor asserted.

Aldon thought for a minute. "We'll have to resort to 'Plan B' - the Casino! Are you up for that?"

"It would be a bit dicey for me to go a second time. They may remember me. Do you think we can risk enlisting a trusted couple of people from the Friendship Club?"

"We'll have to. Let's just hope they don't get caught!" Aldon sighed. "Make sure you take tight security measures and keep everyone unknown to each other. Let me know the exact plan and timing before they go"

Bart, their contact in the casino, was only known to Victor and the Terrans. He was a genetically enhanced hybrid with amazing kinetic abilities. Victor made the secretive arrangements with him, and sought out two of the 'friends' after their next gathering at the bookshop.

Both Mary and Bob had been individually attending the meetings because they were trying to make sense of strange past events in their lives. They knew their fleeting memories involved beings who were not of this world, and felt an extraordinary connection to them. It was comforting to talk to others with similar experiences. At least the people in the secret group did not think they were peculiar or deluded.

They were equally anxious to help. "Our first assignment, I'm so excited!" Mary enthused. "When do we go?"

"Not so fast." Victor cautioned. "This could be dangerous, and you have to follow my instructions to the letter. You must do as you're told and not ask any questions."

To avoid being identified they had to leave their cars at the bookshop. Mary was to wear a red dress, and a disguise of a black wig and glasses. Bob needed a false moustache and grey suit with a bright yellow tie.

The next evening, as they walked up the steps and into the casino, Bob whispered to a very nervous Mary, "It's show-time! Remember this is for a very beneficial cause."

They walked around the poker machines for about 5 minutes, and started playing one, only putting in small amounts as instructed. Soon a waiter came along, and nodded slightly when he gave them the usual complimentary drinks. A couple of minutes later bells were ringing, and their machine was flashing as the reels landed on a major jackpot.

"Oh, wow!" said Mary. "Just as Victor told us."

"Shh!" Bob cautioned. "Just follow the directions. We claim the money in casino chips, and then go to the restaurant for dinner until half past seven."

Chantelle sat at the bar, sipping a glass of wine, and looked across to the restaurant where Mary and Bob were enjoying their meal. Aldon had asked her to check on the young couple in case anything went wrong, and she was wearing an extra communicator button.

Going to another part of the casino she watched as they went to the roulette wheel, and started putting on bets one chip at a time. Just before eight o'clock she noticed Bart was in place near the gambling table.

It was then, at the prearranged time, Bob started the deliberate argument with Mary. "Come on! We have to go home before the baby sitter leaves."

The discussion became heated and Mary dumped the chips onto one spot on the board. "No! Not all of them!" Bob protested. But it was too late, the wheel was already spinning. When it landed on her number, Bart quietly moved away. The couple gave a gasp of astonishment and the croupier pushed a massive pile of chips towards them.

"Oh, my God! I don't believe it," Bob said. "Now we're going home. I'm not going to let you risk gambling it all away again!"

Chantelle watched from a distance as the pair followed their instructions and split the chips between them. The casino would not payout cash above $10,000 per person, and a cheque or electronic transfer would not suit their purposes.

After individually claiming their winnings both went to the rest rooms, and transferred the banknotes into money belts under their clothes. It was only when they entered the foyer, ready to leave, that Chantelle realised all was not well.

Earlier she had spotted two smartly dressed men whom she had suspected as being enemy agents. They were also in the foyer, and seemed intent on leaving the casino behind the young couple. She was glad she had her communicator, and quietly messaged Aldon to get a monitor/teleporter lock on Bob and Mary in case there was trouble.

When they got outside and looked around Mary became apprehensive. "Where's the red taxi cab Victor told us to get into? It's not here. I can't see it anywhere. What do we do now?"

Bob paused. He couldn't see the designated vehicle either. "People inside must know we won all this money. We need to get out of here. Perhaps we should walk to the subway. It's only about half a mile, and we can take a train back to the bookshop. I have to put my arm around you. I hope you don't mind, but Victor told us to stay close together if anything went wrong."

They were only a short way along the street when Mary looked over her shoulder and whispered, "Someone's following us! What do we do?

There aren't many lights – the road will get darker before we reach the station."

Chantelle, under the pretext of smoking a cigarette, was watching from the bottom of the casino steps. "I think they're in trouble," she messaged Aldon. "Have you got a lock on them?"

"Yes," he replied. "Both physically and telepathically. I'll message them to run around the next corner, where they must stand still holding on to each other."

Bob heard the telepathic instructions, and said to Mary, "Quick, run like hell!" They sped up the street and the two men also broke into a fast pace. When the fleeing pair reached the next corner, Bob pushed Mary around into the alley, and grabbed her in a bear hug.

"Bob!" Mary protested, but before she could say anymore they felt a swift whoosh, and after what seemed like a few seconds of darkness, found themselves standing in Victor's bookshop.

Chantelle had to avoid being conspicuous. Once she knew Aldon had rescued their two accomplices, she quietly melted back into the crowd in the casino

Aldon asked Martina and Andy to continue observing and recording the activities of the two suspicious men, who rounded the corner and stopped in surprise to see their prey had disappeared. They raced to the bottom of the dark lane, and realised it was a dead end.

"Perhaps they got over the wall," one suggested, "but it would be a bit high for the woman. I can't see them." After looking in and behind the trash containers, they tried to open all the doors along the side. Eventually they seemed to give-up, and slowly walked back to the casino.

Aldon hoped that perhaps they were just two criminal types, intent on robbing Bob and Mary of their winnings. He turned to Martina, "Although we didn't detect any conversation indicating who these men were, or their motives, I'm still concerned that Bart's abilities and involvement may have been discovered. Worse still, he has defected to the enemy, but that seems unlikely. I still don't know what happened to our contact in the red taxi. We must be very careful if we have to use the Casino again."

Back in the bookshop Bob and Mary stared at each other in amazement. Victor had just come downstairs, relieved that they had got back safely. "What just happened?" Mary asked him.

"I guess our alien friends transported you out of a sticky situation. Just in the nick of time, I'm told. It is a good thing you followed my instructions."

Bob, still a little dazed, suddenly recalled a long forgotten memory. As a young boy, he had been standing in the garden one night, looking at the stars. A huge silver craft, with lots of lights, had appeared above him. Next thing, just like tonight, he experienced that same feeling of zooming through the darkness of time and space.

He had found himself in a strange round, white room and could see little grey beings with big black eyes. There was a man as well, and next thing they put him on a table and started poking at his body.

Before he could relive any more of those past events, Victor interrupted Bob's thoughts. "You know for both my and your own safety's sake you must tell no-one of this – not even your own families or other members of the Friendship Club."

They all sat down to have coffee and the couple handed over their winnings. Victor breathed a sigh of relief. There was nearly $20,000 in nice, non-traceable bank notes, which would keep them financial for some time.

Victor watched Mary and Bob drive away, back to their homes and families. He closed the door, and went back into the now empty premises. A sense of loneliness crept in. Whilst he was born and raised on Solar Base, there must have been genetic material from human biological parents. He wondered who they were. Did he have his own relatives and family somewhere out there?

Although he was prohibited from forming any close bond with the humans, the Guardians had promised that this posting would not last forever. One day he could return to Solar Base, and continue to enjoy the lasting relationship he had with the others. Perhaps he could even find someone to love and marry.

The thought of a family of his own one day only added to Victor's sense of disconnection from his happy childhood and life with the Terrans.

It was as he drew the blinds, before going upstairs, that he heard the faint miaow outside. He opened the door and looked into the dark street – nothing! He thought he must have imagined it until he heard the faint cry again.

Peering into the side alley, Victor spotted a little black furry bundle, huddled in the corner. "Poor little thing out here in the cold,' he thought, and went over to see what he could do.

He picked up the cat and exclaimed, "Oh my goodness, you're about to have kittens! You can't stay here in the cold. Better come inside with me."

After giving her some milk and food, and finding a box and warm blanket, he climbed the stairs to bed. They never had pets on Solar Base, but caring for this little waif shouldn't be too hard.

The next morning he went back downstairs and checked on his new friend. She was purring, and moved to the side to reveal three tiny kittens. Victor felt an unexpected instinct to love and protect this helpless cat and her offspring. He sat down beside them, and stroked her soft fur. She had to have a name. He would call her 'Mishka'.

He went into the kitchen, humming off key. Somehow this little cat had taken the edge of his loneliness. She and her kittens could stay. They could be his family.

It was only a couple of weeks later when Amy wondered who Bob was talking to on the telephone. After he hung up he walked over and glanced at her friend Nancy. "Hi Nancy! Good to see you." He turned to Amy. "I have to pop out for a while, darling. Do you want anything at the shops?"

"Who was it on the phone?" she asked.

"Just one of the guys from work, wanting to discuss a problem without the boss knowing. I won't be long."

As he went out the door, Amy slowly stirred her coffee and paused thoughtfully. She looked across at Nancy. "Sometimes I get scared. Bob is a really good husband and father. Why do I worry about losing him?"

Nancy laughed. "Well, why do you?"

"There's a part of him I cannot reach – a sort of secretive, hidden Bob. I really can't explain it. He can often be quiet, deep in thought, and never opens up. Occasionally he has bad dreams, but won't tell me what they're about. He will arrive home late from work, without ever explaining. A friend recently told me they saw him with a woman in the casino. He denied it, and I have never known him to gamble.

Another night I woke up and he wasn't in bed. The car was gone, and when he came back a couple of hours later, he made an excuse about a friend needing a hand with some renovations to his house – a burst water pipe or something! A likely story! What were they really doing in the middle of the night? Do you think there's someone else? Is he having an affair?"

Nancy, seeing Amy was troubled, tried to reassure her. "No, he loves you and the kids. I can't believe he would be unfaithful. He is a good man. After all, he works in the hospital laboratory doing those medical experiments for new cures. He once said it was 'cutting edge' technology. Maybe some of his work is for the government, secret or classified, and he can't tell you why he gets called out after hours. He would probably get really upset if he thought you didn't trust him, or were checking up behind his back."

Bob drove back to the hospital, and thought it unusual that George, his laboratory assistant, was waiting in the car park.

"We have to talk out here," George cautioned.

Bob paused. "What's up? - Why all the mystery?"

George went on to tell of an accident victim who had been brought into the hospital earlier that day. It was normal procedure to send blood samples to the laboratory in case one of the drivers had drugs or alcohol in their system.

"There were no drugs or alcohol in this patient's system, but his blood wasn't quite right. There were no indicators of any illness, but this sample wasn't quite human."

"Have you told anyone?" Bob asked.

George hesitated. "No, you're the boss. I thought I'd speak to you first. Have I done the right thing?"

"Yes, of course," Bob assured him. "Let's go and take a quiet look at this bloke. If his biology is a little different it might be useful in our research. Hang on a minute – I'll just go to the car and ring Amy to tell her I'll be a while."

Bob went back to the car and rang the bookshop instead. "What shall I do?" he asked.

Victor had him wait on the line while he raced upstairs to contact Aldon, who quickly checked all their agents' communicators and frequency signals. The only malfunction seemed to be coming from Jarod, who had been in the area earlier that day.

"Bob," Victor said, "if this guy is middle-aged, about 5ft 6in, with greying hair and moustache he might be one of our 'colleagues'. Get back to me as soon as possible and tell me what you think."

"What took you so long?" George asked as Bob came back.

"Oh – just Amy complaining again. You know what women are like!"

They went into the hospital and up to the ward where the man was lying semi-conscious in a bed. When he opened his eyes George muttered "He looks ordinary enough. Why the abnormal blood?"

Bob looked at the name card above the bed – 'John Smith'? – and saw that the patient fitted the description Victor had given him. As he gazed upon 'Mr Smith' Bob sensed a faint recognition from somewhere in his past, and was startled when a voice said in his head, "Get me help!"

Bob realised this must be the missing Terran Victor spoke of. "Let's go," he said to George. "We can't do much tonight. Don't tell anyone, and we'll come back first thing in the morning."

Instead of driving home Bob headed straight to the bookshop. He reported back to Victor, who said, "It is Jarod, as we feared. Our Terran friends cannot get a transporter 'lock' on him. They have sent me this locator button, which we need you to put on him as soon as possible."

"Why is his blood different?" Bob asked. "I thought Terrans and humans were essentially the same race."

"They were, thousands of years ago, before our ancestors left Earth." Victor explained. "The intervening evolutionary period since has created slight differences."

Bob was worried about Amy's suspicions and decided he had better return home. He would take the device to the hospital first thing in the morning.

It was only just after dawn when Bob arrived back at the hospital, and he noticed an unusual dark, unmarked ambulance at the side door.

"That's strange," he thought as he made his way to the laboratory and donned his white coat. "Now to deliver this gadget."

Bob reached the ward and could see that 'John Smith' had been loaded on a trolley and was being propelled out the door by two men in dark suits.

He ran over and called out, "Who are you? What are you doing with my patient?" Reaching the trolley he put his hand on 'John Smith's' chest and slipped the locator under his hospital gown.

"This is none of your business. Get out of our way!" snapped one of the men, pushing Bob to the side. They disappeared into the lift, and Bob hoped he had delivered the little device to this poor man in time.

Aldon, Martina and Andy were all gathered anxiously over the transporter system. "No luck so far, Boss." Andy said. "Perhaps all the equipment in the hospital is creating interference."

As soon as the trolley was wheeled outside Martina confirmed a connection. "I've got him – I've got him! It is Jarod!"

When he was placed in the vehicle and the doors closed and secured, Earth Base got their lock on Jarod and transported him out.

Aldon looked at a thankful Jarod, and gave an impish grin. "I'd love to see the look on those government agents' faces when they arrive with an empty trolley in their ambulance!"

"They weren't government agents." Jarod said. "They were private security thugs, employed by one of the big corporations. I had been helping another company develop beneficial advanced Terran technology, and they wanted me to transfer over to them. Their research and development wasn't so benign, and I don't know if they were in league with the Xvars or Katons.

"When I refused to work with them, they tried to kidnap me, and my car crashed while I was escaping. Luckily there were members of the public around who called an ambulance. I'm not sure if anyone, except your friend Bob, recognised my true identity, but somebody would have sooner or later. Thankfully he slipped me the locator, just in the nick of time!"

Martina and Aldon treated what they could of Jarod's injuries, and gave sighs of relief when the shuttle craft arrived to take him back to Solar Base.

"I liked Jarod, he was one of our least troublesome agents here. We probably won't see him again." Aldon commented to Martina. "I guess he can't come back to Earth. His cover has been blown – if only by the disappearing act! Once he's recovered and debriefed, he may go home or perhaps onto another deployment."

Bob wandered back into the laboratory, and George, who had just arrived, looked up from his bench. "Shall we go back and take another look at our 'Mr Smith'?"

"No, I checked and he's either been discharged or transferred somewhere else." Bob answered, hoping the locator had worked.

He was still pondering the events of the past twelve hours. It wasn't the first time Bob had heard a voice in his head. Often when researching new medical innovations sudden ideas would somehow be transmitted to him the same way. He couldn't explain it, but he knew it was connected to his childhood and that night in the garden, when the spaceship took him. He wished he could remember more, other than the strange dreams he kept having.

CHAPTER 3

Chantelle might, as a Terran, have slight physiological differences, but she really enjoyed the more hormonal and carnal attributes of the human species. The overlords had decided she was well suited to the spying activities their presence necessitated, and commenced an advanced training program in the sexual arts. This was her first risky, but important, mission on Earth. She had to present as a credible callgirl, and so far she had been very successful.

A couple of days later, as she sat in the Army officers' favourite bar, Chantelle felt a rising sense of excitement and anticipation. The Colonel was furtively looking across at her, and as their eyes met she gave a little smile of encouragement. When the waiter delivered a cocktail to her table, Chantelle could sense her imminent success. She coyly nodded her thanks to the Colonel, and beckoned. He walked across and sat down. She was well schooled in seductive behaviour and the appropriate conversation. After a couple more drinks they left together.

He was glad this woman had her own apartment, away from spying eyes and nosey desk clerks at the local seedy hotel.

She ran her hands over the Colonel's body, kissing and nibbling his neck. He groaned in pleasure – his loins responding.

"Come into the shower first," she whispered, dropping her satin robe to the floor. He was shaking with anticipation and ripped off his clothes and shoes. Their bodies were almost fused together as they stepped into the tubular see-through recess and the opening slid shut.

She pressed on the side. A beam of light suddenly engulfed them, and he found himself, still merged with Chantelle, in a small white circular room. Before the Colonel could prise himself apart from her, he felt a small metal object clamp upon his forehead, and lost consciousness.

The mind probe only took a few minutes, and the couple were beamed back into Chantelle's transporter tube shower. The water flowed over them and she continued caressing him, as if there had been no interruption. The Colonel felt a little disorientated and confused, but his desire for Chantelle soon overcame any fleeting memory of the unexpected intervention.

When he left she felt rather sorry for him. Not only had she taken his money, they had gained all his military secrets. The damning video record of their sexual encounter had also been transmitted back to their Base. It may prove useful later.

Martina was still looking forward to catching up with Chantelle, and spending some time with her. They were cadets together when they trained in the Galactic Military. Although they had very different attitudes regarding relationships with the opposite sex, they had been the best of friends for many years.

Aldon reluctantly agreed to allow Martina one day's leave to spend with Chantelle, who came to the Base to collect her. Both women could hardly contain their enthusiasm as they prepared to depart.

"Not so fast!" Aldon cautioned. "I want to know your plans for the day and where you are going. You must both wear additional locator devices at all times. Martina is still not familiar with this planet – its customs or dangers. I need you to stay together at all times, and want to get both of you out if there is any trouble. I needn't tell you, no matter what, to stay away from any other of our Terrans. These days, security is more important than ever."

Chantelle suggested a trip into town where they could buy Martina a swimsuit, and later go to the beach.

She glanced across at Martina. "Remember how, when we were at the academy, we both had problems learning swim. Thankfully we got the hang of it in the end."

As they transported back down into Chantelle's apartment, Aldon called out, "Don't draw attention to yourselves!"

Before they ventured out into the street, Martina couldn't help admiring Chantelle's luxurious home. "I earned it," commented Chantelle over a quick coffee. She took Martina down to the lobby and then steered her into a very expensive clothing shop. As they viewed the rather revealing swimwear, both were giggling like they used to in their younger days.

Martina chose a more conservative costume and matching beach-coat, and then whispered, "I don't have any money!"

"No worries. I've always got plenty." Chantelle assured her as she paid for their purchases and they went back onto the street. "Now to get the bus to the beach – it's just over an hour's trip. Gosh, I hate this antiquated mode of transport when we can just zap places in seconds."

Whilst Chantelle was performing an important function for the Terran cause, Martina wanted to counsel her about this risky occupation. She knew that Chantelle had always enjoyed a more extravagant lifestyle, and perhaps the benefits were outweighing her need for more caution.

"This bumpy bus, full of people, is hardly the place to talk," she thought. "I'll wait 'til we're alone."

When they reached their destination Martina was captivated by the sight of a white, sandy, palm lined beach and the great expanse of blue ocean beyond. There were many humans, most scantily clad, on beach chairs or lying on towels.

"Let's find somewhere a little more private," Chantelle suggested, leading the way to a much more secluded cove around the headland.

The water was warmer than Martina expected, and it took her a while to adapt to the waves breaking on the shore. The whole experience was so much better than the small pool where they had practised swimming on Solar Base.

Once they had settled on the sand Martina asked Chantelle about her assignment. "Why do you treat most men, either human or Terran, with what seems like contempt, and take their money without regard to their feelings? Do you ever feel love or some form of emotion for any of your 'clients'?"

"I don't let myself, not anymore." Chantelle replied. "Remember that lecturer in military college? I really cared for him. He just used me and dumped me at the end of the course. Apparently he sought out a naive student every term. I was just a plaything!

"And then there was that witch on Zarcon Base. Her husband, Richard, pursued me for months. I thought he really cared, and said he was going to get a divorce. We could get married and a new posting somewhere else.

"Well, he was lying through his teeth! When push came to shove he claimed it was I who seduced him. His wife forgave him and I was banished! If I'm going to be a 'plaything', then the hormone driven males of this Solar System can pay well for the privilege!"

Martina felt a pang of empathy for Chantelle. She had also been betrayed by a lover, but hoped she would not become this cynical.

"Chantelle," she said, "don't give up on genuine love and affection. I'm sure you'll meet the right person one day."

They lay on the sand for a while, soaking up the sun's balmy warmth. Chantelle looked around at two young men approaching them. "Here's trouble!" she muttered.

"What do you mean?" asked Martina.

"They might not be in uniform, but I think they are from the military base."

They came nearer and one called out, "Why, if it's not the General's whore. Who's your little friend?"

"Not talking?" said the other. "I suppose us two corporals are not good enough for a high and mighty bitch like you."

"Dressed that way, they're asking for it! Let's show them what real men are made of," sniggered the first, grabbing Chantelle and dragging her into the bushes behind the beach.

"You'll do me," the second guy announced, as he picked Martina up and followed his mate into the shrubbery.

Once hidden by the undergrowth the women's training came into play. A few swift manoeuvres had their attackers on the ground. Martina felt a surge of uncontrollable rage, and grabbing each of their assailants by his penis, gave a mighty tug followed by a vice-like crushing squeeze.

Their momentary screams were silenced by the loss of consciousness.

"Oh, my God," said Chantelle, "what have you done? You were always being warned about your temper. We'd better get out of here!"

Racing out onto the sand, they grabbed their bags and took cover under some palm trees. "Quick! Get us out of here!" Martina messaged Base. Andy alerted a bemused Aldon, who soon had them back.

"How on Earth could you get yourself into trouble on a simple trip to the beach?" he sighed, putting his head in his hands. He looked at their scanty swimsuits and muttered to himself, "No – don't tell me."

After hearing their garbled explanation he ordered Chantelle to transport back to her apartment, where she was to quickly change into a fancy day outfit and come straight back to the Base.

About ten minutes later she returned, and Aldon said, "Quite presentable! I'm going to beam you down to an area without cameras near the back door of the Casino. Go inside, make yourself noticeable, and set up an alibi. It's only twenty minutes since you ladies mangled those guys' prize possessions, and you can't be in two places at once."

When she entered the Casino, Chantelle spotted Bart, and he telepathically directed her to where one of her regular clients was sitting at the bar.

She sidled up to him and cooed, "Good afternoon, how's my favourite General?"

"All the better for seeing you," he grinned. "What are you drinking?"

About half an hour later the General's phone rang. "What are you talking about?" he yelled into it. Then he said more softly, "Couldn't have been her. She's sitting right next to me, and has been for some time. The security cameras can confirm it if you are stupid enough to continue any further. I'll get you lot for trying to pull a trick like this!"

Chantelle's expression was one of pure innocence. "What's wrong?" she asked.

"Those bastards in military headquarters are trying to claim that you and a girlfriend seriously injured two soldiers, less than an hour ago, at a beach more than 50 miles away."

She looked at him, her eyes wide with fake astonishment. "Why would they make up a story like that? What have they got against me?"

"It's not you. There is cut-throat competition for positions and promotion among the higher ranks. They'll stop at nothing! I suppose they thought that trying to accuse the General's mistress of assaulting a couple of soldiers could have affected my career.

"Don't you worry your pretty little head about it! Finish your drink and let's go back to your place."

As a relieved Chantelle left, with the General in tow, she thought she might even give him a freebie this time.

Back on the Base Aldon was admonishing Martina, who was protesting that it wasn't their fault. They weren't to know this would happen. She and Chantelle were merely defending themselves.

"There are two major points I want to get across. Firstly self defence, and only self defence, is one thing – you must learn to control your more brutal fighting instinct."

"And second?" asked a subdued Martina.

"Human males do not have the same self-control as their Terran counterparts. They succumb to their basic sexual instincts when they see near naked females. In fact, in some less developed countries, the way you and Chantelle were dressed would be seen as an open invitation."

"Sorry boss," she said. "You were right. I do have a lot to learn!"

CHAPTER 4

Victor was in a good mood and preparing for the next Book Club meeting. He planned to show a documentary on global warming to complement a couple of books they had been discussing. He was also intent on finding a couple of volumes on human rights for later.

As he walked back and forth, he talked to Mishka and her little ones, who were in a basket at the back of the bookshop. Their presence had provided the companionship he had previously been missing.

The members arrived and started clucking over Mishka and her babies, many offering a home for the kittens when they were ready to leave their mother. Although Bob gave Mary a little wink as he passed, they were both totally discreet about their recent assignments.

During the film Victor was also able to talk to some of the people in the more secretive Friendship group. Aldon had updated him on the increased Xvar/Katon threat, and he wanted them to understand the need for greater security.

Mary was also in a turmoil regarding her own family, especially her grandmother. She didn't know quite where to turn, and wondered if she could trust Victor to ask his Terran friends to help. Once approached, he made arrangements for her to come in for coffee a few days later.

"Now why the secrecy, what's the problem?" he asked, sitting down at the table with her.

They had spoken before about her experiences, dating back to her childhood, when she was contacted by the Terrans. Although some of her memories were hazy and incomplete, she could remember being on a big silvery space ship. She used to play games with the little grey entities, and there were other children there as well.

She was not happy about the physical examinations she experienced in her teens, and the realisation they had taken some of the eggs from her ovary. Victor tried to explain there was a program of genetic enhancement involving at least some of the human population. Victor himself, having been born on the Solar Base, thought he must have been a product of this ongoing agenda.

"But why?" she asked.

"When the Terrans gave safe technological and scientific knowledge to your leaders, they were suppressed by your military and large corporations, who wanted to keep them for their own advantage.

"We had to turn to the general population instead. The genetic enhancement of as many people as possible will affect the subsequent generations and contain the evolutionary imperative necessary for your future. My superiors did feel a certain amount of guilt over the deliberate manipulation of a less advanced species, but it was essential. Earth's inhabitants must transcend their own negative history and behaviour if they are to survive."

Mary did not dwell on her indignation at not giving her consent to being part of this experiment. "My main concern is my mother and grandmother. Granny has always made vague comments about seeing and talking to aliens. She used to say that they had been in her life since she was a young girl, and they had given her certain psychic 'gifts'. I must admit she has an incredible ability to predict events before they happened.

"Mum wouldn't discuss it with either me or Granny, whom she was always trying to hush up. Because of that I have never told Mum what happened to me, but I think she has experienced something similar. Granny used to tell me it was 'our secret'.

"I think my mother does know about all of this, and is either in denial or scared of anything alien. My father died when I was young - I don't even remember him. Ever since, she has been overly protective, always checking up on me and nervous if I go out alone at night. I have only told her about the Book Club meetings, and she would have a pink fit if she knew about the 'Friendship' group.

"Granny lived with us and really looked after me more than my own mother. Recently she started talking non-stop about extra-terrestrials and how she had been on their spaceship and wanted to go away with them. Mum was so concerned she called the doctor, who diagnosed dementia and had her consigned to a nursing home.

"She is now 'drugged-up', and kept there like a prisoner. Every so often she is lucid enough to ask me to get her alien friends to save her. I am more concerned about her mentioning a strange new doctor who indicated he was going to move her somewhere else to do some tests. When I asked the nursing home, they were very shifty, and just said this new bloke had something to do with the government and it was out of their control."

Victor needed to inform Aldon immediately. He advised Mary to visit the nursing home to check on Granny as much as possible. She was to leave it to him, and to tell no-one, not even her mother.

Aldon was concerned, and confirmed that Mary's family was part of their genetic enhancement program. They certainly didn't want the security boffins examining Granny. Although she probably wouldn't survive their invasive methods, it was possible she could initially divulge too much information.

"It is not just our human adversaries we must worry about," he said. "It is likely Xvar/Katon agents are also eager to identify, and maybe even eliminate our protégées. We will have to snatch Granny back before she falls into any of their clutches."

For the next few days Mary visited her grandmother every afternoon on the way home from work. The nursing home was on the edge of town, bordering on a State forest. The staff said very little. They were still evasive about Granny's mental capacity and the drugs they were giving her.

On about the third afternoon Mary found her sitting with an old bloke, Leandro, who seemed to be of Mediterranean descent. His unkempt hair and beard gave him a rather scruffy appearance.

"He was homeless, on the street, when he was brought here, suffering in this heatwave," the nurse said disparagingly. "We cleaned him up, and will move him on to a shelter once he regains his health. We aren't at all happy with him associating with the other residents, but your grandmother seems to have taken a liking to him. At least he's had a calming effect on her, and she's stopped garbling on about going away with aliens."

Mary wasn't sure why, but she felt a sense of connection when she was close to Leandro. Granny had whispered in her ear, "My friends up there will rescue me. You wait and see!"

When Mary rose to leave Leandro winked at her, and she wondered who he really was.

The next night alarm bells started to ring in the nursing home. Granny could see nurses running in all directions, gathering up the residents and ushering or carrying them to the front doors and the emergency assembly point.

"What's happening", she whimpered as the staff rushed past.

One of them called across the room. "Nothing to worry about, darling! - Just a bit of a fire in the forest. We'll be back for you in a minute."

Above the commotion of the mayhem all around, she could hear the noise of sirens, coming from the fire brigade and ambulance racing to assist with the fire and evacuations.

Leandro came up behind her, and grabbed the wheelchair. "Here we go - time for the great escape!"

He broke into a run, and pushed Granny to the other end of the building. Once down the ramp and out the back door, he moved her under the cover of the nearby trees.

"The fire! It's coming closer." Granny wailed.

"Don't worry," he reassured her, activating his locator and communication devices. "We'll be out of here in a minute".

Andy, Martina and Aldon were ready and waiting to bring them up. Once they were safely retrieved, Aldon beamed the wheelchair back into the burning undergrowth at the rear of the building.

"Now they'll think she was lost in the fire." Aldon predicted.

Mary and her mother got the telephone call later that night. The nurses thought Granny had been taken away in the ambulance, but later couldn't locate her in the evacuation centres. When the burned remains of her wheelchair had been found, they assumed that, due to her confused state, she must have gone the wrong way and perished.

The next afternoon, as a very downcast Mary made her way to the bookshop, she bumped into a man coming out of the entrance. She gasped in disbelief when she recognised a very clean shaven, smartly dressed Leandro, who winked as he rushed past her.

"Victor! Victor!" she called out. "Tell me that wasn't who I think it was."

"I'm sure I don't know what you're talking about!" Victor cautioned, glancing at the other customers. "I am sorry about the sad loss of your grandmother. Come out the back – I have something to show you."

Once in the privacy of his office, Victor handed Mary a portable monitor, and turned it on. There on the screen was Granny, no longer confined to a wheelchair, and looking twenty years younger.

The tears streamed down Mary's face and Granny said, "Don't you cry darling. I told you they would come for me. I'm very happy, and going away to live on one of their bases. I've got a new job helping with the children in their care.

"Promise me you won't tell your mother about this, even though I know she'll be grieving. You are a good girl to stay with her, and don't judge her too harshly. She was traumatised by her own experiences and other inner demons, and as a result has always been in total denial about our interaction with the aliens.

"Don't let her hold you back from your own future. With their genetic enhancement, and other programs, our Terran friends have gifted you with superior abilities, which you have yet to realise.

"There are other Terran protégées with whom you have a special bond. Some are with that group I know you go to in secret. You are related and connected, as is most of the universe. Once you are absolutely sure someone is who you think they are, you can harmonise your brainwaves into a network. If you forge a link with the others you can combine your powers for good.

"Embrace your destiny, and play your part in helping humanity advance to a better future on planet Earth. Don't neglect your personal happiness. I hope that one day you will find a nice young man and start a family of your own."

The transmission ended all too soon, with Granny promising to try and keep contact. Mary was left trembling. "Look at me," she said to Victor. "My mascara has run down my face from crying. Thank you for granting her wish to 'go away with the aliens', and letting me know she is safe and well."

Leandro had merged back into the crowded city streets. Any risk of detection was outweighed by the satisfaction of saving the old lady from a terrible fate at the hands of their opponents - but it meant his role as a down-and-out homeless man was over. Solar Base would assign him a new task and identity in another town, or maybe even another country.

Victor was still captivated by the little cat and her babies, who had taken up residence in his bookshop. They were quickly growing, and developing personalities of their own. He knew that he would have to part with the kittens soon, but he was going to keep Mishka.

Mary had been coming in after work more often, and Victor found himself enjoying her company. She adopted the pretence of playing with the little bundles of fur and mischief, especially the one he had promised she could take home.

In reality, she was still recovering from the incident with her grandmother. Victor was the only other person who knew what had really happened. It was sort of a secret bond between them.

Mary found it ever more difficult to conceal the truth from her mother, who was consumed with guilt at having allowed Granny to be forcibly confined to the nursing home in the first place. Victor was adamant she must never reveal what she knew.

The funeral was delayed due to police forensic teams investigating the cause of the fire and burned out area behind the facility. One evening two men in suits were waiting for her when she arrived home.

"Where have you been?" her mother demanded. "These detectives have been waiting to interview you."

"Just to the bookshop, Mum," she replied nervously. "I want to have one of the kittens they've got."

"You always want something that costs time and money!" Her mother complained bitterly. "These gentlemen are here to ask you about the death of your grandmother."

Mary's heart gave a little start, but she managed to retain a blank face. "What can I tell you? We were both here when it happened?"

"The fire appears to be very suspicious," the one man explained. "What is of greater concern is that we cannot find your grandmother's body in the ashes; only her wheelchair. There should have been some remains."

"How can we have a funeral if we can't bury her?" sobbed her mother.

Mary just stared at the two policemen. "I can't see how I can help."

One explained about Leandro, he was nowhere to be found, and his body wasn't recovered. "What can you tell us about this man?" He asked. "In fact, we can't be sure if either of them perished in the fire. Could he have escaped and taken your Granny with him?"

Mary feigned total ignorance. "I don't know anything about him, except he was sitting with her one afternoon. The staff at the nursing home should be able to tell you more."

She gave a sigh of relief when they left, and quietly wondered if they were just detectives or from one of the security agencies. She hoped and prayed they didn't know what had really happened.

Her mother was pacing the room in an agitated state. "Mary, could she still be alive? Do you think she really went away with the aliens as she said she would?"

It took all her composure for Mary to shrug her shoulders and say, "You know it was only one of her fantasies. Anyway, she couldn't have gone anywhere without her wheelchair."

CHAPTER 5

Aldon and Martina were enjoying an interlude on the Base. She was glad he had taken to drinking coffee and other non-intoxicating beverages. Solar Command had asked her to check on Aldon's psychological status, and if he was recovering from the loss of his family.

She had noticed several bottles of human alcoholic beverages in his quarters, and although he had confessed to drinking it in the past, he had stopped since she arrived.

"It helped me forget," he admitted, "but I was drinking too much, and it had to end. That liquor clouded my judgement, and can quickly become addictive. I'm glad you are here, to make sure I don't slip back into bad habits."

Just as he was opening up and starting to trust Martina, Aldon was interrupted by Andy bursting through the door.

"Commander! Commander – an urgent message from Solar Base!"

Aldon went to the communications unit: - "Yes Sir! I have already made my daily report. Is there a problem?"

The voice on the other end sounded tense and serious. "The Xvars have attacked and commandeered one of our minor bases in this quadrant of the galaxy. The whole of this Solar System is now on yellow alert."

"What does this mean for Earth?" asked Aldon.

"With a bit of luck, nothing," came the reply, "but we cannot be too careful. We know there are a few Xvars and Katons on Earth, but due to their very different physical appearance they stay in the shadows and cannot openly mingle with the population."

"Agreed," Aldon replied, "but in some ways they are more dangerous, and rely on human agents we cannot identify. They are close to mastering the technique of replicating androids of humanoid appearance. In addition there are reports they have abducted some inhabitants and implanted telepathic monitoring devices. Whilst we can detect most of this, it is more difficult where their human allies are concerned."

"Yes," Solar Base confirmed, "we know that although the vast majority of the population is not involved, they have enlisted the aid of some powerful agencies on the planet. Humans can be very naive. They have been lured to the other side by gifts of dangerous knowledge from the Xvars and Katons.

"Once the general population adopts and depends on this new technology, it can be used by our enemies to control and dominate them. It hasn't got to that stage yet, so for the moment we want to avoid any open conflict. Just be on your guard and warn all of our agents."

Aldon still had a lot more to show and explain to Martina before she would be fully trained in her new duties, and able to take complete command in his absence. Now he realised that time was of the essence to bring her fully up to speed.

They discussed the situation and Aldon agreed that the incidents with Jarod and at the Casino may not be related to the Xvars or Katons. Even so, he insisted that as soon as possible Martina must meet with and be able to identify all their Terran personnel. In addition there were several sub-bases, which were used by their agents to access Earth Base and other distant locations on the planet.

Her first journey was to be to Sub-Base One, which was manned by Tyra, another biological android, and Charra, a little grey worker. The transporter enabled her swift arrival at the base, located high in the Himalayan Mountains.

Tyra, a very attractive female android came to welcome her, followed by Noru, one of their local Terran agents. Martina immediately noticed Noru was wearing a monk's robe, and both were of Asian appearance.

Sensing her surprise, Noru laughed and said, "You know that even us Terrans don't all look the same. We have to go where we will fit in! We were present on this planet many thousands of years ago, where many of our own ancestors originated.

"In fact we had a large population in this very area, and many of us are genetically related. This base is located under an ancient monastery. As well as providing an additional Terran facility, part of my assignment is to locate some of the artefacts our people left behind when they left. We don't want them falling into the hands of either the humans or Xvars.

"So far I've been unsuccessful in locating the old relics and equipment. I'll have to intensify my efforts now we have an increased Xvar threat. Fortunately, some of the higher order monks are assisting us.

"They have inherited some of our past knowledge, passed down through generations of their religious beliefs and practises. At least they advocate peace and love, which is what we wish for all Earthlings if they wish to progress and not destroy themselves in the process.

"The monks' power to levitate huge stones by sound, and their ability to access other dimensions has been well known to other civilisations. They have been persecuted over the years, but have never divulged any of their secrets."

Even though there were some emergency provisions, Sub-Base One did not have a shuttle bay — just the transporter and an exit/entrance tunnel. Martina was intrigued as Noru made her put on a similar robe to his, and took her through a camouflaged, cryptically encoded door going into a cave under the monastery.

"Only a couple of the monks are even aware of this door, or the existence of the base," he reassured her.

After a steep climb up spiral stone steps, she found herself in the cool, crisp mountain air.

She gazed at the white capped mountain peaks rising up into the clear blue sky. It was an entrancing sight. There were several robed monks around the elaborately carved old stone building. Martina could sense the enlightened frequencies and vibrations emanating from a couple of them.

Noru read her thoughts and murmured, "They are the 'masters' — our friends and helpers. Only a few trusted ones know who I am and my mission. They are a little like the friendship clubs we have elsewhere. I suspect they do know about our ancient facility, but so far have failed to acknowledge its existence or location."

The beautiful surrounds combined with the melodic chanting of the monks had lulled Martina into a deep reverie. She jolted back to reality at the sound of shouts coming from the valley below.

Noru looked down and said, "Government soldiers! Every so often they mount expeditions up here, mainly to ensure the community are obeying the strict rules and regulations imposed upon them when they were conquered by a much more powerful country. Unfortunately they can be quite brutal, and given the chance, will steal what little we have."

The monks were scattering. Some ran into the monastery, and appeared to be hiding some of their gold, silver and gemstone encrusted religious icons. Others were locking or obscuring the entrances to their food stores.

"Noru – would the military steal from their own people?" Martina asked.

"Of course," he said, "they are very badly paid themselves. They don't treat any conquered population very well. Our only consolation is that their government is very totalitarian. They have also heard of the relics, but will not allow anyone else in to search. Their officials wish to locate the ruins themselves."

Martina wondered what was so important about finding these artefacts. Noru explained that, several thousand years ago, there was an enormous disaster on the planet. At the same time they were being attacked by a hostile alien race.

Their own large transport craft descended through the atmosphere and rescued most of the Terrans. Some, however, were trapped in their base, which was located inside a network of caves. To avoid capture they had destroyed all the entrances, and probably perished.

Noru continued, "There were some stasis chambers in there, and we don't know if any took refuge in them. There is a slight chance, if located, we may be able to revive them."

"After all this time?" queried a very doubtful Martina.

"You never know," Noru said. "Don't forget the remains of that unfortunate group of our people are also still there. Other than that, a lot of advanced equipment was left behind. It is even rumoured that two shuttlecraft ended up being buried in the base. We need to retrieve everything before anyone else does."

They could hear the sound of the soldiers coming closer. Noru had to remind her that although she was wearing a monk's robe and hood, her blond hair was still rather noticeable. It was time to get out of view.

As they entered the monastery the first of the soldiers had arrived in the courtyard. They could hear shouting and the sounds of monks crying out as the soldiers began an assault.

"Quick! Let's get out of here!" Noru urged, pushing her towards the winding stone steps.

Martina could feel an anxiety attack coming on, and was relieved when they found safety behind the secure hidden door to the sub-base.

Tyra and Noru advised caution before she transported back to Earth Base. They could not risk the local military, or even the astute, highly evolved monks, detecting any transmission frequencies emanating from underground.

Noru was monitoring what was happening above, and appeared quite distressed at what he could see and hear. It was at least a couple of hours before he allowed Martina to return to Earth Base.

As she bid him farewell, she could see he was gathering up some first aid supplies. "Is it as bad as all that?"

"I'm afraid so," he said. "It always is!"

When she arrived she told Aldon of the events. "I was so angry, hearing those monks crying out in pain and fear. All I wanted to do was rush out and zap those soldiers, but Noru stopped me."

"Quite rightly," Aldon responded. "You must forget your warrior days. I know it can be hard at times, but we must not interfere with our agents' missions. We are here to support them, and provide back-up if necessary. We are only supposed to intervene to rescue our own people."

"Not ever?" she sighed.

Aldon paused. "There can be the occasional exception in a crisis. You must remember that here, at Earth Base, we are often not even aware of the true purpose of our own Terrans' postings. Their tasks are set by the Guardians, and often on a covert 'need to know' basis. If we made any unauthorized intervention it could affect the outcome."

He patted her on the shoulder. "This is not always an easy posting. Do you think you can handle it?"

Martina gave a weak smile. "I'm going to have to!"

As she left the room Aldon whispered to Andy, "Make sure the major weapons area is always secure. Other than an emergency, don't give Martina access without checking with me first."

Martina was playing a game of chess with Andy, when Aldon emerged from his quarters wearing his dress uniform.

"Wow!" said Martina. "Don't you look handsome! Going somewhere?"

"Yes," he replied. "The Galactic Council has summoned me to a meeting regarding the growing Xvar/Katon threat. I'm being picked up in an hour, with the first stop-over on Mars Base. From there it's a larger craft to an inter-stellar destination. I'm not sure where it's being held. It's all very hush-hush.

"I will only be gone a few days, but while I'm away you must remain on Base, with Andy, at all times. These are the rules which must be complied with. It would have to be an extreme emergency to justify you abandoning your post."

"Understood!" Martina confirmed, and pushed the chess board to the side. "Never mind Andy, you always beat me anyway."

Aldon's transport arrived, and as they moved away from Earth he experienced the same great sense of liberty he always had when zooming through the black expanse of space.

They neared Mars, and he watched the image of Earth shrinking to a small blue dot. "I hope nothing goes wrong while I'm away," he thought to himself.

When the red planet loomed larger, the shuttle craft decreased speed and turned to enter what appeared to be an empty lava tunnel on the surface. Deep underground, in the hidden base's artificial atmosphere, he alighted to meet some colleagues from other parts of the System.

It was in these buried, simulated environments, with little exposure to the outside, when he appreciated his own posting. They could still see the sky through some of the domes, which appeared to be normal red rock and dirt from the surface. At least, on Earth, he didn't have to get suited up with a helmet whenever he went out.

Mars Base didn't get visitors very often, and treated their guests to what seemed like a banquet compared to normal Earth Base rations.

"We have to put you up for the night," their hosts said. "The interstellar ship doesn't arrive for another fifteen hours. In the meantime, enjoy the facilities in our officers' recreation area."

Mars did not have any indigenous inhabitants, and the Base was considered a little more secure than the one on Earth. It had a sizable population of officers, androids and little grey workers. Aldon thought his own base was more like an outpost by comparison. Up on the main control deck his envious glances were focussed on the monitors and other fancy gadgets. They had much more advanced equipment than the basics allocated to his team.

Pletta, the Mars Commander, glanced across at him. "Don't even think about it!" he warned amiably. "I'm going to frisk you before you return to Earth!"

There was great comradeship in the recreation area. Intoxicating beverages were freely flowing as the various planet commanders exchanged gossip and renewed old friendships. He smiled to himself as he noticed some flirting going on between the opposite sexes. Watching them laughing, joking and drinking together, Aldon realised his space brothers were no different to humans. They all loved a good party.

Aldon was starting to feel a little too merry, when he decided enough was enough. He did not want to go back down the road of addiction.

"I think I'll turn in," he announced. "It'll be a big day tomorrow. Does anyone know our ultimate destination?"

They all shook their heads. "It may be Main Solar Base – I don't know," one suggested.

"Why did they have to locate it way out at the edge of this system?" another complained. "It's the fault of your Earthlings and their exploratory probes to the nearby planets. Even our base on the far side of the Moon has been reduced to a minimum and manned by just one robot. It's a shame the facility will have to self-destruct if located."

The next morning Aldon noticed many of his companions were a little worse for wear, and he was glad he had limited his alcoholic drinks. The shuttle took them up to a much larger craft, hovering above the surface. It was then they were informed that they were, indeed, on their way to Main Solar Base.

They arrived to be greeted not only by Xandra, their own Terran Solar System chief, but also two senior members of their Quadrant Council from the Galactic Ruling Body. They also noticed that there were a couple of representatives from other extraterrestrial races.

Pletta looked sideways at Aldon. "Bloody hell! Must be something important."

Once settled in the conference room, Zadoc, a senior Galactic leader, addressed them.

"I have gathered you all here together to report on the latest incursions the Xvars have made into this Quadrant of the Galaxy. They have attacked and occupied a couple of our outer galaxy bases, and either killed or enslaved the relatively few inhabitants.

"Our intelligence analysts have concluded that the stakes have been raised, and this is just the beginning of an agenda to gain a major military foothold into our cosmic turf. Even though their plans seem to involve a long-term policy of stealth and deception, we must keep in mind that this Solar System is an important outpost in the galaxy's defences.

"We know they have a few illicit emissaries on Earth at the moment, but they stay in the shadows, and are hard to detect. Their obvious strange appearance prevents both the Xvars and Katons from openly mixing with the population, and would also deter most humans from welcoming any co-operation or surrender of power.

"Their tactic is to foster dissent among the various nationalities, and offer them advanced technology to defeat their perceived enemies. By building a secret alliance with the less ethical leaders on Earth, and taking over that same technology, they will effectively claim control over the planet with humanity's unwitting consent.

"We gave the oversight of this Solar System to the Terrans because you have the advantage in being able to openly mix with the human population, without being recognised. The downside is that we are forbidden, by the Galactic Ruling Body, to help them with anything but benign knowledge and expertise.

"For you who command an outer planet base, we don't think an open attack is part of their current strategy, although you need to be prepared for the odd skirmish at times. Neither the Xvars nor the Galactic Government want to start destructive hostilities at this stage"

Zadoc assured all of them that, although there would be extra officers posted to Solar Base to assist the individual Planet Commanders when required, it would be Aldon's Earth needing the most support.

"Still want to swap postings?" Aldon asked Pletta. "Earth may carry a higher pay grade, but it is fraught with difficulties. The humans now have a multitude of 'eyes in the sky' which we always have to evade, and I need to keep a tight rein on our agents, who often behave like a bunch of misfits.

"I had to leave Earth Base under Martina's command, and she hasn't even met all the agents. She is a good officer, but still a little inexperienced to take control. I trust Andy will lend a hand while I'm gone."

Main Solar Base was a much larger facility than those on Earth or Mars – more like a small underground city. Aldon and Pletta enjoyed the extra amenities while they remained a couple of days longer for additional meetings with Xandra and Zadoc. Due to the growing Xvar threat, the stakes had been raised. It was a good opportunity for Aldon to stress his need for additional equipment and personnel.

They promised more workers, androids and agents would be recruited, and he would receive extra provisions as soon as they arrived from the Quadrant Supply Base. In the interim there were a few goodies he could take back with him now.

"What did you score?" Pletta asked as they boarded their transport back to Mars Base.

Aldon grinned, "Some new weapons, communicators, a brand new banknote replica machine and other enviable supplies. They've already been loaded on the craft – just keep your sticky paws off them."

Their arrival on Mars Base was uneventful, and they found a few of their remaining colleagues partying again in the officers' recreation area. Aldon looked at Pletta. "It's been a long few days. I think I'll turn in early, ready for a timely departure tomorrow."

CHAPTER 6

Back on Earth Base Martina was religiously following the daily basic routines. She was still smarting over the lecture she received after her trip to the beach with Chantelle. Although she regretted being reprimanded, in her heart she wasn't at all sorry she had injured those two young men.

"In fact I wouldn't care if they could 'never get it up again'. I bet they won't rape another woman any time soon," she whispered to Delta. The little grey worker looked at her rather puzzled, not quite understanding what she meant.

Earlier, Andy had advised of a message he received from a Terran, 'John', who was one of their genuine agents. Martina had yet to meet him, and was unsure how to deal with any problems he may have.

"Can he wait until Aldon returns?" she asked, checking the records. He was incognito on the surface as a vet, and his premises on the outskirts of the town could, if necessary, suffice as a minor de-facto base.

His consulting rooms and operating theatre could be used in an emergency for any injured personnel if they couldn't be transported back to Base. He also had kennels in the basement, which concealed his transporter 'shower'. He had some specialised weapons and equipment and several underground hiding places.

He was actually an excellent medico, able to treat most species of animals in addition to several extraterrestrial races. Although he could not service the robotic androids, one called Sarah, worked as his receptionist/nurse. There was also a little grey worker, 'Wangi', who always stayed out of sight in the house or basement. The risk of detection was relatively minor. Not many clients actually attended the surgery, and John normally made visits to the small farms outside the urban area.

Andy informed her that John had said a serious problem had cropped up. He had to advise them immediately, and he couldn't risk any transmission being intercepted.

"I cannot leave the Base, he will have to come up here." Martina said, remembering Aldon's strict orders.

Andy greeted a reluctant John as he stepped out of the transporter a few minutes later. "Now, what is so urgent it couldn't wait?" Martina asked going over to meet him.

"It's Wangi – she's missing," he said despairingly. "I've searched and searched but couldn't find her."

A stunned Martina just stared at him in disbelief. "How could you lose Wangi? You know how our 'little greys' must not leave the premises and never be seen in public. And what do you mean -'she'- they are sexless clones!"

John started jabbering his explanations. "I've always thought of Wangi as a she – so quiet and shy. She was in the basement and the door was open. Roger Smither's sheep dog had been admitted for minor surgery and the door to his cage was not fastened properly.

"He must have got out and spotted Wangi. It was quite dreadful. I heard the commotion and raced in. The dog was chasing Wangi around the surgery. He probably meant her no harm. His natural tendency is to herd sheep.

"Somehow the front door must have been ajar, and Wangi fled out into the nearby woodland with the dog in hot pursuit. I ran after them and managed to catch the dog and lock it up, but I can't find Wangi."

Martina was seething, "We must get her back – quickly – before she is seen. We will have the general public yelling 'aliens' to all and sundry. Worse still, have you any idea the trouble we will all be in if she is captured?"

Their little workers could not speak, and were all linked to a master brain. They communicated telepathically, an ability which was woven into their biology.

She turned to Delta and Thelta. "Try to contact Wangi. Let me know what you can sense. Ask her where she is and what she can see. Transmit it to the monitor."

"Lost –hiding – scared," was the response, and a picture of leaves and bushes all around appeared on the screen.

"Oh, shit!" Martina spluttered. "She appears to be cringing in the undergrowth. These creatures are witless at the best of times, and frighten easily. It is not a good idea to ask her to move into the open. Delta, tell her to stay where she is.

"John, where is Sarah?"

John started to fidget and looked at the floor. "I sent her into town to pick up a consignment of medicine"

"You did what?" Martina snapped. "You know your android is not allowed to go out in public, except in an emergency. Even then there must be an escort. You sent her into town alone?"

Martina told herself she must stay calm, and figure something out quickly. "John, get a locator from Andy and take it back down with you. Put it onto your smallest monitor drone, and fly it very low over the nearby woodland. Let us know when it locates Wangi, or her frequency, and we'll beam her back here."

"Can't I take her home with me?" John pleaded.

"No you can't!" Martina shouted in growing frustration. "What are you thinking? Will you walk across the fields, in full view, holding Wangi's hand as you return to your surgery? Please get back to your quarters, and get that drone in the air."

About half an hour later Andy announced, "Lock established!" and Wangi and the drone appeared in the transporter bay. She was curled up in a terrified little ball, and Martina left it to Delta and Thelta to take her into care and calm her down.

Martina was just relieved she had found Wangi before any damage was done and before Aldon returned. She was still shaking when she went into his quarters and raided his liquor stock. As she took a long swig from the bottle, she considered this transgression was justified, and collapsed into her chair.

For the first time, when Aldon arrived back on Earth Base, it felt like coming home. Maybe it was Martina's influence or just a growing sense of belonging. Once the shuttle had been unloaded and headed off, Aldon joined his team.

"Hello honey, I'm home!" he joked.

He started singing, off key, "We're in the money – we're in the money," and handed the banknote replica machine to Andy.

"Make sure you program it carefully. Remember - older, non-sequential serial numbers."

Martina's heart sank a little. Since she arrived, she had not seen Aldon so happy. How was she going to break the news of John's near disaster at the vet surgery? Her mind was still debating the best approach when he noticed there were three little grey entities instead of two.

"Why, it's Wangi. What is John's worker doing here?" he asked.

Martina gulped and tried to explain as diplomatically as possible. Aldon uttered a few choice expletives and the smile left his face.

"I'm sorry you had your first emergency so soon after arriving. Despite not knowing John or meeting him formally, you handled the situation very well. I'll take it from here."

"Are you going to send him back to Solar Base?" she asked.

"I wish," Aldon sighed. "He is very cavalier where standing orders are concerned, and I've always had some nagging doubts about his suitability to blend in with the general population. The problem is we cannot readily replace him with someone who has anywhere near his expertise.

"In addition to his medical skills and the ability to place monitoring implants in animals, he has an extra gift of being able to communicate telepathically with some creatures.

"I'm going to pay him a surprise visit in a couple of days, and it won't be pleasant!"

Aldon beamed down to the garden outside the vet surgery. He wanted his visit to be totally unannounced. As he opened the front door Sarah looked up from the reception desk. "Good morning, Commander. I'll let John know you are here."

"Don't bother," Aldon growled. "I'll show myself in."

When he saw Aldon approaching in the basement, John made a weak gesture. "I suppose you heard what happened," he stammered. "It wasn't my fault. It was an accident."

"An accident?" Aldon roared. "Both the animal's cage, the basement and front doors were left open! To add to your stupidity you sent your android alone into the town. What were you thinking? When you raced outside after the dog and Wangi you left the entire premises open and unattended."

John hung his head and looked at the floor. "Are you going to tell the boss? I promise this will never happen again if you give me another chance."

Aldon glared at him. "I should send you back in disgrace. The only thing saving you is your exceptional medical and surgical skill, which is now needed more than ever. You have a teleporter, and other Terran facilities down here. You must ensure strict security measures from now on.

"This is your last chance. It's not the first time you have flouted the rules. If it happens again I'll have no option but to advise headquarters."

John shuffled his feet, and looking up said, "I still need help around the surgery, and cannot employ a human who may not be trustworthy. Can I have Wangi back?"

Aldon was still glowering. "No, you can't. Wangi is confused, and unable to process what happened. You and Sarah will have to pitch in and do some of the cleaning and housework yourselves. I will allocate a new worker when Solar Base sends me the extra personnel they promised.

"While we're on the subject of staff, Wangi has indicated that Sarah would only perform the nurse/receptionist duties, and regarded Wangi as a menial housemaid. Before I leave, I am going to tell that lazy android that she is only a glorified robot, and unless she starts pulling her weight I'll redeploy her to a less pleasant position."

John's expression turned to one of desperation. "No – please don't do that. I'll make sure nothing else goes wrong. You can depend on me."

"Okay," Aldon said as he was leaving. "Let's make a fresh start. In a couple of weeks Victor will come in to get his new cat, 'Mishka', desexed. I want you to put an implant into her at the same time. Let me know the frequency.

"Don't tell him. He loves that animal and might object, but it will help increase our connection to Victor and surveillance in the bookshop."

After Aldon left John went up to Sarah and put his arms around her shoulders. "Never mind sweetheart. We'll get a replacement for Wangi soon. In the meantime, we've still got each other. I like you better than any of these horrible humans."

Back on Base, Martina asked Aldon if he would really replace Sarah as well?

"Not so easy," he replied. "Androids like Sarah possess an advanced artificial intelligence, which allows them to constantly learn and adapt through experience. We would have to teach a new one all the receptionist and animal husbandry skills she has accumulated.

"I am a little concerned that John was quite distraught when I suggested replacing her. I hope the only reason he wanted to retain Sarah was because of her acquired knowledge. Sometimes when our secluded agents have very little company, they can become too attached to their androids."

Aldon and Martina were relaxing over breakfast and discussing the new equipment he had received from Solar Base.

"More laser guns and stun devices," Aldon gloated, "and what about this cool stuff! These up-dated drones were specially designed to mimic the birds on Earth, even down to their individual calls. They can carry and do a lot more than what we've had to date. Our really miniaturised surveillance units can do little else, and the larger ones are more obvious. Fortunately they are difficult to detect amongst the human versions.

"I'm especially pleased with the latest personal invisibility technology. We really shouldn't be going out without wearing one of those gadgets. It sure confuses those humans when we suddenly seem to disappear into thin air!"

Martina waved her finger at him. "I can understand the need for more precautions as human knowledge and technology starts to catch up. However, you haven't mentioned the several costumes I noticed you stashing away. They strongly resemble some of the features and uniforms of the Xvars and Katons. What are you and Xandra up to? You can't tell me they're just for a fancy dress party."

Aldon explained that it was more important than ever to realise that they must keep a very low profile. "All is fair in love and war, even in this conflict, however covert it may be. The Xvars and Katons have pulled enough dirty tricks on us. It's time we returned the favour, and masqueraded as them when required."

Martina frowned. "As long as our own side don't also make a mistake and lay into you or worse."

Xandra arrived a few days later with another consignment of equipment for Earth Base. "We have a larger craft further away from the surface, and I was able to bring you a couple of the new PVXs."

The PVX was the latest pilotless passenger disc, which could travel by air, land, and on or under the sea. It had a teleporter, a blue beam transfer unit, and both invisibility and armour protection shields. As a bonus, it was not detectable by human radar or other technology. The PVX carried some awesome weaponry and could be either remote controlled or manually operated. Aldon could not contain his excitement at having not one but two of these ready to use.

He was wondering what Solar Base wanted in return, when Xandra said, "I can't stay long. I came here to transport a Guardian delegation to a meeting, at a secret location, with a few of Earth's own intellectuals who share our views. Although I won't be attending the discussions, several android guards have accompanied the Guardians, and strict security precautions will be adhered to. All going well, I will be leaving with our people in a couple of days."

Xandra, needed to conceal both his own presence and that of the emissaries while the conference was taking place. Many of his Terran agents, operating in various locations, were summoned to get together with him on Earth Base where he took the opportunity to exchange information and issue further instructions.

All the agents were also issued with a small device which could detect Xvar transmissions. Each base was to receive even more advanced detection and decryption equipment.

Xandra insisted on meeting Victor, and included Aldon and Martina in the discussions. Due to the increased Xvar/Katon threat, the Guardians had determined that it may be necessary to allocate more covert activities to their protégées in the Friendship Club.

"The negative influences affecting this planet must be countermanded. Our contactees and genetically enhanced humans must be encouraged to combine and utilise the various talents and abilities they have been given." Xandra said. "We will notify you which ones are suitable for further contact. It will only be those who have absolute loyalty and are considered to be psychologically stable.

"Every so often, they are to be taken to our special refuge village. As far as they are concerned it will just be a short stay at a spiritual retreat. There can be no more than a few at a time, and some will come from other friendship groups.

"They must not know the exact location of the village, and you must use a PVX to transfer them there and back."

Xandra reminded them that although they were obviously required to work with and utilise the protégées, these genetically altered/enhanced humans were the product of a strategic operation by the Guardians, who had ultimate control of their telepathic and other interfaces. He must be notified immediately if any problems occurred.

When John arrived, Martina was glad that Aldon had given him a second chance. Although he had logged John's recent transgressions, Aldon didn't bring them to Xandra's attention during their meeting. They explained Wangi's presence as being due to her fear of the animals in the vet surgery.

Xandra decided Wangi could stay at Earth Base as part of the planned extra deployments. He would send John a replacement worker as soon as possible.

Martina was glad Xandra didn't ask any difficult questions, and whispered to Aldon, "At least we didn't lie. We just didn't tell the whole truth!"

"You're learning!" Aldon smirked.

Earth Base team was kept fully occupied with the continual movement of their Terran agents to and from the facility. "At least I can introduce you to them now, in advance of later meetings," Aldon advised Martina.

Xandra insisted on going to the surface alone to confer with their specialised Terran scientific personnel who were working incognito with various high-tech laboratories and establishments.

Aldon had told Martina that she would also get to meet them soon, but extra precautions would have to be taken. "Although we are there to support them, if needed, their actual responsibilities are highly classified. These guys are sometimes a law unto themselves, which is a worry. They take their instructions straight from the Guardians.

"Naturally they did not attend the conference, to which only our human colleagues were invited," he said. "The existence of the Terran infiltrators is known only to us, and if identified they would be in extreme peril due to their advanced knowledge and expertise."

Meanwhile the conference, which was held on a pleasure boat, moored just off shore, had been quite promising.

The android guards were vigilant at all times, and quick to take action when they noticed an unidentified man watching through binoculars from a beachside park. He was in fact a federal agent, following up on his own suspicions that there was more to this 'cruise' than met the eye.

His superiors didn't believe him when he reported that aliens were visiting Earth and posed a threat. This time he was going to get the evidence. He was getting his camera ready when a bolt of light hit him in the chest. Unable to move he watched in terror as a figure suddenly appeared and moved towards him. Everything went black.

When he regained consciousness he was lying in the grass. The boat was nowhere in sight, and his camera was gone. As he groggily staggered to his feet two police constables took him by either arm. "Had a bit too much to drink? You'd better come along with us."

"No," he protested, "I'm a federal policeman. I'm not drunk. I don't know what happened." The two officers just laughed as they took him back to the station, only to later find his identification in his pocket.

"Don't apologise," his colleagues said when they arrived to collect him. "We hope he hasn't been raving on about flying saucers and aliens again. Our psychiatrist thinks the job has been too stressful. He needs a good holiday!"

Xandra told Aldon and Martina about the incident, and assured them that the detective would not recall anything. Their androids had captured him and wiped the last few days from his memory before depositing him back in the park.

Once their mission was over, Xandra and the delegation were ready to leave on their transport ship.

"Before I go," he said to Aldon, "I wanted to discuss your position with you before I select more personnel to be posted here. Supervising Earth Base is not going to get any easier in the future. You have served well, and can move on somewhere else if you wish."

Aldon thought of his lost family and destroyed home. There was nothing to go back to.

He paused for a moment, and said, "No, I may as well stay here. This place has grown on me. There would be a lot for a new Commander to learn. Martina, as second in command, is still not familiar with all our sub-bases, agents and the various customs and problems on this planet."

It had been a demanding time for all on Earth Base, which was restored to peace and quiet once everyone had departed. Aldon swung around in his swivel chair.

"Martina, how about you get the rest of that bottle of whiskey you nicked while I was away. I can understand why you needed it when John lost Wangi. I think, after the last few days, we're entitled to finish it off!"

Andy, even though he was essentially only a biological robot, was able to judge a person by their body language, words and tone of voice. It was part of his programming to continually reassess the mood of his controllers so he could respond accordingly.

As he watched the couple relaxing with their drinks, he noted that Aldon had seemed much happier since Martina arrived. Perhaps it was her presence which had prompted his decision not to accept Xandra's offer of a transfer elsewhere.

CHAPTER 7

Victor had gone up to the apartment for a moment, when he heard a strange noise below. Going downstairs, he found Mishka treading over the keys of a piano at the back of the bookshop.

He picked her up and asked, "Do you like music? Let me play something for you."

The piano was already in the bookshop when he purchased the premises, but it had remained relatively untouched, just gathering dust.

As his fingers touched the keys, his mind went back to his days on Solar Base. The Guardians had encouraged his interest in music, and told him it was one of the gateways to the soul. They decided he had talent, and taught him to play all kinds of beautiful melodies, both human and alien.

Due to his advanced intelligence, he could play the most complicated pieces from memory. He recalled a favourite concerto, and as the notes filled the space around him he felt a peace he had not known since his arrival on Earth.

Mishka was purring on his lap, and it was as if their souls were bonded by the harmony and serenity surrounding them. The music poured out of him for a while before he noticed Mary sitting in a lounge chair, with her eyes closed.

"Don't stop," she said. "That was so beautiful, it took me to another place. How did you learn to play the piano like that?"

He was non-committal. "When I was young."

Mary got up and went over to him. "You belong in a concert hall, not hidden away in a suburban coffee lounge/bookstore."

Victor smiled sadly. "You know why I can never do that. Anyway, I feel safe here. This world frightens me sometimes."

Later, when they sat over their coffee, he thought he'd broach the subject of the Terrans' Refuge Village for their contactees.

"Do you remember what your grandmother said about you forming a closer relationship with some of the other protégées? Would you like to spend a few days with several of them, at a very pleasant retreat?"

Although Mary was interested in learning more about his suggestion, she reminded him about her mother's unsympathetic attitude to anything concerning aliens or visitors from outer space.

"Both Granny and I had contact with the Terrans. I've heard that this genetic and other influences run in families."

Victor gently put his hand over hers. "I know your mother is troubled, and perhaps she has also experienced something that was not of this world. She could still be traumatised and in denial. I also realise that she has clung on to you, and is very possessive and demanding where you are concerned.

"You are already in your early thirties. You have to break the ties sooner or later, and start to look to your future. Consider what Granny said about embracing your destiny, and working for change and good in the world."

Mary gave a quiet nod. "I know you're right, but sometimes things are easier said than done."

"Just think about it," Victor suggested as he rose to serve a couple of customers coming in the door.

When she got home Mary was met with angry criticism from her mother. "Late again! You know I expect you home at five – not six-thirty. You have no thought for others. And while I'm at it, you can forget about bringing that kitten home. I'll end up having to clean up after it, as if I haven't got enough to do."

As she choked back the tears, something snapped inside Mary. Not even allowed a kitten to bring a little love into her life! She couldn't take this anymore.

"If I'm so much trouble, maybe it's time I got a place of my own."

Mary had never seen her mother fly into such a rage. "Go – just go," she screamed. "Get out of here! You're just the bastard child that I never wanted in the first place. Your father didn't die. I don't know who your father was. I was walking the dog in the park one night, and saw a bright light. The dog ran home and I don't remember anything until I woke up lying on the grass hours afterward.

"When I discovered I was pregnant, I didn't know how. Your grandmother wouldn't let me have an abortion, and said she would help look after you. Nine months later you were born."

Mary retreated to her room, and sobbed as she threw her clothes and some possessions into a couple of suitcases. She was so distraught, that she had raced out the door and was halfway down the street, before realising she had nowhere to go.

Victor, with Mishka's help, was enjoying a late supper, when he heard a knock on the front door. Looking through the blinds, he saw the tearful Mary.

"You'd better come in," he said.

It took him a while to get the full story out of her. Victor knew he had to help, and couldn't turn her back out into the street.

"I'm going to make you some dinner, and you can stay in my spare bedroom for the night. In the morning, you can leave your things here while you go to work. Tomorrow I'll see what I can arrange."

When he was sure she was asleep Victor transported to Earth Base to discuss the situation with Aldon and Martina.

After some thought, Aldon asked Victor if he would consider letting Mary live permanently in the spare room of his apartment above the bookshop. It would be good company for him, and another person there would provide a little extra security.

Victor looked thoughtful for a moment. "I wouldn't mind, I like Mary and she has nowhere else to go. What about my transporter shower unit?"

"Luckily it's in the en-suite to your room, and not the main bathroom." Aldon said. "We will attach an extra security device, so it cannot be activated by accident. From now on you will have to remember to lock your bedroom door before beaming up."

Once Victor left, Martina questioned Aldon's decision. He explained his concerns about Victor's loneliness and dissatisfaction with his posting.

"In so far as the Friendship Club is concerned he would be difficult to replace. Perhaps he will feel more settled with Mary for company. Mary herself is one of our more mature and trustworthy protégées. I anticipate her taking a leading role where the others are concerned. This way we will not lose contact with her, and in time she may prove a great help to both us and Victor."

The next morning Victor noticed Mary's eyes were red and swollen, and he knew she had been crying. Over breakfast he suggested that she stay permanently.

"I had been considering advertising for a lodger," he lied. "I would much rather share the flat with someone I know and trust."

That night Mary accepted his offer. Affordable accommodation was hard to come by. At least, for the moment, she had a roof over her head, and felt safe. Time would tell if it would become permanent.

Once settled, they discussed her invitation to the Terran Retreat. "Now I'm no longer under my mother's constant control, I am free to do what I please. Granny has always shown me more affection, so I will take her advice and go to meet some of the others. Finally, I may remember and understand the strange events in my past."

A month had passed, and Mary was happier than she had expected living over the bookshop. Her mother's confession about her unknown father was a shock, but in a way answered some of the questions which had haunted her for years.

She was devastated at being rejected by her mother, but all her efforts at reconciliation were in vain. "It is like she is sinking deeper and deeper into a very angry depression," she told Victor.

He frowned, "I heard about some of these cases when I was on Solar Base. It's regrettable that some of the so-called experts, working with the genetic upgrade program, did not consider the long-term effect on the particular human they were dealing with."

Aldon had been correct in his assumption that Mary and Victor would both benefit by each other's company. Victor had someone to converse with. They would often cook together, and watch a movie or TV in the evenings. Sometimes, on the weekends, she would help him in the bookshop and coffee lounge. Mary also encouraged him to play the piano. Mishka had settled in, and would insist on participating in everything. The bookshop was no longer an empty silent prison every night.

Mary was slowly finding the peace and quiet she had never enjoyed at home. Victor's music transformed her into a state of meditative calm. She persuaded him to share his talent with the others at the next Book Club meeting.

Many at the get-together were asking her why she had moved in with Victor. She did not wish to confide the full details of the argument with her mother, and merely said that she was renting the room until something else came along. In fact, she was not even looking for alternate accommodation. She was quite content where she was.

Aldon was well pleased with his decision to let Mary share the apartment above Victor's bookshop. The regular Book Club met as usual, and it was Victor's responsibility to ensure the protégées were careful what they said in front of the entire group. Some people attending were just an unsuspecting part of the deception, and thought the bookstore meetings were merely a venue for intelligent social dialogue.

Victor had already expressed some reservations about a couple of new members. Although they seemed genuine when discussing various topics of interest and the latest publications, he felt uneasy. He already suspected that one woman was a journalist, interested in more than the literary and current affairs aspects of the get-togethers.

There was always the additional risk of government or Xvar aligned agents infiltrating the group, and he did a regular check of the premises for any hidden 'bugs' or surveillance devices.

At first he had been furious when he inadvertently discovered that John had inserted an additional monitoring/telepathic microchip into

Mishka when she was at the vet surgery. Later he was to realise the advantage of her extra abilities.

Now Mary lived there, her continual presence allowed additional contact with some of the more trusted members of the Friendship Club. Their visits appeared to be personal social occasions, with some of the protégées going up to the privacy of her room. This new arrangement provided complete confidentiality when counselling those who were still trying to come to terms with their extraterrestrial experience.

Back at Earth Base Aldon was finalising arrangements for the first group of their genetically enhanced protégées to visit the 'Retreat'. The facility was in a very remote part of the world. It was originally established as a safe haven for Terrans in danger, who could wait there, undetected, until a rescue craft arrived.

Communications were limited, and access usually only by air, or by several days on foot, negotiating very rough terrain. It was originally a small abandoned mining outpost, comprising several log cabins, which the Terrans had modified. Whilst it was hardly ever used for its principal purpose, there was always an android, Otto, on duty.

Aldon and Martina were required to fully convert these primitive buildings into a presentable, but camouflaged, facility. For the next month they used the PVX to ferry in supplies, and loaned a very reluctant Thelta to Otto to help with the work.

"It's only for a short time," Aldon told Thelta. "As soon as Xandra sends some extra workers you can come back to Base. I thought you'd like the change of scenery!"

Thelta turned and looked at him a little uncertainly. Clones did not really like or dislike anything, but they could be fearful of unfamiliar surroundings. Further, it was a big change to be expected to perform manual work rather than the relatively easy duties on the Base.

The interior of the cabins were modernised, complete with bedrooms, bathrooms and kitchens. Primitive dirt paths were smoothed over, and an inconspicuous jetty constructed on the shore of a nearby lake.

Finally the renovations were completed, and the subsistence long-life rations, provided for any fleeing Terran, were supplemented with food more suitable for their human guests.

Once Aldon was satisfied, he notified Solar Base that the preparations at the 'Retreat' were complete. Xandra seemed rather pleased.

"Good work! I will advise the Guardians. The advancement of the human species, through genetic upgrading, is ultimately their project. I think they are going to send a specialist officer to work with our protégées."

Although Victor had discussed the proposed visit to the 'Retreat' with Mary, the choice of who was to accompany her was partially dependent on his and Aldon's reports to the Guardians.

Victor had only been given limited information about the 'Retreat', as it was strictly on a need to know basis. He was unsure as to the whole extent and purpose of the program. His judgement was to be based on emotional stability, and the loyalty, intelligence and talents of those he considered suitable. Also their current area of employment may affect the final selection.

Two promising contenders were the twins, Lucy and Fiona, who had the added advantage of identical genes. They were so connected that they could already share their thoughts and feel each other's pain and emotions. Like Mary, they were at least third generation 'hybrids'. Once their abilities were further augmented, together they could prove to be quite a formidable force.

Bob, who had already proven himself, was also nominated as a candidate, however his family could prove an obstacle. Amy had already shown a tendency to become jealous and suspicious. If she discovered the truth, she lacked the required discretion, and would certainly 'tell all' to her friend Nancy.

The Guardians relayed their decision to Earth Base. They had agreed with Aldon, and accepted his recommendation of Mary, Lucy and Fiona.

Victor invited the twins to dinner one night after the bookstore was closed. Later, when they gathered upstairs, they were told about the invitation to spend a couple of weeks at the 'Retreat' with Mary.

As was their habit, they exclaimed in unison, "How exciting! Of course we'll go!" Lucy could hardly contain her enthusiasm. "You'll have to tell us when, so we can arrange some recreation leave."

Fiona interrupted. "It's lucky we work for the same company. They know we always go on holidays together."

"What about their family?" Mary asked Victor after the women had left.

"No problem!" Victor assured her. "They don't live at home, and share a flat together in town. They have gone away before, so no-one will suspect anything different this time. They have one of Mishka's kittens, so I guess I'll have to mind it here while you are all living the good life at this 'Retreat'."

Aldon continued working with Xandra and the Guardians as they prepared for the first intake of protégées at the Retreat. A specialist Terran agent, Gareth, had arrived and was finalising the upgrade of the small remote settlement, which was to provide the setting for this new project.

Finally, the night of departure had arrived for the three women. They arrived at the bookstore, and sat down to dinner with Mary and Victor. Mishka seemed happy at the return of one of her babies, and having pinned him down with one paw, was giving him a good motherly wash.

More than once the women had asked Victor if he knew where this 'Retreat' was. He had never been told and all that he could say was that it was some distance away. He was to drive them to a quiet area in the country, where another means of transportation would arrive.

Their trip out of town took about thirty minutes. Victor ushered each woman, with her backpack, into a secluded clearing. It was then that he messaged Aldon, in the PVX, that they were ready to go.

They were standing in the darkness, looking all around, when suddenly a silver saucer materialised overhead. Without warning a blue beam of light descended directly from the craft to the earth below.

"Just stand under the light," Victor instructed. "It will take you up into the ship. We could not risk landing so close to town."

There was some hesitation until Mary stepped forward. "I'll go first."

She walked into the circle of blue light on the ground, and unexpectedly found herself slowly rising through the air and up into an opening under the craft's metal type hull.

Lucy and Fiona were both a little uncertain, but followed Mary into the blue light and then the saucer. They found themselves in a comfortable cabin with bench seats all around the walls. Aldon was at the controls, and as he reactivated the invisibility shields, he smiled to himself at their obvious apprehension.

"Welcome to the 'Retreat Express' girls," he announced in a reassuring tone.

They all stared out of a window, captivated by the multitude of brilliant stars against the black velvet expanse of space. Were they going to another planet? Aldon reassured them that the flight would only take an hour, and they were still on Earth.

Suddenly the darkness faded into daylight. They gasped in amazement.

"My God!" said Lucy. "We're on the other side of the world!"

CHAPTER 8

The PVX started to slowly descend, and the women peered out the windows. Lucy was pointing down below.

"I can see mountains, and a valley with trees. Look, there's some water as well. Where are we?"

Aldon, who was now controlling the craft manually, looked across at her. "Sorry, I can't tell you that. It's classified."

The saucer landed smoothly in the middle of the lake, and then moved over to the small jetty.

"What now? I can't see any 'Retreat'." Fiona complained.

A side door slid open, and Gareth peered in. "Welcome ladies. If you care to follow me I will take you to your holiday home for the next fortnight."

Fiona was still doubtful. "I hope we don't need tents." Gareth started to laugh, and when he helped Mary and Lucy out, a reluctant Fiona followed. As he led them up a dirt path through the trees, they saw the PVX rise into the air, and disappear.

Mary was going to comment on having to make the best of it, even if it was just a tent, when they came into a clearing.

"Oh look!" she said. "What charming little log cabins, and such pretty flowers and bushes. What is that over there? I think it's a chicken coop and vegetable patch. We couldn't even see this from the air!"

Gareth explained that, for obvious reasons, it wasn't meant to be seen. "You are right, but the chickens are for eggs only. We are vegetarians and don't kill anything. The vegetable patch is part of being self sufficient, a skill which will be included in some of your training here. You may find it useful one day.

"This is my assistant Otto; he will show you to your quarters and get you anything you need."

They were given one of the log cabins to share, with an individual bedroom for each of them. All the linen had been provided, and the kitchen was well stocked with provisions. Otto advised the village had its own clean energy power supply, but they must close the shutters at night when they turned on the lights.

Once they had settled in, Fiona admitted it wasn't so bad, after all. "I think I might even enjoy it here. That guy Otto is a bit of a hunk." Lucy, who was taking the clothes and toiletries out of her backpack, agreed.

After a while Gareth knocked on the door and suggested he show them around the community. It was during their short tour that Fiona asked about Otto.

"She thinks he's cute." Lucy teased.

Gareth started to chuckle. "He's actually an android, a very advanced biological robot. I don't know how he'd react if he was told you fancied him!" Mary and Lucy collapsed into fits of giggles.

Fiona blushed and looked embarrassed. "You can laugh all you like. He's probably better than most men we know!"

When they noticed Thelta coming out of the facility's small control room, all three women stopped as forgotten memories came flooding back. The four foot tall little grey being stopped, and tilting its large head to the side, stared at them with big black oval eyes.

"That's Thelta, who will not hurt you." Gareth reassured them. "These little workers are quite shy. They can hear and understand you, but cannot talk themselves, and converse telepathically. During your stay here you may develop the ability to communicate with them."

Fiona looked at Lucy. "Do you remember? We had some friends like that when we were little. We used to go with them at night, when Mum and Dad were asleep. We would go up into the sky and play games together."

Lucy nodded. "Yes, and I remember going up in that blue beam of light, to get to their silver house. Mum would get really angry, and sometimes cry, if we talked about it. In the end, she convinced me it was all in our imaginations."

"It was very real," Gareth assured them. "We have been contacting and monitoring each one of you since you were small children. You are a special part of our plan to help the human race evolve into a more peaceful and spiritual future.

"I want you to rest for the remainder of the day, and tomorrow morning, over a communal breakfast, you can meet others like yourself, who are also here. They include many different races and nationalities, however to safeguard everyone's identity and location, you may neither ask nor tell too many personal details, or your exact places of origin."

During their tour of the small village, Mary had noticed the PVX materialising in the sky every so often, and realised it must have been bringing these other people Gareth had mentioned.

The next morning, they sat down at the large outdoor table spread with a buffet breakfast. There were four other groups of 'students', of varying ages, from the other log cabins. Some of them didn't even speak English, and were obviously of Asian or native origin.

The twins commented that although they didn't recall ever meeting these people before, they somehow seemed familiar. Gareth could sense what they were thinking, and walked over.

"All these people were chosen because they carry the same hereditary 'strain' which dates back thousands of years to when many Terrans were living on Earth. That is why they seem familiar. You can recognise and connect with each other's related frequencies and vibrations.

"Everyone here has what may be called a 'gift' – be it kinetic, the power to heal, predict the future, read others' minds, or communicate telepathically. Human society would classify your various abilities as being 'paranormal'. They are, in fact, the result of our recent 'genetic enhancement' project involving several generations of particular families.

"In fact, most Terrans already possess these powers naturally. We will teach you how to communicate without the need for spoken language. It requires a concentration of the mind - images, emotions and all the senses. Once a telepathic link has been established, it can be tuned into anytime.

"When each one of you has learned to master your individual talents, we will progress to you working in small groups, and combining your skills. Also, when the time is right, we will activate certain additional knowledge, which we placed into your subconscious minds during past contacts."

One of their first lessons involved exercises in 'mindlessness'. The students lay on the lawn, with yoga mats for comfort. Gareth was playing incredible music on an unusual instrument, and before long they all reached a very tranquil meditative state.

Mary found that as her conscious mind and thoughts drifted into a sense of 'peaceful calm', long forgotten and suppressed memories began to surface. When she returned to reality and the present moment she looked at Fiona and Lucy, who were comparing their perceptions of the reverie. It was not surprising that, being identical twins, they also had matching reports. All three commented on a sense of a shift in consciousness.

This morning ritual continued throughout their stay at the 'Retreat', and gradually they realised that they had a heightened awareness of the world around them. Not only could understand what people were thinking and feeling, they could also convey particular thoughts and ideas in return.

They were taught how to control and utilise their mental powers, including the art of what was commonly termed 'psychic self-protection'. Just as they were able 'to get into someone's head', they had to learn how to block anybody else doing the same to them.

Although the students worked in their own individual groups, they shared many meals together, and started forming bonds with the others who were from different parts of the planet. In the evenings there would be sing-songs around a communal camp fire. A dedicated few would take a daily dip in the lake below.

"That mountain water is too cold for us!" The twins lamented.

All the initiates were taken around the 'Retreat' and taught the basics of survival, and how to 'live off the grid'. Gareth was at pains to give them some knowledge of self sufficiency.

"Your planet is too dependent upon digital and other technology, which can be manipulated or used for total control. In a natural disaster or other calamity, such as an enemy attack, the population would not know how to fend for themselves and be totally helpless."

Daily instruction periods also included the use of telepathy. At first Mary, Fiona and Lucy had to work as a group of three, and later they began to communicate with the other students, without the necessity for a common spoken language.

They also practised combining their minds in exercises to move objects kinetically, and predict the outcome of certain events. As their skills improved, Lucy whispered, "I foretold most of the 'winners' in that one exercise. We have to go to the horse races more often!"

Each of them had been given the task of trying to move a stone using the power of their mind. Mary found it impossible, no matter how hard she tried. When she combined her efforts with Lucy and Fiona the rock wobbled slightly.

On the last day Gareth gathered all the students together, and jointly with mass concentration, the stubborn rock rose several meters into the air. There was spontaneous cheering.

"I trust you now understand that while you may not be able to do something alone," he said, "with mutual co-operation you can achieve great results. Keep close to your own small groups, and foster and strengthen the bonds you have formed. You will need each other in the future."

The night before Mary had been summoned to the control room, where Otto placed a small metal device on her head. It created a distinctive vibration which permeated her entire being.

"I know what that does," she grumbled. "I remember from when I was a child. It will wipe my memory."

"On the contrary," Otto explained. "I have just provided your subconscious with an additional amount of knowledge and information. It is similar to downloading data into a computer's memory. You will be able to access it when certain situations arise."

The time had come to leave. They were about to board the PVX, when Gareth farewelled them on the jetty. "Remember all we have taught you, and practise your new skills. Nobody, and I mean nobody - not even the other members of your 'Friendship Club' – must know of the existence of the 'Retreat' or your visit here."

After all the students left, Gareth received a clandestine visit from Zadok, and discussed plans to bring more of their protégées to the Retreat at a later date.

Zadok reminded him that not even Aldon and Martina could be advised of the true purpose behind the 'Retreat'. "Everybody thinks all the people, we have modified through the generations, are here to assist mankind to a better and more spiritually peaceful future.

"This is true for the vast majority of the thousands of humans concerned, however our efforts are being constantly undermined by the covert activities of the Xvars and Katons. They have agents on Earth who do not wish to see the human situation improve.

"Our own Galactic guidelines are ones of non-interference, at least on a direct level, with the inhabitants of this planet. We cannot send our own military here to confront our opponents. These gifted humans will be able to help protect our other 'enhanced' citizens from negative forces. A more disturbing task will be to act as small clandestine insurgent groups if the need arises."

Gareth assured Zadok that Mary, and all the others at the Retreat, were totally unaware of what might be asked of them later.

Victor was waiting in the clearing when Aldon returned the women in the PVX. He noticed a change in all three of them, and an unspoken bond. During Victor's upbringing on Solar Base, he had been trained to use the power of his mind. His capabilities had reached a very high standard and he immediately sensed the improvement in the women's telepathic and other abilities. This would allow him a greater connection with them, which could be advantageous at future Friendship Club meetings and activities.

Before he dropped Lucy and Fiona at their apartment block, they returned to the bookstore and collected their kitten. Victor was glad Mary was back. He was used to living alone, and did not expect to miss her during the two weeks she was away. In fact his evenings seemed lonely without her company.

Mishka gave Mary a warm welcome as she settled in her room. Over the past few weeks, since the clash with her mother, everything had changed for the better. It was only recently that she realised how restrictive her life had been. Now there was a newly found freedom, and a place she could call home. The Terran experience had created a special bond with her new friends Victor, Lucy and Fiona.

Otto had remained at the now locked down Retreat. Zadoc had intended to take Gareth back to Solar Base with him. At the last minute he changed his mind, and thought it better Gareth remain on Earth so he could keep a close eye on a couple of valued Terran scientific agents and their new project. Aldon gave Gareth a lift in the PVX to an insignificant town, where another of their agents was going to accommodate him until he established a false identity.

Eventually Aldon was able to return to Earth Base. He arrived with his last passenger, Thelta, who immediately scuttled off to be with Delta and Wangi.

"Funny little things," he observed, "they seem to prefer being with their own kind."

He had spent a hectic twenty four hours in the PVX, ferrying everybody back to their various countries and destinations. He was glad that he did not have to take anyone back to the sub-base in the Himalayas. The monks in Noru's group did not require additional training. They were already highly evolved due to their genetic heritage and very secluded existence over thousands of years.

Martina noticed that Aldon seemed rather tired. She poured a couple of drinks, and sat down on the lounge with him. "Time to relax.

Nothing of importance has happened. Just take it easy for a while. Andy and I can handle the normal routine matters."

Martina's words had reminded Aldon of his former happier days. He would return home from duty, the children would be in bed and his wife would meet him with a drink.

"Snap out of it! No good feeling miserable, or dwelling on it," he thought. "Those damn Xvars destroyed everything dear to me. One day I'll make them pay!"

CHAPTER 9

Mary, Lucy and Fiona were all adjusting to a new 'awareness' and connection with the world in general. From time to time they would to sense other people's thoughts and emotions, which could be somewhat disturbing.

At the Friendship Club get-together the women were dutifully vague about their holiday, and waffled on about hiking and swimming in the country. Later on, over coffee, Victor was full of praise.

"You did very well ladies! Don't forget to keep practising your new skills – just not anything significant in front of the others!

"I would like you to keep an eye on that woman, Joy Brown, who has recently been attending the meetings. I can't put my finger on it, but there is something about her that makes me uneasy. Our surveillance systems have not detected her doing or saying anything suspicious. On the surface, she is well read, and only interested in the philosophical discussions.

"I think she suspects there is more to our meetings than meets the eye, but I don't know if she is an agent from some authority, a journalist, or just a nosey busybody. She is definitely not one of 'us', but has gone out of her way to try and strike up a personal relationship with some members of the 'Friendship Club'."

Lucy was pleased. "How exciting - our first assignment!"

Later, Mary spoke to Victor about some thoughts she and the twins had regarding the Friendship Club.

"All three of us have been getting the same urge to find a sort of weekend hide-away out of the town. We have suddenly become uneasy at living so close to the sea, and want to find a small self sufficient country property up in the hills. There are several suitable for sale about twenty miles away. I don't know why we are all getting this sudden compulsion. Maybe it is something to do with our time at the Retreat.

"Thinking about your concerns regarding infiltrators at our get-togethers, perhaps a secluded country holiday cottage would be a safer place for the 'inner circle' to hold more confidential discussions. You are right. It is a bit risky having so many of the Terran contactees and experiencers meeting together in such a public place."

Their suggestion had merit, and Victor thought it deserved further consideration. He would need to discuss the idea with Aldon.

"What are you going to do about money?" he asked. "Those farmhouses don't come cheap."

Mary paused, "Lucy has a psychic gift for predicting winners at the race track. She is even more uncannily accurate when she actually sees the horses prior to the event. We thought we could raise the purchase price through gambling."

Victor gave her a bewildered glance. "You know you mustn't use your powers for personal gain, but I suppose for the good of the Friendship Club.........I don't know, but you're going to do it anyway, aren't you? Just use different bookmakers, and don't, under any circumstances, go anywhere near the Casino."

Aldon shared Victor's misgivings, but both agreed that several of their human contactees and protégées meeting at the same time and place was not really safe or advisable.

The three women couldn't wait for their first Saturday at the race course. Half the fun was getting their costumes, hair and make-up just right. Lucy and Fiona picked Mary up in their car. Victor couldn't help smiling to himself as she went teetering out the door in very high heels, with a ridiculous bit of net and feathers on her head.

Fiona didn't want to bet on every race. "If we keep picking the winners, people will get suspicious. Better to stick to one or two with a high return."

Lucy kept scrutinising the horses, pointing out the ones she thought promising. Usually she was accurate, however many were only on short odds. Early in the afternoon they singled out a potential candidate, placing ten dollars for a win. They were screaming encouragement as he raced out in front.

"That was great," Fiona gloated, as she put their one hundred dollar winnings in her bag. "But it is nowhere near what we even need for a deposit on a property."

The last race was due to start, and Lucy was still concentrating on the horses before they were led to the starting boxes.

"That one!" she proclaimed triumphantly.

Mary examined the race guide. "He's an outsider and not given much chance. Are you sure?"

"Yes – yes! Give me the money. Let's get to a 'bookie' quick."

When they reached 'Honest Joe's' stand, Lucy shoved their money into his hand and said, "One hundred dollars on 'Black Prince' to win."

Fiona and Mary gasped, fearing Lucy was about to lose everything they had just gained. When they walked away 'Honest Joe' looked at his offsider.

"A fool and their money are soon parted. That horse hasn't a hope in hell of winning, that's why he's a hundred to one! Silly woman said he looked so nice, and had beautiful eyes!"

The race got underway, and the three women were sending every possible concentrated thought at 'Black Prince' to run faster. Mary had closed her eyes, scared to look, when her two companions started cheering and hugging each other.

"He's won – he's won!"

On the way home Lucy counted their ten thousand dollars with relish. "Honest Joe wasn't very happy. I think we took every last cent he had in his bag! Better not go back there for a while."

A bemused Victor met them as they came bouncing in the door. Aldon had approved their idea for the farm cottage out of town, provided they agreed it could be used as a safe house if the need arose. However, they both had reservations about the fund raising scheme.

"Rather than raising the entire purchase price by dubious means, it would be better to put down a deposit. Pay off a mortgage with your ill gotten gains. That way there won't be questions asked over your sudden influx of cash.

"Avoid the private bookmakers who may start to query your continual good luck. Go individually to three betting shop windows, and each place a smaller amount on your chosen horse. This way your return will be the same without raising suspicions."

The women agreed that may be the wisest course of action. After a couple more rewarding excursions to different, very crowded racing festivals, they started their search for some suitable real estate

For the next few weeks, they said nothing about their plans at the bookstore meetings, which had been without incident. Lucy and Fiona would stay behind, after the rest of the group left, for private discussions with Mary and Victor.

It was late, on one of these evenings, that they heard a loud noise outside and a call for help. They raced out the front door to see two hooligans on motorbikes, circling and terrorising a homeless man and his dog.

Fiona and Lucy experienced an uncontrolled moment of pure outrage, and in unison, without thinking, each stretched out one arm and pointed at the culprits. Mary was so incensed she also directed her anger at the bikies.

"No – don't do that!" Victor cautioned, but it was too late. Both motorbikes went skidding sideways across the road, with the riders flying into the air and hitting the ground with a painful thud. While the two bullies were sitting on the tarmac in stunned disbelief, the man and his dog escaped down a side lane.

The women stared at each other in astonishment. What had they done? Their reaction had been spontaneous and not an intentional directed use of their powers.

Victor quickly ushered them back into the shop. "I can understand your anger, but you have already been told that you must always have complete self control when using your extra abilities. Any emotional response can increase the effect.

"In future, please think first before you do something like that. You were lucky nobody witnessed your little party trick. Our mission is too important to jeopardise with unwanted publicity."

Further up the street Joy Brown stepped out of the shadows. She was still shaking from what she had just seen. Her newspaper editor had said she was wasting her time investigating a small suburban bookstore, and any suspicious activity was a figment of her imagination.

"Maybe now he will stop belittling my efforts," she thought. "On the other hand, I have no proof. He will never believe me."

A few nights later, Mary and Victor were both asleep when Mishka came dashing into their bedrooms. First she jumped up on Mary's bed, crying loudly and patting her face.

Mary sat up. "What on earth's the matter? It's two o'clock in the morning. We've already fed you."

Mishka raced straight into Victor's room. More direct action was required! She landed straight on his face.

Victor and Mary met in the landing. "I think someone is in the bookstore," she whispered.

They crept down the stairs, with Mishka leading the way. When they entered the shop two dark hooded figures fled out the front door.

Joy Brown gasped and caught her breath as she and her colleague ran up the street to their cars parked around the corner. She couldn't understand how they had been discovered so quickly. She had hired a private detective, who turned off the burglar alarms.

'Thank God we weren't caught", she said. "We could both be charged with break and enter, and my editor would certainly kick me off the newspaper. Perhaps I can think of another way."

"You can count me out next time," her companion growled.

Victor looked at Mary as he shut the front door. "I'll have to install better locks. Whoever it was disabled the burglar alarms. They may have overlooked the security cameras, which are too microscopic to be detected.

"Now let's see who it was, and if they present any ongoing threat!"

The security camera footage and the data from Mishka's monitoring chip revealed Joy Brown and an unidentified man. Victor entered special biometric and other recognition programs on his computer. He seemed relieved.

"I don't think they found anything. I checked up, and that Joy Brown is a local reporter. The bloke is a run of the mill private detective."

He gave Mishka a cuddle. "You are such a good girl. Without you we may never have discovered them in time. I'm buying you a special treat for dinner tomorrow."

He turned to Mary. "I must consider some additional precautions. In the meantime keep a close eye on that Joy Brown whenever she is at our Book Club meetings."

Gareth had spent some time finding a suitable home in a cosmopolitan city. Aldon and a couple of their Terran agents, experts in cyber crime, had arranged for his new identity, false papers and employment history.

The Guardians had decided Gareth was to infiltrate into society as an executive, managing agreements with sub-contractors for a large multinational aerospace conglomerate. This provided him with the freedom to move among various crucial locations without suspicion.

He was allocated two assignments. One was to covertly support and liaise with a couple of their Terran scientists, Michael and Tony, who were deeply imbedded into the technological development department of that same company. If their true identities were ever discovered they would be in dire peril. Not only would the Xvar/Katon agents want to eliminate them, the military, government and powerful corporations would stop at nothing to discover all their advance knowledge and everything they knew about the Terran activities.

Gareth was a Terran, and like his colleagues must remain incognito. The sole exception was his second responsibility to monitor their special category of protégées. Of all the Terran agents, he was the only one who had revealed his true identity, and even then, to just a trusted few at the Retreat.

Although Victor was raised on Solar Base, he was not categorised as a true Terran, and considered a genetically enhanced human. Gareth felt that due to his special status, Victor could perhaps continue working on his behalf, and assist in the selection of a few more promising candidates for a future intake at the Retreat.

If the need ever arose, it would be Gareth in command of these small elite groups. One night he made his first clandestine visit to the bookstore. He smiled to himself when Victor recounted the incident with the bikies. The girls had learned well. Victor was unaware of the warrior skills that were to be included as part of their programming.

"Never mind," he said to the crestfallen trio. "Next time think carefully before you do something drastic like that."

The main reason he had dropped in to see them was to discuss the final choice of the country property the women planned purchasing. After the incident with Joy Brown breaking into the premises, they definitely needed a more secluded location for their special group of protégées and the more trustworthy of the genetically enhanced humans and hybrids.

"We need the assistance of some of these people if we are to promote peace on this planet and successfully raise the population to a higher level of spirituality. We do not want them to be identified, harassed or worse by curious researchers, reporters or government agencies." Gareth said.

"I will be much happier when you can hold weekend get-togethers away from town. Your proposed country farmhouse can also provide a safe haven for any of our friends in an unexpected emergency.

"With that in mind my superiors have approved our contribution towards the mortgage every month. Your innovative fund raising efforts are very commendable, but could cause unwanted attention."

Mary, Fiona and Lucy could hardly contain their enthusiasm, and allowed Gareth and Victor to make the final property selection. The entire project was co-ordinated by Aldon and Martina, who also kept

John informed. Over the next few weeks, Victor used his small van to transport their newly acquired furniture and household goodies up to the premises.

The three women were not even aware of the existence of transporter showers, and it was too risky to even consider installing one in their new cottage. If any fugitive took shelter there, a remote back road could be used to reach John's sub-base veterinary surgery, twenty miles away.

CHAPTER 10

Back in his vet surgery John was grumbling to Sarah about their little grey worker no longer being there. Wangi used to do the housework, and clean the animal's accommodation during the day. Now, they had to do all the work themselves, after the surgery was closed.

John, being a Terran agent, did not have to rely on his veterinary occupation to provide a high standard of living. That was a good thing, because he often spent more than he earned.

He loved the wonderful variety of life on this planet, and hated all humans for their cruelty towards them. John was even horrified that these people bred and killed animals, fish and birds to eat. He, like his space brothers, was vegetarian.

Part of his premises served as a wildlife refuge, where he would treat and care for all manner of creatures at his own expense. He would also attend to his clients' pets and livestock, even if they had no money to pay him. Alleviating the suffering of innocent creatures was more important than any financial reward.

He hated it when the duck shooters went berserk with their rifles, and the animal rights volunteers would come in with these poor little innocent creatures. Some of their injuries were horrific, and many would never fly again.

Every time hunters were on the prowl John's finely tuned telepathic abilities would sense the fear and terror of their prey. He had to suppress the urge to go out and give them a taste of their own medicine, but protocol prohibited him from drawing attention to himself.

One night he heard shots coming from the woodland. "That's it! That's the final straw!" he said to Sarah. "It's the hillbilly Jackson family from up the mountain. They don't only kill the wildlife to feed their dogs, they have been slaughtering the local farmers' stock whenever they want to put meat on the dinner table.

"I can't stand this anymore. I've got to do something!"

He transported up to Earth Base, and asked Martina if he could urgently use the PVX for a short while. She was unsure if this would be sanctioned by Aldon, who was on the surface visiting another agent. She was well aware that they were there to assist John and the others, and where possible not to interfere in their assignments.

When he flew off, Martina hoped and prayed John would return, as promised, within the hour. That way Aldon may never know.

John kept the invisibility shields activated as he searched the area for the Jacksons. There they were, in Bert Walters field, stalking one of his cows. He swooped down, allowing the PVX to be seen by those below.

The Jackson boys and their father came to a sudden halt. A strange silver craft was hurtling towards them and skimmed over the top of their heads.

"It's a flying saucer. It's aliens!" one yelled.

John turned the PVX around and made several more low passes. Each time he directed a ray towards them. It had just enough heat to affect all the metal in their rifles and other equipment. John chortled to himself as they stumbled and fell in the mud. As soon as he saw the terrified culprits running towards their old ute, he reactivated the invisibility shields and headed back to Earth Base.

John was glad that Aldon was still away, and had not been around to ask any awkward questions.

"Thanks for that," he said to Martina as he entered the transporter to return to the vet surgery.

Martina was tempted to ask him what he had been up to; - on second thoughts – maybe not.

Sarah looked up as John walked into the lounge room. "Where have you been? I couldn't find you."

"You don't want to know," he grinned, "but it sure was fun."

The next day Bert popped into the surgery. "Have you heard the latest? That Jackson family have been raving on about being chased by flying saucers and aliens. Probably been drinking too much of their homemade moonshine again.

"Nobody believes them, of course, but last night my cows were disturbed, and I'm sure I saw the Jackson's vehicle outside my back paddock fence. I also saw something strange in the sky.

"If it was the aliens, I should like to thank them. I know that family are responsible for a couple of my animals going missing. I just can't prove it."

John felt a little nervous. He didn't need any local gossip about aliens! He just smiled at Bert and said, "If I were you, I wouldn't tell anyone about what you think you saw. People might think you are as barmy as those country retards!"

A few days later, Aldon was expressing the need for greater security, especially where John was concerned.

"His facility is close to a populated area," he told Martina. "Even when Wangi is replaced, John and Sarah are insufficient staffing. We need to deploy at least one more assistant. We also have to devise a safe way of conveying messages, in an emergency, between the veterinary surgery and the newly established farm house.

"You know, I was rather impressed with the role Mishka played in thwarting the break-in at Victor's. That was good thinking to plant that monitoring device in her. Why can't we do something similar for John? After all – there are always animals at his surgery."

Martina looked thoughtful, and was glad she hadn't mentioned John borrowing the PVX. "I have a better idea. Galactic Command have already manufactured all kinds of biological robot animals suitable for various civilisations in this Quadrant. Why not a dog?"

Aldon was quickly warming to the suggestion. "It could monitor and record everything, and communicate with Sarah and John, especially if it had the ability to talk. A large breed, with a fine set of teeth could certainly deter any human intruders."

The Guardians agreed with the plan, and placed an order for the 'animal'. John, however, didn't seem overly enthusiastic. He wondered if this new 'dog' would also be recording and spying on both him and Sarah as well. It seemed futile to argue, the decision had been made.

A few weeks later Aldon arrived in the transporter under the vet surgery. He led a very fine Rottweiler specimen into the waiting room.

"Here you go John, this is your new guard dog. He has been well programmed, and will not speak in the presence of any humans."

"I hope not," said John. "That would certainly cause unnecessary publicity. I guess I will have to give him a name. How about 'Boof'? That sounds innocent enough."

"Whatever," sighed Aldon, a little disappointed by John's lack of enthusiasm. "At least 'Boof' doesn't require feeding, doesn't urinate or make a mess, and won't chase Wangi's replacement when it arrives. He has an incredible strength, is deadly in attack mode, and can run faster than any human.

"An additional benefit will be his ability, in an emergency, to convey messages and information under cover. After all, who is going to suspect a dog, especially one who is so realistic he even slobbers like his breed?"

"I noticed," John grunted.

Aldon was getting annoyed. "You could at least show a little more gratitude. Everyone went to a lot of trouble to design the first robotic android in a biological dog's body. In fact, the Guardians were so pleased with the result, they are seriously considering making some more.

"That is why they have placed a special security collar permanently around his neck. He is a valuable prototype, and we need to be able to track his movements at all times."

"And mine!" John thought as Aldon departed.

John looked at Boof with a little hesitation. "Do you know how to act like a normal dog?"

"Yes," he replied, "I have been programmed for all the appropriate canine behaviour. I can even bark, growl, whine and make all the appropriate sounds."

John shrugged. "Fine! Just don't talk in front of humans. Remember I'm in charge, and don't get in the way!"

That night John made sure that Boof was guarding the surgery when Sarah slipped into his bedroom.

A couple of weeks later, Sarah looked up as Billy Jackson came into the waiting room. "I'm sorry, John's out on a house call. Is there anything I can do to help?"

"All alone," Billy smirked, "a pretty lady like you? How about a real man to keep you company, not a wimp like your boss.....Come on, give us a kiss."

He lunged forward, knocking Sarah off balance. Within seconds of her cry for help, a ferocious growl could be heard from the doorway. As Billy turned around Boof sank his teeth into his ankle, and Sarah took the opportunity to get to her feet.

"Heel Boof!" she shouted. "I'll take it from here."

As Boof sat by her side, Billy looked at his bloodied ankle, and limped towards her. "Look what your dog's done. I'll get you for this!"

Sarah, with her robotic strength, took a swing at Billy, knocking him clean across the room. "That's nothing compared to what I'll do to you if you ever lay a hand on me again."

Old man Jackson came running in, and kicked his son as he lay on the floor. "What did I tell you boy about being nice to the vet. He's cared for the dogs even when we didn't have any money."

"I'm very sorry Miss," he apologised, as he grabbed Billy by the collar and marched him out the door.

When he returned, Sarah and Boof were unusually quiet and John sensed all was not well. "What have I missed?" he asked.

He was seething when he heard of the incident, and for the first time appreciated Boof. Sarah was precious to him personally. More important was the fact she was a valuable android whose true nature must never be revealed. If anything went wrong during this mission, his next posting may be too horrible to contemplate.

A few miles away, Fiona, Lucy and Mary spent several weekends adding the final personal touches to their new homestead. One day, during their absence, Aldon had taken a reluctant Andy to the farm, and together they had dug-up the soil for several vegetable plots.

Victor had to get a couple of gardening books off the bookshelves, and smiled to himself as the women poured through the pages, making copious notes and a long shopping list.

All three were very enthusiastic. "We need gardening tools and things....... and lots of seeds. It's good there was already a stream for fresh water and also an extra tank along with solar panels and wood heaters. Soon we'll be self-sufficient!"

Later, over supper, Mary looked at Victor, and asked him if he knew who had dug the vegetable garden for them.

"Ask me no questions and I'll tell you no lies," he replied.

Mary stood up and patted him on the shoulder. "I know you or Aldon must have had something to do with it. Thank you for what you are not going to tell me!"

Aldon reported the completion of the project to Solar Base, and Xandra congratulated him.

"Well done! We have very few places 'off the grid' as humans say. Although the girls may take their mobile phones for an emergency, as long as they're turned off there will be no detectable technology – ours or theirs.

"There is one more modification Gareth and I want you to make. During the week, when no-one is there, I want you and Andy to construct a camouflaged escape tunnel from the basement into the small cave in the rock face just behind the house. The laser blaster and some of that new gear I gave you should make it relatively easy."

"What's up?" Martina asked as a glum Aldon as he came back into the room.

"Gareth didn't wait around. He's off on his new assignment, playing the high flying corporate executive. It looks like Andy and I are left with the hard slog. Never mind, you win some you lose some!"

Mary, Lucy and Fiona were absorbed in their project at the new farmstead hide-away. Every weekend they practised their newly learned psychic and kinetic abilities, both individually and as a group.

"I think we're improving," Mary said when they managed to levitate a few very small objects into the air

The vegetable garden was full of promising green shoots, and they planned on a few chickens for a newly erected coop. They had dismissed the idea of a pony, and a couple of goats because they were away at work during the week. They had also made friends with an elderly lady who had a property just up the road.

"She is rather eccentric, and has befriended a few of the wild cats that live in the neighbourhood." Mary told the others. "She seems to stay home all the time, except for once a week, when she takes her old car into town for supplies. I offered her a few dollars a week if she would keep an eye on our place. Maybe if we get the pony and two goats she will feed them for us."

Old Mrs McAffrey was more than happy to earn some extra money, and readily agreed to the suggestion. Except for her cats, she had been very lonely. The local families had avoided her, and their children called her a 'witch'. She really appreciated the friendship of these three new neighbours.

Victor had used his van to transport all manner of things, including the chickens and goats. He insisted a proper horse float had to be used for 'Wiggles' their new pony.

He thought his removalist duties were over, until the girls decided that to be truly self-sufficient they would each require a bicycle. They were having coffee one night when Fiona made the suggestion.

"You'll end up falling off and breaking something," Victor warned.

"No," Lucy argued. "Fiona and I both had bikes as kids."

"Me too," Mary said. "Do we have enough money in the kitty?"

Lucy counted out what remained of their winnings. "Not really. We haven't been to the races for a few weeks. Next Saturday we'll go back for another little flutter."

Within the fortnight Victor was co-opted to take the new bicycles up to the farm. He watched in amusement as they wobbled around trying to regain the balance which came naturally when they were children.

After he left, Fiona looked at Mary. "You know, Victor is such a nice guy - one in a million. Men like that don't come along very often, and he obviously likes you."

While Mary denied any romantic attachment, she realised she had become quite fond of Victor.

CHAPTER 11

Aldon told Martina he was thankful that Gareth had been deputised to keep an eye on their Terran scientists, who were often a law onto themselves. Their activities and influence on the human race were essential to the Guardians' overall strategy to effectively bring planet Earth under their authority.

"Let's be honest about this," Aldon said. "Control is what this is really all about - control of this planet and entire Solar System! Whom can we liaise with, when the Earth itself is torn by competing nations, their military, and large corporations? The ordinary population can revolt and overthrow a government. The future here is often unpredictable. Now we have the additional complication of increasing incursions by competing alien interests."

Martina interrupted. "Yes, but due to their different physical appearance the Xvars and Katons are at a disadvantage. Unlike us, they cannot mingle freely with the human population."

Aldon explained that their enemies were mainly confined to living in the underground laboratories of the few corporations or military factions, who welcomed the supremacy their dangerous technology would provide.

Even the various nations' governments were unaware of the Xvar infiltration. Some of the dissident military hierarchy and industrial cabals considered that one day, with the Xvars' assistance, they would be in command, instead of the inefficient elected politicians.

"Of course it will really be the Xvars in control," Martina commented. "Will Gareth's new position visiting the various sub-contractors' premises help locate the concealed Xvars and their underlings? What do we do if we find them?"

Aldon frowned. "What do you think? If we can't safely hand them over to the Guardians, we kill them of course! Why do you think most of our people here have been trained by the military?"

Gareth had purchased his new home in the outskirts of a cosmopolitan city. Once his transporter shower and a few other high tech goodies had been installed, he concentrated on providing support for Tony and Michael, whose high salaries had also enabled them to purchase luxury abodes.

They had mostly been allowed a free reign during their deployment on Earth, but this would have to change. Their input into innovative research and development projects for aerospace and military concerns made them two of the most important Terrans on the planet.

Aldon had, on several occasions, been concerned about their scientists' less than desirable behaviour. They had developed a tendency for too much socialising. While Tony and Michael were required to attend corporate conventions, dinners and other similar events, Tony in particular had a partiality for wild parties and loose women.

Michael was quieter. It wasn't that he disliked the female species, he just didn't trust them. Back on his own planet, his fiancée had jilted him at their marriage ceremony. That was one of the reasons he agreed to this assignment on Earth.

After Gareth had visited several of the sub-contractors' establishments, his suspicions were aroused at one facility in a semi-arid desert area.

"My detector picked up Xvar transmissions from somewhere underground at D.K. Enterprises," he told Aldon.

It did not take Xandra long to get back to them. "Do nothing! We do not want to compromise any of our Terrans on Earth. Solar Base will handle this."

Zadoc, Xandra and Commander Karine planned their raid on D.K. Enterprises. They prepared special android robot warriors, who would be disguised as an unidentified human military unit.

The attack itself was to be led by two of their senior officers, also wearing a similar disguise. They had been told, where possible, not to injure the human employees at the facility, which had to be searched and then destroyed.

Late at night, when the premises only had minimal staff, a shuttle craft was launched from a ship high in orbit. The soldiers beamed down behind a storage shed near the main building. A couple of 'stun' devices were thrown through the front doors before they commenced their assault.

Any security guards, not rendered unconscious, were paralysed by the Terran ray guns before they could reach for their weapons.

A couple of soldiers disengaged the emergency alarms and the rest of their force proceeded down the corridor. After a few minutes their android leader reported that all visible personnel had been neutralised, and Commander Karine ordered his troops to remove the motionless bodies of the employees to safety outside.

"We cannot neutralise this Xvar enterprise until we locate them, and discover what they have been up to. They are somewhere under the building; – Corporal, detonate those couple of concealed security entrances, and let us see where they lead."

Once the doors were destroyed, they were able to enter a tunnel leading down to an enormous brightly lit area. Karine was astounded at the complexity of this underground facility. Their opponents had been far more active than they had realised.

Suddenly they were met by a barrage of laser fire, and he saw a couple of his robot force go down. He spotted an Xvar and three Katons ahead, and when his ray gun failed to paralyse them, ordered his troops to shoot to kill.

He stepped over the lifeless bodies of their enemy and sent a party of soldiers ahead to search the premises. One returned a few minutes later.

"I think you'd better see this Commander."

Karine recoiled in horror when he saw the glass enclosures, containing the mutilated bodies of human beings. "Are any of them alive?"

"Only a couple, Sir, and I don't think we can take them out without disconnecting the tubes and leads attached to their bodies."

Karine felt sick to his stomach, but he knew what he had to do. After removing the incapacitated and lifeless Terran robotic soldiers, they set explosives on a short timer. Once evacuated, the building crumbled into a heap of rubble. With any luck, all evidence would have been destroyed.

Before they left, the Terran militia scattered the bodies of the unconscious employees and erased their memories of the past few hours.

"That way they will hopefully not remember us," Karine said.

The next morning Gareth sat down with Tony and Michael, who were ordering breakfast in the large company executive cafeteria. He noticed Tony was looking decidedly seedy, and had settled on toast and strong black coffee.

"Hard night partying?" Michael ventured. "Who was the lucky girl this time?"

Tony had only just commenced his garbled excuse when Barry, one of the senior company directors, came bursting through the door.

"Attention everybody! Urgent meeting in the conference room in thirty minutes."

Gareth turned around. "What's up, boss?"

"D.K. Enterprises literally exploded sky high last night. Everything was destroyed!"

"Gosh, what happened?" Michael asked.

Barry shrugged. "I don't know. Most of the employees got out unharmed, but can't remember a thing – probably concussion. I always said they were doing unorthodox experiments there. We will have to find another sub-contractor as soon as possible. Our project is already behind schedule."

Xandra contacted Aldon once the military expedition had returned to Solar Base. When they had heard the report, Martina turned to Aldon.

"How serious is this?" she asked.

He shook his head. "Our suspicions were well founded. The Xvars and Katons are already present on this planet, and probably more entrenched than we previously suspected. At least we have disrupted one of their ghastly operations, and with a bit of luck one of the human agencies or military will get the blame!

"Karine was not able to determine everything they were doing under that installation. His report indicated that the remains of the mutilated people suggested that they had been trying to perfect their efforts to create human clones.

"Possibly they were also manufacturing artificial android robots, similar to Andy and Sarah. If they are eventually successful, humans will not be aware of what they are dealing with. Luckily, we should be able to discern the Xvar/Katon frequencies embedded in their formation."

The explosion at D.K. Enterprises required a replacement contractor, and provided Gareth with a valid reason to visit each establishment. He needed to ferret out who else was involved in subversive activities. Next time they located a covert Xvar/Katon operation, perhaps they could capture these interlopers alive. Solar Base would welcome the opportunity to interrogate them.

His position with the corporation allowed him to openly socialise with Tony and Michael. He was concerned that three Terran agents in the same place could prove precarious if any one of them was identified.

Tony's reckless drinking and womanising was a worry, although he assured Gareth that he never took his girlfriends back to his home. Part of the problem was his tendency to get romantically involved with some of the corporation secretaries, who had access to his address. Sometimes he had been known to seduce other men's wives! Gareth knew that he would have to take steps to amend this irresponsible behaviour.

Michael was, in fact, quite the opposite. He was quiet and introverted, often quite grumpy. He would go to some company functions with Tony, but would avoid any emotional interaction with the opposite sex.

While Michael's solitary existence was advantageous from a security perspective, even Terrans had biological 'needs'. His occasional visits to massage parlours were of some concern, and Gareth hoped he had not engaged Chantelle's services, which was strictly against the rules.

He concluded that Michael was deeply affected at being rejected by his Terran lover, and was scared of initiating a new relationship.

Michael had also wanted to indulge himself in a property on a secluded tropical island. He had insisted he needed a second secret location as a safe haven, due to the danger he may find himself in. Gareth thought the need to 'get away' was an extension of his anti-social tendencies, but said nothing.

The Guardians understood his wish for a second home, but were not impressed at his proposed extravagance. Michael argued that, given his generous corporate salary, he could afford it. Further, he guaranteed that nobody, except the Terrans, would know. Eventually a compromise was reached, and he purchased a small estate on a remote island, mainly populated by indigenous inhabitants.

The old fashioned village stone church and attached nuns' quarters was also a small disguised Terran sub-base. The priest, 'Father Paul', one of their agents, was assisted by another posing as 'Sister Jacquita', one of the nuns. They also possessed an underground transporter, however Michael eventually persuaded his superiors to allow him a second special shower unit in his bathroom. That way he could travel, quickly and unseen, between his city home and his undisclosed hide-away.

Aldon and Martina were still waiting for the promised additional personnel, and were disappointed that only a couple more little grey workers had so far arrived. One, called Max, was deployed to John's establishment as a replacement for Wangi.

Max had worked as an animal attendant in installations on other planets in the Quadrant. Like all of his kind, Max could not speak, but was able to communicate telepathically with Sarah and Boof. John found him to be an obedient assistant, and he soon settled into the veterinary practice.

Gareth's hunt for the Xvars was his first priority, and any further intake of protégées to the Retreat was delayed. In the meantime, it was thought unwise to only have one android on duty there. Earth Base may not be aware if he were rendered inoperable, either by accident or attack.

Aldon took the PVX and along with more supplies, delivered the second little grey worker, Tibor, to the Retreat. Gareth came with him and they updated Otto on the current events.

"You have to be even more mindful of security," Gareth told him. "Not just where humans are concerned, but also the increased Xvar/Katon threat. We have installed an extra alarm system, connected to Earth Base, which either you or Tibor can activate in an emergency."

They also left a small independently powered boat at the jetty. "This will provide an additional means of transport or escape," Aldon explained.

Otto assured them that, except for the local wildlife, he had not seen or heard anyone in the area. If somebody unexpectedly happened along, he would stick to the official explanation. It was a spiritual retreat for an obscure religious cult.

If it were investigated any further, digital records would confirm the existence of this particular sect. The Land Records Office also had 'The Followers of the Divine Light' listed as being the registered owners of the property.

On the trip back to Earth Base, Aldon expressed his frustration that the majority of the promised additional personnel had yet to materialise.

"I know Karine took all possible measures to make the raid on D.K. Enterprises look like it was either an accident or initiated by the military or a rival interest. If the Xvars or Katons realise it was us Terrans, we can expect some retaliation."

"And we won't know where or when," Gareth agreed.

"Exactly!" Aldon said. "That's why Earth Base must have at least one more robotic android like Andy."

They knew, if they were under attack, that Xandra and Zadoc would immediately deploy a military response. However, an additional assistant was also needed to be stationed with Aldon and Martina.

When they arrived Andy told them that he had been monitoring all transmissions.

"There has definitely been increased Xvar and Katon traffic," he reported. "They must have a craft somewhere in the vicinity. Martina and I decrypted most of their messages, and it seems they don't really know what happened at D.K.Enterprises.

"We've also been trying to trace the origin of all their communications to various places on Earth. So far we have been able to identify several locations in different countries."

Martina joined Aldon and Gareth, and confirmed Andy's report. "I have already notified Xandra at Solar Base. He and Zadoc have sent a small expeditionary military force to search for any Xvar or Katon craft in the Solar System. I guess we will just have to wait and see what happens!"

Gareth, Michael and Tony were still attempting to detect more of the Xvars and Katons. Unlike the Terrans, their unusual appearance meant they could not appear in public. They were out of sight, restricted to underground laboratories or bases. It was assumed they would have a couple of human looking android robots, which could be identified by the Xvar/Katon frequencies within their programming.

Other than that, their opponents would have to rely on normal humans to operate on their behalf. Usually these people would be provided by the contractor and military establishments whom they were assisting with forbidden technology. Xandra had told them that any human agents would certainly have been implanted with an Xvar control and tracking microchip.

One military officer, Major Robards, whose presence had activated their Xvar detectors, had visited the company on several occasions. Under the pretence of considering the corporation for a sizeable contract, he asked Michael and Tony several suspicious questions.

Gareth was told not to apprehend the Major. Aldon and Xandra were hoping he might lead them back to where his alien masters were based.

"We have to get our own tracking device on Robards," Aldon said. "He is obviously attached to a rogue military faction. We need him to lead us back to the base where the Xvars and Katons are located."

"That should be easy to do," Gareth said.

"Not so fast," interrupted Aldon. "The Xvars also have sophisticated technology. We don't want them knowing where, who and how an extra implant ended up in their Major. It must be done in a public place, by person or persons unknown."

Gareth discussed various ideas with Tony and Michael, and it was decided a bit of a drunken night out on the town may be the appropriate venue.

"Every month the corporation hosts a night out for its clients and contractors. We could invite the Major, along with many other guests," Gareth suggested. "How about we propose the Casino for next month's get-together? That way we can enlist the help of Bart and Chantelle."

Aldon approved the plan, and contacted Chantelle and Bart with final instructions.

Major Robards was delighted to be asked to attend the corporation's function. He could report back to his superiors that he was making progress, and certainly not being suspected of any espionage.

Quite a large party of corporate employees and clients gathered at the Casino, had dinner in the restaurant, and later proceeded to the gaming area. Everyone had been given a few complimentary casino tokens, and Bart and Chantelle discreetly followed a slightly inebriated Robards as he made his way to the roulette wheel.

Some of the other guests joined the throng gathered around the table, and Bart stood a short distance away. Gareth and his co-conspirators moved to the other side of the room, and as Robards sat down to have a little flutter, Chantelle quietly slipped into the crowd behind him.

When Bart's kinetic skill affected the game, the Major jumped from his seat, jubilantly hugging everyone around. "I've won! I've won!" he shouted, not even noticing the small jab as Chantelle, undetected, injected the microchip into his arm.

To avoid any suspicion, Chantelle left the Casino without any further delay, and Michael, Tony and Gareth joined some other clients, a short distance away in the cocktail lounge.

Major Robards was becoming quite noisy and intoxicated. Once he had gambled away his winnings, and made inappropriate suggestions to several women, the security guards escorted him off the premises.

Xandra did not want Earth Base monitoring the Major's microchip. He was well aware that 'tracking' someone was a 'two way street', and had deployed a small drone to follow the Major's movements.

At first Robards returned to his quarters to recover from his eventful night out. Xandra and Aldon waited, and after a few days their patience was rewarded. Major Robards left his own base and travelled alone to a remote government experimental installation over one hundred miles away.

"Gotcha!" gloated a jubilant Xandra.

Xandra explained to Aldon that the Major was not their target. Rather, they wanted to prompt Earth's own armed forces to destroy any Xvars or Katons at the suspect facility. Their Terran cyber experts sent a false message to both the national media and military headquarters.

"Now let the games begin!" Xandra chortled. "Everybody is rushing to this base, thinking an armed insurrection is taking place. A couple of my androids, disguised as Xvars, will transport into the immediate area. In full view of everybody, they will take a couple of pot shots with stun lasers, and then disappear into thin air!"

Aldon and Martina waited impatiently for the results of Xandra's tactics. It had been a success. Once the 'aliens' had fired upon them and 'disappeared', the soldiers from military headquarters stormed the building and extensive concealed basements. They met heavy resistance from both the Xvars and a contingent of militia loyal to a covert secret government faction.

There were multiple injuries and fatalities on both sides. Before the invading forces could secure the area for further investigation the entire structure was destroyed by the remaining Xvars, who preferred suicide to capture or interrogation.

When Michael and Tony were advised of the battle, they were not surprised there was no mention of the incident in the media. All journalists had their films and photographs confiscated, and were threatened with prosecution under national security if they ever breathed a word about the event.

CHAPTER 12

Ever since Victor had arrived on Earth and purchased the bookshop, he had not actually been able to get out into the community and socialise with normal fellow human beings.

Mary often worked overtime in her job, and occasionally her employer would give her a day off in return. She agreed when Aldon asked her if she would manage the bookstore for a while, giving Victor the time to 'get out and about'.

Bart had been unable to liaise with Victor, as he was not permitted to go to the Friendship Club, due to his position at the Casino. Thanks to Mary, they had their first day out together, and Bart took Victor to the local Golf Club.

After their first round Bart commented, "Even though this was your introduction to the game, it hasn't taken you long to 'get the hang of it'. Let's go back to the clubhouse for a drink with the boys."

Back at the bar, some of the other members were engaged in a bit of friendly banter with Bart.

"You always seem to come out in front. Don't know how you do it. If you're teaching your friend to come a close second, there's no hope for the rest of us!"

On his next outing with Bart, they watched a professional tournament being played on the golf course. Bart had placed a small bet on Peter Bistar to win, but his favourite was a couple of holes behind the leader.

Victor was lost for words when after Bart said, "I'd better give him a bit of help," Peter's ball would suddenly give a little jump forward whenever it stopped short of its target.

Victor lectured Bart later. "I know you were moving that ball with your mind. No wonder you're always beating your friends! Just be careful they don't realise what you are doing. They may connect it to your employment at the Casino!"

"Yes, but from the outset, I've always obeyed the rules," Bart said bitterly. "It's not fair! Whenever I've been asked to manipulate the gaming tables or machines, it's always someone else who gets the money. What about me? It's hard trying to manage on a waiter's income."

Victor agreed that Bart was rather isolated in his role at the Casino, and recognised the need for more support. He promised to supplement his income from the Friendship Club's funds, and also to raise the matter with Aldon and Martina.

He was going to socialise with Bart more often, and wondered if he may be considered a suitable candidate for a later visit to their Terran Retreat. He decided to say nothing for the moment. A second protégée school had not been scheduled as Gareth was fully occupied investigating various sub-contractors' premises.

Further, whilst Victor could understand it, perhaps Bart's dissatisfaction was not a firm indicator of his loyalty. What if he succumbed to temptation, and enlisted the help of an acquaintance to win some money for himself?

The casino was controlled by a Mafia type organised crime syndicate. If they detected anything was amiss, the less Bart could say about Terran operations, the better.

John was pleased with his new little grey 'worker' at the vet surgery. Max had settled in well, kept out of sight, and didn't seem disturbed by Boof.

One afternoon, John returned from a trip into town to discover a very lively parrot sitting in bird cage on the reception desk. He turned to Sarah.

"Isn't that old Tom Lacey's bird? What is he doing here?"

Sarah hesitated, not sure how her boss would react. "Tom had a stroke. The hospital has moved him to a nursing home, which doesn't allow any pets. He asked if you could take 'Petie', and maybe find him a new home."

John looked at Petie, who danced up and down on his perch, singing a garbled version of a popular song. "I guess you can stay for the time being. Perhaps you'll keep the waiting room entertained."

Petie did indeed keep the clients amused. He had a great repertoire of bawdy songs and colourful language. John couldn't confine him to the house or basement, because he was terrified of Max's large black oval eyes.

Petie didn't like Boof either, and couldn't understand why, even if he bit him, that dog always ignored his taunts and antics. It wasn't long before Petie could mimic Boof's bark. This was annoying late at night, when John would have to get out of bed to check if there were any intruders on the premises.

His final transgression came one sunny afternoon when several people were sitting in the waiting room. "Hurry up Sarah – come to bed!" Petie screeched.

Several of the customers tried to muffle their laughter, and one man waved a knowing finger at an embarrassed John, and a confused Sarah. That was it! The bird had to go – but where? Certainly not to anyone he knew in the immediate community.

He recalled that Mrs McAffrey was a bit of a recluse and lived some miles away. She loved all animals, and would maybe take Petie. He knew she had experienced some contact with the Terrans, who had helped her develop the gift of healing. She had never discussed her past, and certainly didn't know John's true identity.

A few days later John put Petie in his van and drove up the hill. Mrs McAffrey welcomed him, and as they sat down to afternoon tea, she thanked him for checking on her cats, and not charging for his services.

As John left, he heaved a sigh of relief. Petie was now out of the earshot of the locals, and had a temporary home with Mrs McAffrey.

Mary, Fiona and Lucy spent most of their weekends at the farm. They wondered about the escape tunnel in the basement, and hoped a situation would never arise where they had to use it. Gareth and Victor had explained not only about the danger of the Xvars and Katons, but also the likelihood of certain covert human security organisations wishing to interrogate contactees like themselves.

They had become firm friends with Mrs McAffrey, and were grateful she had agreed to keep an eye on the property and look after the animals during the week.

"Mrs McAffrey is an interesting person," Mary commented. "Even though she has been a very good neighbour, she apparently stays away from most people. I don't know why, but there is something familiar about her."

"Yes, we sensed something too," Lucy said. "I've noticed she seems to have a magic touch with animals. I have heard she often looks after injured wildlife, and has the gift of healing.

"She is not well off, and also cares for all those cats. I suppose the goat's milk and eggs during the week, and the small wage we pay her, must be appreciated."

Fiona came back one day, and was carrying Petie in his cage. "I believe there is a vet, just out of town, who also tends to Mrs McAffrey's cats without charge. She agreed to give this bird a home, as he wasn't happy at the surgery.

"The problem is a parrot doesn't fare very well in a house full of cats. Is it okay if we take him? Mrs McAffrey says she'll feed and clean him while we're away."

The women found Petie's antics and earthy vocabulary quite amusing, and later Mary was recounting some of it to Victor.

"Every so often he says – 'come to bed, Sarah'! I wonder who Sarah was?"

Victor knew who Sarah was, but could say nothing. The three women were also not allowed to know that John was a Terran agent.

A few days later Victor called into the surgery, on the pretext of getting a vaccination for Mishka. When confronted with Victor's suspicions John became defensive.

"A fellow can't stay celibate forever, and I'm here all by myself. It gets lonely, and I'm not supposed to start a relationship with a human woman. What do you expect me to do?"

Victor stared at him in disbelief. "You've been bonking Sarah? But she's not a real person! She's a specialised robot – an android – with a sophisticated artificial intelligence enabling the performance of complex official duties. I know some remote bases have robots specifically for sexual favours, but they have very limited encoding! You have totally degraded Sarah! What on earth will Aldon have to say?"

By this time John was a bundle of nerves. "Please don't tell him. He wouldn't understand. After all, I'm not hurting anyone."

"No, I suppose not," Victor agreed. "If Sarah was ever posted anywhere else, they would discover they had inherited a morally corrupted android!"

Victor decided, perhaps against his better judgement, not to notify Earth Base. After all, it was Aldon who had taught him to bend the rules sometimes. As long as John was getting satisfied, no matter how unconventional his behaviour, at least it was preventing unwanted attention if he became involved in a human relationship.

Aldon turned to Martina as they were enjoying a peaceful breakfast on Earth Base. "We have to tread very carefully from now on. Although we managed to avoid responsibility for the raids, the Xvars will not be happy about the loss of two of their establishments and several personnel. They might attempt to send replacements."

"Xandra mentioned that the Xvars may have a craft in the area. If it comes to Earth we are going to be at the sharp end," Martina said as she poured her second glass of fruit juice. "Our own resources are inadequate for any emergency. I hope Solar Supply sends that additional robot/android they promised Earth Base."

A few days later Zadoc made a surprise visit. "We are actually here to hunt down a couple of suspected enemy ships in this region, and I thought we would deliver your new android 'Gustav' at the same time. He's particularly adept at all forms of technology.

"I know you are still very thin on the ground where both personnel and equipment are concerned. At least, over the last few months, we have given you a few more recruits. We're doing our best to rectify the rest of the deficit."

Zadoc returned to his battle cruiser which was hovering way out of Earth's atmosphere. Within hours he discovered an incoming Xvar supply craft.

It was most important that the enemy ship did not identify the location of any Terran establishments. Zadoc relayed strict orders that, except in an emergency, every Terran Base on Earth was to cease all transporter and other transmissions which may be detected by the craft's powerful sensors.

The Terran battle ship waited, out of sight, behind the Moon, until the Xvars came within range. Zadoc hailed them, and the Xvar leader appeared on screen.

"You have entered Terran territory. Please leave immediately!" Zadoc demanded.

His challenge was met with a torrent of abuse from the Xvar's Captain, and as the screen went blank, a strong blast bounced off the protective shields of the Terran craft.

Zadoc ordered his crew to respond with fire that would damage but not destroy the Xvar vessel. "They're no match for us," he thought. "Let's see where they run to."

After several heavy weapon exchanges, the Xvars retreated.

"I expect they will seek refuge somewhere within the Solar System. They might even lead us to an unknown base they have established." Zadoc predicted.

He was wrong. Their opponents suddenly turned and headed towards Earth at full speed. This was totally unexpected, and Zadoc had to make a quick decision. A crashed or landed extraterrestrial craft and crew was not part of his game plan. It would generate unwanted publicity, and unpleasant results if retrieved by the local population or military. Worse still, the Xvars may escape and team up with their own associates already on the planet.

His next order was reluctant, but explicit. "Destroy them!" A broadside of fire power hit the Xvar ship which disintegrated.

Aldon and Martina were nervously awaiting any news of the confrontation, when a communication arrived from a very reserved Zadoc. He informed them of the situation, and how he had no choice but to annihilate the intruders. Aldon was quite jubilant, and did not share Zadoc's regret over the Xvar fatalities.

For the next couple of weeks, all Terran Earth facilities kept a very low profile and monitored the local world media and military. Although there was some mention of space junk, attributed to a satellite, Zadoc realised a few of the Terran and Xvar contacts would know the true situation.

"Mark my words," he said. "They'll be back, and sooner than we think."

The entire incident had prompted Aldon and Martina to re-examine their own roles at Earth Base.

"Actually, I think we are way down the pecking order," Aldon reflected. "Sure, we operate the main official base, and assist and liaise with particular agents. I have come to believe we're just part of a much larger compartmentalised agenda."

"How much larger?" Martina asked.

He frowned and stared at Gustav, who was fiddling around with one of their monitor screens. "That's a very good question. We know that the Galactic Council and Guardians administer all our activity in this Solar System, particularly on Planet Earth. I think there is a lot more they aren't telling us."

Martina's curiosity was aroused, "Like what?"

"Well, did you ever ask yourself why Zadoc handled the intruding Xvar vessel, rather than leaving it to Xandra, whose military capabilities would have been quite adequate?"

"That may only have been due to the overall situation in this Quadrant of the Galaxy." Martina responded.

He nodded in agreement. "Yes, that is possible, however even during my short time here, I have realised there are other unfamiliar Terran interventions – activities completely separated from Earth Base. I believe we have our own agents deeply imbedded and integrated into this planet's political, military and corporate institutions.

"I don't know anything about them, and wouldn't be surprised if they had their own controller and base in another part of the world. Obviously it has been decided that we do not have a need to know."

In a way, Martina was thankful they were restricted to limited duties on this troublesome planet. On the other hand, what would they do if approached by one of these unknown agents? It was difficult to operate with insufficient information.

She looked at Aldon. "I guess we'll just have to take it one day at a time, and try to figure it out as we go along."

Gareth was still concentrating on his role with Tony and Michael within the aerospace corporation. His position also gave him limited contact with a couple of other Terran scientists who attended the occasional conference.

The intake of more protégées at the Retreat had been placed on hold for the time being. His superiors had determined that discovering the Xvar and Katon bases on Earth had top priority. They had to be eliminated before more of their kind arrived to join them.

There was a second complication. The Xvar and Katons had been abducting some of the human population, and implanting their own microchips in these innocent victims, who could also be unethically manipulated.

In order to flush out the Xvar's human underlings he was required to not only attend all the official company functions, but also accompany their own two agents on various activities.

Gareth was not accustomed to such a hectic night life. Michael was rather reserved, and spent much of his spare time alone. Tony was the opposite, and enjoyed a full social calendar. Gareth had checked out all the female employees at the company. None triggered his Xvar/Katon emission detector, so at least Tony's regular 'flings' with these women, whilst inadvisable, were not dangerous.

His one night stands, a regular occurrence after wild parties, were a different matter. These events were hosted by many of the sub-contractors, and often involved illicit mind altering drugs and other substances. Gareth was fully occupied keeping Tony out of trouble, and often reminded him that he must remain sober and avoid compromising situations.

He had already voiced his concerns to the Guardians, however they suspected that these private shindigs, away from the watchful eyes of corporate security, were an ideal place for Xvar espionage.

They were proven correct. Two or three times, very scantily clad women had activated his emission alert. On each occasion they had been trying to seduce the visiting scientists and company employees. Gareth needed to inject them with a Terran monitor – not so easy when these young females were gyrating around the dance floor.

The only solution was to get close and intimate in a corner of the room, and more than one accused him of pinching her bottom. This gave him a bit of a celebratory status with his fellow workers. If only they knew!

It took some weeks for Aldon and Xandra to track the women back to the Xvars, who were controlling them from afar. As a result one more of their Earth installations was successfully taken out by Zadoc.

The Xvar laboratory ship, which was taking some of the humans, both for experimentation and implants, was a different matter. A galactic battle ship had been laying in wait, but when the Xvars spotted it they hurtled away, down into the Earth's atmosphere, only to be attacked by rocket fire from a nearby country's defence network.

It took a king-hit and plunged into the ocean below. Zadoc did not want any survivors or the wreckage to be retrieved by the local military.

He immediately contacted Aldon, who set out with Andy to the crash site.

The PVX was in invisible mode as they hovered over the ocean and then dived beneath the waves to the Xvar craft. Parts of the saucer were still intact, and Aldon's heart sank as he saw two young women inside, frantically beating on the window for help. It was one thing to slaughter the hated Xvars, but there was no joy in killing innocent females, already brutalised by their alien captors.

"What now, Commander?" Andy asked.

Aldon gulped and then shut his eyes. He didn't want to watch. "Fire until it's no more!"

He regretted what he had done, however they had destroyed all evidence just in time. When they shot back into the sky they could see a fishing trawler on the surface, and two naval destroyers heading towards the site.

The captain of the trawler was still shaking in his boots when approached by the Navy. In between swigs from his bottle of whiskey he gave a garbled explanation of hearing a silent whoosh from something that wasn't there.

"Then there was this giant wave, which nearly sank my boat, and another whoosh!"

The officers stared at each other wondering how to write up their report. They could not locate any large object on the ocean floor, and all they had was the ramblings of a drunken fisherman.

Aldon was very subdued when he returned to Earth Base. Martina could see the tears in his eyes as he recounted the event. She was glad he was starting to open up and show some emotion, rather than retreating into a private inner world.

She put her arm around his shoulder. "I can understand how you must feel. Sometimes you like this job, but today was not a good day!"

Aldon looked up at her. It had been a long time since he had felt a woman's comforting touch and sympathy.

CHAPTER 13

For a few weeks everybody was collectively holding their breath, and trying to be as inconspicuous as possible. There seemed to be no repercussions from the devastation of the Xvar/Katon facilities or the crash and destruction of their craft. Aldon realised however, that Earth's military would still be conducting quiet investigations.

Zadoc reported that his forces had completed a systematic sweep of the entire Solar System. They had located and destroyed a concealed enemy supply base on an insignificant moon. He considered that except for a few remaining Xvar/Katon agents on Earth, everyone could relax, but only for a short time.

Gareth had not detected any more of their opponents on the planet, who by now would be desperate without support. He suspected that they would probably have at least one escape craft, in a small concealed base somewhere. Would their foes stay or flee? Nobody knew. He warned all his colleagues, especially the Terran scientists, to keep vigilant.

The recent events had shaken Tony, and for once he started heeding the warnings and advice of the past couple of months.

"Your immature behaviour has endangered this whole operation. I have too much on my plate to keep checking up on you." Gareth cautioned. "Stop going to parties and sleeping around with women you hardly know. If you can't go without female company, find yourself a steady girlfriend who won't compromise your position and true identity."

Aldon had also warned Tony that, despite his valued position, if he did not mend his ways another Terran scientist could be sought to replace him.

This situation took an unexpected turn when Lucy and Fiona took a trip to the big city, and bumped into Gareth and Tony as they walked down the street.

Tony looked at the very attractive identical twins. "Gareth, aren't you going to introduce me to these lovely ladies."

Lucy giggled and Fiona whispered in her ear. "He's rather charming, isn't he?"

"And quite handsome," Lucy observed.

Despite Gareth's opposition, Tony insisted the girls join them for lunch in a nearby restaurant. By the end of the meal he had made a date with them for that night.

The next morning in the company cafeteria an irritable Gareth looked at Tony. "What do you think you are doing?" he demanded.

"Well you said to find a steady girlfriend, and two for the price of one is even better! We had a great time last night!"

"They live a long distance away, and they must never know who you really are." Gareth said, hoping to dissuade him.

Tony shrugged. "That's okay – they'll never know, and I'll use the transporter to Victor's bookshop. I believe they go there sometimes."

"No way!" Gareth interrupted. "Mary also lives over the bookshop. She will question how you suddenly appear out of nowhere. If you must pursue this irresponsible relationship, you can make arrangements with John to use his transporter at the vet surgery."

"But that's right on the edge of town," Tony protested.

"Yes," Gareth smirked. "Get a bus or walk. It'll do you good and maybe cool your ardour a little."

Tony glared at Gareth. "I don't understand why you are getting so antagonistic about this. I'm doing what you asked – giving up the parties and good-time girls! It's what you wanted, isn't it? I'll settle for the twins. They have their own apartment, so that should keep me out of the public eye!"

Gareth was taken aback by Tony's suggestion, and decided to speak to the women about this unconventional proposal.

"We really like him," said Fiona.

"And we always share everything!" Lucy chuckled. "Haven't you ever tried a threesome?"

Gareth made an unsuccessful appeal to Aldon, who decided not to intervene. Both he and Martina considered that the girls would keep Tony out of mischief, and they could be trusted if they ever discovered his true identity. Also, due to their special protégée status, there could be complications if Fiona and Lucy started relationships with normal human men. It was a win-win situation.

"Who am I to criticise some of the unconventional sexual behaviour on this planet? In some countries a man can have up to four wives." Aldon said. "But tell Tony he is not to visit them for the next few days. Xandra wants you and Victor to make a quick visit to Solar Base."

Gareth smiled, "Victor? He will be happy. He was raised there and considers it his home."

Victor was pleased and excited. He asked Mary not to open the bookshop in his absence. He put up a note saying it was closed for family reasons. He was not lying. Solar Base was his family!

Victor and Gareth waited at Earth Base for their transport to arrive. Gareth was deputising for Aldon, as he and Martina could not leave their post until the ongoing threat from the Xvars and Katons had been minimised. Gareth would update them on the latest situation report.

Martina was a little perplexed; "Aldon, do you know why Victor has also been summoned?"

He shrugged. "Perhaps the selection and training of the protégées at the Retreat is going to take a new direction."

One of Zadoc's larger battle ships picked them up, so there was no stopover at Mars, and they went straight on to Solar Base.

Xandra was there to welcome them, and allowed Victor to hurry off to into the outpost's community to renew old friendships. Gareth was ushered alone into a large conference room where Zadoc, along with several Guardians and members of the Galactic Council were waiting to meet with him.

Their gloomy faces told him the news would not be good. Although they had rid the Solar System of all but a few remnants of the Xvars and Katons, they expected it was only a matter of time before they returned.

There had been a build-up of enemy forces and further skirmishes in this part of the Galaxy. The establishment of a permanent military station on Earth would give the Xvars a tactical advantage. This must not be allowed to happen.

While the Galactic forces would be combating any Xvar incursions into this part of the Quadrant, counter-espionage action had to be taken on Earth. They needed to plan a strategy to discredit these malevolent entities in the eyes of not only their human partners, but the entire population, most of whom were unaware of their existence.

"Some of the planet's influential leaders have been enticed with advanced technology, which they believe will bring them supremacy over all others." Zadoc said. "Instead, they will realise too late, that they have in fact allowed the Xvars and Katons to take control over them."

The Guardians and Galactic Council had also decided to allow Gareth to prepare certain protégées to be used as a resistance force against not only Xvar/Katon intruders, but also any covert human agencies supporting them.

"We will assist you with further resources and equipment, and may need to bring your chosen recruits back to Solar Base for a short period. They will have to be trusted with more classified information than before."

While Gareth was hearing the bad news, Victor was revisiting the haunts of his childhood. All of a sudden, after being on Earth, the confines of Solar Base seemed more restrictive than he had previously remembered.

Xandra invited him into his quarters, and sat him down with a drink. "Victor, I have wanted to talk to you for a long time, and have put it off for far too long. You have a right to know about your true ancestry. I know you have been tempted to search for your biological parents."

Victor fidgeted in his chair. "I am sorry for appearing disloyal or ungrateful. I had the most kind and loving childhood here. This was my family, and I wanted for nothing."

Xandra smiled. "You have nothing to be sorry about. I need to tell you that you were never the result of any genetic manipulation or augmentation. You are half Terran and half human."

"I don't understand," Victor stammered.

Xandra looked at him and hesitated. "Victor, I am your father. Many years ago I was a probationary agent on Earth, and fell in love with a beautiful woman called Lydia. One of the nation's border security guards recognised that my identity papers were false and I was taken into custody.

"I was facing severe interrogation or worse. Lydia organised my escape, and hid me for several months. By the time a rescue craft arrived, she was several months pregnant, and I couldn't leave her behind.

"We were married here on Solar Base, and while we waited for our baby to be born, the Guardians gave us one of their best quarters complete with a little garden. Lydia and I were so happy and in love. We planned on going back to a different identity and country on Earth

"Nobody knows why or how, but she suddenly died during childbirth. We were able to save you, but despite all our expertise, could do nothing for Lydia.

"I was left with a small, helpless little being – my son. I loved you more than anything in the world, and you were all that I had left of Lydia – the love of my life. The Guardians insisted you should be raised with all the other children. Although I was not permitted to tell you I was your father, they allowed me to remain on Solar Base so I could stay with you. Eventually I rose to the position of 'Officer-in-Charge'."

Victor was close to tears. "I never knew. If only I'd known!"

Xandra smiled. "I watched you grow into a man. I was so proud of you. It is only now that the Guardians have relented and allowed me to tell you the truth. I hope you are not angry with me for my silence all these years."

Victor stood up, went over to Xandra, and gave him a bear hug. "No, I'm just so happy and privileged to know who I really am. We have a lot of time to make up together."

On the way back to Earth Gareth wondered why Victor looked so cheerful when the meeting with Zadoc and the Guardians was full of worrying predictions.

Gareth and Victor arrived back at Earth Base, and sat down with Aldon and Martina to brief them on their meeting with the Guardians. Xandra had already indicated that Victor's security classification was now raised to the next level.

"We have to carry on as normal, but be more mindful of the current and potential upcoming situation." Gareth advised. "It's probable that any remaining Xvars or Katons still here will be desperate, and resort to more open espionage and disruptive behaviour.

"We must look to the future and prepare now. I have to recruit more trusted protégées to form a defensive militia, rather than their conventional purpose of peacefully improving the planet and human population. Not all of them will be prepared to accept a more combative role."

After they left Aldon looked worried. "There is a rumour that Victor is actually Xandra's son, so we'd better make sure nothing happens to him."

"Does he know?" Martina asked.

Aldon shrugged, he wasn't sure. "I imagine that is why he was invited back to Solar Base. His attitude must have pleased Xandra, otherwise his status wouldn't have been upgraded."

During Victor's absence, Mary had spent a quiet time with Mishka at the bookstore. She was startled, and jumped up when Gareth and Victor suddenly appeared in the lounge room. "Where did you come from?" she asked.

They could not tell her about the transporter shower in Victor's bedroom. "Didn't you see us come in? You must have been lost in that book."

Mary looked slightly puzzled as she prepared them a quick meal. Mishka decided she liked Gareth and deposited herself on his lap. He had very little experience with animals, and found stroking this warm furry creature a pleasing sensation.

He looked up, "What is that funny noise she is making?"

Victor laughed. "Mishka is purring. Cats do that when they like you and enjoy your touch."

Mary informed them that Bob had visited on a couple of occasions. He seemed to be troubled about something, but hadn't confided much.

Victor met up with him at lunchtime, in the park opposite the hospital.

"How's it going?" Victor asked. "We haven't seen much of you at the Friendship Club recently. Have you been kept busy at work?"

"Yes, the laboratory is making great progress. My assistant, George, and I are doing clinical studies on some new breakthrough cures. We are also trialling some radical medical technologies which will minimise invasive surgery.

"Sometimes, when my research hits the proverbial 'brick wall', I have dreams or visions showing me the solution. In the middle of the night, I will sit up in bed, and I can see a screen with diagrams and pictures. Often I hear a voice, and when I start a conversation Amy wakes up and says there is nothing and nobody there.

"She keeps suggesting I must be having a breakdown and need to see a psychiatrist. But that is not all. She is freaking out because the children are behaving oddly, and strange things are happening in and around the house.

"She is very nervous, and always wants me to come straight home from work. It is difficult to get to the bookstore meetings."

Victor needed to know more about Bob's children and the strange happenings around the house. It was outside his capabilities and he needed to enlist Aldon and Gareth's help.

School holidays were about to begin, and Bob was able to persuade Amy to take the children to a beachside resort for a week. Once they had left, Victor and Gareth moved into the house with Bob.

"I'm glad you are both with me. Amy gets panicky if she is here alone, and I must admit I get a bit nervous as well."

Gareth knew that Bob's family were part of their generational genetic enhancement program, so his children would also be affected.

"Let's start with the kids first."

Dave was seven and Christie only six. Both were very intelligent, and could read and write long before they started formal schooling. They also talked about unseen friends from the age of two. Dave had recently drawn a disquieting picture. It looked very much like a lighted saucer shape object hovering over four people.

"They're my friends who have come to see me. And there's Mummy, Daddy and Christie," he explained in his childish fashion.

Although the school had never notified Bob and Amy, Dave mentioned the nice men in suits that they met in the principal's office.

"They talk to us and ask us questions," he said. "And we read our books out loud for them."

When Amy had asked the teacher what was happening, she was met with evasiveness, and some excuse about evaluating the children's progress.

Soon afterwards, there were episodes during the night when the whole house would inexplicably shake. The dog would bark and whine, and hide under the bed. Electric lights would flash on and off, and disconnected TV and radios started blaring. Outside they could often see strange lights and hear an unusual humming noise.

"The kids have had a couple of nosebleeds and odd marks on their bodies. It might be quite natural at their age. They also refuse to sleep in the dark, and say they'll have bad dreams if the light isn't on."

Gareth said he needed to check with the Terran genetic enhancement team, but he thought they had put their operations on hold since the Xvar scare.

He came back a short time later and said, "No, it wasn't the Terrans, however I don't think it was the Xvars either."

"Then who?" Victor and Bob asked.

Gareth was a little concerned. "Some very secret human organisations have immense interest in the genetics of highly intelligent people, especially children. They are aware of the advanced extraterrestrial programs which have been implemented on Earth. They want to examine the genes, and tap into the frequencies and vibrations associated with these individuals.

"It all depends which government agency they are involved with. Some are very eager to examine these particular contactees so they can investigate further. Others are abducting citizens to conduct their own horrific experiments in secret underground bases."

Bob put his head in his hands. "What can I do to protect my family from these people?"

"Leave it to me," Gareth assured him. "I think most of your problems are being caused by a sophisticated electronic probe. It is a good thing none of you went outside when this was happening. The perpetrators, whoever they are, know we are more powerful. We can get them to back off coming to the house, but unfortunately it may not stop their interest in your kids."

Victor returned to the bookshop, leaving Gareth in the house with Bob. Long after darkness fell the dog started to bark, and then cowered in the corner. When they could see a bright light through the window, Gareth messaged Earth Base.

Aldon piloted the PVX in invisible mode, and spotted a military corporation's primitive prototype of an extraterrestrial disc-shape craft.

It was hovering high above Bob's home. He fired some of his sophisticated weapons – enough to destroy all their technology but still allow them to limp back to base.

"I think they got the message!" he told Gareth. "It's bad enough having to fight the Xvars, without having to deal with half of Earth's affiliated military!"

Bob was relieved when his family got a peaceful night's sleep from then on. He heeded Gareth's advice to forbid the children being interviewed or examined by anyone without their permission. "And that includes any visiting medical officers," he added as he left the school principal's office.

Mary was glad to see Victor back home, and noted that there was something different about him. She couldn't quite figure out what it was. Although he seemed more content, there was definitely something on his mind.

He had been playing the piano one night, and after he finished just sat there, silently staring ahead.

"A penny for your thoughts," she said jokingly.

He walked over and sat next to her. "Remember how I always wanted to find my biological parents? Well, it turns out my father was a Terran, who fell in love with an Earth woman. They were married, but she died on Solar Base while giving birth to me.

"I really want to know about her, but don't know where to start. All I have is a name and the country she came from."

Mary suggested using his computer to try and discover some of her details, but Victor had already dismissed that idea.

"Nobody knew she left with my father, and she would have been listed as a missing person. Any search on the digital network may alert the authorities, even after all these years, and be traced back to me."

Mary thought for a moment. "I can look for you at work. I'll be careful, and go upstairs after everyone has gone home. I'll use someone else's computer. If I put a dust coat over my clothes and wear that wig and glasses I used at the Casino, not even the security cameras will recognise me."

Mary was still shaking when she came in the front door the next night. She was glad she had taken the precaution of appearing to leave the building as herself, and then re-entering wearing her disguise.

She put her hand on Victor's arm and handed him a piece of paper.

"I printed out this picture of your Lydia for you, but only got limited information. She was a very brilliant young scientist who was reported as mysteriously missing all those years ago. They thought she may have been kidnapped."

"I looked at a couple of newspaper articles, but the next site I went to obviously was something to do with the authorities. Once I clicked on, it activated some kind of tracking device. I shut the machine down immediately and got out of there."

The next day Mary noticed two burly men in suits were talking to the office manager on the next floor. After a while they left without even giving her a second glance.

Victor was so appreciative of Mary's efforts and the risk she took. Now he knew who he was, and would always treasure that photo of his mother.

CHAPTER 14

Lucy and Fiona were very satisfied with their relationship with Tony. He would visit on a couple of weeknights and sometimes spend the weekend at the farm. Even Mary felt a slight connection to him, but none of them were allowed to know his true identity, except that he was Gareth's associate, and had some connection to the Terrans.

While Gareth and Victor had informed Tony that his three new friends were valued protégées, he had to remain strictly incognito, especially in regards to his position as a corporate scientist. He was also forbidden to go to the bookshop or Friendship Club meetings.

The women sometimes felt a little apprehensive, alone in their country home. There were only the animals and Mrs McAffrey, with her cats, next door. Tony's presence at the farm gave them all a newfound sense of security.

Aldon was rather pleased with the arrangement. Fiona and Lucy seemed to have moderated Tony's unacceptable behaviour, and his presence on the weekends also allowed him to keep an eye on Mrs McAffrey. She was what he termed 'a closet protégée.'

Tony himself was much happier. This fresh outlet, away from the laboratory, had given new meaning to his life. He found an unexpected peace he had never experienced in the wild parties and nightlife which had previously occupied his spare time.

He enjoyed gardening and watching the vegetables and flowers grow. They went for long walks and explored the nearby countryside. Often, after dinner on a Saturday night, they played their guitars or put on some dance music.

Victor surprised himself when he initially felt a little pang of jealousy. Mary put his mind to rest when she assured him she had no interest in Tony's sexual romps with the twins. She was however, grateful for his assistance around the farm.

It was a Saturday afternoon, and as Mary was brushing Wiggles, she noticed a storm was building in the west. "Come-on my sweet – no more galloping around the field for you. Let's take you back to your stable."

They had all retreated to the house when the brief but violent thunderstorm arrived. As they watched the ferocious rain and lightning from out the window, there was a sudden enormous bang and flash. The entire sky lit up for a few seconds, and they could see a silver craft, plummeting to earth.

"It's not a plane." Fiona exclaimed. "It's a flying saucer."

There was a distinctive thud, and a tremor went through the house. They noticed what appeared to be flames in the woods behind the farm. Tony jumped up, and put on his jacket with a weapon in the pocket.

"You girls are to stay inside while I go and investigate. Don't argue. That's an order!"

Tony contacted Earth Base as soon as he got outside, and Martina advised him that Aldon was already in the PVX and on the way to the crash site.

"It's not one of ours, and our detectors suggest it may be an Xvar escape shuttle. We suspected they may have one or two for the remnants of their infiltrators to get away from the planet in an emergency.

"Try to get close and let us know what you can see – but be careful, this would have also attracted the attention of the local military. Xandra is sending a small warship to intercept any Xvar rescue ship which could be waiting for them above Earth."

The storm had passed, and Tony crept through the residual haze towards the flames. He could hear the sound of planes overhead, and knew armed forces and their vehicles would be arriving soon.

A figure staggered out of the mist, and before the Xvar could raise his weapon Tony fired his laser which was set just below lethal. His opponent crumpled to the ground. A little further up he could see the crashed disc, which had a pathetic little grey clone trapped underneath.

Through the window he could see several alien bodies. It was apparent that only the pilot and his little assistant had escaped the wreck.

He messaged the PVX which was about to land in the field behind. Aldon hurried towards him, and looked with undisguised hatred at the unconscious Xvar.

"Why didn't you kill the bastard?" he growled. "Now I suppose we'll have to treat him as a prisoner of war. Wrap him in an electronic shield, so he cannot be located or contact anyone."

Before setting explosives to destroy the shuttle, they dragged out the little grey worker. He appeared to be badly damaged, and Tony asked what they should do with him.

Aldon paused, wondering whether they should put the little creature out of its misery. "Wrap him in another electronic shield. He may also have some intelligence value to Zadoc."

Once the enemy craft had exploded into a thousand pieces, they knew that the local military would soon arrive.

"I must take precautions to ensure our own security. I cannot take these two prisoners back to Earth Base." Aldon said. "Where can we leave them until Xandra arrives to pick them up?"

"My cats and I can guard them," a voice said from behind. They turned to see Mrs. McAffrey, who insisted they move the limp bodies out of sight into her backyard.

Xandra decided to join Aldon and pick up the prisoners before he searched for the Xvar rescue craft. When he arrived he found one unconscious Xvar, and a terrified grey clone. Each had several snarling felines sitting on top of them.

"Meet my own attack force," announced Mrs McAffrey as she ordered the cats to return to her side.

Xandra took the captives and grinned at Aldon. "Remind me not to mess with her!"

Tony returned to the farm, and was swamped with questions from the anxious women. He gave them an edited version of the events, and instructions on what to say when the authorities arrived.

A short while later there was a knock on the front door, and a scantily dressed Lucy opened it to a rather nice young Major.

"Well, hellooo!" she said in a flirtatious manner, still shaking her hips to the beat of the music inside. "To what do I owe this pleasure?"

The officer was caught off guard and stumbled over his words. "We are investigating a report of a possible plane crash in the area earlier this evening. Did anyone in the house see or hear anything?"

Mary joined Lucy, followed by Fiona who winked at the soldier. "There was a terrible storm – lots of thunder and lightning. I remember one really big bang, and the lights flickered on and off."

The Major listened as the three women went into a lengthy explanation about the storm, how it must have frightened the animals, and how they hoped the stream hadn't flooded.

He was getting irritated, and eventually stammered, "But did you see anything that might have been a plane in trouble?"

"Oh, no! We're scared of storms - stayed inside the whole time." Mary assured him. "Do you want us to come and help you look?"

"No, thank you, ladies. If you'll permit us, my men will quickly check your field, and then we'll be on our way."

"Please just say if there is anything we can do," Lucy added as the Major hurried away down the front path.

They shut the door, and returned to Tony who had remained in the lounge room.

"How did we go?"

He was shaking with suppressed laughter. "Brilliant – just brilliant! You really had the poor fellow off-balance.

"This was all a bit unexpected. I may need to leave early tomorrow morning, if one of you can give me a lift back to town."

For once he was going to bend the rules, and borrow Victor's transporter to get to Earth Base. He needed to file his formal report with Aldon as soon as possible.

Mrs McAffrey also received a visit from the Major. She insisted he come in, said he looked like her grandson, and offered him milk and some of her magic muffins. At first he was tempted. He had left his uneaten dinner on the mess hall table when he received his orders to immediately go and search for the crashed UFO.

Mrs McAffrey did not want the Major to even suspect what had happened, or her involvement. She smiled to herself, when after five minutes of being investigated and jumped on by several inquisitive cats, he gulped down the milk, and grabbed a couple of muffins before fleeing back to his armoured vehicle.

Mrs McAffrey's muffins were starting to take effect, and the Major was feeling a little disoriented when he joined his sergeant. "These locals are all quite strange. No help at all!"

The next day Tony met with Aldon and Martina. They were thankful that Xandra had left with his prisoners before the soldiers arrived. They had not yet discovered whether this particular military unit considered the Xvars friends or foes.

Xandra was exceptionally pleased that Zadoc had also been able to capture the Xvar rescue ship and crew. Solar Base now had several prisoners, and skilful interrogation revealed more details of their enemies' plans and intentions.

The good news was, as far as Earth Base was concerned, the majority of their opponents underground laboratories had been destroyed, along with their corporate/military conspirators. Some of the remaining Xvars and Katons had had fled in their escape shuttles.

The bad news was that a couple of enemy installations still remained on the planet. These needed to be exposed and neutralised. Further, the Xvars unquestionably held imperialistic intentions towards this part of the galaxy, especially the Solar System.

Michael and Tony were feeling a little more protected now that the majority of the Xvars and Katons were in retreat. Everyone, both rogue and Terran approved, were in the race to develop cutting edge technology, including advanced artificial intelligence and exotic weapon and propulsion systems.

They had been warned that the renegade corporate and military factions would not abandon their projects, and were looking for substitute scientists. These powerful conglomerates were quite capable of adopting ruthless methods when it came to recruiting suitable replacements. The Guardians' attention was now focussed on the more possible human agents and minions from the Xvar affiliated military/corporate establishments. These companies also needed to be neutralised.

Gareth attended the regular official corporate functions, and quietly noted any approaches made to Tony or Michael. He was constantly aware of the enemy's tactics, which could include seduction, blackmail, gambling, alcohol and addictive drugs. There had even been some cases of specialists, like Jarod, being abducted and forced to work in a secret underground base.

Gareth also needed to spend time with the rest of their integrated scientists working for other similar Terran approved companies. His role managing Tony and Michael had become easier now that Tony no longer attended wild parties and had multiple girlfriends.

He faced a different challenge with Michael, who was still rather introverted and distant. He rarely socialised, and hadn't made many friends in or out of the workplace. In some ways, to avoid undue scrutiny, their agents needed to assimilate more comprehensively with the local community.

Gareth realised that he had neglected Michael, who was probably still disheartened over being jilted by his Terran fiancée. Perhaps he was avoiding any further emotional attachments. He needed to coax him out of his protective shell.

Tony had confided to Gareth that he thought Angela, one of their laboratory assistants, was attracted to Michael.

"She always rushes to do his bidding, whether it's bringing him a cup of coffee or working late if he wants to finish a particular project. At least he isn't as grumpy with her as he is with everybody else.

"She is rather shy, and although she must be in her mid-thirties, I don't think she has a boyfriend. She shares an apartment with one of the secretaries, and spends her evenings going to college, studying for some higher qualification or science degree'"

The corporation's annual dinner and awards night was coming up, and Gareth organised for Tony and Michael's entire laboratory staff to share the same table with him. There was great jubilation when they received one of the top awards.

After the speeches a pop group came on stage, and Tony and Gareth invited a couple of the secretaries onto the dance floor. As they were gyrating to the music, Gareth noticed both Michael and Angela were sitting alone at the table.

When they returned to their seats he said, "Michael, why don't you ask Angela to dance? She hasn't brought a partner and is sitting there on her own."

Michael mumbled something about not mixing work and pleasure, and begrudgingly asked Angela for the next dance. Gareth could see, by the expression on her face, that Tony was right. Angela's feelings for Michael were more than just those of a work colleague.

The next weekend Gareth and Martina decided to visit 'Father Paul' and 'Sister Jacquita' at their sub-base on the tropical island where Michael also had his secret hideaway.

They entered via the transporter hidden in the crypt of the town's old stone church, and climbed the stairs of the hidden entry into the back of the confessional.

Paul entered the other side, and Gareth said, through the screen, "Forgive us Father, for we have sinned. Snuck in the back way without telling you first!"

Paul met them outside. "Bloody joker! You haven't changed a bit! Good to see you both."

He gave them a tour of the old stone building, which was the main centre of worship for the entire population. The large old fashioned bell not only called the faithful to prayer, it would toll out a warning during any impending disaster. Severe storms often threatened the island paradise.

The sub-base, was well camouflaged in the crypt underneath. Beside the transporter and their technical equipment, it contained a small first aid station/hospital. On the surface, the attached nunnery provided medical attention for the local population. Paul remarked that due to the often heavy burden of their work in the community, they really needed an android or little grey worker to assist with their Terran responsibilities.

"I understand, since we see little if no action here, it puts us very low on the priority list. At least we have an additional asset in Michael's property up the hill."

Gareth agreed, and commented that he thought that is why the boss approved this particular location.

Martina was giggling to herself when Jacquita joined them for a walk in the tropical church grounds.

Jacquita stiffened. "What's so funny?"

"You – in that nun's habit! Last time we were together you were in full Terran military uniform accepting medals for bravery during battle."

"The Xvar Wars took their toll on all of us," said Jacquita. "While being a religious disciple is a far cry from the ruthless soldiers we once were, this posting has been a welcome interlude.

"So far, not much has happened here. I enjoy working with the children. The people need our help, and have very little compared to the outside world. They are mainly self sufficient and live close to nature. They have their animals, fruit trees and vegetable gardens. The men go fishing in those canoe type boats you can see on the beach.

"The official government of these islands is so far away they are rarely seen or heard from. Instead there is local village council which administers the day to day happenings here. Some of their antiquated rules and policies date back to before the influence of modern civilisation.

"We don't seem to be on the Xvar's radar, or anybody else's for that matter. I'm enjoying the peace and quiet while I still can."

Martina and Gareth both felt a little jealous. They looked at the palm trees surrounding the tropical lagoon and the waves breaking on the white sands of the ocean beach. It was indeed an idyllic location.

Over a leisurely lunch they up-dated Paul and Jacquita on the latest skirmishes with the Xvars and their allies.

Martina laughed as she glanced over at Jacquita. "At the moment I'd gladly swap places with you, even it means being celibate and wearing that ridiculous nun's habit."

"Yes, but I get recreation days when I can wear my own clothes and sneak into the city. Besides that, in the nunnery I hold the position of Mother Superior. It's not as restrictive as you think." Jacquita smirked.

After lunch they climbed the hill to Michael's hacienda. It was a beautiful house, painted white in a South American/Mexican style. A local islander met them at the door, and welcomed them in.

"That must be his 'house-boy', Gareth murmured. "Lucky devil! We don't normally get any human servants. I suppose he's a substitute for a little grey worker."

"Sorry to arrive unannounced," Martina said as Michael entered the lounge room. "We came to see Paul and Jacquita, and thought we would call in while we were here."

Michael seemed much more at ease than he was in his work and city environment. He proved a hospitable host, settling them down with a local beverage, which tasted extremely alcoholic.

"No. One's enough, thank you!" Martina said when he offered a refill.

The garden and grounds were tropical but not extensive. Behind a summer house, the small rise at the rear of the property led to the cliffs overlooking the sea. Martina and Gareth could both see the potential for an underground tunnel leading from the house, down to the ocean below.

Michael thought the idea had merit, although he regarded this as his own secret refuge, not official Terran premises. At least his transporter was not restricted. It was fully functioning, and Gareth and Martina beamed straight back to Earth Base.

Aldon was pleased with their report. Paul and Jacquita were two agents he didn't have to worry about. Michael was another matter, and although he fulfilled all of his duties, Aldon was still concerned about his psychological wellbeing.

CHAPTER 15

Mary was sitting in the bookshop, reading the newspaper.

"Oh, look Victor! There's a fairground and circus coming to town on Saturday. I have never really been to one. Mum wouldn't let me."

Victor looked amused. "Never been to the fair...or a circus? I haven't either. We'll have to remedy that. Isn't it your birthday this weekend? Let me take you as a treat."

Bob, who had been coming to the Friendship Club more often, said he had promised to take his kids. When the others heard it was Mary's birthday, they decided to make it a group outing and combine it into a surprise party for her. Victor invited Aldon and Gareth, who arrived with Tony in John's transporter.

"Once I've closed the vet surgery, I'll drive you over to the bookstore," said John. "I want to take a look at that circus. Don't like to see animals held in captivity for human's pleasure."

Victor, along with Mary, Lucy and Fiona were waiting for them, and they met up with Bob, Dave and Christie soon after.

"Where's Amy?" Victor asked.

Bob put an arm around each of his children. "Amy's having a day out with Nancy. It's my turn to have the kids. They're quite excited, and I must admit, I haven't been to something like this since I was young."

Aldon, security minded as usual, thought it unwise for so many of his colleagues to be together in one group. Furthermore, he needed to slip away to an undercover meeting with another incognito agent. He suggested they split up and meet later for Mary's surprise party.

Tony and Gareth went off with the twins, who were insistent on trying out all of the fairground rides. Aldon could hear their shrieks and squeals as they rode the roller coaster. Tony and Gareth had stayed on the ground, and were trying to decide if they really enjoyed this strange fairy floss and toffee apples that the girls had insisted on buying for them.

John had wandered off to investigate the circus animals, in cages at the side of the field, and Victor and Mary were not in sight.

Having made sure he was alone, Aldon went over to the gypsy caravans. He found and entered the tent marked 'Madam Camellia - Your Fortune Told – Only $10'

He sat down opposite a dark haired woman, who was wearing a typical gypsy outfit. "How are we today, Madam Camellia? Will you look into your crystal bowl and predict the future? We all need that more than ever right now."

Camellia stood up and put her arms around Aldon. "Good to see you, old friend. How's life been treating you recently? I was so sorry to hear about the loss of your family."

"Thanks," said Aldon. "I'm more concerned about you, have there been any problems with your assignment?"

Camellia assured him that she had integrated well with this Romany group. Nobody even guessed, or had queried her true identity.

When the fairground was camped near the nation's capital, some high up politicians and members of the Defence Department had brought their families to the circus. A few had wandered into her tent, and later when her carefully moderated predictions came to pass, they privately sought her insights.

"Better than we hoped," Aldon assured her. "The intelligence we have gained was invaluable, and your subtle manipulation of their thoughts has been an added bonus."

As he was leaving, Camellia reminded Aldon that her caravan, travelling around with the gypsies, was still safe and secure for any agent or protégée on the run.

Aldon walked back to the fairground, and found Bob and the children near the typical fairground games of skill and chance. Christie was crying, because she had wanted to win a large teddy bear, and had no more money to play again.

Gareth, who had wandered up with the girls, looked angry. "These fairground stall holders are all unscrupulous. The machines are dishonestly manipulated against the public. Come-on ladies! Remember your training. Let's use some of our kinetic training and get this little girl her toy!"

They gave Christie a few dollars, and she soon came back with a big smile on her face, and carrying the teddy in her arms,

"We'd better do the same for her brother," Fiona said, and they walked over to another stand, where Dave was intent on winning a holographic digital game.

"I don't think we need to," Gareth smirked, as Dave came away clutching his prize. "That kid has great potential. I hope to have him on my team when he is older."

It was time to meet in the picnic area, and Victor produced the previously hidden champagne and birthday cake. Not only was 'Happy Birthday' sung with great gusto, everybody had brought small presents. Mary was quite overwhelmed by this unexpected gesture of love and support from her friends.

As she and Victor walked towards the circus tent, she put her hand in his. "Thank you so much. This is the best birthday ever."

There were mixed reactions to the circus performances. The children were enthralled, however all the adults, while enjoying the clowns and acrobats, had reservations about wild animals being held captive and forced to perform tricks.

Bob and the children had gone home, and a scowling John met the others outside. "Those creatures are being mistreated, particularly the ones confined to small cages. I have been around communicating with all the animals, and very cruel methods are being used on some, especially the lions and tigers. We have to do something to rescue them."

When Mary and the twins passionately agreed Aldon said, "Don't even think about it," and motioned to Victor to take them back to the bookshop.

After they had left, Aldon looked at John. "I have a nasty suspicion you are going to do something silly, regardless of my wishes."

Tony and Gareth both indicated that they shared John's sentiments, and would be willing to assist in any rescue attempt.

"It would be preferable as a joint co-ordinated effort, rather than seeing John being caught trying to do it alone." Tony observed.

Aldon did not like the suggestion at all, but felt he was being outnumbered by his colleagues. If he refused to participate in this hare-brained project, they might go it alone with inadequate support.

"You can forget about the elephants! If you did rescue the lions and tigers, where would you take them?"

John was passionate in his belief that they should be returned to the wild in their natural environment. "I can sedate them, and you could take them back to their homelands in the PVX."

Aldon reluctantly agreed, and wondered just what he had been talked into. They formulated their plans, which were to come to fruition that night. If Xandra ever found out there would be hell to pay!

Late that night Camellia, who agreed with their sentiments, orchestrated a distraction on the other side of the fairground. John, Tony and Sarah, all wearing their invisibility shields, crept into the circus compound.

"It's the lions first," John whispered as he shot three tranquiliser darts into the cage. It took all their strength to carry the beasts out onto the grass.

He messaged Gareth. "Ready! The tranquiliser will last three or four hours. Once they're safely back on the ground, dart them with the antidote, then run!"

Gareth and Gustav, who were in the PVX, hovered low over the area, and transported the lions up one at a time. Gareth was very uneasy about his unconventional cargo, and was not going to waste any time getting to the lion reserve in Africa.

"Tigers next?" asked Tony, as they made their way to the enclosure.

Everything was going to plan when they heard a group of drunken circus folk returning across the field. Having ensured the two predators were lying, safely sedated, next to each other on the grass, Martina and Andy transported Tony, John and Sarah up to the second PVX.

John gave Andy a shove. "Quick! Bring them up on the blue beam!"

Slowly, but surely the two animals were raised up into the craft. With the tigers safely on board, Martina dropped her three co-conspirators off at Earth Base, before she and Andy headed towards the Himalayas.

Noru and a couple of his trusted monks had made their way down to the forests at the base of the mountain, and were waiting with a location beacon. The tigers were gently lowered back down to the ground, in the blue beam. The welcoming arms of their liberators placed them in stretchers, and carried them to a safe area for release.

When Martina and Andy reached Earth Base, she gave a sigh of relief. "You know, Aldon, although we broke the rules, I'm glad we helped those poor creatures find a better life."

Aldon was still anxiously waiting the return of Gareth and Gustav, and he was thankful when the other PVX docked.

"Did it all go to plan?" he asked as he heard them coming in the door.

"Not exactly," said Gareth.

Aldon turned around to see a very battered Gustav. "What the hell.....!"

"We lowered the lions onto the ground in the wildlife sanctuary, and then Gustav went down to administer the revival shots." Gareth explained. "He was ready to come back on board when another wild lion from the reserve unexpectedly came running up and grabbed him.

"I hit the beast with a stun ray, and retrieved Gustav. He seems a little bit the worse for wear. Hopefully we can patch him up, without Xandra finding out."

"Either that, or I'll have to tell Solar Base a few porkies!" Aldon groaned.

For the next couple of days the media was alive with speculative reports about the dangerous missing beasts. Had they escaped into the community? Had they fallen foul of their circus masters? Despite the claims that their animals had been stolen by aliens, the authorities were sceptical of the witness reports that the two tigers were lifted into the air by a blue beam from a flying saucer.

On Sunday night, under the cover of darkness, the circus and fairground community quietly packed up and left town.

After Gareth left, the personnel at Earth base turned their attention to Gustav. They washed his hair and face, removed his torn and tattered clothing, and got him a new uniform. His outer coating was rather scratched and scored, however the lion's claws did not appear to have penetrated his torso.

"The least number of people who know about this, the better." Aldon commented to Martina. "If anyone asks, we will just say Gustav had a heavy fall. I don't like the way his head is slightly skewed to one side. Hopefully his inner circuitry and electronics haven't been damaged."

Martina looked closely at the android. "I see what you mean. His posture is a very slightly off centre. He seems to be talking and behaving normally. I hope nothing will go wrong. Let's restrict him to simple duties for while, and see how he goes. Andy can handle the complicated stuff, as he is confident he has already assimilated Gustav's advance technical knowledge."

Although Gustav performed all his allocated duties, it didn't take long to realise something was wrong. He started wandering around, staring blankly at monitor panels and controls. Andy and the little grey workers were keeping their distance, as every so often he stopped talking, and started making weird noises whenever they came near.

Gustav's computerised brain was actually in a state of confusion. Unlike his Terran controllers he had to comprehend everything, and file it away in digital order. His artificial intelligence was still trying to process suddenly being flung to the ground by a large and powerful, furry creature. Aldon, not wanting Gustav to comprehend the incident, had failed to answer any of his questions.

A couple of days later, Victor and Mary were tidying up the bookshelves ready for that night's meeting.

"Did you hear about the lions and tigers disappearing from the fairground?" she asked. "It's all over the media. A few very inebriated circus workers claimed aliens in a flying saucer abducted them. You wouldn't, by any chance, know anything about that?"

Victor couldn't look her in the eye. He, along with Earth Base and his colleagues, had broken the rules by directly interfering in the circus situation.

"I know nothing...nothing!" he said.

Mary sensed he was lying. "Well, I hope it was your friends. Those poor creatures deserved a better life."

It was the main topic of conversation at the meeting that night. The normal members of the Book Club were full of speculation. The 'Friendship' inner group had their suspicions, and were, for the most part, non-committal.

Most of the people had left when Victor suddenly realised that Gareth was sitting at one of the coffee tables. "Where did you come from? What's up?"

"It's okay," Gareth reassured him. "Only Mishka saw me transport into your shower. We have problems! Gustav and a PVX have gone missing."

Victor stared at Gareth in disbelief. "How .....? Oh, goodness! He must have malfunctioned. Do we know where he is?"

Gareth was explaining the emergency, when Aldon messaged that he had found and retrieved the PVX, which was landed in the field where the circus had been. Gustav, however, was nowhere in sight. They wondered if he was confused, and was retracing some of the locations from the previous 'lion rescue' night.

After a frantic electronic search, Earth Base eventually locked onto him in the middle of town, but there were too many people around to transport him out.

Victor told Mary and the twins that he and Gareth had to go out for a while, and gave them an edited version of the events. He knew that when they eventually apprehended the android, it would be unwise to bring him back to the bookstore.

The plan was to locate Gustav, and as soon as practicable John would de-activate him. They could then take him back to the vet surgery, and return him to Earth Base. Aldon diverted Gustav's tracking frequencies to Gareth's device, and once John's van drove up, they were ready to go.

"He's right in the middle of the shopping district," Gareth groaned. "How are we going to pull this off without drawing attention to ourselves?"

They closed in on Gustav's location, and John pulled over to the side of the road. "Boof's in the back. Put him on the lead, and pretend you're taking him for a walk. With a bit of luck, he may be able to converse with Gustav better than we can."

Victor looked down at Boof. "Just stay by my side. When we reach Gustav, try to communicate telepathically, and tell us what he is thinking."

The metropolitan environment was new for Gustav, who was trying to process the vehicles and large buildings. He was walking along, with a slight lopsided gait, often bumping into other pedestrians. Gareth moved up beside him, and Victor was slightly behind.

"Gustav, what are you doing here? Aldon has ordered you back to Base. Come with us and we'll take you there."

Gustav stared at them, looking slightly confused. Gareth took him by the arm and it seemed like he was going to comply, until he spotted Boof.

"Big furry creature!" he called out in a rasping voice, and took a powerful kick at Boof, who promptly bit him on the leg, and tried to push him up against the wall. As Victor ordered Boof to back off, Gustav fled through the nearest doorway into a late night supermarket.

"Oh, shit!" said Gareth. "That computer brain of his has learned that big furry animals must be avoided. You take Boof back to the van. I'll follow Gustav."

Gareth was now getting worried, as people had stopped and were staring at the scuffle. He wanted to avoid any public scene, and raced into the store after Gustav. He looked up and down the aisles and caught up with Gustav, who was stumbling along, and had already knocked over one display stand.

Gareth was trying to suppress his rising panic, and stay calm. Gustav's speech was fast becoming illogical and incoherent. Gareth put his arm around Gustav's shoulder, and slowly led him towards the entrance.

Whenever Gustav tried to retreat, Gareth murmured, "Big furry creature gone now. You're safe with me."

The checkout operator was calling out for them to stop. "Your drunken friend has just damaged some of our stock. The manager has called the police. They'll be here in a minute."

Victor had returned, and together they propelled the bewildered Gustav out the door, and into John's van waiting outside.

They sped off down the street, and Gareth looked around. "Where's Boof?"

John seemed a little anxious. "I didn't want Gustav to get spooked again. I left Boof, out of harm's way, in a park up the road. Once I've deactivated this troublesome android, we can pick him up and Victor can go home." By the time they pulled up at the park, Gustav was deactivated and slumped motionless in the back.

They searched for Boof, and eventually found him under a tree and in conversation with an Alsatian. He had been playing doggie games with his new found friend, and had now learned and processed new information about how he, as a dog, was supposed to perform.

As John started to disapprove of his behaviour, Boof got into the van and said, "It was only humans you told me not to talk to."

They arrived back at the surgery and carried a lifeless Gustav to the transporter downstairs. A few minutes later Gareth delivered the immobile android back to a relieved Aldon and Martina at Earth Base.

"What are we going to do with him?" asked Martina.

"Good question," said Gareth. "I guess that's your problem. I'm off home now!"

Aldon squinted at Gustav's limp form. "It's a pity no-one here can repair him. We'll have to return him to Solar Base, with some acceptable cover story."

Victor was feeling quite shaken when he finally returned to Mary and the twins. He was glad they had closed the bookshop, and everyone else had gone home. He poured himself a very strong drink, and with a sigh of relief sat down at the table.

"Come on! Tell us what happened," Lucy demanded.

None of the women must ever know the truth about the missing lions and tigers. Victor kept to a brief explanation that they found Gustav after he had malfunctioned, taken the PVX, and got lost.

Fiona chimed in, "Oh my! A rogue robot running amok in town!"

Victor looked particularly stern. "You must promise me, all three of you, that you will never breathe a word of this – ever – to anyone."

CHAPTER 16

A few weeks later Martina came into the control room at Earth Base.

"Aldon, I've got good news and bad news. Which do you want first?"

Aldon frowned. "Just tell me both."

"Xandra is coming to stay a few days. He is bringing a replacement for Gustav, which means we have to figure out what we are going to tell him."

He thought for a moment. "Where possible we'll stick to the truth. Tell him about Gareth's escapade in town, and that his original injuries were due to a fall whilst out in the PVX. We'll omit the bit about the lions. With a bit of luck, when they repair him, any memory of a 'big hairy creature' can be blamed on Boof cornering him in town."

Xandra arrived in a shuttle craft. His main stellar ship had docked on the far side of the Moon, where they were upgrading some of the facilities at their base. Up to date, it had been manned by a single robot. Now Moon Base was to be enlarged, with extra staff and equipment.

"We have a two-fold plan," Xandra explained. "One is to have a better fortified outpost in case more Xvars arrive. Secondly, we anticipate expanding our mining activities. There are some very valuable commodities to be extracted from under the surface.

"Although the base has emergency 'short time' limited life support, it is not the right environment for any Terrans to live or work there. We will increase the personnel by two more androids and several robots."

Since he escaped, all those years ago, Xandra had spent very little time on planet Earth. He wanted to make the most of this opportunity. Martina and Aldon were to take it in turns to escort him on visits to most of the sub-bases, where he could meet with more of the agents and protégées.

"I hope you've brought some civilian clothes with you?" said Aldon. "If not, you can borrow one of my outfits until we get you some of your own."

Martina and Aldon were anticipating that during his visit, they could persuade Xandra to approve more equipment and staff.

For their first trip Aldon and Xandra transported into Tony's home, and went shopping in a city clothing store. Aldon's trousers were much too short and tight, and Xandra was relieved when he purchased some clothes of his own.

"That banknote replicator sure comes in handy," he quipped. "It's a good thing for us, that these people still use old fashioned currency."

Xandra commented to Aldon how he was enjoying the fresh air, sunshine, and scenery. "I enjoyed the time I was here in the past. Earth reminds me of my home planet, and is such a welcome change from the confines of Solar Base. If war doesn't break out, it won't be very long before my tour of duty ends. Hopefully, my next posting will be somewhere else like this."

After dinner at Earth Base, Aldon and Xandra took the PVX to the Refuge, on the other side of the world. It was a winter's day, with the sun peeping through the mountain mist.

Otto and Tibor met them, and led them up the rough path to the cabins. Xandra looked back down at the PVX docked at the jetty on the lake.

"We need to install a basic transporter here. The means of escape are very limited."

After a thorough inspection, Xandra was well pleased with the renovations, and asked Aldon if he could look into the possibility of another suitable site.

"Now we are training some of the protégées, just one refuge is really insufficient. It can be affected by the various seasons. We need a second one in a different part of the planet."

Back on Earth Base, Xandra examined the now defunct Gustav. He seemed to accept their explanation, and decided it was easier not to ask too many questions.

He had brought a new female android. "Her name is Ebony, and she is just as technologically savvy as Gustav. I trust she will not be so much trouble. She does have a darker complexion, which may be advantageous in many of the countries here."

Ebony was wearing the standard android uniform. Sarah, their other female looking android, always wore a white nursing/receptionist outfit at the vet surgery. Martina decided it would be a good idea to have a couple of civilian garments on hand, in case Ebony was ever out in the normal community.

Xandra had expressed a wish to catch up with Chantelle, who was an old friend. The next morning Martina thought she had better check first, and make sure there wasn't a client in her bed. After a couple of messages, Xandra and Martina transported down into Chantelle's shower unit.

"Hello gorgeous! Flash place you've got here," Xandra said, giving Chantelle a big bear hug and a more than friendly kiss.

Martina thought maybe she should leave the two of them alone. She raised her eyebrows at Chantelle, who responded with a wicked grin.

Xandra could not take the chance of her apartment being bugged, and insisted that the three of them should go out together to discuss Chantelle's espionage activities with the local military. He issued Chantelle with a new emergency alarm device, which would instantaneously connect her with Earth Base.

Martina noticed that on a couple nights, while at Earth Base, Xandra transported back to the surface to a secret destination. She strongly suspected he was visiting Chantelle in her apartment.

After a quick lunch, Xandra and Martina had to leave and go to see Noru in the Himalayas. Xandra agreed that Noru needed better facilities at his Himalayan sub-base. He was certainly prepared to provide the monastery with additional equipment and medical supplies.

He emphasised his most important objective. "We must locate the missing ancient base and artefacts, before Xvars, or especially the humans discover them. Apart from dangerous advance technology these people cannot control, a couple of our craft may well be intact and operational. There could also be hazardous radiation or other emissions trapped underground.

"I will need more personnel to find the site, let alone salvage everything. The terrain and local military are the main obstacles when trying to determine a suitable place to install extra facilities." Noru promised to give the matter some thought.

He had privately told Martina that the tigers were doing very well in their natural environment. She was grateful he never mentioned them to Xandra.

On day three Aldon and Michael took Xandra to the island. Aldon had never quite understood the location of a sub-base way out in the ocean.

"It's the island's remote location that gives it an advantage," Xandra explained. "Nobody would suspect that we had a facility here. The local natives have created a self sufficient environment, and Michael's little tropical hideaway allows us the benefit of an additional transporter."

They joined Paul and Jacquita for lunch in the church gardens. The Terran imposter priest and nun had gained the love and respect of the population, who had no idea what lay below in the crypt.

Although, for security reasons, there was certainly no Friendship Club, Paul said he assumed that in an emergency they could rely on the locals for protection and loyalty.

The Terrans had genetically augmented some of their ancestors several generations ago, and he and Jacquita had both recognised that many of the villagers possessed enhanced psychic and other abilities.

"They are already utilising fundamental frequencies and vibrations in their rituals. Most of the civilised world would call it voodoo, but we know better." Paul observed.

Xandra understood their wish for more help and supplies. Their work with these islanders was an important part of the charitable duties they were required to perform as Terrans. He could not provide a little grey worker, who if seen, would totally spook the superstitious congregation. He promised to give some thought to supplying an android.

They climbed the hill to Michael's private hacienda, and were welcomed by his houseboy who had prepared drinks and savouries.

Xandra was impressed by the beautiful home and summer house, with the hill behind leading to the cliffs and azure sea. He had bent the rules, and allowed Michael the luxury of a second property. Now he needed to seek a compromise.

"Michael, will you make one small concession. I know you were not happy with the suggestion of a tunnel from under the house, to a cave at the bottom of the cliff and the ocean below.

"It really would be a great advantage to our operations. Craft and supplies could arrive there, without attracting unwanted attention from the inhabitants. In addition, it would also give you a secondary escape route if you were in danger, and couldn't use the transporter."

Michael was obviously not happy at the prospect of an encroachment on his private paradise, but reluctantly agreed to the proposal.

Xandra's secret nightly trips to town had partly been to see Chantelle. They had known each other, and been good friends, many years before. It was a long, solitary time since Lydia died. He wondered if, one day, the relationship with Chantelle may blossom into something more.

What he wanted, most of all, was to get to know his son, Victor. Xandra would arrive at the bookshop after closing time, and they would sit and talk. Mishka would insist on staying, sitting firmly on Xandra's lap. Mary gave them some personal space, knowing these few stolen hours together were precious. Xandra spoke more about Lydia, and was thrilled when Victor gave him a copy of her picture.

They were both grateful to Mary for having risked her job to search the records and find the photo. Xandra liked Mary, and approved her living at the premises. She was a pleasant woman, and could be trusted. Victor was fond of her, and she had taken the edge off his loneliness and sense of isolation.

Xandra had waited until the weekend, and his last day at Earth Base, to officially talk to Mary and the twins, and visit their self-sufficient farm outside of town.

He also wanted to catch up with John, and went with Martina to visit the vet surgery before opening hours. He was well pleased after his assessment of the sub-base hidden down below. He didn't consider any further personnel were required.

He had little to say to Sarah and Max, but spent quite some time with Boof, who was demonstrating his intelligence and physical dexterity. They communicated verbally and telepathically, and John was relieved that the incident with Gustav was hardly mentioned.

Xandra was concerned regarding John's medical facilities. "The basement of this vet surgery is the ideal place for a small covert hospital/first aid station. It is the only one we have in this area, apart from Earth Base itself. You need much more advanced equipment and medical supplies to cope with any emergencies."

John was only too willing to provide a 'wish list'. Knowing he would not get everything he asked for, he 'padded it out' somewhat.

Later that morning, Victor drove Xandra and Aldon to the country farm. He got out of the van, and admired the solid stone building, with stables and the chicken coop in the field behind.

Mary, Fiona and Lucy were excited that they were to meet with this senior Terran representative. They had prepared a buffet lunch, with much of their home-grown food on display.

"We grew all the salad ourselves," Lucy bragged.

"....and the milk and eggs are from our goats and chickens." Fiona chimed in.

After lunch, he was given a guided tour of the property, including the vegetable garden and farm animals. Xandra was quite impressed with their enterprising spirit.

The women also explained they had been practising everything they had learned at the Retreat, and demonstrated by showing Xandra they could now levitate a small rock. He commented to Aldon that he thought Gareth had taught them well.

Xandra surprised everybody when he took one of their bicycles for a ride around the yard. He was chortling with a boyish delight.

"Many years ago, when I was merely a humble agent here, I had a bicycle of my own."

Victor kept the women occupied in the kitchen, and Aldon and Xandra walked alone across the field. Xandra said he thought the escape tunnel, leading to the cave in the nearby cliff, was an excellent addition. He then asked about Tony and the twins.

Aldon coughed nervously. "Oh ..you know about that? The relationship is a little unconventional, but it's keeping Tony on the straight and narrow. They think he is a friend of Gareth's, and don't know he is a Terran agent. They did the right thing by telling him not to come today."

Xandra nodded in approval. "Nobody must know our scientists are Terran agents. Not even their lovers! There is one more visit I need to make before I'm certain that these three women are suitable for upgrading to more covert activities."

After checking no-one was around, they knocked on Mrs McAffrey's door.

"Well, hello strangers," she said as she opened the door. "Don't just stand there. Come in before anyone sees you."

They carefully stepped over several cats before reaching the lounge room. She shooed off several more before they could sit down.

Xandra began, "Thank you for your help after the Xvar crash. Your feline army deserves great respect. That's not why we're here. We want your honest opinion of the three women on the next property."

Mrs McAffrey smiled as she handed them a cold drink. "Mary, Fiona and Lucy are first rate. I suspected they were also protégées – part hybrid – as I think they suspected me. We could sense each others' vibrations and frequencies. To their credit they never said a word. Not even a hint."

Xandra trusted Mrs McAffrey's judgement. She was the product of several generations of genetic augmentation by the Terrans. When she was twelve, her parents were killed in a suspicious car accident. Rather than let the authorities place her in foster care, or worse, she had been allowed to go away with her 'friends' to live on Solar Base until she was an adult.

Back on Earth, she did not adapt well to normal society, and much preferred her life in the country as a semi-recluse. No-body knew her history, and she wanted to keep it that way. Mrs McAffrey considered herself 'at one' with her Terran contacts and was always available to help when needed.

When they returned to the farm, Xandra gathered everybody together. He asked Mary, Lucy and Fiona to listen carefully to what he had to say, and outlined the problems they were experiencing with the Xvars and Katons, including their dangerous interference with the people of Earth.

"Many of the world's military and their governments have co-operated with these aliens in return for dangerous technology. The Xvars do not have the interests of the human race in mind," he explained. "They create division and hostilities between various nations, races and religions. Their objective is to conquer your planet and turn it into a military outpost to further their imperial ambitions in this part of the galaxy.

"So far you have been trained to expand and use your abilities to assist humanity towards a better and more peaceful future. The Terrans need help from protégées like you to counteract the Xvars, and their human allies. We cannot do it alone."

Mary and the twins were unanimous in their offer to assist in any way possible. Victor motioned them to pause for a moment.

"This will mean using your abilities more aggressively. Remember the time you knocked those two motorbike riders across the road?"

Fiona chuckled, "I know we shouldn't have done that, but they deserved it."

Xandra looked at the three young women. "It is this type of ability we plan to teach you. How are you with that?"

148

Mary turned around to Lucy and Fiona. "What do you think? I'm in if you are. We make a good team, and have always stuck together. All for one, and one for all?"

After whispering to each other for a couple of minutes, the twins announced, "Yes, you've got yourself an anti-Xvar hit team!"

Aldon and Xandra looked very satisfied, but Victor was privately worried about them, especially Mary. This could be dangerous.

Xandra told them that their advanced training would require going to Solar Base. While there they would also be given access to additional information and knowledge, some of which had been implanted in their brains by Otto when they were at the Retreat.

Xandra advised their trip to Solar Base would take about a month. The women needed to get time off work together. Fiona and Lucy said they would put in a request for some of the recreation leave that their company owed them. Mary felt that her boss was easy going, and she would ask for the same time off.

Xandra had treasured the short interlude he had spent with his son. He approached Victor with a suggestion. "Why don't you come as well? You could close the bookshop for a few weeks, and John will look after Mishka. Mary and the twins would feel more secure if you were with them, and we can spend more time together."

Victor was hesitating, but agreed when Mary said, "Do say yes! I'd be much happier if you were with us."

Xandra took Mary into another room. "There's something I have to show you."

He placed a small black box on the floor, and pressed the button. A life-size holographic image of Granny appeared and Xandra had to stop Mary running up to hug it. Mary cried as she heard her grandmother's voice delivering a short message of love and support.

"She is flourishing at Solar Base," Xandra assured her. "The children love her, and now you have agreed to our proposal, you will be able to see her very soon."

It had been a hectic week, and after Xandra departed in his shuttle craft, Martina produced a bag of Aldon's favourite pastries to have with their coffee.

"Why so thoughtful?" she asked him.

Aldon paused, with his mouth half full. "You know how Solar Base and the Guardians always keep everything compartmentalised – on a 'need to know' basis? Has it ever occurred to you that we only seem to be babysitting agents in the 'western' world? What about all the other major, dominant nations?"

"You're right," Martina agreed. "They also have powerful armed forces, and their own military/industrial corporations. It stands to reason that the Xvars must have also tried to manipulate them."

Aldon nodded. "Xvar influence would explain the belligerent behaviour of some governments, let alone the violent and disruptive religious/political factions. Our Terran leaders would not let that go unchallenged, which leads me to believe there is at least one other Earth Base, with their own agents, somewhere else on this planet. We just haven't been told about it!"

CHAPTER 17

The day had arrived for the women to start their journey with Victor to Solar Base. There was great excitement as they decided what to pack in their suitcases.

"One and only one bag each," Aldon had warned them. Victor had no trouble deciding what to put into his. Mary, being the elder of the three women, was normally a very calm and organised person. He watched in amusement as even she kept changing her mind about what to take.

Mishka had been left with John, and once the bookshop was locked up, they were ready to go.

Aldon had chosen Gareth to pick them up, as he was the only other agent whom the women recognised as a Terran. He drove them to a secluded spot out of town, and bid them farewell and a safe trip as, one by one, they slowly rose up in the blue beam to the waiting PVX above.

Once aboard, the craft shot into the sky, to the outer limits of the Earth's atmosphere. It came to a stop, and Aldon announced that they were to be beamed over to a shuttle craft waiting nearby.

"Unlike this larger ship, the PVX does not have protection from all of Earth's space debris or the powerful radiation coming from your Sun," Aldon explained.

Pletta, from Mars Base, who was in command of the shuttle, was trying not to laugh at the three women. Each one was a little uncertain as they stepped out of his transporter. Lucy was pinching herself to make sure she was all there. Fiona was examining her suitcase, to ensure it was intact, and nothing missing.

Unlike Victor, this was a new experience for them. They sat in the passenger area, drinking some pleasant tasting unknown liquid, which had been served by a robot. Most Terran craft had a robotic crew. Androids were expensive and complex, and often reserved for where they may be seen by humans.

Fiona was staring out a window, entranced by the black expanse of space rushing past.

"Look, I can see the Earth. Isn't it beautiful – just like the photos from our astronauts and astronomers? Oh...wow! And there's the moon. We must be going awfully fast – they're starting to get smaller."

After Pletta put the controls on automatic, he came through to talk to his guests. He advised Victor they would be staying over at Mars Base until Xandra came to convey them on the last leg of their journey to Solar Base.

Victor reassured Mary that this was normal procedure. The twins, on the other hand, were jumping up and down like two excited children.

"We're going to Mars! We're going to Mars!" Lucy squealed.

"I can't believe it! It's so exciting," Fiona enthused, "and I guess we can never tell anyone."

"No you can't," said Pletta, "and I've already confiscated that camera you had in your bag. You can have it back when you go home."

Victor followed Pletta back into the flight control area, and pulled a rueful face. "We're going to have to watch those two on Mars Base. Some of our Terran colleagues haven't seen such attractive young women for a long time. Lucy and Fiona are playful flirts when Tony isn't around. The problem is, none of those women know that Tony is a Terran, and he will soon hear of it, if anything inappropriate happens."

Pletta reflected on the potential situation. "I agree, and I don't need any arguments over girlfriends. Two vivacious females will certainly catch the attention of my unattached subordinate officers. I will have to leave it to you and Mary to keep them under control."

Once they arrived at the red planet, Pletta showed everybody to their temporary quarters, and then to the recreation room for a meal. It wasn't long before a group of Terran males joined them, all anxious to meet the women.

Victor made it quite clear he didn't appreciate anyone 'chatting up' Mary, and since, by now, it was common knowledge that he was

Xandra's son, nobody argued with him. On the other hand, it was obvious the twins were enjoying all the attention.

There were male and female Terrans in the recreation area, and in next to no time alcohol was flowing and music playing. Some of the younger officers asked the twins to dance. Victor felt that things could get out of hand, but there might be resentment and heightened tensions if he tried to intervene.

After a quiet word to Mary, she took control of the situation and shepherded Fiona and Lucy back to their quarters, saying they all needed a decent night's sleep.

"But we were enjoying ourselves," they argued.

"Yes," Mary agreed, "a little bit too much for your own good. Flirting with sex starved young Terran officers is not a good idea!"

Pletta was happier when Xandra arrived to collect his four visitors, especially those two lively young women.

Mary gasped when they were taken up to board the craft bound for Solar Base. It was huge, bigger than anything she had ever seen. Victor smiled at her childlike shock and awe.

"Compared to Earth's primitive exploratory vessels, this space ship can travel at phenomenal speeds. We have much larger, faster ones that travel to distant parts of the galaxy. Way out in that vast quadrant, there are also permanent space stations which are the size of a small city."

Xandra's craft was manned by several Terran officers, and a crew of robots and little grey workers. His visitors were impatient to see and explore everything, and one of the officers took them on a quick guided tour of the control centre section only. He told them that the crew quarters and certain technological/engineering areas were strictly 'out of bounds'!

Victor was relieved to hear this. With a bit of luck, the twins would stay out of mischief. After they were shown into their guest quarters, Xandra joined them for refreshments.

"It will take a couple of days to reach Solar Base. In the meantime, make yourselves comfortable in the guest lounge, where there are all kinds of entertainment. I'll keep dropping by, but this is 'J20', a robot attendant who will be here at all times to assist with anything you need."

'J20' prepared a gourmet meal for them, and was more than obliging with some fancy pre-dinner cocktails.

Mary gleefully waved her swizzle stick in the air. "He may have a metallic body and mechanical voice, but I wish we could have a servant like this at the bookshop!"

Lucy spent some time looking out the window, innocently wondering whether they would get to see Jupiter or Saturn. She was disappointed when Victor explained that the planets were not all lined up together. They orbited the Sun in entirely different positions.

Several hours later, they were jolted out of their sleep by a violent lurch of the craft and the sound of a couple of explosions. Victor told the others to stay calm, he would find out what was happening. He was anything but calm. There was an alarm blaring throughout the ship, and a red light above the door was flashing.

'J20' was on the floor, and seemed to be having a problem standing up again. Victor got him back onto his feet, and asked if he could tell them what had happened.

The robot was silent for a couple of minutes, and then announced that he was being told that the vessel had suffered a malfunction. He said that Victor may join the Commander on the main deck, but the other guests must stay in their quarters while the crew initiated repairs.

As Victor left he told both Mary and 'J20' to make sure the twins 'stayed put'. He made his way to where Xandra was at the controls, and transmitting instructions to his team on other parts of the ship. The craft was being operated manually, and Victor could smell a strange odour, as if something had been burning.

"Only a small problem with the propulsion system," Xandra commented. "We are heading towards one of our smaller bases, on a little known moon, while it is repaired."

Victor knew his father was being evasive. "How about you tell me the full story?"

Xandra stiffened. "I suppose you have a right to know, but don't tell the women. We unexpectedly encountered a Katon supply vessel, which fired upon us. Our shields were already activated, so very little damage was done. We blew them into a thousand pieces, but don't know if any of their allies have a larger craft in the vicinity.

"Zadoc is not willing to take any chances. He wants us to wait for him at a nearby moon station until he sends one of his warships to escort us to Solar Base."

Victor looked around at the crew who were obviously stretched to the limit. "What can I do?"

"At the moment, you're our guest. Just stay safe with the others," Xandra said.

"No! At the moment the Terran half of me must come to the fore," Victor asserted. "You are not only my commanding officer, you are my father. I want to be by your side."

Xandra had a lump in his throat. "Thank you, son."

Victor's upbringing on Solar Base had given him enough prior training to be of assistance with much of the craft's technology. This released another officer to help with the minor repairs, which were soon completed.

Victor headed back to the guest quarters, and only mentioned a minor engineering problem, which would soon be fixed.

Fiona pointed through the window. "Look! There's a huge planet coming up! Is this Solar Base?"

Victor mumbled something about it being one of the many planetary moons, in this vicinity, which housed a small base. They were just making a brief stop-over. Mary knew him well enough to know he was not telling the whole truth, however she said nothing.

In order to evade detection by the enemy, Xandra had manoeuvred the craft behind the moon. Lucy, being her usual inquisitive self, wanted to know if they could leave the ship to have a closer look at this mysterious moon, and the base inside.

Victor was unusually blunt. "Certainly not! It is a 'classified' installation, manned by robots, and has no atmosphere or breathable oxygen."

Victor was running out of fabricated excuses as he kept reassuring the women during the long wait for the Terran battle-ship. He joined Xandra back on the main deck when Commander Karine eventually beamed on board, and greeted them.

"Hi fellows! Repairs all done? I guess you are anxious to get underway. We don't expect any problems, but it is safer to have an escort. We aren't aware of any other enemy vessels in the area, but it's impossible to detect everything in this vast cosmic space."

When they had moved off, and gathered speed, Victor returned to the guest quarters. He was behind Mary when she noticed Karine's large ship through the window. Gently putting his hand over her mouth, he whispered, "Shh! I'll tell you all about it after we get to Solar Base."

It was quite some time before the women could see what looked like a rocky planet looming up ahead of them. As they neared the surface, the craft slowed to almost a halt.

"I don't see any Solar Base," Fiona complained.

"Just wait and watch," Victor reassured her.

Underneath their hovering ship, the rocks moved apart, like two huge concealed doors, and they flew into a gigantic underground area. It was massive, and they could see many large 'parked' space vessels inside. Victor, who had grown up with Solar Base facilities, took it in his stride, but Mary and the others were astounded.

"All this makes me feel very insignificant," Lucy murmured, when Xandra ushered them into the base. He put a fatherly arm around her shoulder.

"No need to feel overwhelmed. Except for our robots, and little grey 'workers', everybody here is basically a person, just like you."

They were amazed at the enormity of Solar Base. It was like a small town. Once they were shown to their quarters, and the communal areas, Xandra delegated 'J20' to remain with them during their stay.

"You are already familiar with this robot, it will attend to your everyday needs, and accompany you to scheduled lessons and activities. Once you have settled in you will be taken around our outpost, and it will be explained where you may or may not go."

Solar Base, which was self sufficient, comprised multiple levels. Many of these were totally out of bounds to all but their technicians, laboratory scientists and engineering staff. Besides the resident quarters, there were several shops, restaurants, and recreation spots. There was even an underground parkland, surrounded by a gym, swimming pool, lecture rooms and hobby workshop areas.

"What's in there?" Lucy asked, peering through the doors into what looked like a large auditorium. It was explained that it was the communal entertainment centre, where everyone came together for social events.

During their tour of the various amenities, Mary kept asking where the children were. She was impatient to see Granny. Eventually their guide opened a door to the youngsters' play area, and Mary rushed in.

"Granny – Granny!" she sobbed, and threw her arms around the old lady.

They hugged and cried for several minutes, before regaining their composure. There was lots of news to exchange, and so little time. Granny reminded her that they would have the next four weeks to share together. Mary mentioned her mother, and Granny was sad to hear about the breakdown in the relationship.

"Your mother is still my dearly loved daughter, no matter what! She is in a dark place, so full of hate and anger. She needs help and understanding. Although you must follow your own heart and path, please try to keep in contact with her."

Before their formal training commenced, they were joined by a few more protégées who had been at the Retreat with them. Their first lecture was a comprehensive information session regarding the Xvar and Katon threat, and their political and military interference on planet Earth. The twins were especially shaken when told of the Katon attack on their craft during their journey to Solar Base.

They soon realised that these menacing aliens, along with their human conspirators, had no qualms when it came to eliminating any opposition. Although this had the effect of creating additional fear and concern, it also heightened their resolve to learn how to fight back.

Having been made aware of the dangers of their mission, they were taken to what appeared to be a small hospital, and asked to lie down on low shiny 'tables'. Mary noticed a little being beside her. It had a large grey head, and big elongated shiny black eyes. Its gentle touch brought back a long lost memory, but before she could ask any questions, she, like the others, fell into a deep trance.

When they returned to a conscious state, the little grey creatures helped them back to their feet. Xandra was waiting for them as they were led out the door.

"How do you feel?" he asked.

"Different. I don't know how....just different." Mary said.

The twins agreed, and although Victor was aware of what had happened, he also could recognise new frequencies and vibratory levels within his body.

"We have upgraded your genetic augmentation, and allowed your consciousness to access information and abilities which previously lay dormant." Xandra explained. "You must rest for the next couple of days, and then the essential training will begin."

Solar Base provided a great many social activities for its residents and the other visiting protégées. Xandra and Victor both realised it would be better to provide some structured recreation for the three women. Even though Mary and Victor had lectured the twins regarding proper behaviour during their stay, subtle supervision would be preferable to leaving Fiona and Lucy to their own devices.

Before Xandra could organise an appropriate diversion, the solution came by chance. Mary had accompanied Granny and the children to their singing classes. Victor went as well. It was an opportunity to see his old music teacher, Olivia, who had brought him so much joy during his childhood days.

The twins had tagged along, and suggested the young people try some of the latest songs and melodies from Earth. Olivia approved, and before long the strains of both folk and pop were flooding the studio. Their human guests were in full vocal passion, with the children all joining in the chorus lines. They were about to leave with the children when Olivia beckoned to Granny and her four visitors to stay.

"You have quite promising voices, which blend very harmoniously. Our social club is having a friendly live entertainment competition in a couple of weeks. Why don't you form a group, and participate?"

Victor and Mary were doubtful if they had any talent, but Fiona and Lucy were, as usual, more enthusiastic. Olivia commented that, not only had she previously taught Victor to play several musical instruments, including the guitar, he also had a pleasant singing voice.

"Do think about it. I will coach you. We don't get many human visitors, and our Solar Base community are anxious to get to know you. What better way than to join in one of our shared events."

The twins pleaded with Victor and Mary. "Please say yes! It will be such fun, and we often sing together on Saturday nights at the farm."

With Granny's encouragement, they spent a couple of spare hours every day practising with Olivia. They even appeared with the children when they gave a concert for the base one afternoon. Mary, who was hesitant at first, was slowly gaining more confidence. The singing activity also acted as a relaxation from the intense training exercises they regularly attended.

Telepathy, mind control and kinetic abilities were practised over and over again. Soon their enhanced abilities enabled them to not only read peoples' thoughts, but also to communicate messages to each other. With concentration they could manipulate small objects and affect electricity and electronic devices.

The sessions, requiring concentrated intellectual competence, were interspersed with basic self-defence and military skills. Karine had stayed on to supervise their lessons in unarmed combat and also basic proficiency in firearms, including Terran small ray and pulse weapons.

159

Victor had received some of this training as part of his childhood education, and was able to assist the students during the learning process. He thought it wise to include a fundamental knowledge of Terran communications and other operational devices. Xandra agreed this may prove advantageous in the future.

If they proceeded with their plans to raise small resistance groups around the globe, Victor, Mary and the twins could assist Gareth with the training. Minor genetic augmentation of their hybrid protégées could be performed at the Retreat, but any major implementation required skilled supervision. This would only be reserved for a select few, as they certainly could not bring candidates to Solar Base on a regular basis.

Outside of the training sessions, Victor left the three women to their own devices, while he renewed some old friendships around the Base. Whenever possible he also had dined with Xandra each time he was off duty.

Mary spent her free moments with Granny and the children. Lucy and Fiona, having heeded the warnings about inappropriate behaviour, usually joined them.

In their spare time, the musical training with Olivia continued, and a couple of nights before the entertainment competition, the twins were agonising over what to wear.

"We must have proper costumes," Fiona insisted.

"No," said Mary. "I don't want to look like a tarted up trollop. Let's just be ourselves, who we really are."

Victor agreed, and on the night, when it was their turn to go on stage, they were wearing their normal jeans and t-shirts. Victor played the guitar, and together they sang two recent popular hit songs. The twins, still intent on creating an impression, included some last minute fancy dance moves into their routine.

They noticed the audience was comprised of Terrans, many of whom had varying ethnic appearances, similar to those on Earth. They were given a huge round of applause, and at the end of the night, received a special award.

Xandra joined them for breakfast the next morning. "I was quite proud of you all last night, and have an idea, which I hope you will consider. If, back on Earth, you continued as a casual vocal act, it would provide a wonderful 'cover' for your more illicit activities."

Victor was apprehensive. "I was told not to be conspicuous – to stay out of the limelight."

"I don't think there would be a problem," Xandra reassured him. "A small singing group would not attract the same attention as the talent you have for complicated piano concertos.

"Further, we have a few contacts in the music industry, and they could get you casual bookings in certain venues we want to keep an eye on, for one reason or another."

All too soon it was time to leave. Mary had bid a tearful farewell to Granny, and Xandra gave Victor a more restrained bear-hug. All the protégées were returning on Karine's battle-ship. Xandra did not want to expose his precious son to any more attacks by the enemy on the way back to Earth.

Aldon was waiting with the PVX, and soon Gareth met them at their rendezvous to drive them back to the bookshop. They opened the door to find Mishka on the kitchen table, licking her whiskers.

"John, the vet, must have brought her back and fed her," Mary said. "But how did he get in?"

"Oh, he's fairly trustworthy. I gave him a spare key in case there were any problems." Victor lied, knowing full well that John had saved time by using the transporter from the vet surgery to the shop and back.

CHAPTER 18

The Terrans had warned their scientific team to be more vigilant in regards to their personal safety. The rogue military/industrial corporations had lost most of their Xvar/Katon advisors, and were not above forcibly abducting new experts to replace them.

Gareth was having lunch in the cafeteria, when Michael complained his small laser firearm had been inadvertently damaged. When he got home he would transport to Earth Base for a replacement.

Gareth looked concerned. "Not good enough! You know you must always have a weapon. I have to go to an appointment this afternoon, but will arrange for you to get a new one before you leave tonight."

Gareth went outside and contacted Aldon on his communicator.

"Yes, Michael must be armed at all times." Aldon agreed. "I'll slip into the laboratory late this afternoon and he can have the latest model, just in from the supply ship. Boy, do these babies have some firepower! Don't worry, I'll get you one later"

Michael had stayed back late to finish an assignment, and was bending over his work station when Aldon suddenly appeared before him.

Michael gasped in surprise. "You're taking a bit of a risk, aren't you? Has anybody seen you?"

"Not since we got these personal invisibility gadgets!" Aldon grinned, handing him his new weapon.

After a quick discussion, Aldon said, "Must go. Have some other things to do before I go back. Abracadabra, first you see me – then you don't!" He waved his hand in the air and disappeared.

Michael's heart sank when he turned around and saw Angela standing in the doorway. Before he could reach her, and plead for her discretion, she rushed back down the corridor towards the reception area and front door.

His assistant was a very nice woman – quite sweet in fact. He wasn't sure how much she had seen, and couldn't risk her telling anyone. He knew they could not allow their operation to be jeopardised at this stage. What to do?

He ran down to the car-park, and drove along the route he knew Angela took home from the bus stop. Perhaps he could talk to her? No – he would have to get her right away from here, while he figured something out.

Angela stumbled down the dark street. She wished she had driven to work this morning, rather than getting the bus. It was cold, wet and windy, and all she wanted to do was get home.

Her mind was whirling with the scene she had witnessed. It had been no illusion – that elusive figure, which appeared out of thin air, gave something to Michael, and after a few minutes, just as mysteriously, disappeared again. They seemed to be talking in an unfamiliar language. Who and what was Michael, this scientist, this man she had felt so strongly attracted to?

She knew she was obliged to notify the boss, but her hidden feelings for Michael made her hesitate. How could she betray the man she secretly loved? Distracted by her confused thoughts, she didn't hear the footsteps behind her.

An arm encircled her waist, and just before everything descended into blackness, she felt a strange smelling cloth over her mouth and nose.

When she eventually came to, her mind felt foggy, and her vision blurry. Once her stability returned, she realised she was lying on a large divan, in an unfamiliar room.

Panic set in. Where was she? What had happened? She got up and tried to walk to the nearby metal door, only to discover a handcuff on one wrist led to a chain attached to the floor. The chain allowed her to some space to walk around, and included access to a small en-suite.

She could not quite reach the walls encircling the room, which appeared to be made of woven bamboo. There were no windows, except for a couple of large skylights in the high pitch ceiling above. The room was lit by a large decorative lamp, sitting on a table next to a bowl of fruit and a jug containing some kind of juice. Her surroundings felt like a distinctly tropical prison.

Perhaps she could call for help. She found her bag lying beside the couch. Her phone and corporate personal alarm were gone!

After securing Angela in the summer house, Michael had gone straight to Earth Base. His angry altercation with Aldon had their staff fleeing the control room for quieter areas. The little grey workers were unable to process intense human emotions, especially anger.

Delta peeped around the corner as Aldon was thumping the table with his fist.

"Just what did you think you were doing? You abducted the poor woman, grabbed her off the street, before considering the consequences?"

"It's all your fault," Michael yelled back. "If you'd been more careful, she wouldn't have seen you! I had to stop her before she got home and told her flat mate."

Martina was trying to intervene before the argument got out of hand. "Just quieten down, both of you. We have to figure out what to do now – before she is missed."

Michael had already thought about that, and used Angela's phone to message her flatmate, his own work computer and the company. "I told them she had an emergency. Her friend had a car accident, and she may be away for a few weeks while she helped the family who lived in the country. And yes – I did remember to then de-activate her phone and corporate alarm, so she can't be traced to the island."

Martina was relieved. "At least that will buy us some time to think up a solution. In this case it's probably too late, and not a good idea, to bring her here and try to erase her memory of the entire incident. In the meantime, you had better take good care of her, and make sure she doesn't escape."

Aldon interrupted, "She wouldn't get far. The ferry only goes to the island once every six weeks. We'll have to tell Paul and Jacquita, as the church would be the logical place to seek refuge if she did get away."

After Michael transported back to his island hacienda, Martina walked over at Aldon, who was slumped in his chair.

"I thought you said Michael was one of your less troublesome agents?"

Aldon glared at her and continued muttering obscenities to himself.

Angela tried, to no avail, to escape the handcuff which chained her to the floor. Her imagination was in overload as she tried to guess the identity of her captors. Her family were not wealthy, so ransom could not be the motive. Perhaps it was one of the rival industrial corporations they had been warned about? She prayed to God that she wasn't in the clutches of a white slave trade group.

The door opened and Michael came in carrying a tray of food, which he placed on the table.

"YOU!" she exclaimed. "But why? If it was about that strange disappearing man, I won't say anything."

He didn't reply, so she waved her restrained hand in the air, and tugged at the chain. "You aren't kinky or something...are you?"

Michael smiled to himself, and left the room saying, "Be a good girl, and eat your dinner."

The next morning Michael transported back to his city home, and went to work as if nothing was wrong. He had left instructions with his houseboy, Tuan, to make sure Angela had breakfast and lunch. Under no circumstances could he tell anyone about Angela, or let her escape.

Although Tuan was surprised at the turn of events, he felt great admiration for his boss. In the old days, if the men of his culture fancied a woman from another island, they would just snatch her during the night, and carry her home in their outrigger canoe.

Tony and Michael were having lunch in the cafeteria, when Gareth joined them and nudged Michael in the ribs.

"Aldon is really pissed off. Please tell me you didn't do this. What on earth were you thinking?"

Tony was choking on his lunch as he tried to smother his laughter. "You are a dark horse, after all. Now what are you going to do? Kidnapping might be added to your crimes. You'd better watch out for those indigenous laws on that island of yours. – Of course, if she were your wife, she couldn't be made to testify against you!"

Gareth glared at Tony, "This is serious! Don't encourage him!"

Michael looked rather gloomy. "Aldon says I have to sort this out and put it right. At the moment I'm just blundering along, and haven't the foggiest idea of what to do."

That evening Angela, despite a growing desperation, was trying to keep positive. A young man, who looked like a south sea islander, had brought her breakfast and lunch. She couldn't understand how she could be in a cold, rainy environment one day, and a warm balmy one the next.

Tuan, who said he was the 'house-boy', called her 'Missy' and would not answer any of her questions.

It was getting dark and Tuan was preparing dinner when Michael arrived back at the island. He was still mulling over how to explain everything to Angela when he saw what looked like several flares moving up the hill outside.

"It's okay, boss," Tuan assured him. "They're celebrating the harvest festival – taking fire torches to throw over the cliff for the weather gods."

Michael looked out the window, and exclaimed, "Tuan, just how much fire do they need?"

There were huge flames flaring up from the nearby undergrowth, and the grassy area surrounding the summerhouse was burning. The natives were scooping up pots of water out of the small pond, and running to put out the flames.

One of them called out. "Sorry boss! Abe fell over and dropped his torch."

Michael raced towards the summerhouse, which was starting to catch alight. All he could think of was the helpless Angela inside. If anything happened to her he could never forgive himself. This was all his fault.

He pulled the bolt on the entry. It was already hot. Inside he fought his way through the smoke to Angela, who was cowering on the floor and coughing. He unlocked the handcuff, scooped her up into his arms, and stumbled back to the door. It had swung shut! She clung to his body as he tried to push it open, and heard him cry out as the red hot metal caused a searing pain in both his hands.

Tuan, and a couple of the natives outside, pulled them both through the entrance to safety. As they staggered back to the main house, Michael could see the natives were getting the upper hand on the fire, but the summerhouse had been nearly destroyed.

Angela sat down in the lounge room, still stunned and trying to recover from the smoke inhalation. She looked across at Michael who was obviously in agony. Tuan kept saying, "Your hands, boss – your hands! I get Sister Jacquita."

About fifteen minutes later a nun came rushing in, accompanied by a native looking novice carrying a first aid bag. They gasped in horror at Michael's badly burned hands.

They both spent some time gently applying various creams and a dressing that Angela had never seen before. Sister Jacquita injected something into Michael's arm and turned to Angela.

"I have given him something for the pain, but he needs constant care, and antibiotics to prevent infection.

"Will you be staying here for a while? We haven't got a hospital, and the ferry doesn't come for another four weeks. I will be back in the morning, and can visit every day. Tuan is a nice young man, but he goes home to his family every night, and is not capable of managing this situation."

Angela was in uncertain. She could appeal to this nun, who was obviously not a native, for help. On the other hand, although she still didn't know where she was, it seemed the only escape would be by a ferry which wouldn't arrive for a month.

She glanced across at Michael, who was very pale. He seemed a little unresponsive, which was probably due to the strong pain medication. Angela knew that he was injured while rescuing her. If she had burned to death, no-one back home would have been any the wiser. On the other hand, her imprisonment in that summerhouse was all his doing in the first place!

Angela was obviously giving the matter some thought. Jacquita nervously waited, and eventually she got the answer she had been hoping for.

"I hadn't planned on staying," Angela said, "but I suppose I can. I didn't bring any clothes with me – can I get some around here?"

When Jacquita returned to the church, both she and Paul heaved a sigh of relief. They could tell Aldon and Gareth that the situation had been contained for the moment.

"Before I go back in the morning, I'll pop into town and get her something decent to wear. Gareth can arrange a suitable medical certificate for Michael's company."

Angela woke to the sun streaming through the guest bedroom window. She stretched out and took a deep breath of the balmy early morning air. She could hear the houseboy preparing breakfast, so there was no need to get up immediately. Tuan would have helped Michael out of bed.

Every day Tuan would leave around about sunset. Angela would spend the evening with Michael, and get him refreshments or anything else he needed. Both his hands were heavily bandaged, and he could do nothing for himself. She had to overcome her embarrassment at assisting him in the bathroom before helping him into bed every night.

Sister Jacquita, who had been coming twice a day to tend to Michael's injuries, brought her the promised clothing – several very expensive casual outfits and some glamorous underwear. There were also two very revealing negligees, which made Angela wonder if the Nun thought she and Michael were a couple.

Now she was free from any restraint, Angela was at liberty to explore the hacienda and the surrounding environment. She soon realised it was some form of tropical island, but still had no idea where. The house itself was quite luxurious, and almost Spanish or Mexican in design.

Outside there were palm trees, colourful flowers, and a small fishpond with a fountain. The surrounding paved patio led to the now burned down summer house. She shivered every time she saw it, thinking of what might have happened.

She climbed the grassy slope behind the garden, and found herself on top of the cliffs. Sometimes she would go there to sit, and contemplate her situation, as she gazed at the waves breaking on the rocks below.

Angela had no idea what the future held. Michael had obviously brought her here to prevent her revealing what she had witnessed in the laboratory the other evening. He apparently didn't intend to hurt her, but would he keep her a virtual prisoner on this island forever?

She had tried to tell him she would be missed, but he had given a sly grin, and said everyone thought she had gone to help a friend involved in an accident. Her heart sank a little, but she knew this excuse could not last forever. Sooner or later people would start asking questions.

Angela also had to admit to herself that she was still strongly attracted to Michael. In any other circumstances, she would have been in seventh heaven if, with romantic intentions, he had carried her off to a tropical island.

During their time in the laboratory together, he was very reserved, often quite grumpy. Their discussions usually centred on work. On her first day in the hacienda there had been some periods of uncomfortable silence.

She decided the best approach was to pretend there was nothing wrong, and to take it one day at a time. Bit by bit their conversations became less strained, and slowly he started to open up, revealing more of his genuine personality.

The property had its own power supply, and in the evenings Angela would put on some music. Often he would choose to watch a documentary, usually of wildlife, or different parts of the world. She wondered why, during one screening, he murmured, "What a beautiful planet – such a shame you are all destroying it!"

After a few days Angela ventured down the hill to the village and adjacent lagoon. There was a large settlement of small houses, some on stilts, made of bamboo, and others of stone or brick in a more traditional style. The local natives, who were busy tending their vegetable gardens, gave her a friendly wave or smile, as if they were not surprised by her presence.

Goats and chickens were wandering loose across the dirt road which led to a small jetty. She assumed that was where the ferry docked every six weeks, and made a mental note to find out exactly when it was next due.

Angela made her way across to the old stone church and buildings, and noticed there appeared to be only one local store. It was doubtful that it stocked the up-market clothes that Sister Jacquita brought her.

'Father' Paul, who had been alerted to Angela's arrival, was waiting for her in the church.

"Hello, my dear. You must be Angela. Sister Jacquita has told me how kind you have been, to stay and care for Michael after he was injured in the fire. Abe is very sorry he dropped his fire-torch. It should never have happened, but I'm afraid my parishioners still cling to some of their indigenous beliefs and rituals."

There was something about this priest, she wasn't sure what, that made her hesitant to tell him the true situation and ask for his help. Maybe later.

After some meaningless conversation, she expressed her gratitude for the clothes the church had provided, and made her way back to Michael's villa.

Paul went down to the crypt, and joined Jacquita who was adjusting some of their equipment. He was looking rather despondent.

"We're going to have to resolve this situation – the sooner the better. I don't know what to do about Angela. She is a decent woman, and he can't keep her a prisoner here forever. We mustn't leave this unresolved, and have to sort it out! I need to meet with Aldon and Gareth."

Jacquita shook her head. "I know Aldon has deliberately not visited Michael, and has also told Gareth not to come. Before you officially voice your concerns, perhaps you should leave it for a little while."

Paul was puzzled. "Why? What did you have in mind?"

"Angela is definitely smitten with Michael, and I sense he is quite fond of her. Trust me – I'm a woman and know these things. She has agreed to stay until his burns have healed, and perhaps during that time he will develop stronger feelings. I know his fiancée ran off with someone else some years ago, but it is about time he got over it."

Paul agreed to delay any meeting with Earth Base, but couldn't see what difference it would make. The Guardians discouraged serious relationships between Terrans and normal humans.

Another two weeks went by, and when Jacquita was visiting to care for Michael's hands, she commented that with the advance Terran treatment, they would soon be healed.

"No they won't," he argued, glancing towards Angela, who was outside on the patio.

"Michael, I'm not supposed to lie for you!" Jacquita complained.

"Okay – understood. How about Tuan changes the bandages from here on?"

Jacquita frowned for a moment. "I suspect what you're up to, but since I don't actually know, I'll say nothing. Tuan can collect the dressings from the church every morning. I'll tell Paul he is saving me the trip."

After Jacquita left, Michael walked outside, and quietly watched as Angela was offering bits of left-over food to some of the local wildlife. She was so calm and gentle, the colourful parrots and birds were sitting on her hands and arms.

He had been lonely and resentful of all women for a long time, avoiding any emotional commitment. It wasn't until he thought he would lose Angela in the fire, that he realised he was in love with her.

They were spending the days laughing together under the sunny sky, and in the evenings shared their thoughts. As his shell of isolation and denial started to crumble, his suppressed hormones came to the fore. Every night, as she helped him change for bed, her tender hands would touch him. It took all his self control to prevent his body from making an obvious response. He fantasised about a closer relationship until the longing to have her was almost an obsession.

He was unsure of her feelings towards him, and being scared of rejection, said nothing. Maybe he didn't attract her physically. He was ten years older, and of mixed Terran blood. He had been considered handsome in his youth, well built with slightly tanned, Asian type skin and dark penetrating eyes. An accident with radiation had caused him to lose most of his dark mop of hair, which couldn't be restored until he was able to access the advanced equipment on a Terran home planet or Space Station.

Although Michael knew it must, he didn't want this magical time to end. He was afraid he would lose Angela. She may well reject him like his old girlfriend had done. He wondered if resorting to local island law could provide a solution.

Every day Tuan would change the dressings on his hands, and would give a sly grin as Michael said, "Still burned!" and slid him a few coins.

One morning, when Tuan was preparing breakfast, he looked over at Angela and asked, "One egg or two, Mrs Michael?"

Angela gave a small start. "No! – I'm Angela!"

Tuan gave a high pitch giggle. "Woman in house with man for one month – Island rule says you now married – Mrs Michael!"

Angela was both speechless and bewildered.

Michael walked through the door, with a grin on his face, and a gleam in his eye. "Hello – Wifey!"

The first thing that she noticed was that his hands were perfectly healed, and free of bandages.

Her eyes blazed with indignation. "How long have your hands been better? You did this deliberately – didn't you? Pretending to still be helpless, so I would stay long enough to become your wife under some indigenous law? How could you?

"While I thought there was something special happening between us, you were just keeping me here so I couldn't tell the boss about that strange disappearing man."

Before Michael could tell Angela that he loved her, she had raced out the door.

Running down the hill, she could see the ferry had docked at the small jetty in the village. Her mind was in turmoil. If Michael had asked her to marry him she would have said 'yes'. Instead he chose deception and trickery. Was it really all about ensuring her silence over what she had witnessed in the laboratory?

Did this island's strange marriage customs mean she had to stay? Could a wife desert her husband under their law? She wasn't going to wait to find out. All Angela could think of was getting back home. She had to reach that boat, before it sailed away for another month.

When she arrived at the quayside, she could only find a native deckhand.

"Where's the captain?" she demanded.

"In the church, Missy. He brought the Bishop to see Father Paul, and has to wait for him to come back before we can leave."

Angela found the captain in the church, and was close to collapse when she stumbled up the aisle to ask him for a passage to wherever he was going. Anywhere but here!

Father Paul and the Bishop came over to ask what was wrong. She would need to borrow some money for her fare, but before she could explain she felt an arm encircle her waist. Michael was behind her, and pulled her up close and tight against his body.

He was waving what looked like a gun in his other hand. "She's not going anywhere!"

Angela softly said, "I guess I didn't run soon enough, fast enough or far enough!"

173

"Then why didn't you?" Michael growled.

She looked up at him, over her shoulder. "If you don't know that, you're a bloody idiot!"

Paul felt a rising sense of desperation. Michael, who was obviously out of control, must have come via the transporter, and was close to shooting someone, besides blowing their cover.

"Don't do anything silly, my son. I'm sure we can work this out."

Michael motioned Paul out of the way and pointed the gun at the Bishop. "You – yes you! Get your bible and come over here. You're going to perform a marriage ceremony!"

The startled Bishop was trying to stay composed. "I cannot do this at gun-point!"

"Stop – everyone just stop," a tearful Angela pleaded.

She looked up at Michael. "Why?"

His voice was shaking with emotion. "Because I love you, and can't live without you. This last month has been the happiest of my life."

She looked into his eyes for a few moments, and turned to the Bishop. "It's okay. Go ahead – just do it!"

The service was over in a few minutes. Michael insisted they make it legal and all sign the register. While they were waiting for Paul and the ferry captain to add their own witness signatures, the Bishop whispered in Angela's ear. He would send a rescue party, but the marriage could not be annulled once it was consummated.

Michael still had Angela firmly in his grip when he disappeared somewhere behind the altar.

"Where have they gone?" asked the Bishop.

"Out a side door," said Paul, knowing full well that Michael had headed back to the transporter in the crypt.

"Get your police officers here on the double," the Bishop demanded. "We must rescue that poor woman."

Angela couldn't understand why Michael had carried her down the stairs and under the church. She was even more confused when they entered a small transparent cubicle, only to be inexplicably back in Michael's bedroom at the hacienda.

He gently put her down, and held her in his arms. "Do you believe me now? As of today, we are legally married anywhere in the world. Let's get Tuan to make us a proper 'wedding breakfast'!"

Michael went into the kitchen, and as he was talking to Tuan, he noticed his houseboy's eyes were riveted on the doorway behind him. He turned around to see Angela beckoning to him. She was totally naked except for a black lace filmy negligee.

"The Bishop is going to send a rescue party," she said. "It will be too late if you've already had your wicked way with me!"

The Bishop had wasted no time in calling on the resident police officer, and assembling a group of local natives to form rescue party for a raid on Michael's home. Paul insisted that he and Sister Jacquita accompany him.

About half an hour later they burst into the kitchen. Tuan was smiling and standing at the table. He said nothing, and just pointed at the closed bedroom door.

The Bishop looked rather glum, and suggested it may be more appropriate if Sister Jacquita investigated.

She tentatively peeped in to see Michael and Angela's bodies fused together in sexual unity. She quietly closed the door and turned to the Bishop.

"I'm afraid it's too late!"

CHAPTER 19

Aldon was eating breakfast, and in a decidedly nasty mood after Paul had reported the events on the island.

"What are you going to do?" Martina asked.

"I'm not able to contain the solution to Earth Base Command anymore. We've run out of options, and can't leave this situation up in the air. Gareth is really pissed off! We had to advise Xandra, who will most likely put the whole affair into the hands of Zadoc and the Guardians."

Martina looked up from spreading marmalade on her toast. "What do you think will happen to Michael – and what about Angela?"

Aldon shook his head. "I have no idea. Zadoc doesn't suffer fools gladly. Where Michael is concerned, anything from a demotion and transfer to another planet, to just making the best of the current state of affairs.

"Angela is another matter. Michael already broke the rules by taking her in the transporter – not once, but twice. He has to keep her on the island until this is sorted. She would start asking difficult questions once she realised it takes a long time to get back home by conventional transport."

Within a few days Zadoc and Xandra arrived at Earth Base, and joined them for a very heated and urgent meeting with Gareth, Paul and Michael.

Xandra was pacing up and down the control centre. "Michael, you are one of our most valued scientists, and crucial to our mission on Earth. This wasn't supposed to happen. What were you thinking?

"You threatened the Bishop and your colleagues with a weapon, and entered into a marriage contract which is now valid under human and Terran law."

Michael was arguing his case for being lonely and falling in love with Angela. His emotions, and fear of rejection, had overcome his better judgement.

"We're in no mood for your excuses!" Xandra bellowed.

Michael gave him a scathing glare. "And I suppose it was okay for you and Lydia? I thought you, of all people, would understand!"

There was an uncomfortable silence in the room. Xandra couldn't ignore his own heartbreaking past, and his love for a human woman.

Zadoc sat with folded arms, and eventually made his decision. The final outcome to this dilemma lay with Angela herself. If she could be trusted with limited information and knowledge, Michael could stay. If not he would have to leave Earth immediately.

Angela thought Michael had gone down to the village, and was sitting on the patio when he returned with 'Father' Paul. They looked very serious, and pulled up a couple more chairs to sit down beside her.

At first her heart sank. Was Michael now regretting their rather unusual wedding ceremony, and going to suggest an annulment?

She was initially bewildered when told of Michael and Paul's true identities. They were forbidden to mention Jacquita, Tony or Gareth, all of whom she also knew.

Gradually she came to understand the Terran's mission on the planet, and their need for complete anonymity. If any individual agent, like Michael, came to the attention of the authorities, it would be fatal for both them and their entire family and colleagues.

Michael also explained that his posting to Earth was of a limited duration. Sooner or later he would have to leave, and at that time, she could decide whether to stay here or go away with him and the other Terrans.

Once she had declared her enduring love and loyalty for Michael, they also explained their advance technology, and how the transporter operated. She agreed to undergo certain procedures which would give her some additional Terran biological and mental compatibility.

The next day Aldon arrived in the PVX, and hovering low over the sea, beneath the cliffs, beamed Michael and Angela on board. She immediately recognised Aldon as the strange disappearing man she had seen in the laboratory.

Her augmentation required the more advanced technology on Xandra's ship. The sight of the huge silver craft, high above the Earth, finally confirmed the reality of what Paul and Michael had told her. She had not lost her mind!

As she lay down on the slab, she was taken aback by the two little grey workers who were in attendance. They looked just like the creatures one saw on science fiction movies! Michael reassured her, and when she returned to a groggy consciousness, he was still by her side.

Beside the required biological enhancement, Xandra had also inserted an implant which may be useful to monitor Angela in the future.

"Just to be on the safe side," he told Michael.

The couple transported back from the island to Michael's city home that afternoon. He returned to work, and Angela followed a couple of days later. Nobody queried the official reasons for their absences, and soon after she moved in with him. The company was abuzz with gossip about Michael and Angela living together, and it came as no surprise when they announced they had got married.

Gareth and Tony were both stunned and amused at Michael's recklessness.

"I didn't think he had it in him," said Gareth. "We'll have to watch what we say whenever Angela joins us for lunch in the cafeteria."

Although the couple transported to the island every weekend, Aldon was now free to go ahead with the construction of the proposed tunnel from under the hacienda to the cliffs below. He brought Ebony to help, thinking her darker skin would not cause undue curiosity in the indigenous population.

Angela was made aware that Ebony was actually an android robot, but Tuan thought she was a most attractive woman – one he would like to call his own. It was all they could do to make the infatuated houseboy keep his distance. He offered her alcoholic beverages, but she wouldn't drink them. Perhaps aphrodisiac herbs or island spells and love potions? He tried everything to no avail.

Consumed with unrequited love and longing he decided follow an old island custom, and carry her off to his home. One afternoon, when she was on the patio he grabbed her in a passionate embrace. This behaviour computed as an attack in Ebony's programming, and the next thing Tuan knew he was prostrate in a prickly bush. What a woman!

Everybody was relieved when the project was completed. All Tuan knew was that Ebony was gone, and he was left with his unfulfilled fantasies.

Mary and Victor had re-opened the bookstore, and the members of the Friendship Club were all curious as to where they had been.

Victor was tinkering on the piano, and looked rather sheepishly at Mary. "I didn't know what to say, so I let them continue thinking we went on holidays together. I hope you're not annoyed with me?"

Mary gave a shy smile. "I guess that's better than them knowing the truth, but I don't know if I can get any more time off work for a while."

Aldon hadn't told him of any upcoming trips away, and had suggested that for the time being they think of a stage name for their new group, and keep practising their recently acquired vocal skills and repertoire.

"Let's call ourselves 'The Terrans," Lucy suggested.

"No – bad idea," said Victor. "How about the 'Associates'? We're all part of the Friendship Club."

The 'Associates' spent every Saturday night at the farm improving on what Victor called their 'routine'. Petie would dance up and down on his perch, giving the occasional screech and contributing with his own muddled parrot versions of the songs.

Although they encouraged Tony to join in, he was wary of any public involvement. As far as Victor and the others were concerned, he was still just a friend of Gareth's. Tony was one of the Terran's highly placed scientists, and despite his relationship with Victor, Mary and the twins, his identity still remained in the top secret category.

"This incognito business gets more difficult by the day," he commented to Gareth.

Gareth nodded, "I know, and your and Michael's romantic lives don't make it any easier!"

Tony continued his report about life on the farm. "Victor and the three girls have developed quite a polished performance. Mary has learned to play the guitar, and Victor has bought an electronic keyboard, and some sound equipment.

"Victor said they gave a short performance to a select few at the bookstore, and everybody was very supportive. They've all bought matching outfits of tight black jeans and satin shirts, and I think they are just about ready to quietly go public."

"I believe you have a friendly contact, in an agency which will get them occasional bookings for functions at the companies we suspect have Xvar or Katon connections?"

Gareth needed to infiltrate, one way or another, several establishments that were not connected to the corporation he represented. He also was anxious to gain more information about some military bases that he suspected of collaborating with the enemy.

Intelligence gathering was becoming increasingly difficult. Humans themselves had now developed microchips the size of a grain of sand, although these were susceptible to interference by electromagnetic pulse.

They also had initiated a primitive type of remote mind control, which involved beaming microwave transmissions into a victim, who subsequently 'heard voices in their head'. This was different to the Terrans' ability to communicate verbally 'mind to mind'.

Although Earth Base could secretly monitor all digital traffic and encrypted data, rogue military officers and other collaborators were becoming increasingly cautious with their cyberspace communications. It was going to take some old fashioned eavesdropping espionage to flush them out.

The agency soon contacted Victor, with a request for the 'Associates' to play at a private Saturday night farewell party. Gareth was jubilant – it was to be in the officers' mess at one of the suspicious Army bases.

Before they left for their first ever public performance, Gareth gave them very strict instructions. Extremely minute dormant spying instruments would be smuggled in Victor's electronic keyboard. Fiona and Lucy were to remain sober, and under no circumstances to fraternise with the soldiers, except when it was required to place the listening or monitoring chips.

Each of the women was to wear a pendant which could relay both sound and visual images back to Aldon and Gareth on Earth Base. Once they had passed through the military's screening process, the pendants would be activated, and the girls would be given telepathic instructions as to where to place the eavesdropping devices.

They were all somewhat nervous when they were checked through the guarded gates of the base, and even more so when a security officer scanned them and their equipment as they entered the officers' mess.

They were soon in place to begin the night's entertainment, which was interspersed with various speeches and a presentation to the guest of honour. Victor had slipped them the tiny plungers, which would fasten the gadgets under the edges of tables and other places. The 'Associates' encouraged the lively crowd to sing along, with the twins, who proved very popular, taking a microphone between the tables to various members of the audience.

Fiona found it a little disconcerting, trying to keep singing while hearing a voice in her head giving directions as to where to go to place the next device. It was relatively easy as the plunger fitted, unseen, in the palm of her hand.

Once they were ready to leave, Aldon deactivated their monitor pendants, and they passed back through the military security without incidence.

In the early hours of the morning, when everyone had gone home, a tiny Terran drone flew over the military base, and activated all the microchip spies in the officers' mess.

After they had dropped the twins off at their apartment, Victor and Mary relaxed over a late supper at the bookshop.

"I was so scared we'd be caught out," Mary said. "I hope we don't have to do that too often"

Victor agreed. "But other than that, it was a fun evening – and we are going to get paid some quite generous pocket money for our efforts! I'm off to bed now, so we can all get an early start to the farm tomorrow."

On Earth Base Aldon told Gareth he was relieved everything had gone to plan.

"Have you any idea how much valuable intelligence we can gain from this? A lot of the lower ranking officers have very 'loose lips' when drinking after duty," Gareth gloated. "Zadoc and the Guardians will be well pleased."

Xandra had arrived unexpectedly at Earth Base, supposedly to deliver the new transporter unit for the Retreat, and the extra medical supplies and advanced equipment for John's veterinary surgery/sub-base. Aldon and Martina suspected it might also be an excuse to catch up with his son, Victor.

Martina and Xandra were able to deliver most of John's supplies via the transporter.

"Don't worry if some of these new-fangled machines look unfamiliar," Xandra explained. "They all come with instructions."

John was carefully examining small bottles of an unknown liquid. "What are these for?"

Xandra paused for a moment. "This is something I have to discuss with all our agents. The Xvars have been educating some of their human underlings in biological warfare – something they had already

182

been tinkering with anyway. These are the antidotes to most of these natural and artificial ailments.

"More recently there has been an insidious development into pathogens which only affect certain races of humans. We are concerned that there could be genetically modified diseases to which only those of Terran origin are susceptible. We need to track down and destroy the laboratories manufacturing this biological warfare, but until we do, these are the antidotes. Earth Base also has a supply. Guard them well, you may need them one day."

Xandra also implemented a slight modification to both Boof and Sarah's artificial intelligence. "Now they will also know how to diagnose and treat everybody in a crisis. I will ensure all our androids have acquired this knowledge before I leave."

Back on Earth Base Xandra held discussions with Aldon, Martina and Gareth. Due to his upgraded status Victor was also included.

Xandra was enjoying a glass of Aldon's best malt whiskey. "Just because most of the Xvars and Katons have fled for the time being, it doesn't mean our troubles are over. We still have their human followers to contend with. They don't want to relinquish their own power and control, and will continue maintaining the Xvar bases and secret facilities.

"A lot of the Guardians' original strategies have gone awfully wrong. They thought a one world government was the ideal path for the human race, and certainly didn't take into account the fierce competition between various nations and religious doctrines.

"When we gave them environmentally safe expertise, it was suppressed by industrial interests who wanted to preserve the status quo and profits in their harmful existing products. Driven by the fear of attack by rival countries, those same companies were relied upon by the military to develop more dangerous technology and weapons made available by the Xvars."

Gareth continued clarifying the situation. "These companies, who had a free hand to develop the new technology, have now become massive international corporations, and are more powerful than the governments and military that originally employed them. They are dependent upon the Xvars for their continued supremacy.

"To maintain their dominance, these dark forces are reliant upon some loyal elements in various military and secret service factions. They also have their own private security forces and mercenaries who will stop at nothing to eliminate any opposition. These are the Xvar collaborators we need to identify, and neutralise or eradicate, before their alien masters return."

Martina glanced uncertainly at Xandra and then looked over to Victor. "I hope you realise these undercover activities are highly dangerous?"

Victor gave a wry grin. "Yes, and a bit scary! But while we were away, we received extra training in martial arts and psychic warfare. I'm not sure how much help that would be if we were caught out!"

"Don't be concerned. As long as you follow orders, we will be there to rescue you if anything goes wrong," Xandra assured him. "In the meantime, since our own miniature satellites prevent any digital activity being traced back to Earth Base, Ebony is going to engage in some diverse cyber espionage."

Martina thought to herself that their protégées were little more than amateurs, and 'rescue' would be meaningless if one of the team was killed! Despite her misgivings she agreed to help Gareth to arrange another instruction session at the Retreat for suitable candidates.

She accompanied Xandra, in the PVX to the Retreat, where they constructed a small secret basement under the control centre, and installed the new transporter.

"Due to this remote, relatively unguarded location, there are extra safeguards in place." Xandra told Otto. "In an emergency it will provide a safer means of escape, and at least you will now be able to beam students up and down, rather than landing the PVX in the lake every time."

Xandra did not bring up his previous suggestion of a second Retreat, at a different location. Neither Aldon nor Martina intended reminding him of something which would involve a lot more time and effort.

Before he left, Xandra met with Victor, Mary and the twins one night after the bookshop had closed. He congratulated their successful concert at the military base, and said the Terrans were still listening to conversations which indicated which officers were aligned with the enemy.

He glanced across at Fiona and Lucy. "What's up? You seem to be a little on edge tonight."

"Our parents are coming to visit us for a few days, and we don't know what to tell them," the twins babbled in unison.

Xandra realised that they had been told little of their family's history with the Terrans. "Many years ago we had contact with your grandparents, whom we genetically enhanced. Your parents, who were both highly intelligent professionals, seemed unable to conceive. In order to continue our genetic generational program, we took them on board one of our ships, and implanted two embryos in your mother's womb. You have both of your parent's genes plus a few Terran additions.

"They are in denial about their experiences, and were distressed when you spoke of visiting our ship when you were children. I recommend you say very little about recent events or any interaction with our Terran agents or other protégées."

Victor agreed. "I think you should avoid bringing them to the bookshop whenever a Friendship Club meeting is scheduled. Perhaps they could come when we are practising our 'Associates' musical routine. A quick trip to the farm would probably be okay, but don't let them meet Tony. They would never understand your 'threesome' relationship."

It was a holiday weekend, and the Bookers, Lucy and Fiona's parents, arrived on a Friday morning, and planned to stay with them in the apartment until Monday night.

Their mother was scrutinising everything, including the contents of the cupboards and fridge. "We've been worried about how our girls are doing, living so far away from home. Your father and I miss having you around. Have you made any new friends here?"

"Yes," said Lucy. "We've made several at work, and of course Mary, whom we wrote to you about. Tonight we plan to drive to the little farm we have bought together. We can spend the whole of Saturday there. Mary and her friend Victor run the local bookstore. We're taking you to meet them after dinner."

"And we have another surprise for you!" Fiona added mysteriously.

The Bookers were always wary of any sudden impulses the twins may have. They knew the birth of the two girls had been considered so medically improbable, it was almost a miracle. They desperately tried to block out any memories of their contact with the Terrans. There was always the fear that these aliens would come and take their beloved daughters away; especially when as children they talked about going to play with their little friends on the silver ship in the sky.

It was about 10pm when they all left the bookshop – with the Bookers in Lucy and Fiona's car, and Mary and Victor following in his van. About halfway up the dark country road, the twins' car spluttered and stopped. Victor pulled up behind, and got out to see if he could help.

Whilst he was rummaging under the hood, the whole area lit up, much brighter than his small battery operated lamp. He was so startled he bumped his head as he moved out to look into the sky.

Mrs Booker was cowering and weeping. She was clinging to her husband, who appeared to be terror stricken.

"They've come back......they've come back!" she cried.

Victor managed to restart the car, and peered through the window. "It's alright Mrs. Booker. It's just a police helicopter – probably looking for some lost hikers."

Fiona wasted no time driving up to the farm. Lucy was in the passenger seat trying to calm down their parents, who were sitting behind her. Mr Booker put his arm around his wife, who was trying to regain her composure, and gave a weak smile to his two daughters.

"It's alright! Your mother has been having some bad dreams recently."

That night, when they had retired to the spare bedroom, Mrs Booker put her head on her husband's shoulder.

"That bright light brought it all back. You remembered too, didn't you?"

Mr Booker had never forgotten that night, all those years ago. He had not taken much notice of his mother-in-law waffling on about aliens. That was, until their car had stalled on a similar dark country road. He got out to be surrounded by an intense white light, coming from a huge silver craft overhead.

Everything was misty, and he remembered indistinct figures coming towards him. Three days later they were back in their car, at the side of the road. Neither he nor his wife had much recollection of the intervening period. They would have an occasional 'flashback' memory of lying on a smooth, cold table, and seeing the large faces of little grey creatures with big, black elongated eyes.

They had told nobody. Who would believe them except his eccentric mother-in-law? The discovery of his wife's unexpected pregnancy with Lucy and Fiona had filled them with both joy and fear. They were sure the twins were somehow the result of their encounter with aliens. What if they came back for their children?

The next morning, after breakfast they toured the farm, and met Mrs McAffrey, who gave them a quizzical look. She could sense a Terran connection, but said nothing.

After lunch Victor set-up the electronic keyboard, and with Mary playing the guitar they gave an impromptu 'Associates' performance for the twins' parents. Mrs Booker was quite impressed, and rather proud of her offspring, especially when told they had actually been paid to sing at a function. She and her husband had given their daughters an excellent education, and she was relieved when they assured her they did not intend giving up their day jobs.

Everybody was pleased when the Bookers left on Monday afternoon. They had not mentioned anything about aliens, which was a relief to Lucy and Fiona. Xandra had given them strict instructions that, under no circumstances, could they confide anything to their parents, who were too unstable to be trusted.

"That was very hard," said Fiona. "They love us so much, and gave us everything. I wanted to tell them they had nothing to fear, and the Terrans are our friends."

CHAPTER 20

The Terrans had always been concerned about the Xvars partiality for biological warfare, and the encouragement of their underlings to develop similar weapons on Earth. Whilst they could not negate the entire human biological research facilities, Zadoc and the Guardians had instigated a two pronged agenda to minimize the enormous damage these Xvar programs could cause.

The first was to identify and destroy the establishments responsible for the research and development of some of these dangerous pathogens. This had to be done with immense skill and care, by a special Guardian craft and crew, so as not to discharge any germs into the surrounding environment. There was always the concern that manufactured diseases could also be inadvertently released by careless manufacturing laboratories.

The Guardians' second program required what humans referred to as a 'Noah's Ark' – the collection and safe storage of all healthy plants and the DNA and genetic material of every living creature on the planet.

Both of these courses of action were completely compartmentalised, and conducted by two special laboratory ships under Zadoc's control. Earth Base rarely had any contact with them, and Martina was surprised when the 'Noah's Ark' craft messaged Earth Base for assistance.

She walked over to Aldon who was fiddling around with his newly acquired coffee machine. "I haven't heard much about this operation, because it doesn't involve us. What exactly is their mission?" she asked.

Aldon turned around, "Zadoc has a couple of genetic specialists on a craft which comes in every so often to collect specimens for the storage of all plants and life. So many species have already become extinct on this planet. Our program will help preserve the remaining biodiversity of Earth in the event of cataclysmic disasters, wars or the use of damaging contaminants.

"They usually send robots or our grey workers down to collect the flora and vegetation. Occasionally androids will collect genetic material

189

from living creatures. This can sometimes require what is referred to as 'animal mutilations', as we require a varied unpolluted genetic pool for each species."

"That sounds quite horrible. Although I'm told Terrans are only responsible for a minority of the 'animal mutilations', I'm thankful we have no part in it. It's pleasing to know we get the biological material from most human specimens in more ethical ways," Martina commented.

"We only ever hear from the laboratory ships if they run into any trouble or interference," Aldon said. "I'd better find out what's wrong."

Senior Scientist Godric was insistent that Aldon join him on his ship as soon as possible, and must bring an Electronic Dissolution of Memory device with him.

Aldon took Ebony and set off in the PVX. Godric's craft was high in the atmosphere, and he transported over to the laboratory.

"What's the problem? How can we help?"

Godric was trembling and a little incoherent at first. "I was bringing some plants up in the blue beam, and somehow brought a woman up with them. This has never happened before, and I don't know what to do."

"Where is she now?" Aldon asked.

Godric pointed to the sealed containment area, and when Aldon looked through the viewing area he could see a distraught middle aged woman flapping around in a mass of grape vines.

"Just how much of one particular plant species did you need?" he asked. "It seems to me that you were taking half the bloody vineyard!"

Godric faltered, and stumbled over his words for a while, finally admitting that taking the grape vines was disobeying official procedures.

"The guys back on Space Station Three have developed a taste for the white wine which comes from this particular vineyard. They wanted to grow their own grapes and produce it themselves. I foolishly promised to bring them back a supply of the plants.

"I waited until the middle of the night, thinking I wouldn't be seen, and just scooped up a lot in the blue beam. That way, my android 'Chester' and the little grey worker would have no memory or knowledge of it. This woman suddenly ran out, into the middle, waving her arms and shouting. Next thing I knew it was too late, and she ended up in the containment area along with the vegetation. Perhaps we can erase her memory, and put her back on the property?"

When Godric brought up a magnified view of the winery, Aldon looked at the screen and muttered to himself. "The whole place is lit up, and I can see a couple of police officers examining the damaged surroundings. We can't put her back there with all those witnesses!"

"What now?" Godric groaned. "She can't stay here. How could I ever explain it to Zadoc?"

Down on the ground the police were becoming highly suspicious that some form of foul play was involved in the disappearance of Enid French. The damage to the vines could just be a red herring to throw them off a possible murder! The family's vehicles were still in the garage, and there was no sign of any other means of transport entering or leaving the somewhat remote property. Her husband claimed she had gone outside, and when he went to look for her she was nowhere to be found.

Aldon was desperately considering their options. "They will bring in search helicopters as soon as it is daylight. We must act quickly and leave her somewhere else; somewhere safe - with no surveillance cameras!"

They quickly travelled over the remote countryside, finally locating a suitable spot on a back road near an all night garage. Godric went into the containment area and tried to apologise to Enid, who was becoming hysterical.

He came back out to Aldon. "That didn't go well! What are we going to do now?"

Aldon thought for a moment. "You go back in, and attempt to distract her. I will just have to sneak up behind, and administer a mild sedation. Then we must try to erase her memory, and beam her back down!"

Enid felt dazed and shaken when she unexpectedly found herself sprawled at the side of a country road. What had happened? She still had a vague memory of being in some form of spacecraft, and someone apologising for inadvertently taking her along with the vines.

She staggered to her feet, and could see some lights a short distance away. When a dishevelled Enid stumbled through his door, the garage proprietor immediately called the authorities. She was taken to the nearby hospital, where everyone was initially sceptical of her befuddled story about aliens sucking her up into their space craft.

The local police chief looked at his constable. "Maybe she is not so crazy after all. Her vineyard is hundreds of kilometres away, and yet she was only reported as missing a couple of hours ago."

Aldon and Godric returned to the PVX, where Ebony was waiting.

"I'm back to Earth Base," Aldon told Godric. "I think you had better make yourself scarce for a while. If there's even a hint of what happened tonight, the military will be on the lookout for any suspected extraterrestrial incursions.

"Other than that, there are some bad storms building up over the ocean. They can interrupt transmissions and also be risky if you intend operating, without stabilisers, at a low altitude in Earth's atmosphere."

Godric was grateful when Aldon promised to try to keep the incident from Zadoc, and said he was indebted to Earth Base. Perhaps he could repay the favour one day, or maybe deliver a couple of cases of that prized wine.

"I may hold him to that, if the time ever comes," Aldon told Martina when he finally returned.

They anxiously waited to see if there was any about publicity about the event, but except for an article in a regional newspaper, the incident was soon forgotten.

Aldon was right about the storms, which were an annual occurrence. They interfered with both electronic and transporter transmissions to the affected areas.

Michael and Angela decided to stay in the city that weekend. There was the possibility they could not safely transport to and from the island. Paul and Jacquita had stocked up in anticipation. Often when cyclonic weather events happened, their solid stone church hall provided shelter for the local people.

Within a few days the high winds and torrential rain arrived. The palm trees were nearly bent double, and huge waves crashed around the shores of the small isolated island. While Michael's hacienda, and other stable buildings, remained relatively undamaged, some of the more flimsy houses were not so lucky.

Jacquita and her nuns were singing with the villagers in the temporary church hall shelter. The door suddenly flew open, with the wind and rain blowing in. As Jacquita ran over to shut it, she saw a body lying on the ground outside.

It was a rather wet and battered, middle aged Caucasian man, dressed in an expensive business suit. When they carried him in, he was still struggling for breath.

"Thank heavens I found you," he gasped. "It seemed like a miracle - a message from God – when I heard voices singing a hymn above the noise of the storm."

Finally he was able to explain that his name was Derek Dewitt, and he was the general manager of a large company. He had been flying in a small corporate jet, when the storm forced him off course. It eventually crashed into the lagoon next to the village. He had been able to swim to the beach, but feared his plane and the pilot were lost.

While everyone was fussing over the survivor, Paul drew Jacquita to the side. "I think we have problems. I saw the small craft sink into the lagoon, but it was no ordinary plane. It was some form of prototype, with distinctly Xvar features. We must keep an eye on this fellow, and not let him anywhere near the church or crypt."

"I'll give him a spare room in the nunnery," Jacquita whispered. "In this weather, I don't know if I can get a message through to Earth Base."

The nuns dressed Derek's wounds and put him to bed. Thanks to the sedatives Jaquita put in his coffee, he slept solidly for the next two days. By that time the tempest had subsided sufficiently for Paul to contact Earth Base.

"We need to put some form of tracking device on both your patient and the crashed plane, before any rescue party arrives." Aldon determined. "It is still not safe to use the transporter. I will bring the PVX, unseen, to the other side of the island, and come up the tunnel from below the cliffs and into Michael's place. It's a good thing we got it finished."

Aldon arrived soon after, and left Andy in charge of the PVX. He walked the short distance from Michael's home to the church. Paul was waiting in the crypt, and Aldon gave him the microscopic trackers and applicators.

"How are you going to manage this, with curious natives all around?" he asked.

Paul grinned. "Jacquita will give this Derek bloke an extra dose of sleeping tablets before the injection. I have a scuba diving outfit hidden down here. It should be easy enough to slip into the lagoon, unnoticed, and attach the tracking devices. Once that's done we'll radio the mainland and report the crash."

After Aldon returned to Earth Base, he anxiously awaited Paul's report.

"Everything went to plan," Paul told him, "and guess what? When I swam down to the wreck, it was a Katon grey worker, dead at the controls. After we got all the tracking in place, we took Derek to the island's radio transmitter in the general store and he messaged his people for help.

"Within three or four hours a seaplane came to pick him up, and the next day a huge military aircraft arrived. It literally winched the small craft out of the lagoon and flew off with it."

Aldon was still a little concerned. "Do you think anybody suspected our true identity, or anything else we should be worried about?"

Paul laughed. "Not only are we in the clear, the Bishop is overjoyed because Derek's corporation has donated a very generous sum of money to the Church. Whilst most of it is going into his coffers, some of it has been earmarked for the island to complete storm damage repairs, additions to the school, and a small hospital."

Aldon sat down to morning tea with Martina. "Try some of this coffee from my new machine. It's as good as what we get at Victor's."

He started telling her about the results of the incident on the island. "It's been a win-win situation all around. Paul and Jacquita are getting more amenities for their little community, and we are able to track the previously unknown human Xvar collaborators."

Aldon and Martina were savouring some of Victor's pastries when Gareth joined them. "Just a quick visit before I enjoy a more relaxing weekend," he said, and helped himself to one of the pastries. "I love these, but am not normally allowed to go to Victor's bookshop."

"Other than pinching our goodies, what else can we do for you?" Martina asked, pulling the plate away as he grabbed a second helping.

"I was wondering if you heard anything more about that fellow Derek Dewitt?"

Aldon frowned. "Very little, actually. We have been tracking his movements, and conducting the usual cyber espionage. Other than that, we are under strict instructions to stay out of this. It will be up to Xandra and Zadoc if, how and when they take out any of his laboratories."

"If it were up to me, I'd obliterate all the chemical and biological warfare establishments on this planet," Gareth complained.

"Unfortunately, that isn't as easy as it sounds," said Martina. "All the major countries have similar projects, and that type of operation requires a great deal of skill and care. It would be disastrous if anything escaped and contaminated the local environment or population."

"And I think it's only the Xvar/Katon facilities they are targeting," Aldon added. "They must destroy any 'Anti-Terran' pathogens, and further, they don't want our adversaries to have any secret bases and followers to return to."

Gareth stood up, ready to return home. "Michael and Angela have gone off to the island, and Tony is meeting the girls at the farm. Other than his fancy sports car in the city, he bought himself a second smaller car, which he leaves at John's surgery. It solves some of his country transport hassles."

Before he could step back into the transporter, Andy came rushing in. "An urgent message from Godric, Commander!"

Aldon groaned, "Oh no! Not that bungling scientist again? I was hoping he'd gone back to Solar Base....anywhere but here! What now!"

"He was hovering over the woods, a few miles behind the farm, while Chester was collecting various samples. Suddenly some air force jets appeared on the horizon, heading straight in his direction. He had to cloak his craft and shoot off, leaving Chester behind."

Aldon asked Gareth to wait while he spoke to Godric. "Can you still communicate with Chester?"

"Yes," Godric replied. "I have told him to hide in the bushes."

Aldon transmitted a map of the area. Once the jets had departed, Chester was to quickly get to the cave behind the farmhouse, and enter the tunnel through the secret door. He was to stay there until a rescue could be arranged.

Gareth regretted staying to eat the pastries. Now it was too late to leave.

"I'm sorry to interrupt your peaceful weekend, but would you beam over to John's vet surgery, and wait for further instructions?" Aldon asked. "It's the nearest transporter to the farm, perhaps you can pick up Chester in Tony's car."

John was flustered for a moment, when Gareth entered the treatment room while he was in the middle of examining a somewhat scruffy dog.

He jumped in surprise. "Hello stranger! What brings you here? If you're looking for Tony, he's just about to leave."

Tony had already started the engine when Gareth opened the car door. "Sorry, my friend, but I have to borrow this for a while. I should be back soon."

Aldon thought he had the problem solved, until Martina received another communication from Gareth, who had already arrived at the farm. He was in the middle of explaining the situation to Mary and the twins, when he spotted two or three small military drones in the distance.

"I'm not risking any of my agents for that idiot Godric," Aldon growled. "Tell Gareth to get the car out of sight in Mrs McAffrey's garage. He can stay there until I get this sorted."

As soon as Gareth left, Mary turned to Lucy and Fiona. "Now is the time to put some of our training into practise. We have to do something about those government snoops, otherwise Gareth will be in hiding for hours."

"I know what to do," Lucy chuckled. "Quick! Get your gear off, and grab those bats from behind the door! We're going to have some nudist cricket and baseball practice."

There were clothes coming off all over the lounge room when Mary declared, "I'm still keeping my shoes on!"

"Suit yourself," said Fiona. "It won't be our feet they'll be looking at!"

They raced out into the back field, and as the drones came closer, quickly commenced their pretend game.

Back at the drone control base, the operator looked across at his colleagues monitoring the other screens.

"Hey guys! Get a load of this cricket game!" He manoeuvred in for a closer look.

"Wow - naked women!"

A few of their co-workers crowded around to get a better view, and discussed with boyish enthusiasm which one they would like to 'have it off' with.

Lucy looked up at the three small surveillance craft diving towards them. "Wait until they are really close."

Lucy was the first to swing her cricket bat at the intruder, scoring a king hit. Fiona had disabled the second with a whack from her baseball bat. As they crashed to the ground, the third started to quickly rise out of reach.

Mary took aim with the cricket ball, and using all her Terran training, threw it high into the sky. They all cheered as the last drone wobbled and then veered sideways, hitting a tree as it fell to earth.

Gareth was staring in amusement as he watched the events from Mrs McAffrey's window. Once he was sure the drones were out of action, he raced across the field to the farmhouse. Mary was putting her top back on as she opened the door.

"I need you to do something else for me," he said. "Remove the small control units from each of the drones, and put them into this lead lined container. Be careful, they may still be recording. The military will soon be on their way to retrieve their expensive gadgets, but before they arrive, somebody will also come to rescue the android. After I've made off with this box, you can bash those little spy craft all you like!"

Back in the drone control centre, the operators were in a panic. How were they going to explain this to the boss? Their superiors did not accept any hastily fabricated explanations, especially when they viewed the last transmissions before the drones went down.

"Bloody morons! You were supposed to be looking for any signs of what that alien craft was doing in the woods several miles away – not perving on naked women! You'll hear more about this later! Now I'll have the embarrassment of asking the local army unit to retrieve what's left of our equipment."

Gareth was told to drive back to the bookshop in town, rather than there being any evidence of traffic from the farm to the vet surgery. He arrived, and gave the box to Victor, who beamed it up to Earth Base.

As he drank his coffee and scoffed more pastries, Gareth didn't really mind waiting at the bookshop for more instructions.

Mary was in the back field, watching Fiona and Lucy give the offending drones a few extra wallops, and was startled when she heard a cultured masculine voice behind her.

"Where is the android, Chester? I have come to take him into custody." She looked behind her and could see nobody except a large Rottweiler, who repeated the question. Fiona and Lucy ran over, staring in amazement.

"Oh my goodness – a talking dog!"

Boof tilted his head to one side. "I am a Terran canine android, sent by Aldon. You must take me to your basement, and open the door to the tunnel. I need to escort Chester out of the cave and lead him to safety before the military arrive."

The women watched as Boof and Chester left the cave and took off at incredible speed, faster than any human, through the woods. It only took them a few minutes to reach the vet surgery.

A thankful John and Tony immediately took Chester down to the basement, and transported him back to Earth Base for return to Godric. Gareth returned with Tony's car, and warned him he could not go to the farm until after the expected visit from the military.

Later that afternoon, Mary answered a knock on the door. It was the same Major who had visited on the night of the storm.

He shuffled his feet, and then glowered in feigned bravado as Lucy and Fiona joined her. "I believe you ladies are in possession of some valuable government assets – assets which you have maliciously destroyed!"

"Maliciously destroyed!" Mary protested, as they led him out to the wreckage in the field behind. "These drones were dive-bombing and harassing us. We acted in self defence."

The major was trying to save face in the presence of his platoon, who were gathering up the bits and pieces. "I may have to charge you for damaging government property."

Fiona waved her arms in the air. "Charge us? You were using military equipment to perv on innocent women enjoying the sunshine in the privacy of their own backyard!"

Lucy stared at him. "You're the same officer who came here about that plane crash, aren't you? I didn't realise we had such an effect, that you would use valuable army resources to stalk and spy on us. You should be ashamed of yourself! Go ahead and charge us! My sister and I work for a big legal practice. I'm sure the media would relish this story."

The major's face had turned bright red, and his soldiers were sniggering in the background. He stammered out an apology, and tried to explain that he did not operate the drones, and was merely collecting them. He hadn't known the circumstances, and was sure they would hear no more about it.

When Tony turned up after dusk, he blamed his late arrival on Gareth borrowing his car. He smiled to himself as the women were excitedly describing the events of the day, how they had whacked those drones out of the sky, and their later confrontation with the major. To their credit, they never mentioned Gareth or the stranded android in the tunnel.

The next week Tony arranged a meeting with Gareth and Aldon.

"This whole situation is becoming unnecessarily complicated," he said. "Fiona, Lucy and Mary know who you are but not who I really am. To make matters worse, I have to pretend that I don't know they are highly trained protégées. I want permission to tell them the truth."

Tony's request had to be forwarded to Xandra and Zadoc for careful consideration. Eventually they agreed, with the proviso that the three women must still not know of the whereabouts of Earth Base, or the identity of any other agents, who must remain incognito.

One evening, after the bookshop had closed, Victor invited Lucy and Fiona over for supper. Before they arrived, Mary had gone into the lounge room to find Aldon, Gareth and Xandra sipping glasses of wine. She was in the middle of greeting them when she paused and gave a slight gasp. Tony was also sitting there.

"Yes, my dear," Xandra said. "We thought it was about time we told you that Tony is also a Terran agent."

Mary sat down and wondered why she hadn't realised this herself. She wasn't sure how the twins would react, but Fiona and Lucy accepted the news much better than everyone expected.

Tony started to feel embarrassed when Fiona announced that now they knew why he had enough stamina to keep up with both of them.

Lucy started to giggle and looked at Xandra. "We can still keep him, can't we?"

"I guess so, for the moment," he sighed. "Better you two than half the females in the city!"

Xandra had also given permission for the three women to be told of the transporter in Victor's en-suite. It would be modified, but only to allow them to go to and from Tony's city home.

CHAPTER 21

Aldon and Martina were pleased that most of the Xvars and Katons had fled planet Earth, and Aldon was looking forward to a more peaceful interlude. Provided his agents kept out of trouble, he could get out and about more often.

Martina reminded him that their problems were not completely solved. "Although we have taken out a few of the individual Xvar allies, I know we still have more of their human buddies to deal with," she said. "Now Karine and his colleagues have destroyed most of their covert bases and facilities, it is the top scientists and advanced technology that the intelligence services and these corporations will be after."

Aldon nodded. "That's why I'm so thankful Gareth is here. He has taken on most of the responsibility for our scientists and protégées - a little less for us to worry about! I'm also hoping that Zadoc and the Guardians don't come up with any plans soon regarding that missing ancient base in the Himalayas."

Martina agreed with him. "But it is a beautiful place. I wouldn't mind a holiday in that monastery. It would be a different matter having to do undercover work with such an aggressive military presence."

Their peaceful morning was soon interrupted by an unexpected visit from Victor.

"I don't know whether we have a problem or not," he explained. "Bob contacted me a couple of hours ago to tell me George had noticed a new patient has the same unusual blood as Jarod. He went into the ward, and could not actually converse with the woman. She didn't speak English, but Bob kept saying he could sense a strange familiarity. He doesn't know anything about her except that her name is 'Natalie', and she has an unknown illness. They have put her in isolation until they can diagnose the complaint."

"Never heard of her!" Aldon said. "I suppose I'd better not dismiss it out of hand. I'll check with Gareth first, and if he knows nothing, with Xandra and Solar Base."

Eventually they received an ambiguous reply from Solar Base. Aldon was not happy.

"Apparently she is one of our agents. One we have never been told about! Xandra has made the excuse that she was deployed on another part of the planet." He scowled and looked over at Martina. "I told you I thought there was another base somewhere.

"Xandra is worried she may have contracted that manufactured virus which only affects Terrans, and wants all of us to stay away. We have to somehow get Sarah into the hospital. Being an android, she will not be affected. She can do a quick test, and administer the antidote if required.

"If this 'Natalie' is positive for the virus, she must stay in isolation for a few days before we can rescue her. The rest of us will have to immediately be immunised against that particular type of biological warfare. It will make us feel very seedy for a while."

John drove Sarah, wearing her nurse's uniform and a mask, to the hospital car-park. Bob met her and escorted her quietly to the isolation ward. She soon confirmed a positive result, and administered the antidote. Bob made her walk through a decontamination booth before returning to John in the car-park.

As soon as they got back to the surgery, John immunised himself, and notified Aldon of the bad news. Within a couple of hours Earth Base and Victor had received their shots, and summoned a reluctant Gareth along with Michael, Tony and Chantelle.

Martina transported the vaccine to Noru in the Himalayas and Paul and Jacquita on the island, advising them all to be prepared for a few days of extreme discomfort.

"Are you sure the protégées won't be affected?" Martina asked Xandra.

He was confident they would be spared, and giving them the vaccine could do more harm than good.

Sarah had been able to communicate with Natalie in the Terran language, and reported that she came from a group stationed on the other side of the world. Apparently two of her Terran colleagues had become infected earlier. She thought they were probably dead by now, and she had only escaped just in time, using a false passport to fly out of the country.

Aldon was furious, and determined he would have serious words with Solar Base and the Guardians as soon as they all recovered from the constant nausea, and side effects of the vaccine.

"Xandra said that we have to get Natalie out of that hospital as soon as she recovers," Martina commented. "We know very little about her. What if she was deliberately sent here to infect all of us? I don't think it's wise to take her to any of our own facilities, which she could identify later."

Aldon agreed, and told Xandra that Solar Base would have to come and pick her up directly from the hospital.

For the next five days all the Terrans were feeling decidedly sick and miserable. Michael stayed home in the tender care of Angela, and the twins fussed over Tony. Mary took some time off work to look after Victor, and the unfortunate Gareth and Chantelle were left to suffer alone.

Bob was keeping an eye on Natalie, who was quickly recovering, and no longer infectious. He had promised to assist with her extraction from the hospital, but disaster struck before Xandra arrived.

It was a lucky co-incidence that Bob was passing the Hospital Administrator's office, and through the open door could hear two men in suits discussing Natalie. They were claiming she was an illegal immigrant and needed to be taken into custody.

There was no time to contact Victor. Bob raced up to the isolation ward, and taking Natalie by the hand led her down the back stairs to his car parked underneath. He motioned her to lie down on the back seat before covering her with a rug, and driving out past the security cameras.

What to do now? He had to hide her somewhere, and get back before anyone got suspicious. The only place he could think of was his own house. He sped across town. Nobody was home. He took Natalie into the basement, and hoped that she understood his gestures to stay there and be quiet. With a bit of luck Amy wouldn't find her.

He grabbed some take-away on the way back, and was sitting in the laboratory innocently eating his lunch when the boss came in.

Both Bob and George advised their pathology tests had been unable to determine the nature of Natalie's illness, and they assumed she was still in the isolation ward.

Bob excused himself early that afternoon, and having ensured he wasn't being followed, made his way straight to the bookshop.

He was in a state of panic when he told Victor of Natalie's escape. "What should I do now? She can't stay in my basement. If Amy finds her there will be hell to pay. Our marriage is already on rocky grounds.

"The children have been coming back from school saying that after the class did a few special tests, some more nice men have been coming to talk to them. One night Dave started floating up in the air, and Christie was calling out that her brother was flying. Amy's parents claim their daughter is close to a nervous breakdown, and it is all my fault."

Victor left Bob with a cup of coffee, and raced upstairs to contact Aldon, who told him Xandra's craft was due to arrive in a few hours. Victor instructed Bob to smuggle Natalie out to a nearby park at 11pm, and gave him a locator device to assist in her extraction.

Bob and the family were sitting down to dinner, and he noticed the children were smiling, as if they had a secret. When Amy's back was turned he put his finger up to his lips – "Shhh!"

After the meal he sat in front of the television, as if nothing was wrong. The evening seemed to drag on forever. Eventually Amy put the kids to bed, and went into the bathroom for a shower. He raced down to the basement, gave Natalie the locator, and motioned to her to stay there until he came back.

Amy came out in her nightdress. "I'm off to bed. Don't stay up too late."

Bob nodded, "I just want to watch the end of this program."

It was well after ten o'clock when Bob crept down to the basement, and quietly led Natalie upstairs and outside. Amy heard a slight noise, and going to the hallway, noticed the front door was ajar. She turned around to see Christie standing behind her.

"Where's Daddy?" Amy asked.

Christie looked at the floor. "We're not supposed to say."

Amy grabbed her by the shoulders and shook her. "Not supposed to say what? You tell me right now – or else."

Christie started to cry. "He went out with that lady who was in the basement."

Amy was shaking. "What lady in the basement?"

"She was the same nice lady that we saw in the shiny room in the sky. Dave and I go there sometimes to play."

Amy pulled on her robe, and raced out into the street. She could see Bob and his companion entering the park at the top of the road. How dare he hide another woman in their house! She set off in hot pursuit.

Natalie gave Bob a quick 'thank you' kiss on the cheek, and walked to the middle of the grass. Xandra's craft materialised above her, and she disappeared from sight as he transported her on board.

Bob turned around and headed back home. Thank God that was over! Amy suddenly stepped out in front of him.

She was seething. "That's it! We're through!"

Bob chased after her. "Amy wait! It's not what you think. I can explain!"

She reached the house before him, and slammed and locked the front door. He banged on it loudly. "Amy, please let me in."

The bedroom window opened, and she threw out his car keys. "Go away and don't come back!"

Bob was stunned, and stood motionless in despair and disbelief. The lights were coming on in the neighbours' houses, and a couple were peering out of their windows. He felt so alone and vulnerable, but couldn't stay here. He got into the car, and slowly drove to the bookshop.

Victor had just dropped off to sleep, when he heard a loud thumping on the back door. A distraught Bob came in and emotionally recounted the night's events.

Mary came downstairs. "This is not his fault," she whispered to Victor. "He can't sleep in his car. We'd better make him up a bed on the couch."

The next day Bob went straight to work, and by lunchtime had persuaded the boss to grant him some special leave. He went home to try and reconcile with Amy, but it was too late. She and the children were gone. There was a note on the dining table.

'I have taken the children to my parents' home. Don't try to follow me. I want a divorce. You have one week to get your things and move out.'

Bob sat down, and putting his head in his hands, sobbed like a small child.

Mary and Victor's last customer was finishing his coffee, and they were ready to close for the evening when Bob came through the door. They didn't have to ask him how the situation was with Amy. His expression said it all.

"I bet you haven't eaten," Mary said. "You must stay for dinner."

When they heard about the empty house, and Amy's note, Victor was furious. This was all the fault of the Terrans, and their failure to advise them of the other unknown agents on the planet. Bob could have ignored the situation. Instead, his efforts to help had cost him his marriage.

"I don't really blame our friends," Bob said. "My marriage was already on shaky ground. I think Amy was just looking for an excuse. For a long time her parents have been coming between us, and encouraging her to get a divorce.

"Today I started packing my things, ready to move into a flat or something, when I discovered she has emptied our bank account. How can I rent another place without money?"

Victor tried to reassure him, and insisted on lending him some cash for the next couple of weeks.

After Bob left, Victor turned to Mary. "Can we find him somewhere to live in the meantime? It can't be here, and there's no spare bedroom at the farm on weekends. I'm off to see Aldon. This whole situation is not his fault either, and Terran Command has to find a solution."

Aldon and Martina were just as angry about the whole state of affairs, especially the distressing outcome for Bob. Amy was obviously intent on remaining in their home, which Bob had foolishly put in her name. They discussed buying him a new house, but realised Amy would want to know where the money came from, and also claim part of it in any divorce settlement.

"In fact, we would prefer the case to be settled out of court." Martina said. "We don't need Amy mentioning aliens in any public hearing!"

They sat in thoughtful silence for a while. "What about Mrs McAffrey? She has a spare bedroom," Aldon suggested. "Xandra was never happy about her living alone. Bob has proven himself trustworthy. He could board with her, and has a car to get to and from work."

Victor agreed. "That sounds like a good idea. Bob is fragile at the moment, and shouldn't be living alone. I hope he likes cats!"

The next morning Aldon called on Mrs McAffrey, and explained the situation. She was hesitant at first, but soon warmed to the idea.

"I sometimes feel a little lonely and vulnerable. The local children occasionally harass me and the cats, and Mary and her friends are only next door on the weekends. The garden and building maintenance is often a bit much for an old lady like me. It would be good to have a trustworthy man around the house, but for the moment we must keep our mutual connection a secret."

Aldon agreed, and once the plan was approved by Xandra, Victor took Bob to meet Mrs McAffrey. Within the week he had moved into his temporary home.

The heated discussion between Earth Base and Xandra soon turned into a blazing row, with Zadoc being drawn into the argument.

"How can we be expected to function efficiently when we are not even aware of some of your other operations or agents on this planet?" Aldon demanded. "If it hadn't been for Bob's quick thinking, that virus may have spread into the community and killed all of us."

Zadoc was in no mood to explain or justify the Guardians' reasons for duplicity. Instead he informed Aldon that there were good grounds, in certain circumstances, to have separate undisclosed autonomous facilities. This was not the right time to divulge their existence or purpose.

Aldon's conference with their superiors was over, and he startled Andy and Delta when he threw a chair at the wall of the control room. "I have just been reminded that we are military officers, and must obey orders. Obviously we do not 'have a need to know'! What is it these humans say – 'ours is not to question why, ours is just to do and die!' Something like that!"

Martina patted him on the shoulder, and handed him a large glass of whiskey. "Never mind – at least everything turned out okay! I hope that Zadoc and Karine can take out that unknown laboratory still manufacturing or storing the virus."

Bob was still devastated and struggling with the abrupt change in his life. He missed his kids. At first Amy would not even allow him to see them, but his lawyer forced an agreement which gave him access every Saturday. He had to admit to himself that his marriage to Amy had been a sham for a long time. They had probably only stayed together out of habit, and because of the children.

Mrs McAffrey appreciated Bob's company, and the extra money he gave her every week. In addition, her cats had taken a liking to him, and he cheerfully did lots of odd jobs around the place. She insisted on cooking for him in return.

He enjoyed the fresh country air, and working in the garden on weekends. He soon learned of Mrs McAffrey's hidden talents. She had a few fruit trees, and the apples and pears, along with her rhubarb ended up in the cellar, fermenting into particularly potent beverages.

He was curious about some green leafy plants, which he couldn't identify, but looked familiar. She just smiled. "Never mind about those. Ask me no questions – I'll tell you no lies! I use them in my magic muffins."

Bob had started going back to the Friendship Club meetings, and also welcomed the weekend interaction with Mary and Victor at the farm next door. He became better acquainted with the twins, but not so Tony, who always kept his distance.

Dave and Christie couldn't wait for their weekly visits with Bob. They would go to his new home, where Mrs McAffrey fed them on cakes and all kinds of forbidden goodies. She insisted they call her 'Aunty Ida'. Amy would not allow them to have any pets, and they spent many happy hours playing with the cats. Mary, next door, would let them feed the chickens and ride on Wiggles.

Christie liked to run around with the animals, but Dave took great interest in the women's training sessions, often lying down on the grass and meditating with them. One day when they were practising levitation, he announced that he knew how to do that. He stretched out his hand, and a small pebble rose several inches into the air.

Christie definitely displayed a budding musical talent, and delighted in singing along and dancing whenever 'The Associates' practised their routines. Bob realised that in the past Amy had never allowed him to interact with his children the way he was able to on these special Saturdays.

The children couldn't understand why Bob couldn't come home. They had once asked Amy if they could go and live with their father. They were met with such a torrent of abuse, they never asked again. Bob had noticed a few unexplained bruises on both Dave and Christie, and feared that Amy may be heading for the nervous breakdown that her parents had predicted.

Victor asked Gareth to meet with him and Mary in the bookshop one night. Gareth agreed with them that Bob was now a suitable candidate for a training course at the Retreat, and should be nominated for the next intake. Everybody was concerned about Dave and Christie.

Gareth confirmed that Bob and his children were part of the Terrans generational program of genetic enhancement. "Their hidden knowledge and memories must not fall into the wrong hands. Dave has already displayed paranormal abilities, but he doesn't know how to control them.

"Their school has already noted their advanced intelligence, and this in turn has attracted the attention of certain government departments. Amy cannot protect those kids, and her recent behaviour would be a good excuse for the powers to be to remove them from her care."

"What about Bob's family?" Mary asked. "He never seems to mention them."

Gareth thought for a moment. "They are elderly, and live on the other side of town. Amy didn't like them, and wouldn't let them see their grandchildren very often. They have never disclosed that during their younger days they were also part of our generational program. Their discretion may work to our advantage now."

Gareth was determined to stop Amy having custody of Dave and Christie, and hired the best legal team in town. One of the stumbling blocks was Bob's ability to care for them whilst going to work. Mrs McAffrey was more than happy to take on that role. Bob's parents were overjoyed at the prospect of having their grandchildren any time Bob was away.

That only left the problem of a suitable residence, and with Mrs McAffrey's permission two more rooms were included in the renovations Gareth ordered for her home.

The day of the divorce proceedings arrived, and both sets of lawyers were hotly contesting the custody of the children. Gareth was quietly sitting in the back of the courtroom, and concentrated his thoughts on Amy. Suddenly she jumped up, screaming incoherent abuse at the judge and everybody else around.

The decision went Bob's way, and he left with the children clinging to him in a mixture of both joy and distress. They still loved their mother, despite her often heartless behaviour.

Gareth felt a little ashamed that he felt no remorse for manipulating Amy's mind. He had to protect Dave, who had already shown immense potential. Gareth predicted that one day the young lad would perform very valuable services for the Terrans.

The children settled in with Bob at Mrs McAffrey's, and started attending the local school. They were blossoming, and happier than they had ever been before. Every afternoon they would help her care for the animals on the farm next door. Some weekends Bob would take them to see his parents. Occasionally they would visit Amy, who was still a patient in the town's sanatorium.

One night Christie snuggled up to Mrs McAffrey. "I love you Aunty Ida. I'm so glad we came to live with you."

The old lady felt a sense of joy and fulfilment she had never experienced before. She thought of the children in the nursery and school on Solar Base. If she ever returned, it was there that she wanted to work.

CHAPTER 22

Martina and Aldon were more comfortable now that most of the current Xvar/Katon threat had been eliminated.

"We are both overdue for some leave," Aldon remarked. "It will be good to get away for some peace and relaxation. I don't want to go back to my home planet. There is nothing left there for me except painful memories. It is probably a choice between some very desirable spots on this planet, or one of the Space Stations in this Quadrant of the Galaxy."

Martina was inspecting a map of the Earth. "When my turn comes, it will probably be somewhere quiet here. I don't fancy a closed environment, no matter how much entertainment the Space Stations provide."

Ebony stuck her head around the door. "Message from Xandra. He's on his way here."

"What now?" Aldon complained. "I hope it's nothing to stop my time off!"

"Maybe not," Martina said. "Now that he and Victor have bonded, he uses any excuse he can to visit."

Xandra arrived in time for lunch, and ushered in a new android. "Meet Wilbur. He has a specific purpose, and will be with you for some time."

Aldon frowned. "Enlighten me!"

"The Guardians have decided that now is the time to locate our old hidden base, which we think is in the Himalayas. Wilbur will be examining all human records, literature, ancient maps, myths, artefacts, and ruins. He will then match them to current aerial views to see if he can pinpoint a likely location.

"There have been several so called 'alien races' here in the distant past. There are countless legends of ancient astronauts, supernatural races, semi-divine beings and Vimana craft. We are more concerned

213

with our own Terrans and where their hidden base was located. Because all records were lost when our ancestors escaped the planet, there may be even more than one abandoned base."

Aldon groaned. "That is one enormous task. I suppose if Wilbur's computer brain has been specifically trained for this, he may have some success."

"Not only has he been well programmed, his artificial intelligence can even detect isolated dialects which have Terran similarities." Xandra gloated.

"Most of the history of our ancient Terran ancestors, who lived on this planet, has been lost in the mists of time. Some human scientists have been quietly researching the forbidden and suppressed knowledge. Modern academia is arrogant and bigoted, and has censored and derided anything which does not conform to their thinking. It dictates the current scientific agenda and those who do not comply with the prevailing orthodox theories are ridiculed.

"Wilbur can remotely access most information, but you may have to escort him to a couple of libraries to scan their books and records."

Xandra noticed Aldon's irritated glare. "What's up? I thought you'd be pleased that Wilbur will do all the tedious sleuthing."

"It's not that," Martina said. "Aldon and I were discussing the possibility of having some time off. It has not been easy here, and we both need a break."

Xandra sighed. "I'm sorry. I cannot replace you, and need you together here at Earth Base. Perhaps you can take it in turn to have a few days off, but it must be somewhere you can return from immediately in an emergency."

Xandra went to visit Victor, and Martina set Wilbur and his equipment up on at a spare workstation.

Martina told Aldon he should be the first to spend a little time on the surface. He thought of all the sub-bases or agents who had a transporter. Most were either too remote, or in the middle of a city or town.

"How about the island?" Martina suggested. "Either Paul can put you up, or I'm sure Michael will let you stay in that luxurious hacienda of his."

Aldon had wanted some solitary time to go sailing, or mountaineering. He realised he may have to settle for the island, where he could at least paddle around in a canoe or go swimming.

Michael was very understanding, and made his guest bedroom and houseboy available for Aldon. It took him a couple of days to genuinely relax from the often extreme pressure he had been under for so long.

Tuan thought his boss's guest must be a very devout and religious man. He went to church every day. Aldon really appreciated spending time with Paul and Jaquita – not as their senior officer – but as old friends. They would go scuba diving together, and after sit under the palm trees with a cold drink.

That weekend Angela stayed in the city. Michael and Tony arrived at the hacienda, and took Aldon, along with Paul and Jacquita sailing on Michael's yacht which was docked in a solid stone boat house on the shore. While out on the ocean, they had the chance to communicate freely with each other, as Terran military officers.

Aldon outlined the Guardians' quest for the ancient Terran Bases. "I have a nasty feeling we are going to be asked to search for more than just the buried facility in the Himalayas."

Paul recalled some of the native lore on the island. "Before conversion to Christianity, they used to worship many of their own Gods, who supposedly lived deep under the sea. There could be some connection to alien visitors ages ago.

"They have one myth, which is universal, of seafaring people who were the guardians of advanced knowledge. They also urged humans to progress in harmony and proportion with the sources of all creation. I must admit many of my native congregation have paranormal abilities, and seem to possess that same interconnectedness taught by the ancient sages. I'll try to find out more about it."

Paul asked Aldon, before he left on Sunday morning, to attend the church service with Michael and Tony. He needed their combined influence to convince the natives to believe in the power of the church.

During one hymn Paul made a predetermined gesture and Jacquita and the others concentrated on one statue, which started to move and glow. After the service Aldon prepared to return to Earth Base. He thanked everyone for their hospitality, and winked at Paul who was tending to his wide-eyed and devoted congregation.

"Don't you think that was a bit unethical?" Aldon whispered.

Jacquita walked him to the vestry. "These people have enough kinetic power to manifest some phenomena themselves. You would be surprised at the occurrences during their indigenous ceremonies. We have to keep one step ahead."

Back on Earth Base, Wilbur was still absorbing and processing all the available data on ancient civilisations, megalithic societies, and their celestial deities.

Martina told Aldon that Wilbur hadn't stopped. "He's been working day and night, rambling on about technical feats and stone structures which are beyond human capacity to duplicate. He has even read and translated Sumerian and Sanskrit texts.

"Wilbur is a bit of a pain in the butt, even for an android. He is like a walking, talking computer, and obviously hasn't had much programming in how to relate to humans. He doesn't interact like Andy and Ebony.

"Now he's insisting that he must inspect some ancient maps that are locked up in the basement library of a very secure museum. He wants to compare them with the planet's ley lines and harmonics, which would have been a factor in the location of Terran and other bases!"

When he heard of the actual museum, Aldon was uneasy. "We haven't got a transporter or facility anyplace near. Nothing in that country! We cannot use conventional means to take Wilbur there. He would never clear the border security scanners."

"Can we use the PVX?" Martina suggested. "We could drop him and an agent nearby."

"The local military would detect us almost immediately. The 'in and out' would have to be a very speedy." Aldon said.

Aldon carefully prepared his strategy. Wilbur had to know in advance the blueprint of the museum, and exact location of the maps he required. Once Aldon's plans were in place, he co-opted a very reluctant Gareth, who was multi-lingual, to assist.

Aldon piloted the PVX, and transported Gareth to the outskirts of the city. He felt very alone and vulnerable when he saw it speed off almost immediately. He had enough of the local currency to catch a bus to the museum, and activated his invisibility device before climbing the stone steps to the entrance hall.

Their invisibility technology merely created an optical illusion. It was fortunate there were no body scanners and only security cameras in the reception area. He had committed the building plans to memory, and soon made his way into the basement. This was not going to be as easy as he had hoped.

There were several curators working nearby. He quietly looked around until he spotted a fire alarm, which he kinetically activated. When the siren sounded out, the museum staff stood staring at each other. They couldn't see any smoke or fire. Gareth breathed a sigh of relief when a supervisor entered and ordered them to leave.

As soon as the basement door closed behind them, Gareth raced to the chart cabinet and opened the drawers. He carefully took out the delicate parchments, and was in the middle of indentifying them, when the alarms stopped.

He gathered the maps into his arms, activated his locator, and messaged Aldon. "Quick! Get me out of here!"

It seemed like an eternity before he was beamed back up onto the PVX with Wilbur and Aldon. It only took a couple of minutes for the android to scan and record all the documents in detail.

"We have to put them back, and you'd better make it quick!" Aldon said. "We don't need to arouse any interest in our search."

Aldon was becoming increasingly concerned about the proximity of the local Air Force. "I can only hover for a minute or so. I will transport you down, then straight back. Just dump the charts on the table."

Georgio, the head curator, was met by a young intern when he re-entered the library. She was garbling on about seeing a strange man appearing at the parchment cabinets, then disappearing again. He could see there were several valuable documents scattered on the map table.

He wondered about the false fire alarm, and decided he didn't want any security investigations. Better to say someone forgot to put them away before the evacuation.

Wilbur finally concluded his analysis of the possible sites of the ancient alien bases on planet Earth. As Aldon feared, he had detected more than one.

Zadoc and the Guardians decided they would start by concentrating on the Himalayan location. The search would not be without danger. There was an aggressive ruling military to contend with. They could appear without notice.

Xandra thought it would be better to send Wilbur along with their three female Terran military officers.

"They are well trained, and can hold their own in battle," he said. "They will not cause unwarranted suspicion if they pose as three backpackers going on a spiritual quest."

Martina, Jacquita and Chantelle were both hesitant and excited when told of their new mission.

"It will be like old times together," said Martina, "and it is really beautiful and peaceful at the monastery. There is always Noru's transporter if we have to get out of there in a hurry."

The prospect of mountaineering required a certain degree of physical fitness, and they all spent the next month in the gym getting back in shape.

Aldon transported Wilbur straight to Noru at the base under the monastery. He took the women in the PVX, and dropped them a couple of miles away. They were dressed in jeans and parkas, and had heavy backpacks. When they hiked up the track to meet Noru, they appeared to be like any other hippies who arrived from time to time.

"We cannot be too careful." Noru explained. "While I trust most of my monks, there could always be an undercover government agent in our midst."

Even though, to avoid unwanted attention, Wilbur had been dressed in a monk's robe and hood, Martina accompanied him at all times. He had followed orders, and quietly wandered around the ancient monastery examining all the inscriptions and carvings on the walls and pillars.

He then directed his attention to even older ruins and stone artefacts nearby. Wilbur pointed out to Martina that the gestures depicted in the temple art also provided a great many clues. He came to the conclusion that the elusive Terran base was in a subterranean location a short distance away.

They asked Noru about the area, and he advised there was a large lake, further down the mountain, in that direction. Some landslides, in the past, had made access difficult. The lake itself was considered to be haunted by monsters and evil spirits. Nobody went there.

Wilbur was safely locked up with Tyra and Charra in the base under the monastery. Noru and the three women set off down the mountain to the lake. The track was rough, and littered with huge boulders which had come crashing down in previous avalanches.

"We can get severe earthquakes here." Noru said. "I have often wondered if the ancient base had an entrance which was obliterated by one of these rock falls."

Jacquita thought his theory had merit. "Nearly every base I have been on always had a secret escape tunnel. Maybe our ancestors' facilities were the same."

When they reached the lake Noru had a big smile on his face. "Look! Someone has left an old boat here. It doesn't appear to be leaking, and can carry us further out over the water."

Jacquita insisted that since she was the best swimmer, she should be the one to explore what lay under the surface of this mysterious lake. She had changed into her swimsuit, and as she adjusted the goggles, Noru insisted on attaching a safety rope to her waist.

"This way we won't lose you," he said.

Jacquita took a deep lungful of air and dived into the dark depths of the water. She could see a luminosity down below her, and descending closer realised it was a pulsating sphere, giving off a radiant glow.

She was about to get closer, before she ran out of breath, when she was met by two underwater 'beings'. They appeared to be a combination of man and fish, about ten feet in length, and wearing silver suits. She could not discern their features, as the creatures' heads were covered by silver helmets.

The body language of these 'things' seemed far from friendly. She tugged on the rope and swiftly rose to the surface.

"The monsters?" Noru asked as he helped her back into the boat.

She gulped for air and nodded. "I think they may be some form of androids or robots, designed to frighten off any intruders. If they are guarding what was the entrance to a Terran Base, maybe they will recognise one of our Terran identification devices."

Noru admitted he had never thought of that before. "How could anything like that still be here thousands of years later?"

Jacquita described the pulsating sphere, and suggested that it may be a perpetual power source, left behind when their ancestors fled the planet. Was it even possible that it had survived so long?

He was reluctant to allow Jacquita to dive down again, but she insisted on submerging once more, this time carrying Terran recognition. She was only a few feet below the surface, when the creatures rose up to meet her. She held up the emblem, which was emitting Terran vibrations and frequencies.

They stopped, and swam in circles below her, as if processing a new recognition. One beckoned with what looked like a half arm/half flipper. She motioned in friendship, and indicated that she would return.

Jacquita climbed into the boat. "I was right," she said. "They recognised me as Terran, and stopped being aggressive. I think they are some form of android or artificial entity, but don't know how to communicate with them."

Chantelle looked at Noru. "How about Tyra? She is an android. Perhaps she can extract information from their cognitive processors?"

Noru was hesitant. This meant sending his valuable android into possible danger. She would be underwater with robotic type entities more powerful than her. He insisted they should consider Wilbur instead.

They returned to the monastery, and contacted Aldon for further instructions. Aldon was reluctant to make any decision, and referred the matter to Xandra and Zadoc. The Guardians did not want to risk Wilbur and all the specialised information he had accumulated. On the other hand, he possessed the requisite aptitude and was the most logical candidate for the task. They were glad that Aldon had downloaded a copy of all his knowledge into a storage unit before he was dispatched to the Himalayas.

The next day they returned to the lake with Wilbur. He had been given a description of the silver creatures and how to extract their data. Wilbur looked confused when they placed a helmet on his head, a chain around his waist, and lowered him into the water. He had very little time to process this new experience.

Everyone peered uncertainly down into the depths. They could see some turbulence and flashes of silver in the water below.

"Oh shit!" Martina said. Had the creatures recognised Wilbur as Terran, or were they in the process of annihilating him?

Noru looked at Chantelle. "There's the tug on the chain! Here goes! I hope we're not going to drag out a dismembered android!"

They pulled Wilbur up. Thank goodness he was still intact! They removed his helmet, and he answered their questions in a monotone voice. Obviously the experience was not beneficial to his programming.

They returned to the monastery and transported his data transmission device to Earth Base. Xandra and the Guardians were delighted. Wilbur had extracted all the information from the underwater silver beings.

It confirmed their historical records about the base. Their ancestors had taught Earth's people about the Solar System and galaxy. They had also tried to educate them in the utilisation of the abundant energy already freely available. The planet itself creates sound waves, vibrations, pulse and rhythm. The data download also explained the reasons for their swift departure. It was not just an enemy attack.

Xandra gave Noru and the women more details. "Just as we do today, our ancestors had alerted the ancient humans about the ongoing emanations and cosmic waves from our Milky Way Galaxy during the Earth's 25,776 year procession of the equinoxes. Sometimes they can cause severe weather or geological disturbances. A giant cataclysm was about to occur on the planet.

"The main entry to the facility, which they destroyed, was under the lake. Whilst some, but not all of them escaped, they left the silver robotic guards and perpetual power supply intact. Due to the constant military presence in the area, it will be very difficult for us to covertly gain entry that way.

"There was, as Noru suspected, a secret entry tunnel. It may be easier to locate. I will send the plans of the base to you."

Wilbur analysed the new plans, and led his Terran controllers along a very unstable path around the side of a nearby cliff. The android stopped, and indicated that this was the location of the entry to the concealed escape passageway.

Chantelle stared at Wilbur. "Are you kidding? This is just a huge jumble of rocks and boulders."

Wilbur stared at her with a blank expression. "The entry is here!"

Noru interrupted. "It may well be in the rock face behind, and has merely been concealed by all the landslides over time. It is too difficult for us to try and gain entry."

He slipped a locator behind the rocks. "It's now up to Zadoc and the Guardians to take it from here."

They were edging their way along the narrow rock ledge, towards a clearing, when Noru motioned them to stop. A little ahead, were three government soldiers.

"Stay back! These men are evil," Noru whispered. "They tortured and killed one of my monks. Just for fun!"

Martina and the other two women stiffened, and had their weapons on the ready as their military training came to the fore. One of the soldiers spotted them, and pointed his automatic rifle. He moved towards them with a leer on his face.

Chantelle in particular knew what he had on his mind. She mentally messaged Jacquita and Martina to move forward with her. Noru, who was trying to keep a grip on Wilbur, was unable to hold them back.

"Just stay put, and leave this to us," Martina snarled. "They won't be bothering you anymore!"

Jacquita was the first to reach the soldiers, followed by Martina and Chantelle. Their flirty giggles and body language caught their opponents off guard. Without warning the three women kicked the rifles out of the soldiers' hands, and dealt a fatal blow to the back of their necks.

Noru stared in disbelief. He had almost been indoctrinated to the peaceful ways of his monks.

He was concerned. "Their comrades will retaliate when they find their bodies."

"No they won't," said Martina as she threw her victim's body and rifle over the edge of the cliff. Jacquita and Chantelle did the same.

"They will be washed away, down the river in that gorge, a long way from the monastery."

They felt no regret for their actions. It was a matter of both self defence and justice.

The three women and Wilbur transported back to Earth Base. Martina told Aldon about the events in the Himalayas, and expressed her disappointment at not being allowed to take their search further.

"This is one time Xandra won't let you turn an order into a debate," he said. "Now they have discovered that the perpetual power supply is still active, there is no telling what they may find in that subterranean cavern. Karine and his specialised team are going to take it from here."

CHAPTER 23

Jacquita and Chantelle had never been to the Himalayas before, and along with Martina were a little miffed that they had not been allowed to stay there any longer. The thought of gaining entry to the lost base, and discovering its ancient secrets filled them with so much enthusiasm.

"I cannot fully express our disappointment at being ordered to leave it to the Guardians." Martina complained.

Aldon understood their frustration. "Everyone was appreciative of your efforts, and successful location of the missing base. In fact, you may all be awarded a citation. Zadoc was apologetic about curtailing your expedition. From now on it will take a specialised scientific and military team, along with a purpose built retrieval craft."

"It might have been a change of scenery, but I hope you don't consider it as part of my time off." Martina said.

Aldon assured her she could have her holiday as soon as circumstances permitted. At present he needed to speak with Victor and Chantelle, who were concerned about Bart.

Victor had been meeting Bart on a more regular basis, and every time had given him extra funds to supplement his income. Chantelle, who often attended the Casino with her clients, had sensed that Bart was manipulating the gaming tables and poker machines without authorisation. Had he become envious of the lavish lifestyle of the rich and wealthy, who gambled their money without a second thought?

"Most of these gambling establishments are controlled by powerful criminal organisations," she said. "They would not hesitate to kill anyone they suspected of ripping them off. They have also been known to torture their opponents to discover the identity of their accomplices."

Aldon was even more concerned about Bart's association with the Terrans. He did not want any knowledge of their own activities or agents falling into the wrong hands. He asked Victor, who rarely went to the Casino, to have a serious talk with Bart.

In the meantime Chantelle kept a closer watch, and noticed that it was one particular man, Keith Masters, who was winning the funds. She suspected that he secretly met Bart later on, in a dark lane down the road, where they split the proceeds.

Aldon discussed the matter with Victor. They did not want to compromise Chantelle's position, and advised her to avoid any contact with Bart.

Before Victor had a chance to meet with Bart, their worst fears were realised. Chantelle messaged Aldon that Bart and Keith had run out of the Casino, with a couple of thugs in hot pursuit. There had been a shooting in the lane down the street. Bart was nowhere to be seen and Keith's body was being removed by the police.

Mrs McAffrey was about to do her weekly shopping in the late night supermarket. She had gone to the newsagent first, before it closed. As she walked back down the poorly lit street, she saw a man running through the car park. There were two swarthy ruffians in hot pursuit. Several gunshots rang out and the man fell to the ground.

Her heart was racing as the two assassins stopped and stared at her. She realised that having witnessed an obvious underworld execution, she was also in danger. She turned and ran up the road, taking shelter in the lobby of an apartment building, and hiding in a cupboard under the stairs.

She cowered in the dark when she heard their footsteps and voices in the hallway.

"Can't see her here. Maybe she went into the next building. The boss can download the footage of the security camera outside. If we don't get her now, we will later, when we find out what she looks like."

Mrs McAffrey was so terrified she remained hidden and shaking for what seemed like hours. She heard more sirens, and it was only when all was silent that she crept out.

Victor and Mary were discussing the shock news that a man had been found dead in a lane near the Casino, and Bart's bullet ridden body in the local car park. They were drinking a late cup of cocoa when they heard a tap on their back entry.

"Mrs McAffrey!" Mary exclaimed as she opened the door. "What are you doing here? What's the matter? It's so late, why aren't you home? Bob and the kids will be worried."

They gave the exhausted old lady a hot drink, and listened to her terrified account of the night's events.

"I have spent over an hour getting here by back streets, where there are no security cameras. It is only a matter of time before those gangsters get my photo and try to track me down. They will kill me too! What am I going to do? I can't stay here anymore. I can't even go into town. I want to go back to Solar Base."

Victor took Mrs McAffrey's car keys, and collected her vehicle from near the supermarket. He picked her up from the bookshop and took her home.

"They can't find you yet. You're safe, for the moment, with Bob and the kids."

After he returned, Victor made a late night trip to Earth Base. Aldon and Martina had already heard of Bart's death.

"Bart was a silly fool." Aldon said. "Sad as it is, at least he wouldn't have had the chance to tell them anything. Perhaps it's better for us that those mobsters decided to shoot him first, without asking any questions."

Aldon and Xandra decided that maybe it was advisable, under the circumstances, for Mrs McAffrey to return to Solar Base. She would be good company for Mary's granny, and could help with the children. They advised her to pack whatever she wanted to take with her, and Xandra would pick her up within the week.

Dave and Christie were told that their Aunty Ida was moving to another country. They were in tears, but cheered up when told Mary was going to pay them a small wage to help with the animals on the farm next door.

Mrs McAffrey insisted on drawing up the paperwork, and signing her property over to Bob. At least he and the children would have a home to call their own. Bob had talked to the hospital, and they agreed to alter his working hours so that he could collect the children after school. Another neighbour would take them in the morning.

Ida contacted John to give her cats a check-up before she left. He realised later that he should have been suspicious when she asked for some sedatives.

"Just to settle them. They will be very upset when I'm gone," she said.

Late one evening Xandra hovered overhead. Tearful goodbyes and hugs were being shared all around, and they started taking her luggage up in the blue beam. Mrs McAffrey was teleported aboard and Xandra shot off at high speed.

Xandra went through to the guest cabin and welcomed her. "You never were that adjusted to Earth, were you? We'll be glad to have you back on Solar Base."

Mrs McAffrey was getting agitated, insisting she had to get three large soft carpet bags out of the baggage hold. Xandra sent two crew members to get them. It might calm the old girl down - the last week had been very traumatic for her.

He left the room as the three large bags were placed on the floor. "I'll pop back in later when you're settled and unpacked," he promised.

She ran to the bags, and quickly opened them. "Are you babies okay?" she asked, carefully lifting the furry bundles out onto the floor. The cats were still sleepy, and she gently placed all twelve of them on the bed.

Back on Earth Bob looked at Dave and Christie. "Something is missing besides your Aunty Ida. What is it?" He looked at Soxy and Tiger, two elderly cats who were asleep in the chair.

"The cats! Where are the rest of the cats?"

Christie giggled. "Aunty Ida took them with her. She asked us not to tell anybody. She let us keep two and said they were too old to travel."

Back on his space ship, Xandra took a supper tray into Mrs McAffrey. As he opened the door a bundle of white fur shot through his legs and out into the corridor.

He stared in bewilderment at the eleven other felines spread all over the cabin. "Ida! What were you thinking?"

"But you told me to bring whatever I wanted. They are my most precious possessions. I couldn't leave them behind. It's alright. I've got them enough food for the journey. It's in one of my boxes in the hold."

"But we don't have animals on Solar Base. You know that." Xandra said. "It's too late to take them back. I don't know what to do. For the moment, just catch the one that got away, and make sure they all stay in your quarters."

Keeping twelve active cats contained in Ida's cabin was easier said than done. Xandra allocated J20 to assist. The robot knew very little about these peculiar creatures, and spent most of the journey collecting them from the control centre, engine room and other forbidden areas. It didn't help when the Terran officers, who were not permitted to keep animals, made a big fuss of his bothersome charges.

Xandra was at the controls, and one little tabby feline was leaning over the top of the screen, trying to catch the moving pictures and icons. As J20 took it away, Xandra had to admit that, having interacted with Mishka at the bookshop, he also had a soft spot for these rather cute creatures. He had to figure out what to do with them when he reached their destination, and messaged ahead to Solar Base.

Most of the Base families were delighted that their young ones, who were never allowed a pet, were now going to experience the joy of developing a relationship with Ida's kitties.

There was an unused area, next to the schoolrooms, which was renovated into an apartment and cattery for Ida. The space ship arrived at Solar Base, and it took a couple of hours to round up some of the agitated felines, who had escaped and were hiding in various nooks and crannies. J20 was going into robotic meltdown, and was trying to compute why, when Ida banged the spoon on a can of food, all those pesky creatures came running.

Ida and her furry friends were finally established in her new quarters. They were greeted by Mary's granny and a horde of excited children. Within a few weeks Ida and her pussies had settled in. She became firm friends with Granny, who appreciated her help in the schoolroom.

Xandra had originally despaired over the introduction of any animal on his Base. After a while, he noticed the cats would wander out into the communal areas, where everyone would stop to pet them. They had generated a new ambience and harmony among his officers. Their children were happier, and there was less tension in the families who were cooped up in this relatively small environment.

Everybody was still in shock over the recent events and ultimate fate of Bart. Whilst Aldon was used to casualties of war, this need not have happened. He told Martina and Gareth that in future they had to be more prudent in their use of protégées.

"We must be a thousand percent sure of their loyalty and discretion. Also they must obey orders. If he were captured, Bart may have jeopardised Victor and the Friendship Club. That, in turn, could have led to us."

Martina nodded in agreement. "What will happen regarding our occasional use of the Casino?"

Aldon was thoughtful. "Sometimes it has its uses. It will have to be only when absolutely necessary; even then, nothing to arouse suspicion. Just one 'manipulator' and smaller amounts."

Earth Base was also able to access the footage from the security cameras on the street. They didn't want to leave any 'loose ends'. A few days later a casino vehicle mysteriously exploded into a ball of flame, and both assassins were incinerated. The newspapers covered the story of the two murders for a couple of days, and suggested that it was a gangland war.

Victor didn't go to Bart's funeral, and was glad he had only socialised with him outside the Casino.

Mary was also stunned. "This has really shown how important it is to follow the rules, and keep our secrets. Bart is now dead. In some ways, although Mrs McAffrey had no choice but to flee to Solar Base, she is apparently very happy there, and has become a bosom buddy with Granny. I don't know if your father has come to terms with all her cats!"

Victor went to Earth Base once a week, and was allowed to use their communications station to speak to Xandra for fifteen minutes. Mrs McAffrey's felines had often cropped up in their conversation. While creating the necessary food for their new pets had initially caused some problems, the cats and Terrans had settled in well together. Even the androids and other cyber entities had adjusted to their presence.

During his investigation, Wilbur had identified several hidden alien bases on planet Earth. Some were of unknown origin, and others definitely Terran. Zadoc and the Guardians gave top priority to the ancient Terran Base near the monastery in the Himalayas.

Its existence was already suspected by the humans, and many explorers had searched for the entrance. Xandra advised Aldon and Martina that a specialist team, including Wilbur, had been assembled, and was ready to penetrate the facility.

"Karine will be directing the operations," he said. "Everything must be undertaken with the utmost care and secrecy. Our presence must not attract any attention from the local armed forces or the lamas at the monastery. Our own military will be protecting some of our best scientists.

The dedicated Guardian ship transported two experts to the locator, which had been left at the landslide on the narrow cliff path. They penetrated a small part of the barrier of rocks until they reached the hidden entry. Eventually they had to force the opening, and replace it with a new door which could be accessed with their own more modern technology.

Karine led a team of scientists, wearing protective suits and helmets. They cautiously entered the dark rock tunnel and made their way down the roughly hewn stairs to the caverns below. They were all amazed when they emerged into a huge lighted area. It was enormous!

"Jacquita was right. Their perpetual power plant is still operating. It will make our job much easier, but we must be alert for any alarms or booby traps left to defend against intruders." Karine said.

He could see a small red beam flashing on one wall, and his scientists activated their current Terran frequency/vibration device, plus one of the oldest ones that the Guardians could provide. There was a collective sense of reprieve when the warning light stopped flashing.

The team relaxed and using the plans that Wilbur had previously accessed, started to survey their surroundings. Although it was possible that the power supply was still generating breathable air, Karine had it tested for any build-up of harmful agents or gases before they finally removed their helmets.

"That's better," he said. "I was beginning to feel rather claustrophobic. Just look at this place, and the antiquated equipment. I wonder if any of it still works! Unfortunately their teleporter would never be compatible with our more advanced current models. It belongs in a Terran museum, back on one of our home planets."

They discovered that the historical records were wrong. Their ancestors had not destroyed the base itself, and had merely detonated the main entry under the lake. The saucer 'hanger' inside housed two very ancient craft.

"I would be surprised if they could fly today," said Orani, one of the scientists. "Given we have already encountered the unexpected, I suppose we had better check them out."

Two robots, trained in space vehicles, set to work examining the saucers. They reported that if the supply ship sent them some equipment, and a few spare parts, they were confident the craft could at least be operational within Earth's atmosphere.

While they set to work, Karine and the others searched the rest of the base. The control centre was deserted, and the living quarters empty, except for some personal possessions left strewn around when the occupants had made their hasty exit.

232

Wilbur was slowly making his way around the rock walls. They had a glassy appearance, and were covered with inscriptions, which he was meticulously documenting. They may reveal more than the records contained in the archaic equipment which had been left behind.

The team descended to a lower level, and at long last discovered their Terran ancestors who had not escaped. Their bodies had been mummified in the rarefied atmosphere. Two androids were given the task of gently preparing them for removal. They would be identified later, and given a respectful burial in a Terran garden of honour.

Pavit, one of their geologists, was examining the surrounds, and called the others back. "Wait a minute! These walls over here are not natural. I think they are concealing something." Slowly the team examined the surface.

"Here! Here!" Pavit called out, as his fingers felt a small embedded lever.

They pressed on it, and a section slid open to reveal another space beyond. Pavit and Orani carefully stepped in, unsure of what they may find. They stopped in disbelief when they saw a row of stasis chambers.

Orani looked through one of the transparent tubes, and was rendered speechless when he saw the motionless face of a fellow Terran. They stumbled back into the main lower area and raced up to the base's control centre.

Karine walked over as they approached him, and asked if everything was under control.

Orani was still shaking when he blurted out the news. "I'm afraid not! I think some of them might still be alive. Maybe that is why the perpetual power supply was still operating."

The team returned to their science ship until Zadoc and the Guardians decided what to do next. A medical unit was dispatched to Earth. After close examination, they considered any attempt to revive the survivors would have to be performed on a special hospital ship. This required the re-opening of the main entry under the lake.

Karine and Xandra summoned Noru to an emergency meeting at Earth Base. A decision had been made to deactivate the silver 'guards' and access the primary way into the saucer hanger.

The most important task was to extract the stasis tubes and occupants. After that they intended to remove all the Terran equipment, leaving nothing but empty caverns.

Martina was stunned. "That is a massive job, especially under the noses of the monks and patrolling soldiers."

Aldon was hopeful that since most of the activity would be underneath the mountain and water, they would not attract unwanted attention.

Due to his previous successful interaction with the ten foot silver guards, Wilbur was sent into the depths of the lake to deactivate them. A small 'tunnelling' craft then descended to clear a way into the base. They had to be careful not to damage the power source.

Pavit was waiting with the two ancient saucers, which had already been loaded with much of the salvaged equipment. They were piloted by two robots, who manoeuvred them out into the lake, and then straight up into the sky towards Karine's retrieval craft.

He watched with some foreboding as they wobbled around below his docking aperture. His crew managed to catch one, and then the other, in a gravity beam and drag them on board.

Noru was making sure none of the lamas strayed from the monastery and kept a vigilant watch for any military in the area. After he gave the 'all clear' the hospital ship descended straight into the lake.

It took the medical crew about two hours to safely remove the stasis units which were going to be kept fully functioning until they could be delivered to the best Terran facility in another part of the Quadrant.

Aldon and Martina were also monitoring the situation from Earth base. Martina was becoming increasingly optimistic as the recovery operations progressed.

"Can you imagine how mind blowing it will be if they can actually revive those early Terrans. I wonder how they will react. Will they be able to adapt to life a few thousand years later?"

Once the medical intensive care team had departed, Karine sent down a cargo ship to collect the remaining equipment. After that was accomplished the operation would be complete, except for deactivating the base and collecting the rest of his team. He couldn't believe everything had gone so smoothly.

The cargo ship was slowly ascending into the sky, when a squadron of military jets appeared on the horizon. Karine ordered an immediate retreat, and all his craft immediately shot up into the upper atmosphere and out into space.

Pavit and Orani, along with Wilbur and a couple of robots, were stranded in the subterranean caverns.

"We're trapped!" Orani agonised. "What are we going to do? I'm a scientist – not a soldier."

CHAPTER 24

Karine contacted Aldon and Noru regarding the military jets flying around the Himalayas. He couldn't risk returning to the area to rescue the stranded members of his team.

In addition, Zadoc and the Guardians wanted to alter their original plan, and had devised a new strategy. They required someone to merely close the entrances to the Himalayan base. The perpetual power source was to remain, and their 'monster' guards in the lake were to be reactivated.

It was felt that the facility, now only a covert series of empty caverns, may be of use in the future. Noru was ordered to make his way back there, and once these instructions were complete, to rescue Pavit, Orani, Wilbur and the robots.

"That's alright for him to say," Noru grumbled. "He doesn't have to contend with aggressive military, jets overhead and a whole lot of curious monks."

He waited until late the next night to creep out of the monastery and along to the narrow cliff path leading to the base's escape tunnel. It was not easy, as he was trying to carry five hooded robes which he had smuggled out of the monks' laundry.

He was sure he had been followed, and was getting desperate when he messaged the scientists to hurry up and open the hidden door in the rocks. Once inside, he staggered down the stone staircase to the large space below.

Pavit and Orani were panic stricken. Buried in this subterranean environment, they were sure they had been abandoned to a slow death by starvation

They were both whinging like spoilt children. "Have you got anything to eat?"

Noru glared at them. Wasn't it enough that he had struggled with the five robes to assist in their escape? Obviously they had never lived the Spartan lifestyle his monks adhered to.

Noru didn't mince his words. "Well, the faster you complete these new directives, the faster we can get out of here. It's up to you."

Wilbur dived into the water from the saucer bay, and quickly reactivated the silver guards. After he closed the entry behind him, they all donned the monks' robes and climbed back up the escape tunnel. Once that entry was firmly fastened they edged their way along the narrow ledge.

Noru was startled to find one of the junior lamas waiting in the same clearing that the soldiers were in during Jaquita and the women's visit.

The young man stepped in front of him, blocking their way. "What is going on here? Who are these people? I know you're up to something. Whatever it is, I do not want to anger the soldiers. Better hand over those intruders."

Noru's doubts were confirmed. He had long suspected this particular novice monk of being an informer. While Orani and Pavit were literally shaking in their boots, Wilbur quietly moved forward. The traitor slumped into unconsciousness as soon as the android grabbed the side of his neck.

Noru's recent religious indoctrination came to the fore. "You can't kill him," he said. "Carry him back to the monastery. We'll leave him behind one of the statues and erase his memory."

The five escapees were thankful when Noru quietly led them down into the secret base under the ancient structure. One by one they were transported back to Earth Base.

"Wilbur and the robots aren't much trouble," Martina said, as they watched Pavit and Orani shovelling down huge mouthfuls of food. "But I hope Karine collects these two quick smart!"

The next morning Noru was walking through the monastery courtyard. One of his elderly lamas walked up, and gave him a perceptive smile.

"In times gone by our order gave sanctuary to all kinds of beings. It is pleasing when some of the most precious finally found their way to safety."

Noru did not answer. They both stared at the young novice, still asleep behind the statue. He woke, and looked totally bewildered when one of the older monks walked up.

"Come along, young man. Today we're going on a journey across the country. You are being assigned to another temple for further training."

The monks went about their everyday life for a couple of weeks, until they received an urgent warning that a large military contingent was on its way up the mountain. The government had ordered them to investigate the recent unusual aerial activity in the vicinity.

Noru was ordered to transport Tyra and Charra to Earth Base, and temporarily close and seal the facility under the monastery. All the religious icons, and their main food supplies, were carefully hidden. Two senior monks volunteered to remain, and under the cover of night, Noru led the rest around the cliff edge to refuge in the now deserted Terran Base.

Many were astounded at what had been there all the time. The caverns' had a natural supply of water from the lake, the entry to which remained sealed. They had brought sufficient food with them, so it was just a matter of quietly meditating and waiting for the soldiers to leave.

For the monks this was a spiritual experience like never before. Although the Terran equipment had been removed, the old base itself was a conduit of elevated frequencies and vibrations. Many were experiencing visions and even time travel to both the past and future. Their minds and souls soared to a higher connection and union with the universe and cosmos.

The military arrived in force, and were told all the monks had gone on an annual pilgrimage. The two elder lamas used the excuse that there had been 'Silver Gods' in the sky – it was an omen! Everybody had to go and pray at a larger temple down the mountain.

The lamas pointed the soldiers in the opposite direction to the lake. That was where they had seen the strange craft hovering. Their deception paid off. After several fruitless days of searching, the troops were running short on supplies. Their commanding officer was cold and hungry. He advised his superiors there was nothing to be found, and ordered his men to begin their demanding trip back down the difficult terrain.

A few nights later, Noru and his enlightened companions returned. The monastery base was quietly reactivated, and Tyra and Charra transported back to perform their regular duties.

"Are you sure our security hasn't been breached?" Aldon asked Noru.

He confirmed that much as they would like to return, the monks would not be able to locate the secret entry to the Terran caverns in daylight, and they were still not aware of the facility under the temple.

Several months had passed, and all seemed calm and event free on Earth. On the occasional weekend, Mary and the twins would host a day out at the farm for some of the members of the Friendship Club. Gareth and Tony would attend, and quietly assess the guests' suitability for further training at the Retreat.

Secrecy was still of paramount importance, and only when no-one else was present, Gareth would conduct extra training sessions with Bob and the three women. He was amazed at the abilities of young Dave, who would often join in.

Gareth included the young lad in his reports. "Dave is a product of several generations of augmentation. The Guardians' genetic enhancement program really does seem to work."

Every so often John would visit the farm, supposedly to check on the animals. Actually it gave him a chance to catch up with Tony, Victor and Gareth.

"He is such a nice man," Mary commented. "I believe he has a wildlife refuge, and never charged Mrs McAffrey when her cats needed any treatment."

Victor just grinned to himself, and thought it would be even better if John liked humans as much as animals and his android.

The quiet, incident free period had allowed Martina and Aldon to get out and about a little more. They both wanted to improve the morale of their Terran agents on the planet, and Martina organised fortnightly get-togethers at Earth Base.

These were more like parties than official conferences, and everyone was much more relaxed than they had been for a long time. It was on one of these occasions that Gareth raised his glass and looked at Michael.

"I believe congratulations are in order?"

Michael hesitated for a moment. "I suppose you will find out sooner or later. Angela is pregnant. We are going to have a baby!"

When Jacquita, Chantelle and Martina expressed their interest and offered to help in any way they could, Aldon had some misgivings.

"I hope our female agents aren't going to turn all 'clucky'," he told Xandra. "As it is, they're all demanding they're overdue for some leave. We have no pressing matters on Earth at present, so I have to arrange for their time off. I hope they don't get up to any mischief when left to their own devices. Unplanned pregnancies are not on the current agenda!"

Xandra agreed. "Actually we won't be granting them a traditional holiday. Zadoc is organising a special trip for them. They are to be taken to our nearest Terran home planet, where an exceptional welcome awaits them. Along with Karine and his officers, they are to be honoured for their efforts in locating our ancient base."

Martina, Jacquita and Chantelle may have had other ideas of what to do during their anticipated recreation time together, but realised they couldn't refuse the invitation.

"We have been summoned!" Martina exclaimed. "Gareth is going to assist at Earth Base if Aldon wants to go anywhere."

Chantelle took them on a shopping trip to buy some new alluring outfits.

"My treat," she said. "This trip is supposed to be in lieu of our holiday. Who knows, we may meet some handsome hunks out there in the galaxy! We need something a bit more seductive than our uniforms."

Jacquita was slowly spinning around in front of the mirror. The tight fitting red dress showed a lot of cleavage.

"This is much, much better than that wretched nun's habit!"

They transported back to Earth Base and ignored Aldon's protests when they packed extra suitcases with all their new clothes.

"Zadoc said one case each!" he warned, knowing full well that they were going to do whatever they wanted.

Aldon loaded them into the PVX and took them up to the giant space transport waiting in the upper atmosphere.

Martina gave him a quick kiss on the cheek. "Stay safe! See you in six weeks!"

Zadoc ushered the women into their guest quarters, and wisely never mentioned their excess baggage. He took them on an extended tour of his huge craft, and explained far more of the technology than he ever had before.

"You ladies are soon due for much deserved promotions," he said. "Maybe one day you will be controlling a craft of your own. I will also be making quick stops to give you an idea of the command duties on the Moon, Mars and Jupiter Bases."

Thousands of years ago the Moon had a substantial base. Despite its recent upgrade, it was now no more than a small mining operation with very cramped quarters, and limited life support.

Chantelle whispered to Martina that she would rather forgo any promotion, and didn't want to swap her luxurious lifestyle for a Spartan existence on some rocky planetoid.

They spent a night at Mars Base, which was a much more convivial environment. Pletta told them that their location of the ancient Terran base and survivors was the talk of the Quadrant.

"We didn't do it alone." Martina said. "It was a joint effort."

They were overwhelmed by the attentive males in the bar that evening, and stuck to their agreement to stay together at all times.

"I've had three offers to go to some bloke's quarters and see his space etchings," Martina giggled.

"Me too!" Chantelle laughed. "They must get lonely and bored stuck here!"

Jacquita had also decided it was much nicer living on Earth. She took one look at these constrictive, confined bases and was positive she much preferred the church on her tropical island.

Solar Base, where Noru joined them, was their last stop before zooming into the blackness of space on their way to Excelsior, the nearest Terran home planet.

The women alighted at the Space Port. It was a long time since they had been back to their own families and community. Several relatives had travelled to Excelsior and were waiting to greet them.

The Guardians had arranged luxury accommodation in the city, and a generous amount of free time before any formal ceremonies.

Chantelle, Martina and Jacquita met for breakfast in an outdoor plaza, which was surrounded by strange native plants and flowers. Small sky-craft darted around the large structures, towers and spires which rose into the blue/grey sky and glistened under the two suns.

"I had forgotten how beautiful this is," said Martina.

Jacquita looked around. "A bit different from my home planet, but then no two places are exactly the same."

Chantelle agreed. The best thing was being herself again. No need to be incognito in a fake guise. They parted company for the day. Jacquita and Martina were occupied with family and old friends who had come to Excelsior to be with them.

Chantelle was feeling alone, no-body had arrived to meet her. Zadoc suggested that she join him and Noru on a trip to their Garden of

Honour, where there was to be a private religious service for the ancient Terrans who had perished at the Himalayan Base.

They left the city, and made their way towards a magnificent crystal temple, set in a garden of colourful flowers. There were plaques and memorials for various Terran heroes. Zadoc stopped at a small tomb with an epitaph dedicated to the Terrans who had died on planet Earth.

As Chantelle bowed her head in silent prayer, she felt a presence beside her. She looked, but no-one was there.

She could hear a quiet voice. "Thank you, my child, for bringing us home."

During the later ceremony everybody sensed an atmosphere of peace and love. Chantelle looked across at a grove of trees, and was sure she could see several figures in long flowing white robes. She looked again and they seemed to melt away and disappear. Zadoc said the spirits of the departed were often seen here.

The women were thankful to Chantelle for their new evening costumes. Karine and his crew, who had also come for the celebrations, hosted a couple of lively parties. Their tours of duty often involved dangerous battles, and like most soldiers, they welcomed a chance to relax and put it out of mind.

The special night arrived, and Zadoc insisted they had to be in full dress uniform. They were seated at the front of the large crowd, along with Karine and his crew. Pavit and Orani were also there with several scientists and the medical team.

"Where's Wilbur?" Jacquita asked. "He deserves the same recognition as everybody else."

Zadoc agreed, and went away for a while. He returned with a smiling Wilbur, who sat alongside them.

"He's smiling!" Martina commented. "He was always so sombre and mechanical. Why is he smiling?"

"He's been upgraded to the highest class of android." Zadoc explained. "That was his reward. He can now relate to humans!"

Martina looked around at the audience. Besides the Guardians, who comprised several different races, there were many other entities present from various parts of the Quadrant.

The proceedings were starting on a raised area at the end of the large hall. News reporters were gathered around recording the event. An orchestra played the national anthem and a celebratory fanfare as one by one the Terran officers were called up. The Guardians presented them with recognition awards for valour and service to the Terrans.

Near the end of the ceremony the music changed to a mystical ancient refrain. The curtains parted behind the Guardians, and a group of several figures stepped forward. They were dressed in white robes, and their long blond hair was like a halo around their glowing faces.

Everybody gasped when they realised they were their ancient Terran ancestors who had been revived after thousands of years. They addressed the audience and thanked everybody for their rescue and return.

The Guardians explained that their transition to a new life was not easy, and they would be living in the temple under the care of the wise elders.

The ancient Terrans had requested a meeting with Noru, Jacquita, Martina and Chantelle, and the next day they were taken to a private sanctuary.

Their leader told of how they had been regarded as Gods, and had taught and educated primitive man in astronomy and peaceful co-existence. When they had to flee, they had inscribed much of their knowledge on the rock faces of their base and ancient temples. They were especially grateful to Noru, and the lamas before him, for protecting and preserving their legacy.

In the grand scale of the cosmos, planet Earth was not of any great importance. It troubled them to learn that during their absence, mankind had slipped back, and it had taken many centuries for any technological progress to occur.

The leader was sad that many humans had reverted to their cruel and barbaric ways, and noted that everything in the Universe was a balance of good and evil. He hoped that the latest Terran interventions would prove beneficial in leading the planet away from the dark side.

Later that day Chantelle commented that it was times like this that made her feel it was all worth it. The Terrans who had been involved with the rescue were constantly besieged by well wishers and news reporters, and any hope of privacy was long gone.

Before they left they were called to a couple of private meetings with the Guardians and senior Terran leaders. The situation on Earth was discussed, and several confidential messages given for Xandra, Aldon and Gareth.

They were enjoying a final meal with the conference delegates when an aide came in the door and whispered in the senior Guardian's ear. He abruptly jumped up and went outside. Zadoc followed him, and they could hear voices and people rushing about in the corridor.

Jacquita was trying to perceive what the commotion was all about. "Something's going on – that's for sure."

It was a while before a very sombre looking Zadoc returned.

"We have to leave early. Hurry up and get your luggage, and meet me at the Space Port."

"What's happening?" Chantelle asked.

"It's classified. I'll tell you when we get underway," he said and rushed back out.

They obeyed orders and were embarking on Zadoc's craft within the hour. After they shot away from Excelsior Martina joined Zadoc in the control centre.

"Two days early and no time to even say goodbye! This must be something serious?"

"Our worst fears have just been realised. The Xvars have just attacked and overwhelmed Space Station Nine. The whole Quadrant is on war footing!"

Zadoc took them back to Solar Base, and quickly departed. He had more important duties to attend to.

"I wonder how long we'll be here for?" Chantelle said. "At least we're back in the Solar System!"

They spent a couple of nights with Mrs McAffrey and Granny, and tried to maintain a cheerful attitude in front of the children. A rather antiquated transport saucer eventually took them back to meet Aldon in the PVX above Earth.

Andy had the coffee ready when they reached Earth Base. Martina poured herself a stiff drink instead, and turned to Aldon.

"Have you heard the news?"

"Yes," he sighed. "Our worst fears have been realised. Perhaps it was a good thing that we rid this planet of all the Xvars and Katons."

The others were about to leave and as Martina bade them farewell, she took another swig of her whiskey.

"Just when we thought we were in the clear – they're back! Life wasn't meant to be easy!"

CHAPTER 25

Martina glanced across the control centre at Aldon, who was muttering obscenities to himself. Ever since they received the news about their enemies, the Xvars and Katons, capturing their distant Terran Space Station, he had been very irritable.

"Anything I can do?" she ventured.

Aldon hesitated and looked up. "No, I'm sorry. It's not your fault. I just get so frustrated. We have always thought that we are the only Terran Base on Earth, but we both know that somewhere on this planet there is at least one other Base which we haven't been told about."

Martina sighed, and placed a calming hand on Aldon's shoulder. "I agree, but it is no use getting all steamed up about it. We need to talk to Xandra again, and get this sorted once and for all!"

It was only a few days later when everyone could hear shouting coming from the control room. Ebony was trying to reassure Delta and her fellow workers who were hiding in a room at the back of the Base. Wondering what all the commotion was about, Andy tentatively peeked around the corner.

Xandra and Aldon were yelling at each other, and Martina seemed to be trying to calm things down before it came to blows. She stepped between her two senior Terran officers.

"Stop it! Sit down – both of you!" The men were a little taken aback by Martina's intervention, and meekly sat opposite each other, still glowering across the room.

Martina continued; "Xandra – there is something you're not telling us! Up until recently you led us to believe that our Base was the only Terran installation on the planet, and we were responsible for all our agents here. When we rescued Natalie from the hospital, we realised she had escaped from another Base on Earth – a Terran Base we had no knowledge of!"

Xandra fidgeted and looked at the floor for a couple of minutes. "Yes, you do have a right to know, but I am limited with what I can disclose."

"We're listening!" Aldon growled.

Xandra took a deep breath. "Your Base, which the Guardians have named 'Earth Base One', has mainly been occupied with our Terran agents who have temporarily integrated with what humans refer to as the 'Western' societies. There are two other technologically advanced major powers in this world. Since they have also developed dangerous weapons and are venturing into space they are of equal concern to us.

"We have established at least another two Earth Bases to specifically keep an eye on these nations. Our agents there have been expressly trained to integrate with these diverse cultures, and their various languages and politics."

"But why were we not told about this?" Martina interrupted.

Xandra glanced across at his two colleagues. "We are all military officers, and well know the necessity for security and compartmentalisation. Everything is on a 'need to know' basis. If one base is captured or infiltrated, there must be no possibility of the remaining facilities being betrayed and discovered."

Aldon frowned and thumped the table. "I understand, but it was not fair that up until recently we were totally unaware of their existence. We were under the impression that we had got rid of all the Xvars and Katons on the planet. Are they present in other parts of the world?

"In our sector, they didn't have their own bases, and only maintained a presence deep below some corporate and military establishments. I know that they may well come back, but at present we thought there were only the humans to worry about."

Xandra looked tired and drawn. "Unfortunately, that is not the case. While the Xvars and Katons have been hunted down, there is another threat. The Ibearns have been detected in this Solar System. They are an aggressive species, and the Guardians are concerned that they are very opportunistic and taking advantage of the recent interstellar hostilities to make some territorial gains of their own."

Martina looked up. "I remember them! Ugly looking blighters with elongated heads and very sharp, angular features! I met a couple when on duty in the outer boundaries – never liked them much!"

"Yes," Xandra agreed, "but human looking enough to blend in to a limited extent. They also use IABES (Intelligent Artificial Biological Entities) to interact with indigenous populations. We know that many humans have already been abducted by these very advanced tall grey creatures, who have taken genetic material and inserted implants in their victims.

"They have also had a couple of initial clandestine meetings with some heads of government. Due to their large heads and big black eyes they are openly recognised as genuine living, advanced 'alien beings', and somehow trusted.

"Very few humans have seen or realised that these 'tall greys' have less than pleasant 'masters', or queried the motives behind the promised gifts of superior and dangerous technology. The Guardians need to gain any and all information regarding the Ibearns' activities, intentions and plans."

Martina pulled a wry face. "Here I was thinking we might have some 'down time' and breathing space before the Xvars and Katons returned. I thought it must be too good to be true. Now we have to worry about those pesky 'tall greys' and the Ibearns themselves! Do we know where they're based?"

Xandra didn't really know, and advised that Solar Base and the Guardians were tracking and monitoring the Ibearns' craft and movements to determine if they had any hidden bases on Earth. He was insistent that all their Terran agents were to avoid any interaction with the Ibearns and their tall 'grey underlings'.

His instructions were quite explicit. "Remember, we are not at war with the Ibearns, even though it is an uneasy peace. You must report all contact and intelligence directly to Solar Base. I will try to keep you abreast of developments, but you must not take matters into your own hands unless you have no option and are forced to defend yourselves."

Xandra stood up. He was glad that the situation had simmered down, but could still sense Aldon's underlying resentment. Perhaps this was not the right time to tell him that the Guardians had future plans to send a delegation on a field trip to Earth.

He decided to take his leave, and visit his son before he returned to Solar Base. Victor had to be advised of the increasing security threat, and the need to carefully vet all members of the Friendship Club, especially any newcomers.

It was several days later, and Aldon and Martina were working in the control centre.

"I've had a sudden thought," she said.

"What's that?"

"Gareth is one person who must know more about our other Bases on Earth. Apparently there are protégées from many different countries attending his training courses at the Retreat – countries we are not linked with."

Aldon frowned. "You know you're right. Why didn't I think of that? He only accepts candidates after they've been vetted by the local Base Commander, and they weren't nominated by us."

Martina didn't feel positive about extracting any information from Gareth. "He's always been a bit of a 'dark horse', and ultimately answers to Xandra – not us."

Aldon wondered about the new transporter, which Solar Base recently installed at the Retreat.

"All our transporters are synchronised to connect with each other and our own Earth Base. It stands to reason that because there are international students, the transporter at the Retreat must have access to the other Bases which nominated them.

"Yes, but they are obviously three distinct systems, and not compatible with each other." Martina interrupted. "There must be some safeguard programmed in to keep the networks separate."

There was a smirk on Aldon's face. "While I'm sure you're right, and it is configured with security modifications to keep the frequencies separate, there are always secret overrides built in for emergencies. I wonder if I could go from Earth Base One to the Retreat and then use the transporter to reach Earth Base Two or Three?"

"You wouldn't – would you?" Martina said. "If you tried something like that Xandra would be furious. You could well find yourself redeployed to some remote mining outpost."

"No, I'm not that foolish," he sighed. "But in an unforeseen situation it would be worth keeping in mind."

The funfair/circus had set up on the outskirts of a large town, and several customers had already visited Camellia's fortune telling tent. She stretched out in her chair, gave her crystal ball a quick rub, and relaxed with a cup of gypsy herbal tea.

Camellia possessed not only a natural psychic capacity, but also mind reading and telepathic abilities. These were, to a certain extent, inherent traits in most Terrans. Camellia and her ancestors were exceptionally gifted due to a genetic modification program which had been initiated by the Guardians.

On her own planet Terrans like herself were highly thought of. Some often entered religious establishments, and they all lived a very comfortable life. Being a valuable asset Camellia had been overly protected and monitored at home. She had often felt stifled by the constant supervision, and longed for freedom.

Camellia had always wanted to escape the constant restrictions, and dreamed of using her unique talents to make a difference, and help bring peace in the galaxy. She saw an opportunity when she volunteered to serve on planet Earth, but unlike her Terran colleagues Camellia had never fought in the military. She was considered too important to risk in battle, and had always been restricted to intelligence and espionage duties.

Never, in her wildest dreams, had she imagined she would end up as a fortune teller, living in a caravan with a travelling funfair/circus. She always maintained her masquerade as a gypsy, complete with her tarot cards and crystal ball, but often worried that her true identity may, one day, be discovered.

It hadn't helped when the Terrans had recently used a space craft to steal the lions and tigers from the circus. The entire incident had caused much unwanted publicity.

While those poor creatures had been given their freedom in nature reserves, there were still elephants, bears, horses and monkeys imprisoned and forced to perform tricks for the paying public. She often walked or just sat with them, silently communicating. Often she had been called upon to calm the animals when they got disturbed.

Aldon and the Guardians had told her to keep a low profile, but reports of her accurate predictions and insights had led many government officials and military personnel to her tent. This helped her gain a great deal of sensitive information of value to the Terrans. She was also able to gently suggest certain courses of action to her superstitious customers.

Camellia worried that a combination of these factors might eventuate in unwanted scrutiny by the local intelligence agencies. While she enjoyed her new found freedom, sometimes Camellia felt very alone. She had little contact with the other Terrans who were incognito on Earth. Although she occasionally saw Aldon and her colleagues, all her reports were made directly to Xandra.

She had made many friends among the circus folk, who were always loyal to their own people. She often warned them when she sensed something was wrong or about to happen. On one occasion she prevented a possible disaster after advising that there was a problem with the tightrope supports. Perhaps they would help her if she faced any difficulties.

She was still reminiscing when Xandra rushed in. He appeared to be very flustered.

"What's wrong?" she asked. "It's not our normal meeting time."

Xandra caught his breath and sat down. "I'm safe for the moment, but I need to hide out for a short while. I was on a mission to speak to an informer – an ex military guy. When I neared the rendezvous I could see his car crashed at the side of the road. Sensing it could be a trap, I turned my vehicle around and headed the other way.

"I think I was followed, possibly by opposing intelligence agents. I couldn't get myself beamed out, because I may have been captured or killed while I stopped and waited for someone to get a transporter lock on me."

Camellia was worried. "Did they see your face – can they recognise you?"

Xandra shook his head. "I don't think so, but can't be sure. I ditched my rental car in a nearby street and made my way here."

Camellia looked out of her tent flap. "I can see some official looking men on the other side of the park. They seem to be heading in this direction. Make your way through the crowd and lock yourself in my caravan. I'll be there in a couple of minutes."

Xandra gave a sigh of relief when Camellia joined him.

"I can't risk putting you in danger or breaking your cover," he said.

Camellia made her way to an old trunk, and started pulling out some colourful clothing.

"Never fear! When I'm finished, not even your own mother will recognise you. Quickly – put these on!"

Xandra looked in dismay at the padded clown costume. "You must be joking! I hate clowns – used to have nightmares about them."

Camellia threw the outfit onto his lap. "There is no time to waste. Just shut up and do as you're told."

Xandra meekly obeyed her, but Camellia was still not satisfied until she had placed a comical wig on his head. Before he could protest she added insult to injury and painted his face white, his eyebrows black and his lips bright red. The finishing touch was the large red nose stuck to the middle of his face.

Xandra groaned as she stood back, admired her handiwork, and then placed a large yellow rose on his chest.

"There you are. I think that will work fine!"

Within a couple of minutes there was a loud banging on the side of her caravan.

"Open up!"

Camellia stuck her head out of the door. "What now? I'm going back to the tent in a minute. Can't a girl take a break every so often?"

One called out, "Police – looking for a dangerous fugitive!" They pushed passed her and peered into the van, hardly giving Xandra a second glance.

After the men moved on, checking the crowd and other tents and caravans, Camellia went back to her fortune telling duties. She made Xandra promise to stay put and do nothing until she returned. He was not happy, but followed her instructions and sat there silently in his bizarre clown outfit.

Xandra fidgeted around for a while, not knowing what to do until he found some tasty biscuits and delicious home-made wine. He was sure Camellia wouldn't mind if he helped himself. In next to no time he felt much calmer, and settled down to read one of the books lying on the table.

It was a couple of hours before Camellia returned from seeing the last of her customers. Her heart sank when she saw the empty wine bottle, and biscuits crumbs scattered over the table. She had kept them expressly for drugging any difficult clients or unwanted visitors!

Xandra was slurring his speech and giggling to himself. The greasepaint on his face was smudged and he was much too unstable on his feet to walk outside without attracting unwanted attention. She communicated with Aldon, who thought it rather risky to ask the larger Solar Base shuttle craft to come and recover him. If Camellia attached a locator device on Xandra, Aldon was sure if they hovered above in the smaller PVX they could get a lock onto him and beam him out of the caravan.

About an hour later Xandra disappeared from his chair, and Aldon messaged Camellia that they had successfully retrieved him. The PVX was a little cramped, so Andy piloted it back to Earth Base while Aldon kept Xandra under control.

Martina had been advised in advance of Xandra's condition, and was ordered not to comment on his unusual garb. When she saw Aldon helping a ridiculous looking clown through the door, she had to stifle her laughter and rush out of sight into the corridor.

Delta and her little grey friends ran in fright, and Ebony just stared, trying to comprehend this strange looking being. Her computer generated brain had not been processed to recognise clowns!

After she had regained her composure Martina returned.

"What are we going to do with 'Bozo'?" she asked Aldon. "Is there an antidote to whatever is affecting him?"

"I haven't got a clue what Camellia puts in her concoctions," he replied. "Perhaps we should just let him sleep it off. Do you think we should call Victor? After all he is Xandra's next-of-kin."

Martina hesitated. "We had better play it safe, and get his permission to lock his father up for the night. On the other hand, I'm not sure Xandra would be happy if his son saw him like this."

Victor arrived soon after, and his incoherent father gave him a hug.

Trying to suppress a smile Victor held Xandra at arm's length. "I always wanted to run away and join the circus. It looks like you have actually done just that! It must run in the family."

He turned to Aldon and Martina. "I agree we must confine him until he regains his senses. Let's get him out of this silly costume and clean him up, but first let me take a couple of pictures, in case he doesn't remember or believe us later."

The next morning Ebony switched off the containment field around Xandra's guest quarters, and brought him a cup of coffee.

He staggered out to the control room. "What on earth happened? I feel so groggy – like a giant hangover!"

Aldon and Martina joined him for breakfast and started to explain the events of the previous day. He was horrified when he saw the photographs that Victor had taken.

"Give me those right now! I'll be the laughing stock of the galaxy if anyone finds out or sees me in that stupid outfit. Promise you'll say nothing to anyone about the entire incident."

Later that day Xandra's craft took him back to Solar Base. Aldon and Martina were a little miffed that Xandra had been, without their knowledge, meeting with an unknown human informant.

"I regret not asking him about it while he was high on Camellia's doctored wine and cookies." Aldon grumbled. "Under normal circumstances I suppose he would say that we didn't have a 'need to know'! It's all about these increased security measures. How can we do our jobs properly when the 'powers to be' keep us in the dark?"

He continued muttering to himself as he walked across the room, opened his safe, and slipped in some duplicate photos of their boss dressed like a clown. One never knew when they may come in handy!

CHAPTER 26

Mary and Victor, along with the twins, wanted to expand the repertoire of their group the 'Associates', and started practising on a regular basis every Friday night in the bookshop/coffee lounge. Some of the protégées in the 'Friendship Club' would stay back after closing time, and join in singing with the group, which was becoming very popular.

Lucy and Fiona told Gareth how much they enjoyed belonging to the band, especially the occasional public performances and extra money.

"Be careful," he warned. "We don't want you attracting too much unwanted attention. I've heard that a couple of talent scouts have been enquiring about the 'Associates'. Although larger venues would allow you to move about more freely, it would also attract unwanted publicity and scrutiny. It is crucial that your espionage activities aren't exposed!"

Gareth decided that he must confer with Aldon and Xandra. Victor and the 'Associates' must not accept any bookings without permission. Further, they must perform in some venues which were perfectly innocent. Too many appearances at military and corporate events could also give rise to suspicion.

Everybody was pleased about invitations for the 'Associates' to appear at charity events. Even though they involved no payment, it was good to support worthy causes.

Not long after they were asked to sing at a fund raising concert for the local orphanage. It was well attended with many of the children in the audience. Everyone was in high spirits, with the Saturday night crowd enthusiastically singing along with the various performers.

When the 'Associates' came off stage for their break, one of the stagehands stopped Victor and whispered in his ear.

"There were three strange fellows mooching around your dressing room. They were well dressed in dark suits, but I didn't like the look of them. When I approached one, they scuttled out the side door and back into the audience, saying they had taken a wrong turn."

Victor gathered the others together, and although nothing seemed to have been disturbed, communicated with Aldon immediately. Martina transported down, and did a quick electronic sweep of the area.

"You are obviously in their sights, and I don't think they're talent scouts," she announced. "I've detected two monitoring devices in your dressing room, and disabled both of them. Your van seems to be clear. How long before the concert finishes?"

Mary thought it would be a couple of hours before they would be leaving, and although the three men appeared to be sitting in the audience, she was concerned these unknown intruders may be waiting outside later.

"Just leave it to me, and carry on as if nothing is wrong." Martina said. "I will get help and take a few counter measures. When you come out go to your van. I will be nearby, but be prepared to use some of your new fighting skills."

The 'Associates' were back on stage, and trying to mask their nervousness with robust singing. They couldn't help noticing the three dark haired suspects, all wearing similar black suits, were now sitting in the front row.

"Who are they, and what do they want?" Lucy whispered to Mary.

"I don't know," she muttered. "I'm just as scared as you. Keep singing, and try not to stare at them. I hope Martina comes back soon."

Martina had quickly returned to Earth Base, and after appraising Aldon of the situation, returned to the concert with Ebony. They settled down in seats at the back of the hall. Both were dressed in rather alluring modern garb, and in next to no time attracted some interest from nearby males, who tried to approach them as they left.

"Just ignore them and keep going," Martina instructed Ebony, who was loitering behind her, trying to assimilate and comprehend this new experience.

Trying to evade their insistent admirers was harder than she thought. Eventually Martina grabbed Ebony by the hand and propelled her behind a couple of stationary cars. She swiftly activated their invisibility devices, leaving a couple of disappointed followers staring into empty space.

"Where did those hot chicks go?"

"Beats me," said his friend. "They were here only a few seconds ago! No idea where they went!"

Martina and Ebony made their way over to Victor's van and waited. The three suspect men slowly walked over and began talking quietly amongst themselves.

"We don't want to draw attention to ourselves, or be noticed when we capture the four targets. We aren't sure if they are implicated in anything untoward, but the company suspects they may have been involved with placing monitoring devices in one of our establishments where they were performing."

"The boss wants them relatively unharmed," the other said. "He needs us to implant them with tracking devices, then wipe their minds before sending them on their way – none the wiser! If they have been up to no good they may lead us to their controllers."

The third opened his briefcase. "I have the sedatives and implants here. Wait until they have loaded up the van and are ready to go before we move in. Better hide behind those bushes before they come out."

Martina was trying to eavesdrop. Perhaps they would disclose whom they were working for? She could see Victor and the women exiting the venue, and quickly devised a plan.

The 'Associates' had crept out of the back door, tentatively looking around. There was no-one in sight, and most of the vehicles had left the car-park.

"I'm frightened," Lucy whispered. "Where's Martina? She promised to be here."

"And so I am," said a disembodied voice behind them. "Just keep going as if nothing is wrong. Once you have loaded the van, be prepared to take action."

Victor was just as apprehensive as everybody else, but followed Martina's instructions. As they placed the last of the equipment into the vehicle, they saw the three strangers closing in fast from behind. Suddenly one went sprawling on the ground, and Martina and Ebony materialised out of thin air.

The other two men king-hit Victor before quickly producing guns. Before they could aim at anyone the four women and Ebony pounced, sending their weapons flying out of reach. The battle was swift and brutal, with the women receiving several vicious blows before finally disabling their opponents with a mixture of martial arts and psychic warfare.

"What now?" Mary asked, looking at their three semi-conscious assailants.

Martina grinned and reached into the discarded briefcase. "I'll give them a dose of their own sedatives, and then remove them. You people go home, as if nothing has happened. We'll be in contact later."

Ebony was transported back to Base with the first male and his briefcase, and Martina followed with the other two men. Aldon and Andy were waiting.

Martina recovered her breath. "I suppose I'm not at liberty to extract a bit of physical payback?"

Aldon grinned and shook his head. He decided that they would give each of their drugged opponents a brain scan, and administer a Terran implant before wiping their immediate memories and leaving them somewhere out of the way to recover.

The procedures didn't take long, and they discovered that these were mercenaries working for both the government and one of the large 'black-op' corporations.

Martina was nursing her fast appearing bruises. "Even if it is remotely possible they remember tonight or their original mission, we have to leave them somewhere they cannot get back from in a hurry."

Aldon laughed. "Okay – I'll leave it up to you. Think of something inventive!"

The three motionless bodies were loaded into the PVX and it set off with Ebony at the controls. Martina accompanied her, and was giving the co-ordinates of their destination. She was intent on revenge, and had devised a plan which would more than compensate for the injuries she sustained in the brief battle.

When they finally came to a halt, Ebony was puzzled and turned around. "But this is not a friendly country?"

"Definitely not!" Martina smirked. "They are a very aggressive and hostile people, who distrust the other nations. Let's leave these guys in the front garden of their army headquarters. I don't think we'll be seeing them again for a long time!"

A few minutes later the three men recovered, groggily staggered to their feet, and stared at each other in total confusion. Before they could comprehend what had happened or where they were, they were surrounded by armed soldiers, shouting in a foreign language.

Martina knew that some ex-military in the West joined up with special privatised mercenary bodies for unauthorised activities. That way their government could deny any knowledge or responsibility if things went wrong. Nobody was going to come to these guys' rescue, and their captors would hardly believe any garbled tales about 'aliens'.

When Martina and Ebony returned to Earth Base Aldon was a little perplexed.

"You left them where?? When I told you to be inventive – I wasn't thinking of anything quite so drastic. Oh well - I suppose I did leave it up to you," he said, and quietly reminded himself not to get on Martina's bad side in the future.

Fiona was driving the van back to the bookshop, with the others in the back. Lucy was still shaking, while Mary cradled the concussed Victor in her arms.

"Will he be alright, or should we take him to hospital?" Fiona asked.

"Let's get him back home, and take it from there," Mary decided.

They settled Victor down on the lounge, and a very concerned Mishka jumped up beside him, gently patting his face. He seemed to regain his composure and announced that he didn't think his jaw was broken, after all. A stiff drink would surely make him feel better.

Mary sent the twins home, and helped Victor up to bed.

She was still concerned. "Are you sure you'll be okay?"

He gave a little smile. "I have you and Mishka fussing over me. Except for a headache and a few bruises I'll be fine in the morning. Thank God we don't open the bookshop on weekends."

The next morning she took him breakfast in bed, and was glad to see him much improved.

"We must all act as if nothing has happened," he said. "Whoever those guys were, some of their colleagues may come looking for them."

Mary agreed. "Fiona and Lucy have made their normal Sunday trip to the farm, and I will take the day off work tomorrow. That way the bookshop will be open as usual."

Victor was grateful he had Mary to rely on. "I'm so sorry you and the others were put in harms' way."

"It was what we all agreed to, and were trained for," she replied. "Except for my bruises, it was really quite exciting. I suppose someone will come to debrief us."

As soon as Mary went back downstairs Victor quickly transported to Earth Base. Martina was looking a little frazzled, and Aldon rather concerned.

He turned to greet Victor. "Have you recovered enough to go to the country today? That way no-one will notice anything untoward, and Gareth can discreetly come and talk to you."

Victor agreed, and beamed straight back to his room, before Mary missed him. She was a little surprised when he insisted on driving up to the farm.

"We must all follow our normal routines," he said.

The twins raced out to meet them. "Gareth's here, and he has this miraculous gadget which heals the bruises. You should try it."

"I wouldn't mind," Mary muttered as she limped in the front door.

Gareth's little device was indeed magical. Mary and Victor just had to place it over the injured areas and press the trigger.

"I want one of those!" Mary exclaimed as she stretched her limbs in sheer relief.

Gareth laughed and motioned them all to gather in the lounge room. They had to get down to business!

Everyone wanted to know if those three violent men would come looking for them?

Gareth grinned. "I don't think they will be back for a long time – if ever. Martina left them in the clutches of a hostile foreign power who thinks they are spies."

Victor was still concerned. "What about whoever sent them?"

"The car park didn't have any security cameras and we moved their vehicle to a spot a couple of hundred miles away. There is little evidence they were ever at the concert.

"As for their employers, they only suspected you were up to no good. It seems they weren't really sure. If any strangers or suspicious persons come into the bookshop, just carry on as if nothing is wrong."

Lucy was a little dejected. "What about our performances? I really enjoyed being on stage."

Gareth got up, ready to leave. "Don't worry Lucy, there are plenty of opportunities for fame and fortune. Xandra has indicated that the 'Associates' will still have a role to play, but there is to be a change in direction. He is going to come and talk to you all about his new plans."

Xandra arrived at the bookshop a few days later, and spoke to everybody upstairs. He didn't want to be seen by anyone lurking around outside.

He had decided that the 'Associates' would attract less suspicion if they were a well known group rather than only performing at small functions with military and similar connections.

"From now onwards most of your bookings will be at public events. It will only be the very rare occasion where you will be called upon to be engaged in covert activities.

"To assist in your promotion and exposure as a trendy vocal group, Gareth will arrange a recording contract for you. Olivia, from Solar Base has sent some original songs for you to learn."

Lucy and Fiona couldn't contain their excitement. They were going to be famous! Xandra couldn't help smiling at their childlike enthusiasm. He had one more task for them.

"Earth could be in for some rocky times in the near future. We need to attract and recruit more protégées. This song I am giving to you now must not be recorded. You must learn and rehearse it where no one else can hear – perhaps on the farm. Once you have committed it to memory you must destroy this copy so it doesn't fall into the wrong hands. You are only allowed to sing it publicly when specifically instructed to."

Everybody was a little mystified. What was so special about this piece of music?

Xandra explained. "This melody has been programmed into the subconscious of our protégées. When they hear it they will recall their past extra terrestrial experiences and be prompted to make contact. It also triggers their enhanced ability to access cosmic quantum awareness. We call it 'the knowing'. I will tell you more when the time comes."

Xandra departed, leaving everyone in a highly elated mood.

Lucy and Fiona were cavorting around the room. "A recording contract – we can't believe it! Come on Victor! We have to open a bottle of wine to celebrate."

As they made their way downstairs Victor and Mary were both having some misgivings. Who knew where this may lead? It could well mean the end of their relatively peaceful life at the bookshop and on the farm.

Gareth had been arranging for the 'Associates' to be recognised as a normal vocal group within the local musical society. After they had performed at a few neighbourhood venues, he advised them that they had been entered in an important music festival.

"If you win an award, it will make you eligible to enter a nationwide contest, which may facilitate the record contract I have been telling you about."

They started expanding upon and practising their repertoire, both in the bookshop after closing, and at the farm on weekends. Tony also had a good voice, and often joined in. Everybody wanted him to become a permanent addition to the 'Associates', but Gareth put his foot down.

"Tony is one of our most valuable undercover scientists. While the boss has allowed his unconventional 'ménage à trois' relationship with Fiona and Lucy, we don't want a publicly visible connection between him and the 'Associates' or the Friendship Club."

Tony would like to have been closer to the twins while they were performing, and attracting unwanted attention from other males. Instead he had to settle with staying in the background as their unofficial coach and mentor.

The group required new outfits, and also a synchronized choreographed routine to accompany their singing. Tony co-ordinated the costume fittings and supervised their twice weekly dance lessons.

Mary was relaxing after a strenuous practice session. "Tony, you can sing and dance just as well, if not better than the rest of us. It's not fair that you can't be involved in our live performances."

"I think I would really enjoy that, but I must follow orders," he said.

Victor had a mischievous grin on his face. "Never mind, maybe one night I might get sick - then they'll have to let you go on in my place! Just make sure you have a disguise on hand. A false moustache and glasses should suffice."

The weekend of the Music Festival was fast approaching, and the 'Associates' had been polishing up their act. The competition involved elimination rounds, and they had three songs prepared.

All around the main stage, the local parkland was filled with tents and carnival attractions. Camellia's circus and fairground were situated to the one side.

Every contestant was to perform on the Saturday afternoon and evening. The semi-final was Sunday morning, followed up by the final in the afternoon.

Gareth was pleased they were scheduled for six o'clock in the evening. "That way the audience will probably have had a few to drink, and will be in a happy, receptive mood. Any later and the event might be marred by the occasional drunk who may start trouble in the crowd."

They were ready to go on stage when Gareth gave them a last 'once over'.

"Everybody ready to rock and roll?"

Victor was a bundle of nerves, his inherent shyness coming to the fore. Fiona and Lucy were definitely over excited, and Mary was trying to remain calm. Her throat felt dry as she saw the large number of spectators outside. They had never performed in front of so many people before.

Gareth was proven right. The audience were all in good spirits, and cheered and danced along to the 'Associates' routine. A couple of hours later, a small altercation in the crowd turned nasty, and the last two acts were cancelled.

At the end of the night the panel of judges announced their decision. The 'Associates' had made it to the semi-finals the next day.

That night the twins stayed in the spare bedroom above the bookshop. They had to be up early on Sunday morning, and prepare for what could be one of the most important days of their lives.

Victor was glad for the privacy of his en-suite. The women had taken over his bathroom, and there was much giggling and laughter as makeup was applied and hairdos perfected.

Victor complimented them on their appearance when they eventually emerged ready to go.

"We had to look 'just right'. The media will be there today." Mary explained.

Bob had brought Dave and Christie to lend moral support, and Gareth was sure he saw Aldon nipping into Camellia's tent.

The semi-finals tested everybody's commitment. There were local TV cameras and newspaper reporters camped at the side of the stage.

Fiona glanced at the other contestants. "Some of them are very talented. I'm surprised we've made it this far."

Victor tended to agree with her. "We can only do our best, and have the added benefit of Olivia's compositions. Gareth said he is saving the best of the three for last. That is if we reach the final."

The 'Associates' were trying to suppress their wavering confidence as they climbed on stage for their second song. It went down well with both the audience and the judges, and they could hardly believe it when told they had been selected to sing in the final that afternoon.

Many people gathered around them during the break, including the journalists, who were trying to interview both the finalist acts in advance. They had deadlines to meet that evening. Victor was becoming increasingly nervous, and eventually insisted that they all needed to retire to the performers' tent for lunch.

Gareth arrived and realised his vocal group were becoming increasingly uptight. He took them into a quiet corner and ordered them to meditate and practise all they had learned at the Retreat.

"Remember, you don't have to win to get your record contract. That's guaranteed by now."

They shut their eyes, relaxed and continued rhythmic slow breathing. All the tension that they had accumulated slowly melted away.

When they returned to the stage there was tumultuous applause. Fiona and Lucy were so overwhelmed they weren't even sure they could sing anymore.

Sensing their growing stage fright, Mary turned to her colleagues. "Remember, we don't have to win. Our record contract is already assured. Let's just pretend we are back at home, and sing for ourselves."

Their final song was not the lively tune the crowd had expected. Instead it was a haunting love ballad – one of Olivia's best compositions. The audience was mesmerised, and fell into silence as if in a trance. At the end, when the last strains of the melody faded away, there was thunderous applause and everyone rose to their feet.

The 'Associates' could hardly believe they had won. The media were crowded around, all asking questions at once. Victor was trying to fend off inquiries about the composer of their songs and music, when a disturbance on the other side of the park was a welcome distraction.

One of the camera men had grabbed the reporter by her arm. "Come quick! A bear at the circus has escaped from its enclosure."

Camellia and Aldon had been sitting quietly and talking when they heard the ruckus outside. They ran out of the tent, and bumped into Bob who was frantically calling to Christie.

She was walking between the pavilions alongside a very large bear, and they were now stopped next to a cake stall.

The bear was quite peaceful and seemed to be silently communing with the little girl, whose hand was gently resting on its side. A policeman approached with his gun drawn, but was hindered by Camellia who insisted he stop.

"I know this animal. Let me try before you start shooting with all these people around."

When she reached them she could hear that Christie was singing to her new friend.

"Where are you two going? 'Brutus' is not supposed to be out of his cage." Camellia said. "He may get into trouble."

Christie smiled with childhood innocence. "He told me he was lonely, and would like to go for a walk and get something nice to eat. He said he likes cakes. Can we get him some?"

The stall holder was cowering behind the stand. "Take whatever he wants!"

Camellia grabbed a plate of cream buns off the table. "I think 'Brutus' will like these."

The bear was becoming agitated by the noise of the gathering throng, and Camellia hoped her telepathic powers would calm the animal down while she led him and Christie to safety.

"Well, you keep singing, and we'll take him back to his home. He can eat his goodies there."

There were huge sighs of relief when Camellia left 'Brutus' back in his enclosure, enjoying his treats.

Bob clutched his daughter in his arms. "Don't you ever do that again," he gasped.

"But Daddy, he was a nice bear, and we were talking to each other!"

Bob turned around to thank Camellia, but she had blended back into the crowd before the media had a chance to identify her. He thought it was just as wise for him and the children to also disappear whilst all the attention was on photographing 'Brutus' with his cream buns.

Gareth and Aldon began to realise that Christie was exceptionally gifted, however she didn't yet have the maturity to understand or control her latent powers.

"Her telepathic abilities are amazing for one so young." Gareth said. "We may have to commence her education much earlier than usual."

CHAPTER 27

The sky was an angry colour, with lightning flashes and clouds swirling in all directions. Sarah looked out of the surgery window and called to John. One of the horses, frightened by the loud thunder, had broken free from the stable and was loose in the field.

Max, their little grey 'worker', seemed to be the only one who could hear her. Sarah, being an android, only followed her programming in what she may or may not do. Thunderstorms had not been encoded into her data design as something to be avoided.

She knew her duties were to assist with the animals. She decided to venture out the front door herself, and take the horse back to shelter.

She was halfway across the field when she heard John calling her to come back. As she turned to obey his command, there was a massive flash and the ground shook as a lightning bolt hit a nearby tree.

Sarah was thrown into the air, and one of the tree branches landed on top of her crumpled body which was lying motionless on the grass.

"Sarah – Sarah!" called out a distressed John. He ran through the wind and rain and carried her lifeless form back to the waiting room.

Aldon waited until the storm had passed before he answered John's frantic calls for help, and came down to the veterinary clinic. He also tried to revive Sarah, but she was totally unresponsive to any of their efforts.

"I'm afraid this one's done for," he declared. "We'll have to get you a replacement as soon as possible."

John was trying to fight back the tears. "No! She must be repaired," he demanded.

Aldon gave John a quizzical look. "She was only an android, and we shouldn't get attached to them. After all, one is as good as another."

John knew he couldn't admit his relationship with Sarah. "She has specialised knowledge and skills. It would take me far too long to train a new one."

Aldon promised he would see what could be done, and took Sarah back with him to Earth Base. Xandra was due to visit in a couple of days. Perhaps the technicians on Solar Base could repair her.

In the meantime, John told everyone that Sarah had gone on holidays for a few weeks. While Max, his little grey worker, could assist with the actual surgical operations, he needed a temporary receptionist for the waiting room. He had to find someone, preferably a young girl, who would not suspect the true nature of his premises.

John had never liked humans very much. When he was a child his Terran father, who was a skilled doctor, was also deployed incognito to Earth. Contrary to normal guidelines he had brought his wife and son with him.

John was sent to the neighbourhood school, but soon discovered that dark skinned families, like his own, were discriminated against by the mainly white community. He was constantly ostracised by the other children and subjected to cruel racial taunts. His only true companion was Snoopy, his pet dog. Animals seemed to be the only creatures who accepted him and offered unconditional love.

When he was a teenager he was befriended by a local girl, and after a while, became infatuated with her. Once her father discovered the budding relationship, he stormed down to John's home, and ordered him never to see his daughter again.

After a tirade of racial abuse, he turned around and shot Snoopy.

"That's what will happen to the rest of you **** dogs if I see you near my daughter again!"

John, broken hearted and close to a mental breakdown, found solace in the surgery's medical supplies. When his father discovered that John was developing a morphine habit, he asked the Terrans to terminate his assignment on the planet, and they left soon after.

All these years later John was reluctantly back on Earth. The painful memories still lingered and he avoided interacting with the general community.

Chris Cuthbert, a friendly dark skinned local farmer, had a teenage daughter. He was concerned that Clare, just out of school, was having problems securing a job. John thought he would offer Clare a few weeks employment until Sarah was returned.

Clare settled into the receptionist job fairly well. John ensured Max remained in the securely locked basement during opening hours. Boof was allowed to sit in the corner of the waiting room. Whilst he could keep watch on everything that was said and happened, John told him not to talk to anyone, especially Clare.

John knew that Clare had also experienced racial discrimination in the past, and went out of his way to make her feel welcome and of importance. He later realised that this was perhaps not such a good idea after all.

She kept hanging around after closing time, trying to access the locked basement. Boof reported that she had also been telling people that she was at the surgery permanently and Sarah wasn't coming back. The last straw was when her younger brother dropped by, and indicated that he was under the impression Clare and John were involved in a romantic relationship.

John called Chris Cuthbert, and explained that Clare had obviously misunderstood his kindness, and there was no love affair! Chris seemed to understand, saying his daughter was a disturbed young teenager, often prone to flights of fantasy.

They both agreed that it would be better if Clare ceased working at the surgery. John gave him Clare's final wages, and Chris would tell her not to come back.

The next morning a tearful Clare was on the doorstep. "My father is trying to split us up – I won't let him!"

When John tried to explain there was no 'us', she became angry and traumatised. "But I love you – and I know you love me. You can't just lead me on and then send me away! If Sarah is coming back – then where is she?"

When John was unable to answer with any certainty, Clare stomped off. She was consumed with fury. How dare he reject her! A plan of revenge formulated in her mind.

An anxious John contacted Aldon. "Has Sarah been repaired yet? When are they sending her back? I'm having problems here!"

Aldon promised to try and speed things up, and later confirmed that Sarah had been successfully restored with 'added extras'. Xandra would return her on a transport craft as soon as possible.

For the next week Ebony filled in as receptionist. Every so often she would notice Clare loitering outside and peering through the window. John thought it wise to just ignore her. Perhaps Chris could reign in his troubled daughter.

It was early Monday morning when Ebony arrived to help open the surgery for business. "Sarah is back at Earth Base," she said. "After Aldon and Martina have finished briefing and testing her, she will arrive in the transporter."

John's elation was cut short when two local detectives walked in the door. He noticed that their police dog was not with them.

"Hello guys. Where's 'Prince' today?"

They looked uneasy, and after hesitating one said, "I'm sorry John. We're not here about the dog. We have to query Sarah's whereabouts. We've had an anonymous report that something bad has happened to her, and she is either locked or buried in the basement."

As John stared in disbelief Ebony slipped outside and messaged Earth Base.

"Sarah went on her holidays. She is due back anytime now – perhaps even today. Who on Earth would tell such a lie?"

The other detective looked uncomfortable. "It's not personal. We just have to investigate all the complaints we receive. Perhaps we can look in your basement?"

John was getting agitated. He could not let them see the advanced Terran equipment hidden down there. What if they stumbled upon Max or the transporter?

"Not without a warrant! I have sick animals down there – some in quarantine. Certain sterilization procedures will have to be undertaken first! Further, I would like to know who has made these unfounded and malicious allegations."

The officers looked a bit taken aback. Then one said, "I'm sorry John, we do understand, but will return in a couple of hours with a warrant."

Ebony came back in, and said that only one policeman had driven away, leaving the other watching the surgery from behind the bushes. About half an hour later Martina beamed down with Sarah.

John gave a gasp of relief. "I am just so glad to see you!"

He detailed the situation, and Sarah was instructed to say she had been on holiday. Martina returned to Earth Base with Ebony, and asked

John to come and see her later. They needed to discuss the enhancements that had been made to Sarah.

When the detectives returned, Sarah was sitting behind the reception desk. "Good morning, gentlemen! I believe you have been looking for me?"

They stared in astonishment, and one whispered, "I never saw her come in!"

After making their apologies the two police officers left, determined to never again believe that little liar Clare Cuthbert.

John was delighted to have Sarah back in both the surgery and his bed! After dinner, as requested, he visited Aldon and Martina.

"That was a close call today," Martina remarked. "Sarah came back just in time. We certainly don't want any humans rummaging around in the basement!"

"What modifications did Solar Base make to Sarah?" John asked. "I can't quite explain it, but somehow she seems different."

"She is," said Aldon. "As you know androids like Sarah are essentially organic computers, with a limited lifespan. She had a complete overhaul and was upgraded and given the ability to understand human emotions.

"This is a reasonably new innovation. While the boffins did not introduce any hormones into her system, they are not sure to what extent she will experience emotions herself. We need you to advise of any noticeable change in her behaviour."

When John got back to the surgery, he found Sarah waiting in his bedroom. The sex was as good as ever – if not better. He was disappointed that she still didn't display any signs of physical enjoyment. Everything was just as mechanical as before.

He realised that having physical relations with his android was strictly forbidden. Her recent upgrading increased the possibility of his degenerate behaviour being discovered. He resolved to change his ways, and seek gratification elsewhere.

The next morning Aldon was deep in reflection. He stared across at Martina and asked her what she thought about this new idea of giving androids an understanding of emotions, especially if they may also be able to experience them.

"I'm not so sure it is a good idea," she said. "There is such a vast array of 'feelings' - everything from love to hate, happiness to despair, and pride to shame. That's not to mention anger, jealousy, fear, greed and a multitude of other responses dependent upon the situation and the individual person.

"From the time of birth both humans and Terrans are taught to recognise and appropriately respond to these emotions. Androids do not have the same beneficial background of education and experience. Who knows how they may react in any given circumstance."

Both Boof and Sarah had been programmed to communicate telepathically, and the Terrans instructed Boof to report on any change in her state of mind. He would stretch out next to the reception desk and tune into her thoughts every so often.

Sarah could not understand why John no longer invited her into his bedroom. Every night, once her duties were over, he sent her back to her capsule in the basement, saying she needed the android regeneration emissions.

Up until now John never realised how much he had relied on Sarah's companionship. He missed having her close every night. He tried to compensate by slipping out and visiting the local brothel, but it was an empty satisfaction. Sometimes, to his great shame, he could not even rise to the occasion.

He was lonely and craved a meaningful relationship with someone of the opposite sex. While there were some attractive women amongst his clients, he was wary of involvement with anyone local. Clare's unwanted obsession with him had been of great concern.

Boof didn't fully appreciate the situation, but he noticed Sarah displayed some resentment when John payed special attention to attractive ladies who brought their pets to the surgery. She seemed to be comparing their make-up and colourful clothes with her own drab uniform and appearance. He saw her looking through the fashion pages in the waiting room magazines; but why was she making a mental note of various department stores?

Sarah, with her limited comprehension, was convinced that her boss was not satisfied with her. Perhaps if she looked more attractive like those human females? She knew that she had no money to buy clothes and could not understand how that dreadful Clare got paid wages and she didn't. John had just laughed and told Sarah that androids didn't need any money.

Once a week the surgery was closed for the afternoon, and John would go into town. Sarah saw this as her chance to sneak out without anyone knowing. She locked Boof in the basement, then borrowed John's leather jacket to cover her uniform. As an after-thought she grabbed a belt with an invisibility box attached.

She sped unseen across the fields, and was soon in the local city centre. There was a wonderful sense of freedom as she walked along the pavement staring at all the beautiful outfits in the shop windows. She was used to following instructions, and paused before entering one department store. After all, she hadn't actually been told not to! Better to remain in invisible mode!

She cautiously walked inside, and found the clothes and cosmetics which had been featured in the magazines. Overcome by temptation she slipped the items under the leather jacket or into the pockets. The security guard monitoring the shop's cameras thought he must have had too much to drink at lunchtime. How could the stock just float off the racks and disappear into thin air?

He looked again and saw an indistinct figure in the aisle. It was fading in and out of view. Sarah realised her invisibility device was running out of power. She should have checked it was fully charged before she left the surgery! Better leave as quickly as possible. As she passed through the front doors the security detectors sounded a warning. The staff looked around but could see no-one. It must have only been a malfunction.

She managed to get back to the surgery unnoticed. The thought of getting caught was her first experience of fear. She didn't like it!

She hid her ill-gotten gains, put the invisibility box onto recharge, and let Boof out of the basement. Her sense of relief was also a new emotion to be experienced.

The next morning the local newspaper featured a story about the 'Dombles' ghost striking again. The old building was reputed to be haunted – here was the proof! Luckily for Sarah the hazy photograph did not show any distinct facial features. She was safe!

It took a couple of days for Sarah to master the art of applying cosmetics. One morning she slid behind the reception desk to the sound of wolf whistles from the waiting clients. John stuck his head around his office door and did a double-take.

What with the heavy make-up and puffed up hair, he could hardly recognise her. Sarah did indeed look very appealing. She was wearing a very tight red dress, and matching high heel shoes which caused her to walk with an unstable wobble.

"What the hell....." he exclaimed. "Sarah, go back downstairs and change into your uniform."

She went into the corridor and said, "You don't like me anymore. You're always nice to the ladies who dress like this."

She was only an android, and John didn't really know why he was feeling sorry for her. He tried reassuring Sarah that he did indeed like her, but she had to wear her vet nurse uniform when on duty.

That evening he demanded to know where the new clothes had come from. He explained that stealing was not allowed, and was pleased she had told the truth and displayed some indications of remorse and conscience.

She promised not to go out without permission again. John could hardly return anything to 'Dombles'. Better to let the unidentified 'ghost' take the blame. He didn't want any repeat performance, so he agreed that Sarah could 'get dressed up' in private after hours.

He realised that giving androids 'emotions' made them seem like genuine living beings. Sarah was no longer just an advanced robot. She was turning into a 'person' and he was developing feelings for her childlike innocence and devotion.

He retired to his lonesome bedroom, and a wave of isolation and depression swept over him. He remembered his childhood, and the comfort and escape the morphine had provided. Surely one tablet now wouldn't hurt.

As time went by John and Sarah became closer. Although he had to resist the temptation to invite her back into his bed, he began to realise that, having no hormone supplementation, sex was meaningless to her.

Sarah was happy that John paid her more attention, and they often spent the evening just talking or tending to the animals in their care. Due to her new ability to understand and experience emotions she ceased being just an android, an underling, and fulfilled the role of friend and companion.

The Guardians had wanted to know if Sarah's experimental upgrade had altered her programmed intelligence into a more personal 'self awareness'. John was beginning to think it had. He was not about to tell them – they may take her away.

CHAPTER 28

Paul was quite content to impersonate a priest on the island. He had firm religious beliefs of his own and never liked hurting or killing anyone. The Terran military had decided he was much better suited to this current posting than serving on a battleship or any other section of the armed forces.

He had a wife and family on his own planet, and was determined to remain faithful to them. This deployment would not last forever, and then he could return home. He was only a normal male, and although his celibacy was difficult at times, he remained resolute.

Some of the native girls were quite wayward, and often tried to seduce him. He was glad he had Jacquita by his side to ward off the unwanted advances. Michael and Angela up the hill had also provided much welcome companionship, which helped alleviate his occasional slide into depression and loneliness.

Tending to a flock of superstitious villagers was no easy task. Often they came rushing into the church at night, insisting that there were 'ghosts' or demons' nearby.

He was sometimes very unethical, and used Terran technology to manifest holographic 'angels' and other deities to chase away the evil spirits. He had quite a bag of 'magic' tricks to make his gullible congregation feel protected.

He had become very attached to these simple people, and wanted to help them as much as possible. They believed in him and he knew that irreparable damage would occur if they discovered his true identity. They may totally reject him, or even advise the local authorities. It would also be detrimental if they started to regard him as a god.

He and Jacquita always kept the door to the crypt firmly locked. They didn't want any curious parishioner sighting or fiddling with the array of technological equipment.

Angela's pregnancy was starting to become noticeable, and Michael was very protective. He constantly hovered over her at work, and urged her to go on leave until their baby was born. In fact, he wanted her to retire permanently. He was making enough money for both of them, and they also had Terran funding to fall back on.

"But I will be bored sitting at home all day," she argued.

He was determined. "Why not stay on the island? Tuan will do all the housework and look after you."

"I will be alone at night!"

"No you won't." Michael reassured her. "I will use the transporter to come over nearly every evening. Paul and Jacquita are just down the hill. I'll have an alarm system connected from the villa to the church."

Angela had run out of all her excuses, except for a reluctance to use the transporter. She didn't want anything affecting her baby. Aldon came to the rescue and agreed to take her there in the PVX. Within a couple of weeks she was living semi-permanently in Michael's tropical hide-away.

Tuan catered to her every wish, but after a while, relaxing under a palm tree on the patio became monotonous. She started walking down to the village, getting to know the natives. Often she would stop to have some refreshments with Paul and Jacquita, who spent most of their day teaching the local kids, and dispensing essential medicine and care from a small first aid/hospital facility.

She really enjoyed interacting with the children, who had little chance of a meaningful future without education. Although they were happy, they knew nothing of the world outside of their secluded island.

Jacquita had brought in a lot of basic equipment for the school, but her nuns in the little convent were not well educated. It was a difficult task coaching all the students who were at varying levels of literacy. Angela began helping with the lessons, and before too long became a permanent assistant in the classroom.

Michael encouraged her new found interest. "I'm so proud of you."

Their island formed part of a small archipelago nation. Jacquita wanted to take the children for a trip to the main town, several hundred miles across the sea. Most of them had only been out, an insignificant distance from shore, in their families' fishing boats. The thought of such an exciting excursion was more than enough incentive to encourage their students to attend the makeshift school.

The local ferry captain had accepted a charter for a three day return trip, and agreed to take some of the children and two teachers. The Bishop had arranged for them to stay a couple of nights with the nuns at the town's convent.

Jacquita begged a hesitant Angela to accompany them. "What if something went wrong? I don't want to be alone with all those kids. There are no storms forecast, so you shouldn't get seasick! Further, I will make sure we have communicator devices to call both Paul and Earth Base for help in an emergency."

Against her better judgement, and with Michael's encouragement, Angela reluctantly agreed. She had everything she needed on the island, but it would be nice to get back to civilisation and look around the shops.

Early one morning Angela and Jacquita, (fully disguised in her nun's habit), followed a dozen excited youngsters up the gangplank, and soon they were on their way. As anticipated, the sea was very calm, and they reached their destination at dusk.

They were met by the local priest and nuns, and soon the children were settled down for the night. After dinner, Jacquita said the next day the nuns from the convent were taking the children on an outing while she called into the local hospital for medical provisions.

"Well, you can't carry them all back yourself." Angela said. "I'll come with you."

They were about to leave with their new supplies when Angela noticed a naval officer exiting a nearby ward. "I wonder what he's doing here?"

"Let's go and see," Jacquita murmured.

There were only a few natives in the beds, but up at the end was a heavily curtained area. As they approached a nurse said that this patient wasn't allowed any visitors, but she supposed that didn't apply to someone from the church.

They were shocked to see a badly burned man, swathed in bandages.

He seemed to be very traumatised, and for a few minutes Jacquita spoke to him in his own language. Every so often Angela could hear the words 'demons' and 'devil'.

"Let's get out of here", Jacquita whispered. "I'll tell you later."

As they walked back to the convent, Jacquita detailed the man's account of how, while he was fishing in the lagoon, a huge silver object had risen from the water. His boat capsized and his friends had rescued him. He had burns to eighty percent of his body.

He came from the very last in the chain of islands, and for several years his people had been menaced by 'demons'. They had big grey heads and black eyes, and lived somewhere up in one of the nearby mountains.

Sometimes, at night, they would come into the village and abduct the young women, who would later give birth to strange looking babies. He had also mentioned 'the devil', an ugly man with fearful powers, and a weapon he could point at people to render them paralysed.

Jacquita needed to make a formal report to Paul and Earth Base as soon as possible. There was little chance to make any detailed contact with the children constantly present. She would have to wait until they returned to their own little island.

The next day the ferry trip back was without incident. As soon as the kids had returned to their homes, Jacquita insisted Paul hear her account without delay.

Once he realised the gravity of the situation, he messaged Aldon, who beamed down to join them.

"It sounds like the Ibearns to me," he said. "While it must be investigated, it's above my security level. This is a matter for Xandra, Zadoc and the Guardians."

Once back at Earth Base, he sent Ebony in the PVX to the island. She left it below the cliff and climbed the tunnel to Michael's villa. Ignoring the infatuated grin on Tuan's face, she told Angela to get her bag, and be ready to return to the city.

"It's no use arguing. Aldon is insistent, and I'm just doing his bidding. It's bad enough that you won't use the transporter, so just get a move on."

Ebony wouldn't have dared to speak to a Terran like that, but Angela was just a human after all.

While she wasn't impressed, Angela decided that she may as well do as she was told. She wondered what was going on, but realised Aldon must have his reasons for her sudden departure.

Several days later Xandra and Zadoc arrived for a preliminary conference. They had already arranged for some very covert surveillance, and determined that the island in question held some very rare properties and minerals. It was possible there was some kind of facility with entries from the cliff face and adjacent sea bed.

"The Guardians suspect that this might be an illegal Ibearn mining operation." Zadoc said. "The fact that a naval officer had most probably been talking to the injured native is of some concern. The Xvars and Katons were bad enough. We don't want any of the human agencies or governments forming new alliances with the Ibearns, if they haven't done so already."

Aldon interrupted. "But what can we do? I thought we were not allowed to attack the Ibearns?"

Zadoc sighed. "That's correct. We have to be devious. Perhaps we can persuade our human allies to hound them out for us."

Paul expressed his concern that, in the light of the new information, perhaps his own natives' reports of 'ghosts' and 'demons' in the graveyard and the surrounding area had more credence. Could they have encountered the Ibearns or their underlings?

"Yes, that is another worry," Zadoc said. "It is only logical that they will not contain themselves to one island. Sooner or later they will want to expand their operations and sphere of influence to neighbouring areas."

Paul and Jacquita were ordered to monitor the surrounding region, and a few days later detected a small naval contingent heading towards the Ibearns' island. Were they going to investigate the injured native's report?

Xandra returned immediately, and outlined the proposed course of action. "We have to do something about the Ibearns right now, but we cannot be seen or even suspected of attacking them. The Guardians do not want to provoke any more galactic hostilities."

Paul was relieved that all the Earth based Terrans were to remain, free from suspicion, in their various control centres. Solar Base was arriving with some military personnel disguised as human naval officers. They mounted a limited assault on the Ibearns' mountain stronghold, restricted their weapons to conventional explosives, and withdrew just before the genuine naval vessels arrived.

The ruse had the desired effect. The Ibearns, thinking they were still under attack by a human military force, came out with their weapons blazing.

The navy personnel retreated to their boats and alerted their command centre. A few days later several large battleships arrived off the coast and fired upon the rocky entrance to Ibearns' hidden base.

The natives fled into hiding as several waves of marines landed on the shore and charged up the mountain. The Ibearns' mine had already been blown wide open. It had not been fortified to withstand such an intensive onslaught, as none was expected. Many of the occupants had been killed or destroyed in the initial bombardment. The battle was noisy and bloody, with casualties strewn everywhere.

Suddenly there was a loud humming sound, which nearly deafened all on the ground. Two enormous silver craft rose out of the sea and sped upwards into the sky.

"My God, my wife will never believe this," gasped one of the soldiers, as he stared at the partially dismembered corpse of an obvious alien entity.

"Your wife will never hear of this," growled his commanding officer. "No-one will. Understood?"

The naval team remained for a few days, and were astounded at the extent of the Ibearns' mining operations. Several metal mechanical robots were quickly disabled and taken away for analysis by military intelligence and their technicians.

The troops didn't leave until they had removed all evidence of the battle and the aliens' presence. As a final gesture they sealed the entrance to the Ibearns' mine, and warned the locals of a fate worse than death if they ever breathed a word about the incident.

Xandra called a debrief meeting with his Terran officers. Paul was concerned about the well being of the indigenous population. Although the island had been sealed off, some reports had filtered in. While none of the natives had been harmed, they had been confined to their homes. The village chief had insisted that their unusual looking hybrid children were to be hidden in case they attracted unwanted attention.

Xandra was delighted. "Mission accomplished, and we seem to have escaped any blame or involvement! Unfortunately I don't think that was their only intrusion on this planet!"

Jacquita spoke up. She was still concerned. "We're forgetting about our own island. One or two in the community have mentioned seeing the 'demons' in the last couple of days. The Ibearns made a very hasty escape. We should check that none of their tall grey 'underlings' have been left behind."

Xandra looked nervous. "Good point. I hadn't thought of that. I have a detector which can identify and track their electronic emissions. We can even get the local natives to assist us capture their 'evil spirits'!"

Michael, who had been sitting quietly at the side, joined in the conversation. "Count me in - they must be captured. I cannot allow Angela to come back until I am sure they are all gone."

The men of the village were eager to assist Michael and Father Paul to rid their island of these nasty entities which had often haunted the local area and graveyard.

A small contingent of Terran soldiers arrived at Earth Base, and they were not impressed when told to wear monk's robes over their uniforms.

"The natives must think that the church is cleansing their village." Aldon explained.

Xandra and the soldiers landed out of sight, and crept down the hill to join the others. It didn't take long before there was shouting and a scuffle from the mangroves. A 'tall grey' ran out and was immediately tackled by several island men, who promptly sat on top of him to hold him down.

They were extremely angry, hitting and kicking the wretched creature. Xandra and his troops raced over and disabled their captive before carrying him away.

"We want these entities in one piece for interrogation," he grumbled. "My sensor says there is one more around here. If it knows what happened to its buddy, then we may have to use a ray gun from a distance."

They tracked the remaining 'alien' through the bushes to the shoreline. Before it could make its escape into the water, Xandra fired his ray-gun and it crumpled into a lifeless heap.

"Unfortunately I've disrupted its electronic circuits. Hopefully it can be repaired and we can extract vital information and intelligence. Now to get out of here without the natives seeing our space ship!"

Paul gathered his flock together. Everyone must go to the church to give thanks for the monks annihilating these wicked intruders.

The next weekend Angela and Michael relaxed on the patio. Tuan was very attentive. His boss was a hero, and had helped Father Paul get rid of the evil ones who had troubled their island.

CHAPTER 29

Xandra looked up from his desk as Leandro entered the room.

"Hello stranger! Congratulations on completing your second Earth deployment. Looking forward to going home at long last?"

Leandro shuffled about for a couple of minutes.

Xandra was puzzled. "Will you sit down, you're making me nervous. What's the problem?"

Leandro shrank into his chair and put his head in his hands. "I have to return to Earth – to Aldon's area - and put something right."

Xandra was worried. He didn't think it was a good idea for Leandro to go back to that part of the world. He had snatched Granny from the nursing home, right under the noses of an intelligence organization who were curious about her talk of 'alien friends'.

"Do you think that would be prudent? You are possibly on a secret 'watch list'. Our anonymity has precedence to anything personal. Is there something I can do?"

Leandro shook his head. "No, you don't understand. Many years ago, during my first mission, I did something terrible. I cannot leave until I at least try to make amends."

Leandro had been an exemplary Terran agent, with a commendable record of service. Xandra had never received any complaints about him.

"Perhaps you'd better tell me. I cannot give you permission to go back without good reason."

Leandro was trembling as he started to explain. "When I first arrived on Earth, there was a different commander on Earth Base One. My task was to liaise with our human protégées and helpers. Granny was one of them, and for a short while I even stayed with Granny and her daughter."

Xandra interrupted. "You mean Vera, Mary's mother?"

"Yes, and I became very fond of her. It was more than that. I was young and away from home. Relationships with human women were strictly forbidden. My attraction turned into infatuation. I was obsessed with desire for Vera.

"I knew she took the dog for a walk in the park. One night I borrowed a small craft and followed her. When she was alone, with no-one in sight, I beamed her up. Our encounter was consensual and passionate, to say the least!

"Afterwards I was so scared I would be in trouble, and knowing I'd done the wrong thing, I wiped her memory and left her back in the park! I've lived with the guilt ever since. Soon after, the Guardians reassigned me to another division in the galaxy. I had no idea that Vera was pregnant."

Xandra stared at him in disbelief. "You do realise that you must be Mary's father? Your actions have also contributed to years of trauma and grief to Vera and the whole family."

Leandro hung his head in shame. "That's why I had to go back and rescue Granny. Not only had she reared Mary, I had always promised that we would come back for her one day."

Xandra felt some sympathy for Leandro. "I do know how it feels to be a secret father, but my situation was slightly different to yours. Victor's mother and I were married, but she died in childbirth. You seduced Mary's mother, then abandoned her!

"I'm not sure that you can 'put things right'. Vera is very angry with the whole world. After you rescued Granny, she threw Mary out of the house. My son Victor took her in. She has brought him out of his loneliness and depression, and I've become quite fond of her. Perhaps she has a right to know the truth, but I'm not sure how she will react."

Xandra decided that the best course of action was to first consult with Granny.

She was astounded when Leandro admitted to what he had done. "It was you!! I can hardly believe it! How could you?"

"I loved her, and it was only the once. I would never have left if I'd known she was pregnant."

Granny thought that her granddaughter, Mary, should know that she was conceived out of love and lust, rather than a random rape one night in the park.

"I am not so sure about Vera. My daughter is very bitter and hostile. She has always considered herself a victim. How do you intend to make it up to her?"

Leandro took a deep breath. "I will do the honourable thing, tell her the truth and marry her – even if it means staying on Earth."

Granny sadly shook her head. "Don't you realise that all this happened well over thirty years ago? Terrans don't age as quickly as humans. You never saw each other when you were by my side at the nursing home. My daughter is not a young woman any more. With the passing of time, she has matured. In fact, even though Vera has some genetic enhancement, she now looks older than you."

Leandro said that didn't matter. He was determined to be accountable for his actions and 'set things right'. Xandra tended to concur with Granny. Too much time had passed. While Mary needed to know who her father was, any attempt to get Leandro and Vera to reconnect could prove disastrous.

Victor and Mary were surprised when late one evening Xandra arrived with Leandro at the bookshop.

The conversation was awkward as Leandro stumbled through his guilty confession. At first Mary said nothing. She was stunned and completely overwhelmed by the revelation.

"I don't know what to say! I do believe that you loved my mother, and wouldn't have left if you had known she was pregnant, but have you any idea the misery your actions have caused? Her status as an unmarried mother caused her great anguish over the years, and I always knew I was an unwanted child."

A crestfallen Leandro rose from his chair, and Xandra thought that this was not going well.

Mary wiped a tear from her face. "No – don't go. You can't blame me for being a little angry, but I do understand the circumstances all those years ago. This has been totally unexpected, and it will take me some time to adjust. I suddenly have a father that I want to get to know."

Everybody relaxed, and Xandra remembered how Victor was never told, until recently, that he was his father. It was so important for him to bond with his son. Leandro and Mary had the same need to form a relationship with each other. Mary also agreed that it would be unwise for her mentally unstable mother to know the truth.

Xandra decided he would allow Leandro to stay for the time being. There were conditions. He was to keep out of public view, and mustn't try to contact Vera.

Except for giving a sanitised briefing to Aldon, Martina and Gareth, Xandra would keep Leandro's secret. He would justify his remaining at Solar Base by appointing him a temporary aide.

Victor announced that this called for a celebratory drink, and produced a bottle of champagne. He was smiling and looked over at Mary.

"Well, beside our friendship, we now have something else in common."

"What's that?"

"We're both half Terran, half human!"

Xandra paused. "Do you realise that having Terran fathers means that you also have Terran nationality and citizenship? I will make a creative amendment of the records to validate Mary's status."

Mary had often been confused by Terran visitors seemingly arriving 'out of nowhere' in the bookshop. She was now allowed to know about the transporter in the shower in Victor's room, but was not permitted to use it unless accompanied by a Terran, or in an absolute emergency.

She often worried about her mother, who had locked herself away from the world, and was becoming increasingly paranoid and antagonistic.

It had been a long while since Mary had seen Vera, and she told Victor she was going over to make another attempt to reunite with her.

He had some misgivings. "Do you think that's wise?"

She sighed. "I still love her, and it's so sad that she will be all alone on her Birthday. I must keep trying, especially now I understand more about her tragic situation in the past. She and Leandro obviously had feelings for each other. Don't worry - I promise not to mention him."

Mary arrived at the house and rang the bell. While she could hear some movement inside, and the curtains parted for a moment, her mother didn't answer the door. Mary left a gift on the step and walked away.

Several months had gone by when Mary received a telephone call from one of the neighbours.

"I'm sorry to bother you, but it's about Vera, your mother. Recently she has been behaving very strangely, and the police came to my home last night. They were asking questions about her."

Mary's heart sank. "Why? What is she supposed to have done?"

"I don't really know, but she was screaming abuse at some people in the street. Later their cars were covered in paint and graffiti– something about aliens!"

Mary gave a reassurance that she would look into the matter without delay. Victor, seeing Mary's despair, enlisted Aldon's aid. A quick check of police records showed that Vera was due to appear in court in two weeks time.

She was being charged with malicious damage, but that was not the worst of it. The authorities had secretly convinced her public defence lawyer to plead 'not guilty' on mental grounds. They were going to apply for an order to commit Vera to an institution, where they could hold her hostage and probe her mind and forgotten memories.

"This must not happen," declared Aldon. "We need to contact Xandra and devise a rescue plan."

The day of the hearing arrived. Vera was waiting with the lawyer in the vestibule when Mary walked up. "I've come to support you, Mum."

"I don't want your help," Vera muttered.

Her lawyer was not expecting any complications. "You heard the lady," he growled, and shoved Mary away.

Ebony was standing right behind and moved between the lawyer and his client. "Leave her alone you big bully!"

In the ensuing argument Mary propelled Vera into the ladies room and locked the door. They were both astonished to see a near naked female standing before them.

"But that's me!" Vera exclaimed, staring at her android 'double'. Before she could call out, Mary had zapped her mother into unconsciousness, and hurriedly helped the android dress in her clothes. They quickly put a locator device on Vera so Aldon could beam her out.

Mary and the imposter joined the irate lawyer, who pushed them into the courtroom. His unusually quiet client suddenly kicked him in the groin, and made a run for the door. She raced down the street with Mary and a couple of law enforcement officers in hot pursuit.

The android had reached a nearby river, and was teetering on the railing of the bridge. One of the policemen pulled his gun. A shot rang out and Vera's 'double' fell over the edge into the waters below.

Mary gave an excellent performance as she played her part of the distraught and angry relative. A police launch searched the river, and came to the conclusion that the body must have been washed out to sea.

Mary was later allowed a rare visit to Earth Base, where her mother was sedated in the guest quarters. The containment field had been activated as an extra precaution.

Xandra assured her that the android had been retrieved, and he had come to take Vera back to Solar Base, where she would receive excellent treatment. She would also be able to be with Granny.

When Mary asked about Leandro everybody was doubtful of any future relationship. The consensus of opinion was that it would do more harm than good.

Xandra smiled gently, and patted Mary on the shoulder. "I'm afraid not everything has a happy ending, my dear. Over the years your mother has become a very negative person. It is too late to go back in time and alter the past."

There was a subsequent inquest, and the Coroner proclaimed Vera to be presumed dead. The authorities tried to keep the incident away from the media. They did not want people asking why a woman was shot when she had been running away from a trivial accusation of malicious graffiti.

Mary was informed that as the next of kin she had inherited Vera's house and property.

"What shall I do?" she asked Victor. "After all Mum isn't dead!"

Victor shrugged. "Well, she won't ever be coming back to Earth. If you really think about it the house was originally Granny's, and she is also alive and well on Solar Base. Your mother only owned it because the court thought Granny perished in the nursing home fire."

Mary was still unsure until a few days later, when Victor took her into his office and produced his portable monitor. Granny appeared on screen and assured Mary that Vera was doing as well as could be expected on Solar Base

"She is still angry and confused, but receiving the best of care. The experts here are treating her psychological problems, and given time, are hoping for a partial or complete recovery.

"Leandro is still trying to reconnect with her. She hasn't been very receptive, so I doubt if there will be any meaningful reconciliation. In the meantime all the property etc. is yours to do with as you wish."

After the transmission ended Victor sat down with Mary. "What now? You can't just leave the house empty for vandals or squatters. Are you going back to live there?"

He was used to her being around, and silently hoping she would stay with him at the bookshop.

"No," she said. "I want to put that part of my life behind me."

Victor was relieved. "You may as well just settle the estate, and sell the house. What are you going to do with the money?"

Mary paused for a moment. "I suppose I should buy my own place. I have imposed on your hospitality for far too long."

This was not what Victor wanted to hear. After reassuring her that he enjoyed her company, and would be very lonely if she left, he made a suggestion.

"Why don't you pay off what is left of the mortgage on the farm? The twins have always wanted to buy their own apartment, rather than renting. If you also reimbursed their share of the property, they would have a sizable deposit for the first place of their own."

At first, Fiona and Lucy were hesitant. While they loved their shared country property, there was no security in having to pay rent on their city residence.

"But the farm will always be 'ours'." Mary assured them. "This way it will be a 'win-win' situation all around. What you used to pay in rent can now be used to reduce any mortgage on your own place."

Lucy giggled. "I like the idea. After all, we should be able to pay off any loan fairly quickly."

"How so?" Victor asked.

"Well, we are starting to get paid for our 'Associate's' performances, and hopefully some later record deals. On top of that, we can use some of our special abilities at the Casino!"

Victor was immediately concerned. "You must stay away from the Casino. Perhaps the occasional visit to the race track – but that's all!"

It took a few weeks to sort out everything in the house. They all pitched in, with van loads of possessions being moved to the bookshop and farm. A small container of Vera's personal effects made their way to her permanent home on Solar Base.

It didn't take long for the property to be sold, and Gareth, along with Tony, accompanied Fiona and Lucy on their search for a suitable city apartment.

They soon found one in an ideal location, close to the bookshop, and within walking distance to the law firm where the twins worked. It was on the top floor of a three storey building, with patio access to the roof.

"It's away from a potential ground floor break-in and easier for an emergency extraction." Gareth commented.

There was some indecision and hesitation from Lucy in particular.

Tony was getting frustrated. "Oh, for heaven's sake stop banging on about the colour scheme. Gareth and I will redecorate it whatever colours you want."

"Thanks for that." Gareth growled. "I'm a senior Terran military officer – not a bloody painter! Well...okay, if it gets them to agree."

The contracts were signed, and before the twins moved in, everybody gathered for the day to give the apartment a complete makeover. There was great merriment and camaraderie before they finally finished and retired to the bookshop for a late supper.

Mary looked at Victor and giggled. "You've got paint smeared on your face."

"And there's some in your hair," he teased.

Gareth rose to leave. "I think we all need to go home and clean up. I actually enjoyed today, and Fiona and Lucy seem happy with the results. Now I hope we can, without any further ado, get them settled into their new residence!"

CHAPTER 30

Angela loved living in a tropical paradise, and was reluctant to return to an urban lifestyle. Before he left for work, Michael put his foot down. He was concerned that Angela was experiencing her first pregnancy in her late thirties.

"Our baby is due in two weeks. I want you back in town – close to the hospital and specialist," he said. "You must have your things ready to leave in the morning. Martina will come in the PVX to take you back, and I will be waiting to drive you home."

Angela set off down the hill to the church. She was going to miss Paul, Jacquita and all the children. Next time she saw them she would be a mother herself.

She entered the church, and stepped over a young nun who was washing the floor. Suddenly she slipped on the wet surface, and before she could regain her balance fell forward onto the hard flagstones.

"Missy Angela – Missy Angela!" called the novice. "I'm sorry – not dry yet!"

Angela didn't move and Paul and Jacquita came running in. As they bent over her, she opened her eyes. "I'm okay – just a bit winded."

They helped her to her feet and she let out a gasp of pain. "Oh my God – the baby!"

Paul picked her up and carried her to a bed in their small hospital. Angela was still making small moans of apparent distress.

"I think she's going into labour," Jacquita whispered. "Try to get Michael back as soon as possible."

As soon as he arrived Michael rushed into the little medical centre. "We must get her back to town and specialised care."

"It's too late for that," snapped a flustered Jacquita. "It would be more dangerous to move her. You forget that we have advanced Terran medical equipment in the crypt, and we can always call on John. His medical expertise and surgical abilities aren't just restricted to animals.

"Anyway, village women have babies here all the time. My nuns and I know what we're doing. This is women's business – just get out from underfoot!"

Jacquita and the nuns had pushed Michael out of the infirmary. He was pacing the floor in the corridor and every so often could hear Angela's cries of anguish. It sounded like the birth was imminent.

"She is suffering! I must be by her side," he said.

Paul tried to pull him away from the door. "Come and have a drink. I must tell you of the local custom before you go charging back in!"

Paul handed him a glass of his extra strong communal wine. "In this community, when a woman is giving birth, she hangs onto her husband's 'old boy'. By the time the baby has arrived he is in more pain than she is. I am sure the females of the village initiated this tradition. The poor bloke is incapable of bothering her for the next couple of weeks."

"But Angela wouldn't do that to me.....would she?"

Paul just grinned and Michael gulped down his drink. He must be brave. After all Angela seemed to be in agony giving birth to his child. He hoped she hadn't heard of the natives' custom!

He took a deep breath, and as he made his way back to be by her side, he heard the faint cry of his new born baby.

A few minutes later Jacquita opened the door and Michael rushed in with Paul just behind. Angela was worn out, but as she looked down at the little bundle in her arms, there was a tender smile on her face.

"It's all over and I'm fine Michael. Say 'hello' to your son."

Michael tentatively held this tiny being, and was consumed by a sense of love and tenderness he had never experienced before.

"We have already decided to call him Matthew," he murmured. "He is perfect; my dark hair and his mother's eyes."

"This might have happened for the best," Jacquita said. "His blood test shows he has your Terran blood group, which may have raised questions in the city hospital. Because he was born here, Paul will sign the usual local birth certificate. Matthew will have the advantage of dual citizenship, from both Angela and the island."

"That's just on Earth," insisted Michael. "Don't forget his claim to Terran parentage."

Dusk was falling and Jacquita was preparing a meal for Angela. "Michael – go home! Angela will be hospitalised for a couple of days – just to be on the safe side. You can come back and visit in the morning."

When he arrived the next day, he stopped in bewilderment. Her room was already overflowing with tropical flowers and fruit. He was clutching a small bunch of flowers picked from their garden. They suddenly seemed rather paltry by comparison.

"Don't look so surprised," Jacquita said. "All the villagers love Angela, and are very grateful that she has been helping educate their children."

A short while later Martina arrived with a tiny gold Terran amulet for Matthew. Michael left her to sit with Angela and nurse the baby. He joined Paul in the church.

"I see Martina's arrived," Paul observed. "I believe Chantelle is coming this afternoon, and Camellia is talking about getting here somehow. Earth Base may be in trouble. All our female officers are getting 'clucky'!"

Aldon also visited with his congratulations and a rather unusual present. It was a miniature invisibility unit. "You never know when he might need this. Better to be safe than sorry!"

He smiled at the serenely happy Angela, and took the baby in his arms. When Aldon gazed down at the sleeping infant he recalled cradling his own offspring, just after birth. He thought of his lost family and the tears welled up in his eyes.

Michael had never seen his boss like this before, and then remembered that Aldon's wife and children had been killed, some years ago, in an Xvar attack.

That night Martina, sensing Aldon was lost in sad memories, put her arm around him. You aren't alone. Michael and all of us Terrans on Earth are your family now. We care about each other."

Aldon buried his head in her shoulder and sobbed. Martina gently held him, and realised he had probably never been able to release the pent up grief and emotion before.

Gareth was feeling a little despondent. Everybody else had plans for Christmas. Even though the Terrans themselves didn't follow any earthly religion, they joined in the festivities and respected the beliefs of their human contemporaries.

Gareth had been raised in a military family. His father was a high ranking Terran officer, and he was expected to follow in his footsteps. His time in an armed forces academy was devoid of emotional attachments. As a result he found it difficult to relate to others, and was frequently considered to be cold and officious. In fact, he often craved the closeness his Terran colleagues and other humans seemed to enjoy.

His parents had been very controlling to the extent they had even chosen a suitable bride for him. Gareth needed a quick escape, and enlisted for this mission to Earth.

The laboratory was closing over the holidays, and he was enjoying a drink with his colleagues at the cafeteria's Christmas party.

"Michael and Angela are going to the island for a few days. What are your plans?" Tony asked.

Gareth mumbled something unintelligible.

Tony stared at him with a sudden realisation. "You haven't got anywhere to go, have you?"

Gareth looked embarrassed and shook his head. "I might take some presents to Earth Base, but that's about all."

Tony finished his whiskey. "Then it's decided. You're coming to the countryside with the rest of us. There is no way we will let you spend Christmas alone."

The bookshop was closed for the holidays, and Mary and Victor had finished packing, ready to go to the farm. Gareth was out of sight in the back of the van, and Tony and the twins were to follow in their car.

That night their cottage was a buzz of activity as the decorations were put in place. The rustle of paper could be heard from several bedrooms as last minute presents were secretly wrapped and left under the Xmas tree.

Christmas morning arrived, and it seemed like any other day at Earth Base. John had messaged that he would be coming over soon, so Aldon told Ebony to make something extra for breakfast.

Before he left the vet surgery, John noticed Sarah seemed a little dejected. She liked this human tradition of giving gifts, and some of the clients had brought her chocolates. It was disappointing, as being an android, she couldn't eat them!

"Never mind," John said. "I have brought you a present I know you'll like."

She opened the velvet box and took out a matching set of crystal earrings, pendant and ring. Her face broke into a smile. They were nicer than any of the jewellery she had seen in the fashion magazines.

He realised that he was probably being silly and sentimental to even think of giving Boof and Max anything for Christmas. After all, they also were only forms of glorified artificial intelligence. Still, it made him feel good to give Boof a doggy toy and Max a new soft bed.

He arrived at Earth Base shortly after, and put several boxes of chocolates down on the table.

"Oh yummy!" Martina said as she grabbed a handful. "Peppermint creams – my favourites."

They were halfway through their meal when Andy announced an incoming craft, and Xandra and Leandro suddenly appeared.

They sat down and Xandra said, "I know our visit is unexpected but this is one of the most important festival days on Earth. For the first time we are going to spend it with our children, Mary and Victor. If hostilities with the Xvars and Katons get out of hand, it may be a while before we get another chance.

"Before we beam down we want to share in your meal, and also honour the human custom of giving a token of friendship at this time of the year."

Xandra pointed to the shuttle bay, and Aldon could see a new PVX parked there. Martina was thrilled, and Aldon and John raced out to inspect the new vehicle. Several bottles of wine were consumed before a slightly tipsy Xandra and Leandro, clutching clumsily wrapped presents, made their way to the farm.

Gareth had woken to the sounds of laughter and shrieks of delight coming from the lounge room. He went out to see a mess of torn wrapping paper strewn everywhere.

"Happy Christmas, Gareth!"

Suddenly several colourful parcels were placed in his arms. There was a lump in his throat as he sat down to open them. He had never experienced such a warm sense of 'belonging' and companionship before.

Xandra and Leandro arrived at the same time as Bob and the children. After Dave and Christie had opened their presents, they went outside to see the animals. Bob took the opportunity to tell everyone of an unfortunate episode that had happened at the school a few days earlier.

"There was a Christmas celebration for the end of term, and all the children took a plate of food and some drinks. I didn't know Christie had also taken a tin of cookies which she found in the pantry. They had been left there by Ida McAffrey, who used to live in the house."

"Oh, my goodness!" Lucy giggled. "I hope they weren't the ones she laced with illegal herbs and stuff."

"Indeed they were," Bob groaned. "When I got there all the kids were as high as kites and running amok!"

"What about their teacher?" Gareth asked.

"At first I couldn't see Miss Smith, but then I found her. She was stoned out of her mind, and under a desk with one of the fathers who was dressed as Santa Claus. I couldn't resist taking a quick photo – may come in useful later!

"I grabbed Dave and Christie, and took what was left of the offending cookies away with me as well. I thought it wasn't wise to leave any evidence behind!"

Everyone was still laughing when they sat down to an enormous spread of food and goodies.

Tony apologised. "Sorry it is all vegetarian. There is no way the girls would allow one of their chickens or ducks to end up on the dinner plate."

After the leisurely meal everyone relaxed and sang along to the music Victor played on his keyboard. It had been a perfect day – one which would remain in the memories for a long time to come.

It was also Christmas on the island, and for Paul and Jacquita it was the most important time of the year. The natives decorated the church in anticipation of the big event. One of the traditional highlights was a tableau of the holy birth. As they attended midnight mass, the villagers would stop at the manger and leave offerings for the church and convent.

The stable was lovingly recreated, complete with a donkey and several goats. Some of the children would be dressed as angels, shepherds and the three wise men. This year Paul knew who he was going to enlist as Mary, Joseph and the baby Jesus.

It took some persuasion to get Michael to agree, but come Christmas Eve, he and Angela were dressed in the appropriate costumes. Matthew was wrapped in a shawl, and happily gurgling to himself in the wooden crib.

As the locals arrived, smiling at the baby and leaving their gifts, a sudden realisation swept over Michael.

"We don't have just a tropical hide-away," he whispered to Angela. "We're part of a community. It's such a good feeling, something I haven't experienced for a very long time."

Paul and Michael had devised one extra 'magic' trick to keep the congregation faithful. Suddenly beautiful music filled the air, and two holographic angels appeared in the sky above. It had the desired effect and the natives fell to their knees in awe and devotion.

Paul was correct in his observation that the birth of Matthew had aroused the maternal instincts in their female Terran officers. Jacquita was constantly visiting to fuss over mother and child, and Chantelle arrived on the island on Christmas Day.

She had brought expensive gifts, and sat nursing the baby for quite some time. Angela noticed she was very quiet. There was sadness in her eyes as she gazed down at Matthew, who was sleeping in her arms.

"Have you ever thought of settling down and having a family of your own?" Angela asked.

Chantelle seemed a little dejected. "I know I'm not getting any younger, and should look to forming a permanent relationship with someone suitable. That's hardly possible given my current deployment."

Before she returned to the city, Chantelle went down to the little church to catch-up with Paul and Jacquita. After sharing Christmas lunch with the nuns in the convent, they retired to the garden to enjoy a glass of wine.

"You are so fortunate Paul, to have a family of your own," Chantelle murmured.

He pointed out that they were on his home planet, a great distance away. He hadn't seen them for a long time. Silently he was hopeful that his wife still loved him and had remained faithful.

Chantelle was thoughtful for a while, and then took another sip from her drink. "I have begun to realise that having nice possessions and an extravagant lifestyle can become meaningless and unfulfilling. A family with children of one's own is more important. I don't think that is going to happen as long as I'm in my present role on Earth."

Jacquita gave a rueful smile. "We're both in a similar position. I'm not sure which is worse – posing as a nun or a high class escort. Either way, there is little chance of attracting a suitable husband!"

CHAPTER 31

It was a sunny afternoon when Bob and the children went for their weekend walk. Christie had insisted they stop off at the farm to see Mary and the twins. She wanted to check on one of the hens who had become broody, constantly sitting on a clutch of eggs.

"Oh look!" she squealed in delight. "There are tiny little fluffy chicks cuddling up under her feathers."

Bob pulled her hand back. "Don't touch them or Mummy will peck you really hard!"

He looked up. There was no-one around. The sound of music was coming from the house. They made their way to the back door and Bob was overcome with a sense of déjà-vu. Where had he heard that song before?

While the children were excitedly telling Mary that the eggs had hatched, Bob was staring into space.

"Dad – Dad!" Christie was tugging at his sleeve.

"Are you okay?" Mary asked. "You seemed to be miles away."

"That music, and your singing.....I've heard it somewhere before."

She gave him a curious look, and invited them in. As they settled down to some cold drinks, Mary went over to Gareth and whispered in his ear.

Gareth smiled and looked over at Bob. "You have heard that melody before. Let's play it for you again."

As the familiar tune flowed from their voices and instruments, Bob felt as if he was in a trance. Memories came flooding back. He recalled the 'visitors' and spaceship of his childhood. There were other children as well, and they would play games with funny little grey 'friends' who had big heads and large black eyes.

He could still feel the same joy he had experienced as they tossed magical coloured balls into the air. Gareth gently shook his shoulder and brought him back to reality.

"You remember now, don't you?"

Bob gulped, and nervously nodded his head. "I didn't want to. Denial was easier. That way I didn't have to accept that what happened to me probably affects my kids as well."

They both looked over at Christie, who was humming the same tune to herself.

"Yes, for the children's sake, I think it's time to embrace your calling - what went before and what is to come. You need to stay for dinner, and we can talk."

After the meal Dave and Christie were sent into the lounge to play a video game, while the others sat down in the kitchen.

They told Bob about the Refuge, and how a short stay there would be of enormous assistance to him in understanding his heritage and paranormal abilities. He could also discover the special gifts the Terrans had endowed upon his family, and learn how to control and use them responsibly.

The twins were quite passionate when recommending the Retreat and its benefits. "We learned so much!"

Lucy gave him a sly look. "Lots of ladies go there. Maybe you'll meet someone nice."

"What about my kids while I'm gone?" Bob asked.

"They can stay with their grandparents," Gareth said. "After all, many years ago they were also part of our program. They still are. With each generation our protégées become more significant and aware.

"Because your species are biologically almost identical to that of the Terrans, some families, like yours, are gradually being upgraded. The Guardians regard it as essential if we are to preserve your people and your planet."

Bob was a little perplexed. "Preserve them from what?"

Gareth frowned. "Initially from themselves, but also from other dangerous alien species out there in the galaxy. Somehow humans have this naive belief that everything extra terrestrial must be good and have their best interests at heart. Nothing could be further from the truth."

A few weeks later Gareth advised Bob that he was about to conduct another training course at the Retreat. He was to arrange for a couple of weeks off work, and be ready to join him in the PVX when, at the appointed time, it landed near the farm.

Bob went across town to talk to his parents. For the very first time both his mother and father confirmed their interaction with the Terrans.

"I wish we had been able to have the benefit of somewhere like the Retreat," his mother said.

"Yes," his father confirmed, "you must go. Dave and Christie can stay with us. We will understand any unusual behaviour. What's more, we can protect them from Amy if she ever comes calling!"

Bob was pleased with the timing of his anticipated journey to the Retreat. When he advised that the children were going to their grandparents for a fortnight, their teacher expressed some disappointment.

"What a pity," she said. "There are some people coming from the government to test the pupils' intelligence levels. Dave and Christie will miss it, and I'm sure they would have scored very well."

Bob certainly didn't want a repetition of the inquisitive officials who frequented their previous school.

"No," he said. "They are still recovering from the family breakup, and their mother's mental illness. I don't want them subjected to any unnecessary scrutiny."

Miss Smith walked away, quietly determined to try again at a later date. Genius level kiddies were always a credit to a school, and often attracted extra funding.

Dave and Christie were very excited about going to stay with their grandparents.

"What about the animals?" Dave asked.

Mary assured him one of the neighbours had agreed to take over their feeding and care duties during the time they would be away.

She gave them both some extra money. "You have both been so good and conscientious looking after the farm during the week, I think you deserve some 'holiday pay', just like normal employees."

Bob drove them to the welcoming arms of his mother, and then went home to finish packing his case and wait for Gareth.

As he walked across the field to the PVX he experienced a mixture of trepidation and excitement. Gareth had picked up a couple of other students along the way, and they all seemed to 'connect' immediately. Bob was exhilarated as their craft zoomed through the night sky and headed for the Retreat.

This was the start of a new phase in his life.

Bob settled into his log cabin, along with three other male students. They immediately set out to explore their surrounds, and agreed that every morning they would go swimming in the lake together – no matter how cold the water.

At the first communal breakfast Bob noticed that many of those present were not speaking English, and were definitely from other parts of the world. Gareth assured them that by the end of the fortnight's training they would be able to understand each other, if only telepathically.

Bob was amazed that, even after the initial meditation session, how many memories had come flooding back. It was as if someone had flicked a switch in his mind, and he started to recall the details of his early childhood interactions with the Terrans.

The next morning, when he and the others went down to the lake for their first swim, he could see one of the women struggling a short way from shore.

Without a second thought he plunged into the icy water, and helped her to safety. She lay on the sand, gasping for air.

"Thank you for saving me. I got a cramp and thought I was going to drown."

Bob was surprised. "You speak English?"

"Yes, I've been bilingual since I was young. My parents insisted. They always wanted to leave our country and migrate to one of the western nations. Unfortunately, when I was a teenager, they were killed trying to escape, and I was sent to live with an Aunt."

Her name was Rebecca, and she suddenly seemed conscious about her lack of clothing. Bob could see was shivering. She hadn't packed a swimsuit, and was only dressed in scanty underwear.

He wrapped his towel around her, and helped her back to the cabins.

Bob felt drawn to this attractive woman. On the pretext of checking that she had fully recovered, he sat down next to her at lunchtime. They just chatted for a while, and then began to share their life stories. Rebecca showed a great interest in his children, and understood his concerns about the Terran influence on Dave and Christie.

Within a couple of days Bob and Rebecca were spending most of their time together. At first they couldn't understand the sense of familiarity they seemed to share. Following their 'mindfulness' training and the recovery of lost childhood memories they both recalled playing together on a visiting Terran spaceship.

Bob stared at Rebecca. "Fancy that! It's like we were meant to be together."

She blushed. Her shyness prevented her admitting, even to herself, that she was developing strong feelings for him. The spark of sexual attraction was growing by the day.

Neither had intended the relationship to get out of hand. In another week they would return to their own countries. Better treat it as a harmless holiday friendship.

Everything changed on an evening walk along the shore of the lake. Bob couldn't resist giving Rebecca a kiss, and before they knew it their mutual loneliness and longing came to the fore. The beach was quiet and secluded enough for their mutual passion to take over.

Late one night, after Gareth had retired for the evening, Bob was returning to his cabin. He was startled to see a strange man leave the Retreat's control centre and make his way into a nearby grove of trees.

He was met by Gabriel, who was from one of the Asian countries. They spoke in another language, but Bob didn't need to understand what they were saying. Things were getting very hot and steamy. He felt embarrassed and retreated before he was a voyeur to some very serious love making.

The next day, when they sat down to the communal breakfast, Bob asked Gabriel about the whereabouts her boyfriend. He couldn't see him in any of the outdoor areas.

She gave a shy smile. "You must have seen him arrive last night. His name is Richard, and he is an important Terran officer, so nobody was supposed to know he was visiting me. We are in love, and when he goes back to his home planet he will take me with him."

During the morning break Bob drew Gareth to the side, and told him what he had witnessed the previous night, and Gabriel's later confession. Gareth didn't have to say anything. The furious expression on his face said it all.

The next night, when he and Rebecca went for their usual stroll, Bob could hear shouting coming from the control cabin. Otto and Tibor were hiding outside.

Bob tried to eavesdrop, and whilst he couldn't understand exactly what was being said, he gathered that Gareth had caught that Richard fellow coming from the transporter. Obviously he had no right to be there.

The following morning Bob was on the shore of the lake, drying himself with his towel after his daily swim. One of his foreign classmates, Sylvia, sat down beside him.

"I'm so glad you and Rebecca have paired up," she said. "Will you keep in contact with each other after you go home?"

Bob said that he hoped to continue the relationship, and asked Sylvia if she had someone special in her life. Maybe she had also met a potential soul mate during the last fortnight?

Sylvia blushed and whispered in his ear. "Don't tell anyone, because it's a secret. Back home I have been seeing a senior Terran officer for quite some time. His name is Richard, and we are going to get married. He will take me with him when he returns to his own planet."

Bob was greatly troubled by the confidences the two women had individually shared. He didn't want to betray Sylvia's trust by saying anything else to Gareth. He decided to ask the Retreat control centre if he could make an urgent private communication to his own Friendship Club.

Thinking it was something personal, or regarding the children, Gareth granted his request. As soon as he was connected to Victor, Bob detailed his concerns about this previously unknown Terran officer called Richard.

"Say nothing to anyone, and leave it with me." Victor cautioned. He was going to speak to his father about this.

Xandra had already heard from Gareth about Richard's unauthorised use of the transporter to the Retreat. When he learned about the relationships with at least two of the female protégées, he was fuming.

"Richard has a reputation for disrespecting the opposite sex. Several years ago he was a senior officer on Zarcon Base, and he persisted in having affairs with innocent recruits. His wife was all too trusting, and when she eventually discovered the truth she divorced him.

"I've heard many tales of his romantic exploits, and he has often openly bragged about his many conquests. I never wanted him here. Hopefully this latest episode means I can get him reassigned to some other part of the galaxy – the further away the better."

Xandra was not about to tell Victor that in the past, Chantelle was one of Richard's victims. When she was a junior officer, under Richard's Zarcon command, he had started a romantic relationship with her. She had believed his promises of a future life together. After their liaisons were discovered he accused her of seducing him, and she was banished from the Base.

Xandra was also unable to reveal that, against his wishes, Solar Base had appointed Richard to the position of Commander of Earth Base Two. As such, he was specifically forbidden to have any liaisons with their human protégées.

Zadoc needed to be informed of Richard's latest exploits, especially his serious breach of protocol by using the restricted transporter and entering the Retreat, which was in Earth Base One's domain.

A few days later a transport ship arrived unexpectedly at Earth Base Two. Richard pushed passed his android, swaggered to the shuttle bay, and greeted his senior officers like long lost friends.

"We aren't here on a social visit!" Xandra snarled angrily.

Zadoc and Xandra outlined the possible charges against Richard. He maintained a somewhat amiable response to their questions and accusations. There was an excuse for everything.

"Those protégées are just silly women who are infatuated and fantasising about me," he declared. At that moment his Terran assistant entered the room.

"Tell them, Carol, how you and I are in love. We are getting married after our posting here is over."

Carol smiled and nodded, and Zadoc felt his blood pressure rising.

"Still up to your old tricks, Richard? That's what you told Chantelle on Zarcon Base, wasn't it?"

Richard gave a nervous laugh. "You don't believe anything that little slut says, do you?"

Zadoc held Xandra back as he clenched his fist and lurched forward towards Richard.

"And what about breaching regulations and using the transporter to visit the Retreat?"

Richard feigned regret and claimed it was only once to deliver an important message to one of his protégées.

Carol looked a little taken aback. "No – you went there nearly every night over the past week. Come to think of it, you've always had an excuse to go out at night, and often at odd times during the day."

Richard didn't take kindly to criticism or rejection and his mask of camaraderie started to drop. He stood up and glared at everybody around him.

"Come on fellows. These out of the way postings need to have some side benefits!"

"You know that doesn't include open slather on every gullible female in sight!' Xandra said.

Zadoc was now also resisting the urge to whack Richard in the mouth. An enraged Carol beat him to it and lashed out with an office chair, knocking him to the floor.

"You lousy two-timing bastard - to think that I was stupid enough to believe you!"

Richard staggered to his feet, somewhat the worse for wear. Once he had regained his balance he decided that a remorseful apology might resolve the situation.

"I am truly sorry if I may have done the wrong thing. It won't happen again."

"You can bet on that," Zadoc growled. "You could have compromised our whole operation here. You're relieved of duty, and Carol will take over as Commander. You have five minutes to collect your possessions before we take you back to Solar Base with us. There are several charges you will have to answer to."

Richard realised this could eventuate in his being exiled, in disgrace, to the obscurity of some remote outpost. The very thought filled him with dread. What to do? Perhaps his human allies would give him refuge.

Instead of going to his quarters, Richard raced straight to the operations centre, and messaged the local military headquarters. He had already started downloading files when Xandra raced in and disengaged the communication facilities.

"Right now womanising is the least of your worries. This is possible treason."

Richard turned and made a run for the back of the Base. Zadoc called out, a little too late, for the android to disable the transporter. Richard jumped in, and activated the transmission as it was shutting down. Everyone watched in dismay as his image faded in and out.

Carol started to cry and they realised it was too late to recover him. Richard was no more – his particles had not reached their destination and were scattered into the void.

Xandra and Zadoc were in a race to minimise the potential harm their treacherous officer had caused. The Base had to be closed down, and temporarily sealed up. Before an urgent evacuation they needed to discover how much information Richard had relayed to his human counterparts. All Earth Base Two agents and scientists had to be warned, and possibly extracted.

The android traced Richard's illicit communication and launched a cyber attack to erase all digital information from the destination processor.

Zadoc was concerned. "It appears they have already received details about this Base and some of our agents. I'm not sure about the local protégées and other assets. We may have wiped the data before anyone made copies, but we cannot take any chances.

"Earth Base Two must be secured. That includes all transporters and equipment. Get moving people, there is no time to lose."

Everybody was familiar with the emergency procedures, and within a short time everything, including the equipment, was shut down and locked. All transporters in the sector were deactivated, which left their agents in a precarious position.

Every one of the Base personnel was loaded aboard the two PVXs in the shuttle bay, and they left along with Zadoc's transport ship. The final act was to lower two fortified imitation rock barricades to seal the cliff entrances. The facility was now a disguised and impregnable fortress.

As they sped away Xandra sat with his head in his hands. This had not been a good day!

"What about our protégées who are still at the Retreat?" Carol asked. "I forgot about them in all the excitement. The PVXs we used for transfers are gone and Earth Base Two and its transporter network are inactive."

Zadoc knew this was yet a further problem that he needed to deal with, but felt they should be safe at the Retreat for the next few days.

Carol and her staff, along with their PVXs, were kept aboard Zadoc's transport ship. They would go back with him to Solar Base. First they had to safely return Earth Base Two's protégées to their own countries, and arrange protection for any of their Terran agents whose identity may have been compromised.

Zadoc and Xandra arrived unexpectedly at Earth Base One and notified Aldon and Martina of the recent developments and closure of Earth Base Two.

"Our main concern is the safety of our agents in that part of the world." Zadoc said. "While we have extracted a couple of them, the others have been told to disable their transporters and discreetly travel to safer neutral countries. They must be as inconspicuous as possible.

"The problem is that, after our initial message and warning, we have lost all communication with them. We have to wait for them to make it to safety on their own.

"We cannot endanger Earth Base One or any of our people here, so we have arranged for a couple of emergency contacts. They in turn will notify Camellia. She, along with yourselves, has all the details to identify our genuine agents, and will advise you if she is approached.

"I cannot stress enough the need for security and compartmentalisation at this time. Although you may already be familiar with some of these incognito Terrans, having previously served in the military together, they must not be allowed access to this Base or any personnel or facilities in your sphere of influence.

"We have stationed a craft on Moon Base, and where possible will rescue them ourselves."

Aldon was looking rather glum after Zadoc and Xandra left.

"We'd better not waste any time before we advise all our people of the situation," he said. "I never liked that Richard – arrogant bastard. Pity he got disintegrated into oblivion. He deserved to spend the rest of his sorry life in a penal colony."

Bob was having lunch with Rebecca when Gareth demanded that the students quieten down and pay attention to what he had to say.

"I must stress upon you all the necessity for certain security measures while you are here. If any strangers, or worse, military personnel, arrive and start asking questions, you are 'The Followers of the Divine Light', who are gathered with fellow devotees to practice mindful meditation and other religious rituals."

He then beckoned to Rebecca and some of her foreign classmates and walked towards the control cabin.

Rebecca got up to follow the others. "Something's going on," she whispered.

Bob agreed. "Obviously they're not going to tell the rest of us. Perhaps you'll be allowed to fill me in later."

She returned after a few minutes, and Bob could tell she was anxious.

"Our Terran Base has been compromised and closed down. They don't think the identities of any of the protégées have been revealed, but they can't be sure. We are going to be taken home as soon as possible."

Rebecca had good reason to be worried. Her Aunt thought she had gone on holiday with a girlfriend, and didn't understand anything about her own family's extra terrestrial contacts. She would give her up to the authorities if there was any trouble. There would be nobody to turn to for help. Bob couldn't bear the thought of Rebecca falling into the hands of one of those foreign intelligence agencies.

He paused for a moment. "Rebecca, would you consider coming back with me. It has only been a short time, but I have already fallen in love with you. Perhaps we could get married?"

Gareth had been aware of the love affair between Bob and Rebecca, but it still came as a surprise when they advised their intentions and requested his consent.

Xandra and Zadoc discussed the matter with him, and agreed that Rebecca was in a more vulnerable position than the other isolated protégées. She was very trustworthy, but could create more problems by trying to leave her own country in order to reach Bob in Earth Base One's territory.

The lovers held their breath as the PVXs flew in and out, taking the students back to their homelands. Would Rebecca be the next to leave?

Gareth and Aldon arrived and announced that they had generated a new identity and documents for Rebecca. There were conditions to her being allowed to leave with Bob. She could never return to her country of origin or get in touch with anyone there. Further, she must report any attempts to contact her. It was similar to being in a witness protection program.

Gareth officiated at an impromptu wedding ceremony in the gardens of the Retreat, before they were taken aboard Aldon's PVX and left in a grove of trees near Bob's country home.

As they walked across the field towards his house, Bob wondered how he was going to explain this to everyone.

Mary and the twins had just cleared up after dinner, when there was a knock on the door.

"Could you answer that Victor? We don't normally get visitors to the farm at this time on a Saturday night."

A few minutes later Bob entered the lounge. He was accompanied by an attractive dark haired woman. She seemed rather timid and nervous. They were all curious, and could immediately sense her Terran connections.

He took a deep breath. "Everybody – I would like you to meet my new wife, Rebecca."

Mary and Victor were stunned, and lost for words. Fiona and Lucy reacted to the news with typical enthusiasm.

"Oh Bob! How wonderful!"

They all sat down and Victor produced a bottle of champagne. "I think this calls for a celebration. Now tell us all about it."

Everybody was shaken when told about the events which caused the closure of Earth Base Two, and how the foreign protégées had to return to their own countries and go into temporary hiding.

Rebecca explained how she and Bob had fallen in love at the Retreat. They had intended to keep in contact, however the unforeseen circumstances meant they may never see each other again.

"Gareth and the Terrans approved our hasty marriage, and provided me with the appropriate identity and documents to come back with Bob."

Victor smiled. "Well, we are all Terran affiliates. You are in safe hands here."

Rebecca relaxed and took a gulp of her wine. "Thank you so much for making me feel welcome. I didn't know if Bob's friends would accept me. I hope his children will not resent my becoming part of their family."

Bob was intending to pick his children up from their grandparent's house the next day. He was a little unsure of how everybody would react to the news.

After they left, Victor grinned at Mary. "Well that was unexpected. Do you realise that everybody living here and next door has a Terran connection. That's ten people every weekend if you count Tony and Gareth visiting."

"Even more if Xandra and Leandro drop by." Mary said.

Fiona heard them and looked around the corner. "We could form our own 'Country Friendship Club'." Victor thought that the idea had some merit, especially if the bookshop came under suspicion.

Bob and Rebecca were both tense when his father opened the door to them the following morning.

"Come in son," the older man said. "And who is this lovely lady?"

Before Bob could answer Dave and Christie came running up.

"Daddy – Daddy!" They shouted, throwing themselves into his arms.

Rebecca left it to Bob to break the news to his parents, who were understandably surprised, but pleased for Bob.

They were both reassuring. "You deserve some happiness."

His mother turned to Rebecca. "Welcome to our family. You are one of us – in more ways than you know."

It was decided that the news should be broken to the children gradually. At first they were told that Rebecca was a friend who was coming to live with them, and could be there when Daddy was at work.

Dave looked a little unsure, but Christie immediately climbed onto Rebecca's lap. "You're nice; shall I call you 'Auntie' or Mrs Somebody?"

"No. You can call me Rebecca, like everyone else."

They drove home that afternoon, and as soon as they got out of the car the children raced across the field to reunite with the animals on Mary's farm. Bob turned to Rebecca and asked if she thought she would be happy here.

"Oh yes! In my own country we lived in a big city. Our flat was small and crowded, and the air outside very polluted. I love these green fields, the fresh air, and this wonderful sense of freedom.

"Our government put a lot of restrictions on where we could go and what we may say or do. We all had to work hard to make enough money to buy food and a few little luxuries. I promise not to be a burden on you, and will find paid employment as soon as possible."

Bob felt that it would be better if he resumed full time employment at the hospital. He could earn enough money for the whole family, and in addition, the Terrans were giving the displaced protégées a weekly allowance.

"I will be much happier if you remain safe in our cottage and care for Dave and Christie, before and after school. They have not had any beneficial maternal influence in their lives for quite a long time, and you will understand them better than anyone else."

Bob reminded Rebecca that her only possessions were the contents of her backpack which she had brought from the Retreat.

"In a few days I go back to work. In the meantime I will take you into town. You can become familiar with the area, and we will buy you some new clothes and whatever else you want."

Rebecca settled in very well. Whilst Christie was very warm and loving, Rebecca sensed a certain level of uncertainty and distrust in Dave. She began paying extra attention to him. After school they would all go to feed and care for Mary's animals. She would then take time to help him with his homework.

He also liked video games and found Rebecca a worthwhile opponent. Slowly he changed his perception of Rebecca being an intruder, and his resistance melted away.

CHAPTER 32

Zadoc was thankful that due to the problems with Earth Base Two, the Guardians proposed field trip to the planet was delayed. Everything had seemed peaceful for several months, and he was unable to postpone their tour any longer.

He had avoided mentioning the subject to Aldon and Martina, knowing that it was the last thing they wanted to hear. Xandra was also not overly enthusiastic over the prospect of having to 'baby-sit' a group of assorted alien leaders.

"They have never fully understood all the problems they may encounter on an often hostile planet with so many varying cultures. I suppose we will have to start preparing some contingency plans."

He and Zadoc visited Earth Base, and there were several awkward moments when they broke the news.

"Why? Why now?" Aldon complained.

Zadoc was the Terran ambassador to the Space Council, and as such also the Guardians' appointed administrator of this planetary region. He explained that they wanted to re-evaluate their future plans as they applied to the Solar System and its only habitable planet.

"For many thousands of years the Space Council has been sending delegates to Earth. The Terrans, who look completely human, took over the supervisory role relatively recently. In the past our representatives had a distinctly alien appearance.

"When mankind was somewhat primitive, they treated our envoys as Gods to be worshipped and obeyed. Those societies quickly prospered and became civilised. Unfortunately some interbreeding occurred, and due to the existence of part alien progeny, later we genetically augmented and upgraded some of the inhabitants. Their offspring often became great leaders.

"We wanted to keep the genetic strain pure and unadulterated for further supplementation in later generations. That was no problem when human communities were comparatively contained. In recent centuries, exploration, modern industrial progress and urbanisation has led to the population migrating to all parts of the globe.

"This resulted in the dilution of the genes in the specific bloodlines we had altered. We renewed our efforts and concentrated on the descendants and families of the previously enhanced people. This project is still continuing today."

"While we at Earth Base are directly involved with the augmented humans, this has not resulted in the entire human race becoming agreeable or well behaved." Aldon said. "It may take a long time, if ever, to get them to conduct themselves in an acceptable manner. And what of your liaisons with various countries and their scientists? These have not always gone according to plan."

Zadoc reluctantly agreed. "One error of judgement was the Guardians' well intentioned proposal to encourage a one world government, which would be easier to manipulate and control. This mistake led several countries to think that they were the 'chosen ones'. The resultant global conflicts cost millions of lives."

Martina could appreciate the benefits of the proposed field trip. "It is no good the Guardians making decisions from afar. Perhaps it is better that they spend a little time here and get some firsthand experience and understanding of human behaviour."

Xandra and Aldon were still not happy about the proposed visit. They respected, but didn't always agree with, the detailed explanations they were being given. They both realised that it didn't matter what they thought. They had to obey orders. Beneath Zadoc's calm demure lay a warrior with a capacity for ruthless devotion to duty. It would be unwise to disagree with him or oppose his plans.

Xandra was concerned that their visitors, whose appearances were distinctly out of the ordinary, could cause unimaginable problems if left to their own devices on planet Earth. They needed to be in his care, and he suggested that the delegation be accommodated at Solar Base. They could make their field trips under his strict supervision.

Aldon and Martina did not meet with the first two delegates, who were taken to Earth Base Three. They had scheduled discussions with the officers stationed there, followed by an undercover meeting with several allied scientists and diplomats.

That part of the world was subject to strict authoritarian government and military control. Even with invisibility devices, their guests could not go wandering about in public view. Xandra was relieved that it had all occurred without incident.

The first Guardian Xandra brought to Earth Base One was Yannick, who was interested in learning more about humans' social life.

"I have studied a great deal about humans' behaviour," he said, "but no amount of data and screen footage allows me to experience and share in their actual emotions."

Yannick's own species considered him to be a handsome fellow, however by earthly standards he was decidedly strange. He was tall and well built, with piercing black eyes. His outsized bald head, streaked with large bony ridges, was somewhat out of proportion to the rest of his body.

Aldon suggested that perhaps a visit to a night spot, where humans enjoyed themselves, would be a good start. It was Halloween, and all the parties were in full swing. Xandra and Yannick transported down to Chantelle's apartment. They were both in high spirits.

Chantelle, whilst honoured at being chosen to escort her guests for the evening, was terrified of something going wrong on her watch. She messaged Gareth and asked him to join them at a local nightclub, just in case they needed any back-up.

It was essentially a masquerade party. Chantelle was very glamorous in a long black dress with matching cloak, and Gareth had borrowed a white lab coat and stethoscope from Tony. Xandra was wearing his Terran outfit minus any insignia, and Yannick, who was also in uniform, was instructed to keep his invisibility gadget turned on.

They reached the crowded venue, and Chantelle, who didn't want her guests to be standing outside in a queue, slipped the doorman a sizable tip which enabled immediate entry.

The supposedly invisible Yannick, who was hanging on to Chantelle's arm, was enthralled by the modern music and dancing. After about five minutes she couldn't feel him next to her anymore.

Chantelle poked Xandra in the ribs. "Where's he gone?"

Xandra groaned. Yannick was a very jocular chap, with a mischievous nature, and a penchant for liquor. What was he up to now?

Chantelle panicked. "How can we find him if we can't see him?"

Xandra reached into his pocket and pulled out a pair of special glasses. They enabled him to see through the screen which produced the optical illusion of invisibility around Yannick.

"There he is – over near the bar. Oh, my goodness! He's up in the corner next to a half empty bottle of vodka. Let's get to him quick!"

Yannick saw his companions moving in, and merged back onto the crowded dance floor. Although he was still in an invisible mode, and attempting to avoid a collision with the other patrons, his feet and arms were moving in time to the disco beat, which he found quite exhilarating.

He was attracted to Earth women, and couldn't resist a couple of very striking females in flimsy revealing costumes. Every so often he created a disturbance by fondling them as he boogied past. Xandra was having difficulty catching up with him, when suddenly Yannick materialised. Being slightly inebriated he had bumped into a waiter, and his invisibility device had fallen to the floor.

Yannick stumbled as he bent down to pick it up, and collided with one of the dancers, who lost his balance and fell over. He got up and gave Yannick a shove.

"You ugly sod! Look where you're going!"

Yannick pushed back – a little too hard. The other fellow toppled into a nearby patron dressed as a knight in a suit of armour. There was an almighty crash as he hit the floor, tripping several others as he went down.

An altercation started and Chantelle raced up, grabbed Yannick's arm, and propelled him away. She snatched the invisibility unit from his hand, and clipped it back onto his belt.

"Damn! It doesn't work! You must have damaged it."

Gareth and Xandra joined her, and not wanting to be blamed for the increasing mêlée, they hustled a rather wobbly Yannick out the front door and back into the street.

"What do we do now?" Xandra asked as they tried to blend in with the pedestrians. "Does anyone else have their invisibility unit? I left mine behind."

Chantelle gave a rueful grin. "Don't look at me. Gareth and I didn't bring ours either."

Gareth looked around. Up and down the road there were lots of families, all clad in Halloween fancy-dress. He had a sudden thought and walked up to a little boy.

"I'll give you ten dollars for your bucket." The kid hesitated. After agreeing on twenty dollars, Gareth returned with the container, and gave it to Yannick.

"Here – just hold this in front of you."

As they walked back to Chantelle's place, several passers-by stopped and placed donations into the can. One even commented on what a good mask Yannick was wearing, and asked where he had bought it.

When they finally reached the safety of her apartment, Yannick looked into his bucket.

"Why have people given me money, chocolates and lollies? Did I look hungry or something? Humans are kind, but very strange!"

Chantelle didn't bother to explain, and merely handed him a cup of strong black coffee before Xandra took him back to Earth Base to sleep it off.

The following morning Yannick was unusually quiet and feeling a little embarrassed. He tried to justify his behaviour by saying that part of his mission was to gain a better understanding of how modern day humans think and behave.

His next assignment was to contact a particular media entrepreneur, who produced science fiction motion pictures.

"Although this society does not possess our interactive holograph entertainment, their authors and the movie industry, through books and films, have provided an excellent method to familiarise people with the possibility of life in other parts of the universe. When we do eventually make open contact, humans will hopefully be more accepting of our presence, and varied physical appearances."

Aldon tracked down Yannick's film maker to a remote location where his crew were shooting some footage for his latest 'blockbuster'. Andy took Martina and Yannick in the PVX, and beamed them down behind some trees.

As they walked across an open sandy area, Martina felt very exposed. When they reached the film set an aide grabbed both of them.

"You two are late. Get over there with the rest of the cast!" He glanced at Yannick. "Make-up did a really good job on you!"

Martina was becoming increasingly uneasy, and backed away from any possibility of recognition. Yannick seemed to be revelling at the thought of being included in the production, and joined the other actors who were dressed as various alien characters.

The producer recognised Yannick, but could not say or do anything until after they finished shooting that particular scene. It was some time before he had the opportunity to quietly liaise with his extra-terrestrial friend, and Martina was thankful when they eventually went back behind the trees and waited for Andy to pick them up.

Yannick was chuckling to himself. "I bet the audience will never know that there was also a real alien appearing on the screen!"

Yannick was quite fascinated by human sexuality. Perhaps Chantelle could enlighten him. He visited her and started asking some very suggestive questions.

She gave him a sideways glance. "Forget it Yannick! Anyway I'm Terran – not human. What else did you have in mind?"

Yannick confided a lifelong fantasy of being chased, captured and ravaged by primitive human cavewomen. Chantelle immediately thought of a high class establishment called 'The House of Erotica'. Dare she take him there?

She contacted the proprietor, and after some negotiations advised Yannick he could experience his slightly wacky desires – for a price.

He was excited. "I have plenty of spending money that your Base gave me for expenses. It will cover the fee."

Chantelle was sure that these were not the kind of expenses that Aldon had in mind, however she went ahead and made the arrangements.

She had told the 'escorts' that Yannick was a very deformed man who could not find romance or a partner. Three beautiful young women, clad only in bearskins, welcomed him as they discreetly entered through a side door.

Chantelle waited in the reception area. The giggling females led Yannick into their 'dungeon-cave'. "No rough stuff," she whispered. "Be sure not to hurt him."

She could hear the sounds of what seemed to be a rigorous chase and laughter occurring downstairs. It was followed by silence, and then the noises of some exuberant fornication.

Yannick was gone for over two hours, and returned with a beaming smile from ear to ear.

"Thank you ladies," he murmured as he bid them goodbye.

One of the women pulled Chantelle to the side. "You never told us just how deformed he was. Did you know he has two penises – one back and front! We had a threesome with Babs underneath and me on top. We normally have to fake satisfaction, but not this time!

"It was the most incredible sex I have ever had. We should be paying him – not the other way around."

Chantelle made a hasty, embarrassed exit, and counselled Yannick before his return to Earth Base One.

"You must remember that mankind has only flourished because society had dictated that men and women restrict their sex lives to lifelong partnerships which involve love as well as lust.

"Although many ignore these guidelines, it is this arrangement which enables children to flourish within a family unit with both a mother and a father."

Yannick indicated that he did understand, and then gave her a cheeky grin. "Promise me you'll say nothing of my little escapade to anyone else."

Chantelle tried to keep a straight face as she gave him her word.

Yannick was also interested in the effect religion had played on human society. Xandra thought that a meeting with Paul and Jacquita would be advantageous, and one sunny afternoon they visited the little island.

Their discussions proved very informative, and Yannick was pleased when Paul advised that most faiths lived in harmony with each other. Only one creed was violent, and tried force their beliefs on others.

Xandra had not seen Yannick so serious and thoughtful before. "Yes, when we sent emissaries to Earth it was merely to show humans the right way to live. We had no idea that their teachings would give birth to religious cults and power structures, which usually deviated from the lessons of peace and love."

Their meeting had taken place in Paul's small manse. No one wanted the natives to see their visitor. It only took a couple of minutes, when everybody's attention was diverted, for Yannick to wander back into the little stone church.

A young nun was praying at the altar. She looked up, saw Yannick, and ran out of the door in fright. He followed, intending to assure her that he meant no harm, but she had disappeared into the convent.

He stood outside in the warm sunlight, admiring the colourful tropical vegetation and sparkling lagoon. A few natives were tending their vegetable plots and fishing nets. This was indeed a beautiful planet.

How could the Guardians prevent it being systematically destroyed by its human population?

His quiet contemplations were disturbed by the sounds of excited inhabitants emerging from the adjoining village. Jacquita heard the muffled shouts coming from outside and turned around.

"Where's Yannick?"

Xandra jumped up from his seat. "Oh no! He's wandered off again!"

Paul raced outside, and pulled a protesting Yannick back into the church, shutting the door behind them.

"I don't know if the locals will think you are a god or a demon," he said. "Perhaps it's time for you and Xandra to leave before we have a major incident."

Once Yannick and Xandra had entered the crypt and beamed back to Earth Base, Paul opened the church door. The mystified natives had to see for themselves that there was nobody there.

That night Yannick was deep in thought. "There is such a vast difference between your technically advanced civilisations and the indigenous populations. It is an enormous gap which needs to be bridged before there can be any integration with the wider cosmic community."

Xandra decided it was about time that Yannick met some more 'normal' human beings. A visit to the farm with Victor and the protégées seemed the ideal opportunity. Surely he couldn't get into mischief there!

Early on Saturday morning they transported down to the bookshop, and were soon on their way to the country.

Mary and the twins were excited that they were having an important guest for the weekend. The cottage was cleaned from top to bottom, and special meals prepared.

Saturday was spent enjoying the great outdoors. Yannick did not have to remain 'invisible'. He was surrounded by friends, and there were no members of the public to worry about.

In the afternoon he wandered through the field, familiarising himself with the animals. Christie and Dave came over, and he soon found the little girl holding his hand as they patted Wiggles and the goats.

"I like you Uncle Yannick," she said. "I wish you could stay here and be my friend." He realised that she hadn't recoiled or judged him by his unusual appearance.

That night was a very social occasion, and Yannick enjoyed talking to everybody who had gathered at the cottage. Bob had come with Rebecca and the children, and Xandra, Tony, Victor, Mary and the twins completed the get-together.

When some of their discussions became quite serious, Fiona and Lucy couldn't resist the urge to ease the tension with friendly banter and flirting a little with their guest. Victor started playing some of the 'Associates' music, and soon they were all singing along to the popular songs of the day.

On Sunday the group practised their meditation and telepathic training, and the 'melding' of their minds was quite powerful.

When they were about to leave, Christie ran up to Yannick and gave him a kiss on the cheek. "I hope you come back soon."

He felt a lump in his throat, and realised that the innocence, love and trust of one small child was teaching him more about the admirable character and qualities of human beings than any of his other contacts.

Aldon was pleased when Yannick returned to Solar Base to compile his reports. "He was a very amiable bloke, but a real handful when it came to keeping him out of trouble."

Martina agreed. "But he would suddenly show enormous insight into the problems besetting mankind. He mentioned that babies are pure spiritual beings. They only develop undesirable traits as they grow and learn from the world around them. The problems of this planet are not only the result of ego and greed. From the lone individual up to nations, most conflicts are caused by their fear of each other."

Aldon nodded. "To a certain extent he's probably correct. Right now my main concern is that I believe Xandra is returning with two more delegates before this 'field trip' is over."

CHAPTER 33

A couple of days later Xandra arrived with Gorg and Oni, the two remaining delegates.

Gorg's appearance was such that he must be disguised, or wear an invisibility device at all times. He was average height, but his ears and nose were almost non-existent and his skin a decidedly green colour.

Xandra and Gareth were to accompany him to several secret meetings with some of the region's scientists and select military chiefs. Due to his highly classified status he would not be allowed to visit any other locations.

Aldon was curious about Oni, a petite little woman who resembled a pixie. She was only four feet tall, with long black hair, creamy skin, pointy ears, and vivid violet coloured eyes.

"Xandra hasn't told me why she is here," he said.

Martina nodded. "I'm just as much in the dark as you. She took quite a bulky case into her guest quarters. If you keep her preoccupied I'll sneak a look inside."

Martina eventually got a chance to investigate Oni's luggage, and was puzzled to find several 'fly' drones and a remote control along with a monitor screen. They were all packed into a large velvet sack.

"Oni obviously intends to spy on someone or something," she told Aldon later. "Why haven't we been informed?"

Before they could quiz Xandra, Ebony came rushing into the control centre. "The PVX is gone, and I can't find Oni!"

Aldon ordered Andy to track the location of the PVX, and was astounded to learn it was flying over the ocean towards the jungles of South America.

Xandra was just as perplexed as everybody else, and tried, without success to contact Oni. He had no choice but to call upon his reserve forces to help him recover the PVX and his wayward delegate.

By the time his larger craft arrived and found the PVX, it was hovering, unmanned, over some of the thickest, impenetrable Amazon rainforest.

"Bloody hell!!" Xandra bellowed. "What is she up to?"

He noticed a couple of the 'fly' drones and the monitoring device in the PVX cabin. The data history indicated that she had been searching a rocky outcrop under the tropical forest canopy of trees and vines.

Xandra's larger craft had access to his Solar Base records and archives. A quick search revealed that, in ancient times gone by, Oni's people had a base on Earth. It had been located in the vicinity she had been scanning with the miniature drones. Was that what she was looking for?

He tried messaging her again. This time he received a weak indistinct response. All he could make out was that she was trapped in a cave down below. He asked her to turn on her locator, and was thankful when the signal was detected.

He readied a search party, and insisted on his soldiers carrying extra weapons and wearing special protective garments.

"That jungle is not as benign as it seems. There are cannibalistic natives, predatory animals, and vicious insects that can torment a person into madness. Whatever you do, stay out of the water. The piranhas can strip your flesh in seconds!"

Xandra and his jittery men beamed down to the surface, and examined the cliff face in an attempt to find the entrance to Oni's 'cave'. They found some very old petro-glyphs which they followed as they crawled around the rubble of rocks and boulders. Every so often they caught quick glimpses of dark malignant eyes peering at them from the surrounding jungle.

"Here Commander," one called out as he came upon a small opening in the rocks. Xandra shouted through the gap and heard a faint reply from inside. The entry may have been large enough for Oni to squeeze through, but it was far too small for Xandra and his militia.

They blasted into the rock face, and eventually accessed a roughly hewn tunnel, which led to a large cavern. Oni was lying on the ground, covered in blood and bite marks. She was obviously in pain. The whole area was lit by a large glowing crystal, which she held in her arms.

"Be careful – vampire bats," she gasped.

She was still clinging onto the crystal when the soldiers carried her out. Xandra was thankful once they were back on board his craft, which returned him and Oni, along with the PVX to Earth Base.

Martina met them, and helped Oni to her quarters.

"I need an explanation, and it had better be a good one." Xandra growled. "I suppose you'd better get her cleaned up and attend to her injuries first."

While Oni was recuperating, she told Martina that she was from the planet 'Karn'. The large glowing crystal was her people's magical 'Karnia Stone', which brought good luck and prosperity to their planet. It was the cornerstone of their religion.

Many years ago, when their homeland was under attack, and risked enemy occupation, a craft was sent to Earth to hide the artefact in one of their abandoned bases. Its location was a closely guarded secret that they would entrust to no-one.

When she was included in the Guardians' trip to Earth, the Karn government had asked her to covertly retrieve their icon and return it to its rightful home.

Xandra and Zadoc held a meeting at Earth Base to decide what to do in this rather delicate situation. They did not want to offend their Karn allies, and felt any decision should be made by the Space Council. The Guardians quickly determined that Oni and the crystal should be safely returned to Karn under escort, and a military craft arrived soon after.

Zadoc remained to see Oni safely on board. As she waved goodbye through the porthole, she was still clutching the glowing rock to her chest.

"Well, I'm glad that's over," said Martina as they all relaxed over a drink. "I didn't know that the Karns had previously been present on Earth."

Zadoc detailed how, over time, several species of cosmic visitors had founded settlements in South and Central America. Many of Earth's archaeologists are aware that the indigenous people had help and guidance in building their impressive cities.

"Think of Machu Picchu, the Aztec's Tenochtitlian, and the Inca's Cuzco – to name a few. Others exist in Bolivia and the Amazon. These settlements were crafted from precision cut huge stone blocks, and the carvings and pottery indicated an advanced knowledge of astronomy, mathematics and music.

"Many native people have legends of their ancestors' interaction with the 'Gods'. Those tribes who lived close to our bases have high intelligence levels and unusually pale skin compared to others. They are often referred to as 'White Indians', and indicate some possible interbreeding."

"Why have all these bases been abandoned?" Martina asked.

Zadoc shrugged. "Some of our colleagues just wanted to return to their home planets. In many cases they found Earth's tropical areas to be anything but 'Paradise'. The local inhabitants were aggressive and brutal, and the jungles unrelenting and remorseless. The wildlife will sting, bite or eat you, and many species are highly venomous or carry dangerous parasites and bacteria."

"During the sixteenth century many explorers, including Cortes, Pizarro and Walter Raleigh sought out these civilisations and often massacred the inhabitants for their gold and jewels.

"Even today explorers still seek the legendary city of El Dorado and its fabled riches. Chronicles and old scrolls in libraries and churches describe it as having a narrow entry between two mountains."

Xandra had been sitting quietly, lost in thought. "When Oni took off on her own mission, she obviously didn't complete the task she was given on this field trip. What was she supposed to be doing?"

Zadoc looked uncomfortable. "I knew you would ask that sooner or later. Oni is an archaeologist/historian and was charged with locating a self sufficient base which the Guardians had established and colonised thousands of years ago. Now she has gone, it will be up to the rest of us to complete that task."

Aldon was not happy. "Oni never had any intention of fulfilling her official assignment. How can she get away with such deception and disregard for the command structure?"

Zadoc shrugged. "She is not part of our military hierarchy, and participated, as a Kahn representative, in the Guardians' 'field trip'. Oni's errant behaviour was overlooked in the name of diplomacy."

He handed over all Oni's research. "We can start by collating all this information. It seems the area of interest is below the icecap covering the continent situated at the southern extremity of this planet."

"You must be kidding!" Xandra complained. "The South Pole – Antarctica? It's freezing down there!"

Zadoc grinned. "We also have to go in winter, when there is less chance of being detected. Don't look so worried. It is not as cold as

347

outer space. I will be heading the expedition, and will provide all the necessary equipment."

"When this facility was originally built Antarctica had much warmer weather. Over time the climate has changed, and constant layers of snow and ice have altered the landscape considerably. Oni was only tasked with determining the exact location of the entrance to the Base."

Martina knew little about Antarctica except that it was a bleak frozen wilderness. Aldon displayed a detailed image on the monitor screen.

"It is actually a very large continent, entombed in ice, with only two percent exposed as bedrock, mountain peaks or coastal strips during summer. The personnel attached to the various nations' research stations only venture out during the summer months when there is twenty four hours of daylight, and more settled conditions. Even then there is always the risk of earthquakes, and sudden changes in the weather. There are often massive storms with driving rain, ferocious winds and huge seas."

Zadoc interrupted. "We won't have the benefit of any summer respite, and will be going during the long pink twilight of mid-winter, when the sun does not come over the horizon. The one advantage is that the humans will all be bunkered down and covered by a relentless accumulation of snow and ice.

"This is currently the most inhospitable environment on Earth. Up until now, although contemporary human exploration of the interior has been limited, they have developed more efficient methods of polar transportation. Their brief inland expeditions are still hindered by perilous massed ice packs, hidden crevasses, and unexpected blizzards."

Zadoc paused for a moment. He could only divulge limited information, and measured his next words very carefully.

"We believe our own monitoring facility, which belongs to the Space Council and Guardians alone, was built at the most secure place on

Earth. It is deep in the Trans-Antarctic Mountains, at the heart of the continent. It also provides a safe haven for any of our people evading capture, especially those with a distinctive alien appearance."

Xandra nodded. "I must admit that is an excellent choice of location – I thought I knew about every base in the Solar System – that was my job! Up until now, even I wasn't aware of its existence!"

Aldon smirked. "I know just how you feel! Remember what you told us? It's called 'compartmentalisation' – on a 'need to know' basis."

Zadoc ignored the jibes and outlined their most pressing problem. "We don't think it has been compromised, but have not heard from them for some time. Perhaps there is just a minor problem, but without direct contact we cannot accurately determine the exact location needed to access the site.

"Recent satellite, digital and drone technology has enabled humans to conduct much better surveillance and given them immediate connection with the outside world. It is our mission to surreptitiously confirm that our base is still unidentified and intact.

"If everything is okay, we will install new undetectable communication and other systems, relieve our officer, and replenish supplies and equipment."

After Zadoc and Xandra departed for Solar Base Aldon decided he would ask Ebony to look up the history and politics of the area. The next night he read out her report to Martina over dinner.

"Earth's scientific community is insistent that the Antarctic has been a harsh frozen continent for millions of years. Individual scholars have contradicted that opinion, and cite ancient maps and records which indicate this wasn't the case. Some covert agencies have been paying close attention to their alternative theories.

"It wasn't until the early nineteenth century that the first modern humans even circumnavigated the Antarctic. Fifty years later the 'sealers' and whaling ships plied their cruel slaughters off the shore. In the early twentieth century explorers landed and built primitive huts on the coast.

"There was later activity around the Sub-Antarctic islands, and during World War Two the Germans used the island of Kerguelen as a base for their raiders which were attacking enemy shipping.

"Immediately after that war there were two expeditions to the Antarctica, one heavily armed, and a serious confrontation with some of our less than pleasant alien colleagues. They also had a base, situated on the coast, with a point of entry under the sea ice-pack zone. The human military totally destroyed it.

"In the following three years there was a rush on, by many countries, to lay competing claims to the territory by establishing permanent stations on the edges of the continent. We initially had grave concerns. Some nations even proposed using the area to test atom bombs and also store radioactive waste. Luckily some of our highly placed undercover agents were able to influence the negotiations and in 1959 the *Antarctic Treaty*, which prohibited these crazy suggestions, was signed.

"The real motivations of the competing world powers were those of military strategy, with the later possibility of exploiting the minerals lying beneath the surface. They were already aware of massive coal seams, and oil and iron ore deposits."

Martina laughed. "Their ambitions don't seem dissimilar to some of our own outer space contemporaries."

Aldon agreed. "Not so different! They had to content themselves with scientific projects, mainly concentrating on studying the wildlife plus cosmic rays, the ozone layer, and the orientation of the earth's magnetic field. It is a hostile environment. They were forced to depend upon each other, especially during emergencies, and learned that they could all live and work harmoniously together."

Martina noticed that after their meeting with Zadoc and Xandra, Aldon had become very moody. He cheered up considerably when they were advised that the Guardians' expedition would not involve Earth Base. It would consist mainly of Space Council personnel and military. Xandra would also be accompanying them as the only Solar System representative.

It was midwinter, and Zadoc arrived in two huge silver spaceships, shielded against detection by spy satellites. They moved silently over the Antarctic coastline of heavily glaciated cliffs. *'Operation Guardian Base'* had begun.

Both of the craft, concealed in the cloud and fog, hovered low over the frozen mountainous terrain. Their powerful beams melted the ice dome underneath, creating a long shaft to the base far below.

Karine had assembled his soldiers at the exit hatch. "Quickly men! It will freeze back over within minutes."

The advance landing team, dressed in protective gear against the paralysing cold, descended into the dark abyss. They wasted no time in reaching the hidden entry, and activating the reinforced doors. A large silver robot blocked their way in, and would not let them continue without satisfactory security checks.

"Do not remove your breathing masks," it warned in a rasping voice. "There are dangerous fumes within this area."

Karine proceeded straight to the operations centre. The records indicated that the Guardian's duty officer had collapsed some months ago. The robot and other artificial intelligence entities had revived him and placed him into the safety of a stasis chamber.

Karine's experts quickly repaired a problem in one of the facility's ventilation tubes, and flushed the toxins from the area. After the air was safe to breathe, they reopened the shaft to the surface and extended a long access tube and 'space elevator' to the surface. Zadoc and Xandra joined their colleagues down below.

Zadoc opened the stasis cubicle. "Hello Hulwa – time to wake up!"

Hulwa staggered out. He couldn't remember much about what had happened to him. He ran his hands over his long unkempt hair and straggly beard, and realised he must have been encapsulated for some time. He made his way to his quarters, and while he was improving his personal appearance and body odour, Karine explained about the fumes.

"That is one of the many dangers here," Hulwa said. "Further across the continent there are several active volcanoes. They often emit hazardous gases which can be trapped below the surface and travel a long distance underground. Luckily they don't affect the robots!"

Karine was a little uneasy. "There's no chance of us being blown sky-high, is there?"

Hulwa didn't think so. The volcanoes only ran down one side of the continent, and nowhere near the base.

The specialised team immediately got to work, and started unloading replacement provisions and a more modernized perpetual power supply. All the equipment was checked, repaired and renewed when required. While the new communications system and updated technology were being installed, Hulwa took Preton and Qura, his two replacement officers, around the facility.

"I want to be sure you are totally familiarised with every facet of our operations," he said. "You will be the only living beings here. Despite the robots and other artificial entities, it can be an isolated existence. I was here by myself. It was very lonely, and created untold problems when I collapsed, leaving just the robots in charge. I am glad there will be two of you in future."

The facility had another elevator which sped up a steep tunnel to the parking dock for a space saucer and specialised PVX. Hulwa explained that both craft could send a heat blast into the accumulated ice barrier which blocked the exit passageway to the sky above.

"Better warm up the engines first. It's mighty cold out there, especially at this time of the year!"

Karine and Zadoc also advised that they had installed a special two way emergency alarm system connected to their other Earth Bases. An alert was only to be activated in the event of an urgent situation.

Xandra was amazed at the size of the facility. How could he have not known of its existence? How much more were the Guardians hiding from him?

He looked at Zadoc. "There is something you are not telling me. What is it? What is so important about this top-secret project?"

Zadoc pointed to several tunnels which led out of the control centre. "Come with me. What you are about to see is way above top secret."

A moving platform whisked them along to a huge chamber where several robots were bringing out a heavily laden trolley.

Xandra gasped. "Is that what I think it is?"

Zadoc nodded. "Yes – diamonds and gold. Space Council, the Guardians, and even your own bases need financing. Whilst all our cosmic allies support the cost of our joint efforts, it is not sufficient."

"But you are stealing resources from the people of this planet!" Xandra protested.

"Perhaps," said Zadoc. "Look at it this way. The Space Council is protecting them against the more evil entities out there. It is only our presence which has prevented them invading and ravaging Earth.

"Further, this is a vast continent with enormous amounts of important natural resources. We have only taken a small percentage, leaving ample reserves for the inhabitants. When they eventually commence mining operations of their own, it will probably be at the expense of vast areas of the pristine environment."

Xandra sadly nodded his head in agreement.

Zadoc continued. "Nobody else must know about the true nature of this facility. We only visit occasionally, so as not to raise suspicion when we transport our valuable shipment back to the Guardians. Even our allies could be tempted to hijack the cargo."

Xandra was lost for words. He had thought this was just a 'sleeper' base. It was much more than that! Rather ironic that whilst he was deceiving Aldon and Martina about the other Earth Bases, he himself was being misled about Zadoc's activity on the planet. It was indeed a hierarchy of compartmentalisation and 'need to know'.

"I wonder what else I don't know about," he muttered to himself.

Hulwa's tour of duty was over. As he packed his bags ready to return to Space Base, the robots were bringing huge chests of uncut diamonds to the loading dock. From there they were safely stowed away on Zadoc's ship.

Xandra wondered at the chances of pinching one for Solar Base. Those gems could finance countless operations.

Zadoc read his mind. "Forget it my friend! I may be the boss, but even I have to account for it all."

Preton and Qura were securely locked back down into their icy location before Xandra, Zadoc and Karine's troops headed away.

Back on Earth Base Aldon and Martina went about their daily tasks, blissfully unaware that the 'small base' at the South Pole was anything but an insignificant facility!

Zadoc and Karine sped back to Solar Base, where they left Xandra and picked up a couple of passengers who were returning to their headquarters in outer space.

Karine was uneasy. "I don't like having these two on board your ship when it is carrying such a valuable cargo."

Zadoc was not worried. "They are minor members of the Space Council. Furthermore, they are not aware that we are carrying a fortune in uncut diamonds."

Karine did not want to take any chances. It was his duty to escort the consignment and personnel safely to their final destination. Before he returned to his own craft he took the precaution of leaving two undercover soldiers on board with Zadoc.

They sped off, headed for Space Base some distance away across the dark infinite cosmos. Zadoc was looking forward to getting back, and busied himself with routine tasks.

The two passengers had been accommodated in the guest quarters, next door to the disguised commandos. They reported to Zadoc and Karine that although these individuals had done nothing wrong, there was something about them which 'didn't feel right'.

"What do you mean?" Zadoc asked.

"Well, for one thing, they keep wandering around the unrestricted parts of the ship asking our officers operational type questions. My offsider also noticed that one was trying to open the entry to a classified area."

Karine was concerned, and placed his ship and team on alert. Both craft were to keep their defensive shields activated at all times, and Zadoc instructed his crew to carry additional concealed weapons.

A robot was placed on duty in the corridor outside their cabin, and from then onwards the two guests were closely scrutinised. Zadoc reluctantly breached normal discretion and ordered that their private quarters also be monitored.

"They are up to something," Zadoc concluded. "While they seem to be very careful in what they say, there have been several mentions of unspecified 'colleagues' arriving. One of them has some form of communications device hidden under his clothing."

A few hours later Zadoc received a distress signal from a vessel some distance from their flight plan. He was suspicious, but duty bound to respond. Whilst Karine maintained a safer holding pattern, further away and out of sight, Zadoc moved closer and contacted the ship's captain.

A rather rough looking individual appeared on the screen. He claimed to be aboard a trading vessel whose engines had broken down, leaving him and his crew drifting aimlessly in space.

Zadoc asked if they needed any spare parts, but the captain kept requesting someone transport on board his ship. At the same time as Karine was suggesting caution, a second vessel was detected in the distance. It was closing in fast.

He issued an immediate warning. "Do not activate the transporter or lower any defence shields."

One of Zadoc's suspicious guests burst into the command centre. He waved a weapon in the air, and grabbed the nearest officer.

"Do not move anyone, or he gets it! I'm taking control of this ship!"

Karine's covert officer came up from behind. "Oh no you're not!"

The intruder crumpled into a heap, and a couple of minutes later Karine's other soldier dragged the body of the second passenger through the door.

"I caught this fellow messaging someone on that ship."

Zadoc looked back to his screen. The 'trading' vessel's captain had witnessed some of the action in the command centre. His attitude had changed. There was no more pretence of being a ship in distress.

"Prepare to be boarded. Hand over your freight, and we'll let you all live."

The second heavily armed craft swooped in firing its weapons. Zadoc and his crew hung on as the entire structure shook.

"Our shields are still intact," said the operator, "but I don't know for how long."

"Come on Karine! Where are you?" Zadoc muttered.

His spirits soared when his attacker suddenly veered away, with flames pouring from beneath. It shuddered violently, obviously out of control, and plunged downwards into oblivion.

The 'Trader' had also aimed its weapons at them, and lowered its own shields ready to fire. A blast from Karine's ship hit them broadside, and a simultaneous assault from Zadoc's armaments seemed to create a cataclysmic chain reaction. It exploded into pieces which quickly floated away into space.

An immediate check indicated that no significant damage had been done to the Terran craft.

Both Zadoc and Karine would have preferred to capture their assailants. There were a lot of unanswered questions. Were they just space pirates, or did they have specific information about the important payload of uncut diamonds?

At least they still had their two 'guests', who were now lying unconscious on the floor. Zadoc had them confined, under guard, in a secure unit. They were obviously in cahoots with their assailants. He would hand them over to the Guardians at Space Base.

While it was safe to assume that both the enemy craft had been annihilated, everyone was still shaken by the unexpected confrontation. They were all thankful when they reached their destination and handed over the shipment without further incident.

The Guardians were disappointed and concerned that two members of their own Space Council, albeit only minor diplomats, may have betrayed them. After intense questioning the culprits admitted they had been acting on their own initiative.

They had heard rumours about a valuable shipment secretly coming from Solar Base, and thought it was an excellent opportunity to become richer than they could have imagined in their wildest dreams. They struck a deal with a group of space pirates to commandeer Zarcon's craft and make off with the cargo.

Karine thought that they were lucky to have been taken prisoner by the Terrans. Their co-conspirators were nothing but outlaw ruffians, who would have killed them once they got their hands on the diamonds.

They were discussing the matter later with Xandra.

"I hope that they were sent to a penal colony," he said.

"Unfortunately not," Zarcon growled. "The diamonds are strictly hush-hush. We couldn't put them on trial without the facts coming out. The Guardians wiped their memories and sent them back to their home planets with so-called 'nervous breakdowns'."

Xandra was concerned about fortune hunters searching for Earth's Antarctic Base.

Zadoc reassured him. "It's safe. Our villains picked up on some idle chatter at Space Base. They only knew that there was a consignment worth a 'king's ransom' coming from Solar Base – not that it consisted of several chests of Earth diamonds.

"It won't happen again. Where this kind of information is concerned, security has really been tightened up."

CHAPTER 34

After the 'Associates' won the Music Festival, Gareth, acting as their manager/agent, started negotiations with a couple of record companies. Everyone was anxious to get their first contract, but Gareth was delaying the signing of any agreement.

"We will get a better deal once you've appeared in the National Contest," he said. "Just keep practising and polishing up your repertoire. You'll be facing some stiff competition."

Rehearsing every weekend on the farm was not enough if they wanted to perfect their act. Everybody still had their day jobs to go to, so the twins called by the bookshop a couple of evenings after work.

Victor found this was good for business, as many of their patrons stayed back to listen to the music and singing. He often played the piano, which the customers found relaxing after a hard day.

He grinned at Mary. "Our coffee and snack sales have quadrupled, and I'm selling a lot more books and other products."

Mary squeezed onto the sofa next to Mishka. "Yes, we are attracting quite a following. We'll end up with our own fan club soon. The problem is that some people are virtual strangers. We have to be more cautious than ever."

Gareth was also mindful of the risks unwanted publicity could bring, and resisted the temptation to accept premature media interviews before the national competition.

Fiona and Lucy noticed that Tony often looked a little dejected and realised that he was very much on the 'sidelines'. They were determined that he should not feel 'left out'. On the nights they weren't at the bookshop, they started including him in their practice sessions on the rooftop of their apartment block.

There was a mixed reaction from their neighbours, some of whom enjoyed the free concert. A few were too elderly and deaf to hear, but they had to make allowances for a couple of young families, and finish off by nine o'clock.

Tony soon mastered Victor's role on the keyboard and guitar, and was an excellent substitute for the male vocal part. Up until then his brilliant mind had always concentrated on science and technical innovations. He found a peaceful escape and fulfilment in the music, and often remained alone on the roof, quietly playing the guitar under the starry sky.

"You wait and see," Fiona said. "There'll come a day when Victor cannot perform, and the 'Associates' routine is dependent upon his musical and singing complement. Tony is well equipped to 'stand-in' for him."

Lucy agreed. "In fact, if we were without both Victor and Mary, the three of us could put on a reasonably good show. Don't get me wrong – I'm not suggesting for one minute that we should go it alone."

Every weekend all five of them would gather at the farm and practice together. Gareth had to admit that the extra male voice Tony provided gave the 'Associates' a better vocal tone and depth than before.

"I can't give in to your pleading for Tony to be permanently included in the group," he said. "The media will start profiling the band members, and would start asking questions about him. You know he cannot draw unnecessary attention to himself, and must always 'stay under the radar'."

Occasionally Tony went for a walk at lunchtime. One day, while sitting on the park bench and eating his sandwiches, he could hear some familiar music coming from the nearby footpath. Where had he heard that song before?

He walked over and found a shabbily dressed fellow playing a guitar. Tony stopped and listened for a while, and then put a few spare coins into the hat at the man's feet. He looked up to thank him, and as soon as their eyes met, there was an instant recognition.

Underneath the unkempt hair and beard, there was another Terran. What was he doing here? Tony made some polite conversation, and learned that the street busker went by the name of 'Teddy'. He strummed a new melody on his guitar. It was one of Olivia's compositions, and Tony found it hard to walk away without identifying himself. He immediately contacted Earth Base.

"I can account for all our people," Aldon said. "Perhaps he's escaped from one of the countries in Earth Base Two's area. Leave it to me, and I will check with Xandra."

Xandra was anxious to follow up on Tony's report as soon as possible. "We have lost contact with several of our agents from that part of the world. If he is one of 'ours', and living on the street, he must be in hiding from some kind of danger."

A few days later Xandra, disguised with a hat and glasses, accompanied Tony back to the park. There was a different transient playing a piano accordion in the same spot.

It took some persuasion, and a generous financial bribe, before Tony could persuade him to tell them that 'Teddy' wasn't well, and apparently living with many other homeless people in one of the disused subway tunnels.

Tony was annoyed that Xandra would not allow him to continue the search. This may be a trap. He could not permit a second Terran scientist or Earth Base One to risk exposure.

That night, Xandra and one of his soldiers, dressed as hobos, descended into the labyrinth of disused passages and cellars under the city. What confronted them was not a pretty sight. Dozens of destitute men and women were living rough in appalling conditions. Each had their own little space, with some basic bedding and their few possessions.

They approached a small group, who were huddled around a makeshift fire constructed out of an old metal garbage can.

"Does anyone know where we can find 'Teddy'?" Aldon asked.

There was dead silence, followed by a stream of abuse and threats. Xandra's offer of money was also met by anger and hostility.

"You may be dressed like vagrants, but you're not one of us! It's the same as we told those officials who came snooping around. We don't know any 'Teddy' – he's not here!"

Xandra told his soldier to walk away with him. He needed a different strategy, and pulled a small device from his pocket. Suddenly the sounds of Terran music echoed through the tunnels. Embedded in the notes were certain frequencies which their agent would recognise.

They were about to leave when a scruffy looking man cautiously emerged from the shadows. It was 'Teddy', who immediately recognised Xandra.

"Thank God you're here," he said. "I was nearly captured on more than one occasion, and have been in hiding for some time."

The other 'tunnel' residents advanced menacingly towards them.

"Our friend has saved us from all manner of intruders in the past. Leave him alone or you'll never get out of here alive," one said.

Xandra clipped an extra invisibility device on 'Teddy', and at the given signal all three Terrans suddenly disappeared from view. Once out into the street they clung closely together as Xandra's team transported them straight up into his waiting shuttle craft.

Their agent's actual name was 'Edward', and he had been on the run for several months.

"I had been working in a physics laboratory when I received your message that we may have been betrayed by Richard when he started downloading Terran records to his human counterparts in the military. I rushed back to my accommodation, disabled or destroyed all equipment, and packed my identity papers and a few personal possessions.

"I could see a vehicle pulling up outside the front door, and several military officers getting out," Edward said. "I fled through a back window, and sought refuge with one of the protégées. Our own Friendship Club was a wonderful help. They smuggled me from place to place until I was close to the border, where I slipped across, hopefully undetected.

"By that time I had grown a beard, and what with longer hair and a pair of glasses I was harder to recognise. I followed your instructions and eventually managed to reach this country."

Xandra wanted to know why Edward had not approached either of the two emergency contacts he had nominated.

"I was worried that their identity may have been compromised. Before I escaped to the West, I heard that another Terran agent, Rodriguez, had been captured. Who knows what he may have divulged under torture or mind probing methods? He could have taken the easy way out and betrayed us to save himself.

"After I arrived here I cut my hair and shaved off my beard, only to find strange people following me. Perhaps I had been identified by facial recognition from your street cameras. I joined the dispossessed in their underground community until my unkempt appearance returned."

Xandra was concerned, and immediately advised both Camellia and the two emergency contacts to be extra vigilant. If approached they must pretend to know nothing and send a coded message to him immediately.

A short time later a communication arrived stating that an Earth Base Two agent, named Rodriguez, was awaiting rescue.

"Something's not right." Xandra said, turning to his operations officer. "We'll set a meeting time at night, in a remote and open location. Tell our emergency contact that this 'Rodriguez' has to come alone."

It was the early hours of the morning when Xandra arrived at the rendezvous, two hours ahead of time. He secreted himself among some bushes, and quietly waited.

His shuttle craft was hovering some distance away, and another armed vessel was monitoring the area from high in the atmosphere overhead. Before long they messaged that three figures were approaching from one side, and two more from the other. They appeared to have taken cover under some nearby trees.

"Be careful," his officer warned. "Your suspicions were well founded. The two on your right seem to have some form of mobile rocket launcher. Do you want us to take them out?"

Xandra told them to wait until he gave the order. "Keep the shuttle's transporter locked upon me, and activate it immediately I give the word. At the same time our military can simultaneously hit the apparently hostile individuals."

Someone walked forward into the clearing, and stood in the middle, looking around. Xandra activated his invisibility device, and crept ahead until he was close enough to identify the individual. He had been expecting an imposter, and was taken aback that it was indeed Rodriguez.

How could a trusted Terran agent have betrayed them like this, and placed his colleagues at risk? Xandra moved in behind Rodriguez, who sensed his presence.

"Is someone there? I know someone's there! Show yourself!"

Xandra grabbed onto Rodriguez, and yelled 'Now!' into his communicator. The mercenaries hiding in the trees leapt forward as their quarry suddenly disappeared in a beam of light. It was too late, and few seconds later they were annihilated by several large explosions.

Rodriguez found himself aboard Xandra's shuttle craft, and once he had recovered his wits, started thanking everybody for rescuing him.

"Save your breath," Xandra snarled. "We had the meeting spot under surveillance long before you arrived with your friends."

Rodriguez first tried to excuse his duplicity by stating he had been forced into it. Then he claimed the authorities where he had been based wanted to meet the Terrans and make a deal to work with them.

"That's why they set up an ambush and came armed with weapons which could have disabled our shuttle craft?" Xandra asked.

"I didn't know....I didn't know!" Rodriguez wailed.

Xandra was in no mood to listen to anymore lies. He needed to place Rodriguez into a containment field in case he had been implanted with any human tracking devices. Later they would utilise every means at their disposal to discover how much information their treacherous agent had disclosed to his accomplices.

Aggressive mind probing soon revealed the extent of Rodriguez's betrayal. The authoritarian government in the country where he had been assigned were anxious to obtain even more advanced Terran technology for their own benefit. It would give them instant dominance over other nations.

The information the military had received from Richard resulted in Rodriguez being apprehended. He had buckled under their threats, and then co-operated when they gave him a choice; a prolonged and painful death or wealth and the status of a prominent position within their scientific community. His most shameful act was to lead his captors to a couple of other Terran agents who were in hiding.

Xandra immediately sought Zadoc's help. "We must rescue our two officers as soon as possible. Rodriguez has revealed where they are being held prisoner, but it is a heavily fortified underground facility. Furthermore, they will be expecting us!"

Zadoc arrived a few days later with one of his battleships. As it hovered, high over the enemy prison, it was cloaked and shielded against attack. Tiny spy drones were sent down on a survey mission. Some scouted the surrounding area and others entered through the ventilation shafts and transmitted footage of the interior command centre and confined prisoners.

Zadoc scanned his monitoring screens. "It all looks comparatively easy – too easy! It could well be a trap. We need to resort to our automated devices and soldiers."

His first mode of attack was to disable all power to the facility. They could see the guards and other personnel panicking as their lights went out, and all emergency and electronic systems failed.

Zadoc knew they had to act swiftly. He dispatched three remote controlled, large metallic 'balls' - his equivalent of mechanized tanks. They rolled across the ground and breached the heavily fortified entry. Once inside they moved quickly through the rooms and corridors, spraying a mist which anaesthetised all personnel. Any soldiers who tried to resist were disabled by the inbuilt pulse weapons.

The final phase of the action was to deploy several robotic warriors, who stood guard while Terran soldiers released the captives and gently carried them to a suitable spot for transportation to safety on Zadoc's craft. The operation was in its final stages when an enemy tank and contingent of troops approached with weapons blazing.

The bullets ricocheted off the huge metallic automatons, which started moving forward. Flames and laser bursts were coming from their outstretched arms. Their feet and limbs made an ominous grating, thumping sound as they closed in on their assailants, who fled in terror.

Minutes later several incoming enemy aircraft were detected. Zadoc only just managed to get everyone back on board in time to raise his shields against this second violent onslaught.

He had been unsure whether he should destroy this unpleasant covert prison, which obviously tortured its detainees. Fate made the decision for him. In the ensuing battle one of his adversary's fighter planes plummeted into the facility. The impact caused a chain reaction with weapons and explosives decimating the entire complex.

His agents had been repeatedly tortured and were close to death. Despite intense medical treatment one lost his life soon after. The other would need months of rehabilitation before he fully recovered.

Zadoc knew that all Earth Base Two activities had been permanently compromised. This alone would seriously disrupt the delicate balance of technological progress amongst the competing nations on Earth. Richard had paid the ultimate price for his treachery. Rodriguez would be tried for treason by the Space Council, and would probably spend the remainder of his life in a penal colony.

CHAPTER 35

Gareth was surprised when he received an urgent order to report to Earth Base ready to attend a meeting with the Guardians. He packed a few clothes, and met with Aldon.

They sat down for a quick meal, and waited for Zadoc, who was due to arrive with their transport.

"What's going on?" Gareth asked. "Why the urgency?"

Aldon had no idea. "Maybe Zadoc will fill us in."

Zadoc didn't seem to know either. All he had been told was that he had to report to the Guardians immediately, and pick Xandra up along the way. They were to then transfer to an inter-galactic ship for the final leg of their journey.

The Guardians' command centre was in a different star system, a vast distance from Space Base. Even at the phenomenal speeds the new craft was capable of, it took some days to reach their destination.

They all wondered what was going on, but in the absence of any information or answers, decided to avail themselves of the facilities which were available on the large vessel.

There was an excellent gymnasium, and after their first workout, they collapsed in one of the many leisure areas.

"Every muscle in my body hurts." Aldon complained. The others chorused their full agreement.

"I think we are all out of shape." Xandra said. "Not like our time in the military, when there were mandatory training sessions everyday!"

Gareth also took the opportunity to visit the ship's small science facility. He soon became firm friends with Tasha, one of the Terran female technical officers. Their mutual knowledge and interests soon overcame his natural reserve, and they spent many hours in long conversation.

There was an excellent recreation centre where they met with the rest of the ship's complement for refreshments and various forms of entertainment. The crew were a diverse group of different alien races, but they all got on well together. At times Zadoc and his colleagues were enjoying themselves so much they put aside their concerns about the reason they had been summoned.

Tasha often joined them, and when some lively music was provided, she occasionally danced with Gareth.

"She's a very good-looking woman!" Zadoc commented. "Sure there's nothing going on?" Gareth was attracted to Tasha, and he avoided Zadoc's eye contact.

"No – we are just good friends." Xandra and Aldon exchanged knowing glances. They would be happy for Gareth if he found some love and companionship in his life.

When they arrived at the Guardians' planet, they were accommodated in the visitor facilities, and told to be ready to meet with the High Council the following day.

They were eventually ushered into the assembly chamber, and found the magnitude of their surroundings overwhelming. The assorted alien parliamentary leaders were seated above them, on a long high console.

One of them realised their four guests were very tense. He tried to put them at their ease by outlining some of the Guardians' interaction with the people of Earth. He looked down at them in a wise and kindly manner.

"Mankind has forgotten its origins. We have been with them for many thousands of years. Often, by design, our envoys were of such different or exotic appearance, they were regarded as Gods. Many historical records and legends describe strange deities such as Quetzalcoatl, the Dragonfae and the Rainbow Serpent. Others were much revered 'giants' and similar diverse beings. Our advanced knowledge of science and technology reinforced their elevated status.

"Numerous scholars talk of Sumeria, but that was not the first or only civilisation we founded. Cosmic visitors were involved in ancient Atlantis and Lemuria, and much later Egypt and other cultures on all the continents. Evidence of our presence still exists in the pyramids, temples, standing stones and carvings around the globe."

He paused. "However, we are often powerless against natural cataclysms which have occurred with repeated regularity, and frequently destroyed these great cities. The civilisations we had nourished were wiped out, leaving the few remaining inhabitants with nothing but memories and a few artefacts. Within a couple of generations they had forgotten all we taught them, and had to start all over again.

"There is ample evidence of massive asteroid impacts, and the great flood and legend of Noah. Much of it is recorded in *The Book of Enoch*, which is treasured by many of Earth's secret societies.

"Take the wonderful civilisation of Atlantis. The poet Plato described its sudden destruction when he wrote the words; 'There occurred violent earthquakes and floods; and in a single day and night of misfortune.....the island of Atlantis disappeared into the depths of the sea.

"Soon a rogue asteroid will present yet another danger to the planet. It is still some distance away, but has already been detected by the world's astronomers and space satellites and telescopes."

Another Guardian leaned forward. His huge forehead and eyebrows were accentuated by a worried frown. "Its trajectory puts it on a heading straight for Earth. If their scientists deploy nuclear weapons to

371

destroy or turn it aside, they could inadvertently cause untold damage to the Solar System and even other nearby planetary systems."

The Guardians normally adhered to a strict policy of non-interference. This time they had to make an exception. Their Space allies had already commenced complex calculations to determine what was necessary for them to safely deflect the large body of rock which was hurtling through the Solar System. It would be their craft, and their craft only, to take the remedial action.

One of Oni's colleagues from Karn also leaned over the console. "We will regretfully be obliged to counteract any human attempts to destroy this oversized space rock. You must monitor and detect all their intentions and prevent any clumsy missions to intercept the asteroid. Since the Terrans have jurisdiction over the Solar System, this will be your responsibility."

When the Guardians indicated that the conference was over, and were about to leave, Xandra requested a few more minutes of their time.

He broached the subject of the Xvars and Katons. "As you are aware, in the past they caused many problems on planet Earth. We were involved in several armed conflicts, and thought we had finally got rid of them. Later information revealed they had mounted several attacks in the outer galaxy, including an assault on one of your space stations. Do they pose any current threat to us?"

The president of the forum gazed down at his anxious underlings. "Much of the information regarding this unfortunate conflict is classified, however I suppose you have a right to know what may affect your own area.

"We have managed to contain the Xvars and Katons to another part of the galaxy. We have been combating them somewhat successfully, however we must all be vigilant. There is the remote chance that they could slip through our defences. Everyone still needs to be on their guard for any incursions."

Xandra was thankful that, for the moment, he didn't have any additional problems with their previous adversaries.

Once the meetings were over Zadoc collected his replacement equipment and provisions. There were also some personal parcels for his Terran officers, including an item for Gareth. It was a package with a present from his parents, and included a personal letter from his father.

"Son....we were all dismayed at your sudden deployment, so far away. We are endeavouring to get you transferred back home, where my colleague's daughter is eagerly awaiting your return and later marriage." Gareth's heart sank. What was he to do?

While the intergalactic craft was waiting to return them to the Solar System, the crew had 'shore leave'. Gareth and Tasha had taken the opportunity to explore the spectacular city where they were based. As they walked through the beautiful gardens, admiring the surrounding buildings, Tasha confided her frustration at being continually confined to a spaceship – no matter how large and modern.

"I wish I could live on firm ground and breathe fresh air."

Gareth stopped. A thought he dared not even contemplate came into his mind.

"I'm sure you'd like it on planet Earth. Why don't you come back with me?"

Tasha smiled, and then looked disheartened. "They will never allow that."

Gareth took a deep breath. "They would if we were married!"

Tasha was speechless for a moment. She gathered herself together and stared at Gareth.

"Are you asking me to marry you?"

Gareth nodded. "I realise we have only known each other a short time, but we have so much in common. I more than like you already, in fact I think I am falling in love. It is rare to meet a true soul mate, and after a few more days, we may never see each other again."

Tasha put her arms around his neck and kissed him gently on the cheek. "I must be mad, but yes I'll marry you."

Zadoc, Xandra and Aldon were all dumbfounded when Gareth and Tasha returned with their news.

Many of the Guardians were, at heart, quite sentimental. They responded by organising a wedding in the same garden where Gareth had proposed. A brief celebration followed, and as everybody left to return to the Solar System, Tasha was given permission to redeploy as a scientist on planet Earth.

Before he boarded their inter-galactic ship, Gareth sent a message to his parents; - *"Sorry, I have to go back to Earth. I have got married, so please send my apologies to your friend and his daughter."*

After they were returned to Space Base, Zadoc unloaded his supplies, and Tasha collected her possessions and joined Gareth. Nervous and unsure of herself, she watched her own ship depart. This was a new unknown chapter in her life.

Everyone reassured her that all would be well. She would be taught the basic knowledge required to live on Earth, and have a de-facto Terran family to rely upon. She spoke good English, but had a noticeable accent, so Aldon intended giving her a foreign 'cover' identity and documents.

They returned to Earth Base where Tasha remained for the first few days after her arrival. Martina was pleased that Gareth had, at long last, found someone to share his previously lonely life. It was an added benefit that she was also a scientist, and could contribute to their often difficult assignments.

Chantelle and John made excuses to visit Earth Base. They had heard about Gareth's sudden marriage and were both curious and anxious to meet Tasha.

Martina also took her to the island, to see Paul, Jacquita and Angela, and then to the bookshop to get acquainted with Victor, Mary and the twins. A few trips to the local department stores provided some more suitable clothing, and a familiarity with the city.

She moved into Gareth's home, and he laughed as she gleefully danced from room to room.

"There is so much space and freedom compared to my little cubbyhole cabin on the craft!"

The next day Gareth took her to the new job he had arranged for her. Since Angela had retired to have the baby, Tasha could replace her and work alongside Michael and Tony in the same company. His two colleagues were astounded. Gareth's marriage was the last thing they had expected.

"He's a bit of a dark horse." Michael observed.

Tony choked on his mouthful of coffee. "You're the last one to talk," he spluttered. "You abducted your future wife at gunpoint!"

They were both glad that Tasha would be joining them in the laboratory. Her expertise would be greatly appreciated. Together they could surreptitiously search all government, military and corporate communications to determine what the humans were planning in relation to the incoming asteroid.

Gareth reported to Aldon a few days later. "Earth's astrophysicists and scientists are aware of the threat, but keeping it secret. They don't want to scare the public, and further have very limited shelter and supplies in the event of an impact."

"Why does that not surprise me?" Aldon said. "The hierarchy and billionaires only care about their own survival – not that of the man in the street.

"Well, in the event of an impact, their shelters will provide little protection, and are more likely to collapse on top of them. They are sending a probe up next week. I suppose their planned response will depend upon the information they receive back."

Aldon was glad he did not have to make the ethical decision regarding any interference with the probe. All the data was to be forwarded to Xandra and Zadoc. It was up to them.

Solving the problem was no easy matter. The Guardians' specialists had to account for the size, trajectory and speed of the asteroid. Any deviation from its current path could create a chain reaction and result in a later collision with other space debris or even another planet.

Earth's experts had not identified all the possible threats lurking in the Solar System, and were not capable of safely solving this current situation. If they decided to send up a nuclear armed rocket, the chances of them impacting the massive asteroid were limited. If they did manage to hit it, there would be a multitude of smaller dangerous boulders flying off in all directions.

Aldon and Gareth had contacted one of their incognito Terran scientists who had been included in a special international working party, formed to decide how best to save mankind from the impending disaster.

He advised that nobody could understand why their first probe had failed, and were planning to launch a second one as soon as possible. He was also concerned that if remedial action was not taken soon, his human counterparts may resort to the nuclear option.

In order to turn the asteroid onto a safer course, it would take split second timing with several space craft acting in precise co-ordination. Many of the required calculations were complex, and the Guardians were still debating the best solution when Aldon sent an urgent message to Xandra.

"The joint Earth taskforce is preparing to launch a nuclear warhead into space eight days from now. We are unable to dissuade them. These are the details of the proposed timing and trajectory."

Zadoc reported to the Guardians. A decision had to be made very soon, and eventually a second best solution was agreed upon.

The nuclear warhead would have to be deactivated during flight. Also the asteroid would be diverted from its orbit and thrust directly into the Sun, where the impact and intense heat would hopefully destroy it.

There was no margin for error and more calculations were swiftly undertaken. They had to allow for the asteroid's velocity as well as the Sun's rotating and gravitational force.

The downside of this strategy was the distinct possibility that the impact could cause a localised but brief transient energy release. While these complex diverse and rapid waves, commonly referred to as 'Solar Flares', were not expected to actually create any fires on Earth, they could disrupt and even destroy all electronic and digital technology.

Any facilities which may be affected would have to immobilize all their equipment at the appropriate moment.

Once the details were finalised, Xandra was responsible for notifying the Moon, Mars and any other Bases which may be threatened. The side of the Earth, facing the Sun at the time, would also be at risk. Aldon and Gareth had the unenviable task of not only ensuring the safety of their own facilities, but also those of Earth's population.

"This is going to be a nightmare." Aldon groaned. "Even though only part of our area will be vulnerable, I cannot take risks with Earth Base One or any of our Terrans. That means we have to disable as many human networks as we can before we ourselves have to turn everything off. The timing had to be absolutely accurate.

"Andy and Ebony will send numerous anonymous messages to world governments and military, saying that a Solar Flare is imminent. Gareth and his colleagues will utilise their cyber skills to temporarily put out of action all important services such as power grids and electricity supplies."

"Xandra will attend to the human satellites and space stations orbiting the Earth, while Zadoc and Karine, along with a couple of Space Base craft are going to deal with the nuclear warhead and then the asteroid."

The nominated moment arrived, and as Earth Base temporarily shut down, Aldon hoped he had done enough to save society from the devastating effects of an unexpected Solar Flare.

Martina tried to reassure him. "I know that during the few hours people will be without electricity and communications everything will be affected. It will not be your fault if this results in the deaths of a few people. We have done everything possible.

"At least our shields will protect us, and we have our emergency power to rely upon. There will be chaos out there in this part of the world. It is only for a short time and then once we have restored their facilities, undamaged, they can get back to life as normal."

Aldon grunted. "I suppose the few inevitable casualties are preferable to half of Earth being wiped out by that enormous space boulder."

Bob was busy at the hospital, and Gareth, Michael, Tony and Tasha were in their respective establishments assisting with the joint project.

Victor had remained at the bookshop to ensure security, and to make sure all technology was switched off. He would reactivate everything once the operation was over.

Rebecca and the children, along with the twins, had retreated to the farm, where Mary had prepared a meal for everyone whilst they avoided the anticipated mayhem.

Fiona was unusually thoughtful. "I heard Tony talking about an ongoing Terran project to take a lot of Earth's literature and scientific books. Now I understand why they are going to so much trouble to keep them in a safe place. We humans have stored so much of our knowledge on digital technology. It would all be lost in a major cataclysm."

Lucy agreed. "Tony also told me that some of our governments have large underground facilities where they hoard millions of plant seeds. I believe they also save human and animal tissue to preserve the world's genetic diversity."

"I'm glad we are relatively self sufficient." Mary commented. "I wonder how everyone else is coping with all their services suddenly failing. Most of them just take everything for granted."

Down in the town there was disorder and confusion everywhere. Nothing worked without electricity and the digital networks so many relied on.

No traffic lights meant the streets were jammed solid with trucks and cars. Honking got them nowhere. Anything which relied upon digital technology had stopped working. Banks and shops were left in darkness, and staff were manually locking the doors to prevent the pilfering and robberies which had already commenced.

Zadoc and his team out in space worked frantically and with precision to bring the operation to a successful conclusion. A great cheer went up when the rogue asteroid disappeared into the fiery clutches of the Sun.

The impact produced a flaming surge of turbulence and the subsequent cosmic waves raced towards anything in their path. Once Zadoc's squad were sure the danger was over they bid Xandra goodbye and left him to restore Earth's dormant satellites and space station.

Aldon reactivated his Base and other Terran facilities, and Gareth and his team did their best to covertly reverse their previous cyber attacks. Bit by bit the lights came back on as the electricity and other services were reinstated. The general population were confused as to what had happened and why. Perhaps it was a hostile act by a rival nation. Only a few privileged military and government officials knew the truth. They were grateful for the alien's intervention, but could never breathe a word about it. Not ever!

CHAPTER 36

Mary was curled up on the sofa when Xandra came down the stairs. She put down the book she was reading and went to greet him.

"Hello, we weren't expecting you. I hope nothing is wrong."

He followed her as she went into the kitchen to make a cup of coffee. "I don't know. It depends which way you look at it."

"Look at what?"

"Well I have some news, and an invitation for you to come to a wedding."

Mary smiled. "A wedding? I love weddings. Who's getting married?"

Xandra gulped. "Your Granny!"

For a moment Mary stared at him in stunned silence. "I don't believe it! Granny's been a widow for over thirty years, and has never shown any interest in men or finding a new husband. She's too old now to be thinking of getting up to hanky-panky with some geriatric geezer."

Victor came into the room and tried to suppress his amusement. "I didn't think the old girl had it in her. Who's the lucky fellow?"

Mary glared at him. "This isn't funny. Xandra, tell me everything right now!"

Xandra explained that Granny had gained a new lease of life since living with the Terrans. Her new beau and intended husband was actually one of the Terran diplomats who had retired from active duty. He had met Granny while he was resting over on Solar Base.

"His name is Peter, and he really is a decent fellow. He and your grandmother hit it off immediately. Don't be angry. They both have been alone for many years, and have found contentment and fulfilment with each other."

Mary was still scowling. "What does my mother have to say about this?"

Xandra sighed. "Vera is still very hostile and under care and medication. I was hoping you would give Granny and Peter your support and blessing. It would mean so much to them."

Mary hesitated, and remembered how Granny had loved and raised her. Perhaps she had missed out on happiness due to caring for a young child.

"Yes. For many years she neglected her own personal life for my sake. If this Peter is as good as you think, I won't stand in Granny's way."

Xandra suggested that, if she could get some leave from work, Mary could go back to Solar Base with him and spend a few days there before the wedding.

"In fact, if you could get a month off, there is a favour I may need from you for the remaining two or three weeks. We can talk about it later."

Victor urged her to go. "Mishka and I will be fine. The bookshop is usually quiet this time of the year."

This was an excuse for Mary to buy a new outfit for the wedding, and Victor watched as she twirled around in her new dress.

"You look really beautiful," he said. "I could marry you myself!"

Mary blushed, and wondered if he really meant it.

She set off with Xandra the next day, and enjoyed a stopover with Pletta and his Mars crew. They were all enjoying a quiet drink when the discussion turned to the recent emergency over the asteroid.

"I'm glad Zadoc's people solved the problem," he said. "We were terrified the humans' nuclear rocket would either blow us all up or send that rock in our direction."

Xandra agreed. "Tell me about it. The more they start venturing off their own planet, the more problems we are going to have!"

As soon as they reached Solar Base, Mary left her bags in her room, and raced off the see her grandmother. When she found her with Ida and the children, she was amazed at the change in her appearance. She was wearing a very fashionable outfit and her hairdo and makeup made her seem at least twenty years younger.

She gave her grandmother a big hug then stepped back and looked at her. "You look wonderful. If the Terrans have a secret 'Youth Potion' I want to know about it! What's this I hear about you finding yourself a toy-boy?"

Granny gave a big smile. "Yes my dear, I am so happy. His name is Peter, and you'll meet him later. I do hope you like him, as your approval is very important to me."

Ida was sitting nearby, with a large tabby cat resting on her lap. Mary looked around the children's area and noticed a couple more felines and several kittens playing with the youngsters.

"Ida – your furry family seems to be multiplying. What does Xandra think about that?"

Ida assured her that the situation was under control, and several of the Solar Base families wanted the new kittens. In fact there was a waiting list! Xandra had relaxed his 'no pets' rule, as it was unfair that the children who lived permanently on the base had no contact with any other living creatures.

Granny had planned to take Mary to meet her future husband later that day, but as they were talking Peter walked into the room. He was, as she expected, an older man but still quite handsome. He had twinkling blue eyes, a kindly face, and his previously blond hair had turned to a distinguished silvery-white colour.

Mary felt drawn to him immediately. After the initial introductions he sat down, picked up one of the kittens and gently stroked it.

"There is a multitude of birds, fish and animals out there in the galaxy," he said. "Up until now some of the children have only ever seen digital images and holograms. Even though the opportunities are limited, your grandmother and I hope to change that."

He explained that children who had parents on the base often went back to their home planets with their families. Others were orphans or hybrids rejected by their human mothers. They rarely escaped the confines of Solar Base.

Ida looked up. "They need to feel the sun on their face, the wind in their hair and the grass beneath their feet. I think it is wonderful what your grandmother and Peter are planning to do."

Mary turned to Granny. "And what's that?"

"Well, for starters, Peter and I are taking a few of them with us when we go to his own planet for our honeymoon. It will be the first holiday some of them have ever had."

Peter nodded. "Yes we want to share our happiness with these little ones."

Mary began to think that whilst no-one could ever be sure what the future held, her grandmother had made a good choice in her new husband. She changed the subject to her mother, Vera.

Granny sighed. "My daughter is still very aggressive. She resents being 'snatched' from the clutches of Earth's authorities, and can't understand it was for her own good. Her recovery will take some time, and she is still in the care of a specialised team here.

"Perhaps you should delay any attempted reconciliation until a later visit. She is not very amiable at the moment. Even though Peter will become her step-father, she refuses to meet with him or come to the wedding."

Mary went back to her accommodation to change, and later accepted an invitation from Xandra to have dinner with him and the happy couple.

This was an intimate affair in the privacy of Xandra's quarters. A little grey worker served a splendid meal followed by some excellent vintage wine. As they relaxed in his leisure room, Mary thought this was the ideal time to ask all the questions which had puzzled her for so long.

She wanted understand more about the Guardians activity on Earth, and how it affected her and Granny's family. What was it all about and why? She thought that Peter might give her the answers.

The old man took a deep breath. "All life is the result of evolved organisms. In nature they adapt and modify in accordance with the environment and current conditions.

"In the world's hunter-gatherer days it was always about the survival of the fittest. Stone Age societies had to struggle to survive. It was all down to natural selection. The strongest, and often most violent, were the ones to pass their genes on to the next generation."

Mary agreed that the Earth's cave men were regarded as being no more than primitive savages.

Peter paused. "This is true, but even in those days the Guardians were intent upon improving the quality of human life and saving them from undeserved suffering. The propagation of desirable genes was difficult. It can take thousands of years for naturally beneficial traits to spread through the population.

"The long term strategic plan was to ameliorate the bad features without destroying the good ones. The plans were controversial and not all of the delegates to the Space Council approved. The bioethics incorporated into the initial program insisted upon a slow, measured incremental change to certain aspects of seriously flawed human nature. It was designed to improve particular capabilities, which would have a cumulative effect on community networks."

Mary was curious as to how they went about implementing genetic tinkering in ancient mankind, who led a primitive, nomadic lifestyle.

"It wasn't easy," Peter said. 'Initially, they concentrated on specific societies, who soon became much more civilised. Just when they thought their plans were succeeding - wars, plagues and natural disasters decimated the inhabitants, and the beneficial gene pool along with them.

"It wasn't until the last few centuries that they were able to recommence any meaningful modifications. Within a short time secret organisations sprang up, primarily to protect the recipients and their knowledge. The connection and the intellectual capability of some individuals was so improved that their scientific discoveries led to great leaps forward."

Mary nodded. "By the beginning of the twentieth century we had trains, automobiles, electricity and were taking to the air with simple flying machines."

Xandra continued the narrative and explained that the Guardians realised it was only a matter of time before humans would be venturing out into space. The entire agenda had to be fast tracked.

"A brutal world war displayed mankind's continued propensity to violence, and the Guardians concentrated on a couple of genetically suitable nations. Perhaps they could evolve into responsible leaders. Many of the population were enhanced and their human scientists introduced to new technology, including instructions on how to modify the viability of the human gamete.

"It was a mistake, which left everyone with a bitter aftertaste. These people had an appetite for perfection, and considered everybody outside of their racial profile to be inferior. They committed mass murder and practised their own perverted version of genetic manipulation and eugenics."

Peter sadly shook his head as he also recalled what had happened. "They were defeated in the resultant war which was even more atrocious than the previous conflict. Their scientists, who were privy to the advanced technology, escaped to several countries that availed themselves of the knowledge the Guardians had imparted.

"This led to many unintended consequences including a substantial progression in their space program. They were aware of the practice of inserting genes into embryos and proceeded with intentional genetic modifications.

"They also began to experiment with the effects of vibration and certain frequencies upon the human autonomic nervous system and brain. Their expertise has already progressed from basic implants to nano size devices and neural dust motes.

"Some nations were concentrating on producing super soldiers who would not be constrained by any ethics or emotions. It is fortunate that they have not fully discovered the secrets of quantum biology and neurology. Regrettably it will only be a matter of time before they unlock the mysteries of telepathy and mind control."

Peter said that at about the time he was elected to the Space Council, he participated in crisis talks about the evolving predicament on planet Earth. Humans were misusing some of their new knowledge and not yet ready to participate in the cosmic community.

"We realised that some of the problems were due to our own errors in judgement, and tried to counteract the adverse results by performing a basic augmentation on as many suitable inhabitants as possible. We concentrated on improving their cognitive abilities and favourable traits such as empathy, emotions and other values.

"A mass deployment of our specialist teams snatched thousands of people, most of whom had no memory of the encounter. It was easy to avoid detection during the confusion and aftermath of the war and other conflicts.

"The beneficial results became evident at a human festival held in a place called 'Woodstock'. Thousands of young people gathered together and professed love towards their fellow man, concern about the environment, and compassion for animals and their fellow creatures. Their influence on society continues today. We thought maybe mankind was worth saving after all!

"Normally the Guardians will not directly intervene in human affairs. We were glad they made an exception where the asteroid was concerned. Had it hit the Earth all our efforts would have been back to square one!"

Mary was a little confused. "What about families, like my own, and those of Bob and the twins? How do they fit into the overall picture?"

Peter noted her concern and smiled. "There is no need to worry, my dear. Our original Terran program involving the complicated and gradual generational augmentation of particular families and bloodlines continues. They are in an entirely different 'full upgrade' category. Their skills, and yours, include enhanced intelligence combined with psychic and telepathic abilities. Many, but not all, of these protégées belong to Friendship Clubs around the world."

Mary was grateful that Peter and Xandra trusted her enough to tell her more about the Guardians' long term program. She had to agree that mankind certainly wasn't ready to participate in the cosmic community.

The wedding day arrived, and Mary went to help Granny change. She looked amazing in a long white dress with flowers in her hair.

She glanced over at Mary. "Stop dithering girl! You're more nervous than the bride. And talking about weddings, when are you going to settle down with a nice young man? How about that young chap – Victor - whom you're staying with?"

Mary mumbled an incoherent reply, and pretended to be busy doing something else. She had always been independent, and didn't want to face the fact that she cared for Victor, and couldn't imagine life without him.

Zadoc was going to perform the wedding commitment ceremony, and as Mary escorted Granny into the large communal assembly area she stopped in surprise. The whole of Solar Base was gathered there and broke into spontaneous applause as the bride made her way across to the podium where her groom was waiting.

There were decorations of flowers, specially smuggled in a few days earlier. Ida was wearing a long embroidered robe. All around her were the children who looked angelic in matching white costumes. They softly sang a Terran love ballad as Granny and Peter exchanged their vows.

Mary wiped the tears of emotion from her eyes as the simple but beautiful ceremony came to an end.

Suddenly the mood changed, and upbeat music filled the air. Androids and little workers were bringing platters of food out to the tables at the side. Everybody was in a party mood, which was improved by a very potent fruit punch.

There were speeches and toasts, and when it came time for the traditional bridal waltz, Granny and Peter took to the dance floor to perform a very energetic boogie.

"Wow!" Mary thought. "I think those two are going to grow old disgracefully! I wish Victor was here to share this entire uplifting experience."

Zadoc asked for some quiet while he made his final speech. "This happy couple has won the hearts of everybody on Solar Base. We have all contributed to your wedding present, so please come with me now."

He led them to the accommodation area and opened the door to a fully renovated residence. It was furnished with everything they would need for their married life together.

The newly-weds were speechless and they noticed there were even pictures on the wall and colourful cushions on the sofa. Zadoc and Xandra left Granny and Peter in their new home, and reminded them they would be leaving early next morning for their honeymoon.

Mary went to the Space Port to bid them farewell as they left to visit Peter's relatives on his own planet. Granny and Peter asked her to grant them a very special favour, and pointed to six animated youngsters also gathered beside the waiting craft.

"Of course," said Mary. "Anything!"

Her heart sank when they revealed that there were another six children who were disappointed at not being able to go. Would Mary take them back with her, for a fortnight's holiday on planet Earth? Zadoc and Xandra had both approved the plan.

She hesitated, thinking of several excuses. "But they only speak Terran, not English. Where would they stay without causing suspicion?"

Zadoc had joined them, and assured Mary that, in addition to her own ability to communicate with them telepathically, Martina and Jacquita had also agreed to assist. The proposed itinerary was for the kids to spend one week on Mary's farm followed by a few days on the island.

Mary was hesitating when one of the boys walked over and took her by the hand. "Please say 'yes' Miss. Our friends will be so unhappy if they have to stay here."

His heartfelt plea prevailed over Mary's reservations. "Okay....okay!"

A cheer went up, and Mary returned to Xandra's command centre to finalise the arrangements. What had she let herself in for?

Ida brought in the other six orphans, ready to go. Each one was clutching a backpack, and excitedly anticipating the adventure to come.

"That was quick," said Mary.

Ida smiled. "We knew you wouldn't say no."

Xandra ushered them aboard his ship, and soon they were zooming through the darkness on their way back to Earth.

CHAPTER 37

The children, whose ages ranged between eleven and fourteen, were just as excited about the journey on a spaceship as they were about their visit to planet Earth.

They crowded around the controls in the command centre until Xandra ordered them back into the observation lounge under Mary's supervision. The little grey worker looked confused when she ordered ice-cream for everyone. Perhaps spaceships didn't carry ice-cream. Milk and cookies would have to suffice!

Bedding down six exuberant adolescents was no easy task. When Mary eventually got them all settled, she decided to sleep in the dormitory cabin with them. As an afterthought she had one of the robots stand guard outside the door, just in case anyone decided to go exploring on the sly!

The brief stopover at Mars Base was without incident, mainly because Xandra had sternly told them to 'look, but don't touch!' He had also threatened to take any miscreants back to Solar Base in disgrace. Mary wondered how they were going to behave when Xandra was no longer around.

Once at Earth Base the passengers and luggage were unloaded. Aldon did not need six energetic youngsters in his operations centre. He wasted no time in ushering everybody into the PVX, with Andy at the controls. Martina, who spoke the Terran language, was to accompany Mary and the children for the week.

They landed among the trees behind the farm, and Mary felt humbled when she saw the kids' delight in experiencing what she took for granted every day. They rolled in the grass, and lay staring at the blue sky and clouds above.

"Up until now, their main experience has been via virtual reality and similar holographic means." Martina said. "Let's get them settled before they run off exploring."

The accommodation was a little cramped in the cottage, as Mary had not anticipated six extra guests. Petie was dancing up and down on his perch, shrieking with excitement. The children were enthralled as he warbled snatches of the Terran songs which he had learned from the 'Associates' practice sessions every weekend.

Once it was all sorted out, the children were taken outside to meet the other animals. Martina didn't need to tell them to be gentle and not to frighten them. They patted and stroked everything, even the chooks and ducks. Mary realised that with their paranormal abilities they were immediately connecting and communicating with her farmyard menagerie.

Martina told them how humans partnered with animals in their everyday life; the goats for milk, and poultry for eggs. They wanted to know about Wiggles. What did horses do? Mary climbed onto his back and cantered around the field. It wasn't long before she slowly led them, one by one, for a short ride.

It was late afternoon, and Rebecca arrived with Bob's children to perform their regular feeding and care duties. She wasn't expecting to find Mary had returned with Martina and several visitors. While they were explaining the situation, Martina noticed that although the Solar Base kids did not speak English, they seemed to be communicating on another level with Dave and Christie.

The next morning Tony and the twins drove up for the weekend, and Victor arrived soon after. Martina was glad that Tony also spoke the Terran language. Now there were two of them to handle the youngsters, and overhear any mischief they might be planning!

Saturday was spent with a joint meditation and practice session. Bob's family joined them and, after an outdoor picnic, Victor played the guitar and everybody had a sing-along to all the tunes Olivia had taught them on Solar Base.

"What are we going to do tomorrow?" Fiona asked. "I believe these children have never seen the more exotic animals that live on Earth. How about we all go to the zoo? It should be great fun."

It was agreed, and the next morning three car loads of Terrans and their colleagues set off for the zoo.

As they passed through the turnstiles, Tony looked round. "We are sixteen in number. Let's agree that each of the eight adults has responsibility for one of the eight kids."

Everyone thought that was a very sensible idea, and they proceeded around the park, with the spellbound children marvelling at the different species. The 'petting' area was particularly popular. Much as the adults disliked animals being kept in captivity, all the kids insisted on a ride on the elephant.

Multiple photographs were being taken, and Mary was consulting with Victor and Tony over her camera when she noticed the young lad in her care was nowhere to be seen.

"Where is Benny? He was here a minute ago."

Martina asked his friends, and one pointed towards a nearby enclosure. "He's gone to pat the pussycat. It is much bigger than the ones we've got on Solar Base. It's all by itself, and Benny thought it might be lonely."

Everybody raced to the fence, and realised that somehow Benny had managed to climb down into the deep stone-lined pit. He was sitting next to a fairly large leopard, which was purring loudly as he stroked it under the chin, the way one would do with a moggy.

Mary was panic stricken. "This is my fault for not watching him more carefully. It is a steep drop down; how can we get him out safely before the zoo keepers find out?"

Martina had an idea. She called to Benny to stay calm and walk very slowly towards the wall. The leopard followed him, still purring.

Martina and Tony prepared everyone, including Benny, to mutually activate their levitation skills and raise him up, away from the big cat. It took every bit of their combined mental powers to slowly lift the boy above the ground. There was a heart stopping moment when the leopard seemed to awake from its trance and lunged upwards into the air towards Benny, who was just within reach. Victor and Tony quickly grabbed him by both arms and pulled him to safety.

Tony addressed them all in Terran; didn't they understand that some of the animals were vicious and ate people in the wild? The kids looked so scared that Bob and Rebecca decided it was time to calm down and indulge in rather large ice-creams. They tightened their supervision of all the children as they finalised their tour of the remaining exhibits.

Martina had considered taking everybody to town, so her guests could see the shops, and perhaps buy some souvenirs. Maybe that was not such a good idea after all. She did not want anymore catastrophes. Instead, on the way home, they drove through the city streets. The kids pressed their faces against the car windows and looked longingly at all those wonders they were not going to be allowed to investigate.

Fiona and Lucy felt sorry for them, and drove back up to the farm later with some gifts. Bob had the same idea, and the youngsters had accumulated quite a stash of keepsakes by the end of their stay.

On their last day, Rebecca was held up in town. She asked Mary if she would collect Christie and Dave from their local school.

"It's such a pleasant sunny afternoon," said Martina, and looked towards their young guests. "We will come with you. They will enjoy the walk."

They set off across the field with the children laughing and chasing each other. Mary called them back as they reached the small stone building.

"We don't want them drawing attention to themselves," she said. "That teacher sometimes asks awkward questions."

Miss Smith was scowling and waiting outside the front door with Dave and Christie.

"I want to talk to you or his parents about Dave. He's been cheating on his tests!"

"No I haven't!" Dave protested.

"You couldn't possibly know all the answers," she snapped, grabbing him by the arm and shaking him.

Christie kicked her in the shins. "Leave my brother alone."

Miss Smith released her hold on Dave and went to slap Christie. Her arm suddenly froze mid-air, and before Mary could intervene, she started to rise off the ground.

"Oh no!" Martina gasped as a squawking Miss Smith rose higher and higher into the air. She turned to her six charges. They were standing in a line together, telepathically connected and concentrating on Miss Smith. She realised the children had acted in unison to protect Christie.

"My goodness!" Mary exclaimed, trying not to laugh. "Their levitation skills are much better than mine."

Christie momentarily forgot that her teacher had intended to smack her. "Miss Smith – you're flying! You must flap your arms like a bird if you want to go anywhere!"

Mary couldn't contain herself anymore and collapsed into fits of giggles. It was left to Martina to intervene, and she persuaded the children to gently lower the unfortunate woman back down to firm ground.

As Miss Smith fled into the school house and locked the door, Mary was glad there had been no witnesses to the regrettable event.

They all rushed back to the farm, and realised that after levitating Benny out of the leopard's pit, the children didn't know this was not normal behaviour on Earth. They agreed that it was maybe prudent for Martina and her Solar Base charges to leave for the island a few hours earlier than intended.

A hurried message to Aldon and he arrived down behind the trees. Once the youngsters had collected their belongings, and boarded the PVX, there was no real evidence that they had ever even been there.

Rebecca and Bob also hurried home, and along with Mary awaited any possible repercussions from the afternoon's incident. Sure enough, just after dinner there was a knock on the door.

The two local police officers looked embarrassed as they advised that they were investigating a complaint made by the school teacher.

Bob said that his two children were in bed; perhaps they could tell him the problem. They related Miss Smith's account of how six alien children had lifted her into the air, and left her helplessly floating above the ground.

The constable coughed nervously. "She said they were intimidating and staring at her with expressionless faces. They reminded her of the kids in that movie 'The Village of the Damned." Later, she saw a silver flying saucer moving across the sky, near the bordering forest."

Mary stepped forward and said that she had picked Dave and Christie up from school, and she didn't know anything about 'alien children'.

"Miss Smith was behaving rather strangely, and accusing young Dave of cheating on some test. If anything, it is I who should have a grievance. She shook young Dave and threatened to hit little Christie. We left fairly quickly, and I don't recall any 'flying saucers'!"

Bob realised he was being unethical, but his kids' wellbeing was paramount. He produced a copy of the photo from the Christmas party.

"Here's that same teacher, under the table with 'Santa'. I don't know what she is smoking. Perhaps she has been watching too many horror movies, or maybe all those 'ankle-biting' pupils are driving her to a nervous breakdown."

"I'm so sorry for the inconvenience. You understand we had to investigate," said the other constable as he and his colleague hastily returned to their patrol car

Bob and Rebecca were concerned about the complications an inquisitive and hostile Miss Smith could cause.

"Just leave it to me," Rebecca said.

The next morning, after walking the kids to school, she took their teacher to one side. "I must show you this happy Xmas school photo. Isn't 'Santa' Sam Hilton's father? His wife and the education authorities wouldn't be pleased if they saw this."

Miss Smith's face dropped, and turned a strange colour. She nodded when Rebecca asked if they understood each other.

Once the PVX reached Earth Base, Jacquita was waiting to transport the children to the island. Martina related the unfortunate incidents during their stay at the farm, and wished Jacquita the 'best of luck'.

Jacquita wasn't worried. She was sure she and Paul could manage. The nuns had been told that they were orphans, on holiday from a foreign country. They would be staying under their care in the convent.

The island was remote, and surely there was not much mischief they could get up to.

The children were enthralled by the tropical island. The community took a liking to these foreign children, and Paul asked them to keep an eye on them at all times. Some of the village men took them out in their canoes, and others let them frolic in the gardens, and help themselves to any fruit they wanted.

Although they did not speak the same language, they played happily with the local youngsters. Often they would race across the sand together, followed by an assortment of neighbourhood dogs.

They had never seen the ocean before, and had learned to swim in the pool at Solar Base. They were only allowed to go into the water as long as an adult was present. The natives decided that these kiddies were special, and reported that every time they were splashing around in the lagoon, the dolphins would swim up and interact with them.

The youngsters were obliged to attend the Sunday church service. Although they failed identify with the ceremony, they behaved well, and Paul asked them to sing one of the songs Olivia had taught them on Solar Base. Whilst the villagers didn't understand the Terran words, after the incidents with the dolphins, they were sure those sweet young voices must belong to little angels in disguise.

While Jacquita was busy keeping a watchful eye on things, Angela had been filling in for her at the church school. She would always get an escort home, and once their visitors had raced up the hill with her, Tuan would give them fruit juice and homemade biscuits.

They liked Tuan as he let them go to his home and play with his dog and her litter of puppies. Angela thought it was a pity they had no pets on Solar Base; that was not until Ida McAffrey smuggled her cats on board Xandra's ship.

The holiday came to an end all too soon. Paul and Jacquita were gathering the children and their belongings together, ready to transport back to Earth Base and transfer to Xandra's ship for their trip home.

It was rather chaotic as the kids, loaded down with their backpacks and clutching extra baggage and gifts, were sent on their way. Jacquita and Paul had enjoyed their visit, but were glad that life could get back to normal.

Xandra settled his young passengers into the dormitory cabin, and left one of his crew to attend to them. He was halfway to Mars when his officer approached him in the control centre.

"I have fed the children, but what do I give to the two little furry creatures they brought with them?"

Xandra groaned. "What furry creatures?"

A hurried visit to their quarters reminded him that, in his haste to get underway, he had failed to check the luggage being brought on board. After the incident with Ida and her cats, he should have known better. There were two small puppies running around the cabin.

The smallest boy eventually broke the guilty silence. "Please Sir, say we can keep them. They won't be any trouble, and we'll look after them."

His heart started to melt as he looked into six pairs of pleading eyes. What could he do? Now he would have both cats and dogs on his once orderly Base!

CHAPTER 38

Aldon frowned as he read the message Ebony gave him.

Martina looked up. "What's wrong?"

"Nothing, I suppose. Pletta is coming from Mars Base for a few days, and he is bringing his son Nathan with him."

Martina was curious. "Pletta is such good fun. I didn't know that he was married, and has a son. Why are they coming here?"

Aldon hesitated. "Pletta doesn't like to talk about it, but he and his wife parted company many years ago. Their son is a young man now. He recently graduated as a cadet from military college. I met him once, and unfortunately he had a less than pleasant personality.

"Zadoc could not allocate Pletta any extended leave to attend Nathan's graduation. Instead he has allowed the boy to spend some time with his father on Mars Base, combined with a short trip to Earth together."

They arrived the next day, and Martina began to understand why Aldon was cautious where Nathan was concerned. He was a brash young man, who obviously had no respect for the androids or little grey workers. In fact, although she was a senior officer, Martina sensed a barely concealed arrogance when he spoke to her.

Pletta already had false identity documents, and Andy was busy creating a set for Nathan before they could set out on their sightseeing trip. Martina walked in just as the young cadet gave Andy an aggressive shove.

"Hurry up, you moron! I haven't got all day!"

Martina was seething. "Don't you dare!"

He turned around. "I'll do what I want. These androids have to learn their place. What's more, I don't take any orders from a woman!"

Martina snapped. This intolerable cadet was no more than a boy! She strode across the room and knocked him to the floor. Before he could get up she grabbed him by the collar and dragged him bodily into the recreation area where Pletta and Aldon were sitting.

"Pletta, as long as you're here, I hold you responsible for Nathan's behaviour. He may have been a senior in his last year of military college, and able to lord it over the younger cadets. Now he is back down at the bottom of the pecking order. He needs to lose the self-importance and learn the chain of command."

Pletta cringed and ordered Nathan to wait for him in quarters.

"I must apologise," he said. "Before college he lived with his mother, who spoiled him. I wasn't around to exert any discipline or set an example of how he should behave. I thought the military academy would straighten him out. I was wrong. Perhaps with some time together now, I can steer him on the right track."

They determined that, to be on the safe side, Pletta must always be present with Nathan both on the Base and during excursions outside on Earth. It would also be preferable that Nathan didn't know the identity of any Terran agents or protégées during his stay.

This decision meant that while Aldon kept Nathan under strict supervision on the Base, Martina took Pletta, on his own, for a very quick trip to visit Victor, their three scientists and the island. This way he could identify where their personnel and transporters were located. One never knew when they might be needed in an emergency.

Pletta was sitting with Paul and Jacquita outside the little stone church. He was entranced by the island and the tropical, simplistic way of life, and welcomed their promise that he could come back by himself for a vacation one day.

Pletta finished his intoxicating fruit drink and rose to leave. "I have a better idea," he chuckled. "If either of you finish your tour of duty, and want to go back home, I'm going to have my name on the top of the list as a replacement!"

He met with Victor and Mary that night after the bookshop had closed. Gareth and the twins joined them. The much anticipated musical competition was about to take place, and they were in all in high spirits. Pletta remembered how popular Fiona and Lucy had been with his crew when they stopped over at Mars Base on their way to visit Xandra.

His first joint trip with Nathan was to be special. It was the evening of the National Singing Contest, and the 'Associates' were appearing in the preliminary rounds. Pletta had taken a liking to those young people, and wanted to lend his support.

Aldon accompanied him and a very sullen Nathan to the large entertainment centre where their friends were performing.

"Why are we here?" Nathan asked.

Aldon made the excuse that he wanted him to experience the concerts young people of his age enjoyed on planet Earth. The music was loud and lively. Pletta was optimistic when his son started to applaud and sing along with the rest of the audience.

Mary, Victor and the twins were a bundle of nerves. They had a completely new repertoire as Gareth had forbidden the use of any Terran songs, which may be recognised. Olivia had composed a new program of popular type music, especially for the competition. Gareth did not allow them to sing their favourite number, and said it must be saved for the Grand Final.

The event was to be televised and held in three stages. There were three judges who awarded half the votes. The rest were up to the viewing public, who had until five minutes after the last act to lodge their choice. The 'Associates' performed half way through the show, and it was a long anxious wait until the voting numbers were revealed.

They hugged each other in excitement when they were told they had made the Semi-Finals to be held the next night. Gareth ushered them out of a side door, and whisked them off, back to the bookshop for a good night's rest.

The Semi-Finals were hotly contested. All the acts were of such a high standard, the Associates didn't think they stood much chance of progressing to the Grand Final.

Victor was pessimistic. "Some of these groups have campaigned for a lot of friends and acquaintances to vote for them."

Gareth gave a perceptive smirk. "Don't you think I already know that? I've also made certain arrangements."

"Isn't that cheating?" Mary asked.

Gareth didn't think so, not when everybody else was doing the same thing. He wanted the 'Associates' to succeed. It was essential for his future espionage plans.

When the results were announced, the 'Associates' had made it to the Grand Final, which was to be held the following Saturday night. They had already attracted a gathering of young fans, and had to struggle through the crowds and media to leave the venue.

It was very late when they were all recovering in the bookshop, and they were all due back at work the next morning. Before he went home Gareth reminded them they only had five days to perfect their act for the most important performance of all. He would be expecting rehearsals every night.

He was also obtaining the services of a friend to act as their agent. Gareth needed an intermediary to deal with the media. He couldn't risk too much exposure or publicity himself.

As soon as Xandra heard the news he advised Aldon that he and Leandro would be coming to Earth Base in time for the Grand Final. They were both very proud of their children, and had to give them moral support. Pletta agreed that he should return to Mars Base with Nathan before they arrived.

Ebony called Martina over to the banknote replicator device. "I think it's malfunctioning again. All the one hundred dollar notes have the same serial number."

Martina yawned. "We certainly can't use those. Leave them on the side. I'm off to bed. I'll show Aldon in the morning."

The Base was quiet, and Nathan ensured his father and everybody else was asleep before he crept out of his quarters. Andy and Martina were nowhere in sight. He had been taken on a couple of excursions to the city, and also a national park and the beach. It was all a bit boring. He liked his own planet better.

He was much more interested in those attractive Earth women. Now his father was taking him back to Mars Base, this was his last chance to go and have some fun. He had checked up where the young people congregated, and decided he would go to one of the popular nightclubs.

Nathan couldn't believe his luck when he found a pile of one hundred dollar banknotes sitting on the desk in the operations centre. They would never miss a few of them. In fact, he may as well take the lot!

He was capable of piloting a PVX; one of the skills he had learned at the academy. Nobody would know if he borrowed it for a few hours. As quietly as possible he slipped into the craft and flew away in silent mode.

He landed in the same spot Aldon had used for their previous trips, and made his way to the nearest nightspot.

His excitement rose as he went inside. He purchased a large drink from the bar, and got a lot of change from the hundred dollar bill. That should see him through the rest of the evening. He could put the rest back when he returned to Earth Base in a couple of hours.

The music was exhilarating, and he found himself gyrating around the dance floor with hundreds of other young people. Many of the girls were scantily dressed, and he tried to make clumsy conversation with a couple.

He was buying his second drink when a particularly attractive female sidled up to him. She had noticed the large amount of money Nathan had put back into his pocket.

"Hello handsome," she said, giving him a provocative upward glance. "All alone tonight?"

Nathan looked down. Her ample breasts were nearly fully exposed under her flimsy blouse. He hesitated and bashfully nodded. Sensing his immaturity, she moved closer, pressing up against his thigh.

"My name is Fifi. You know, I can show you a good time if you want."

Nathan could smell her musky perfume, and already felt his body responding to her tempting behaviour. She led him towards the door and suggested they go back to her place. He felt slightly groggy after his last drink, which he had gulped down while she was standing next to him.

Fifi led him down a couple of unfamiliar streets to a large three story house, with a red light over the porch.

"You have a beautiful home," he commented.

She gave him a puzzled look, and as they went up the stairs, explained that she just had a room in the premises.

Once inside she disappeared behind a screen, and emerged a couple of minutes later wearing a white satin robe. She smiled enticingly at him and undid the tie. It fell open, revealing her nakedness underneath.

Nathan's legs had turned to jelly. The promise of sexual delights filled him with eager anticipation. Fifi put her arms around him and drew him close, her body melting into his. Their lips met in hungry demanding passion and he struggled to rid himself of his outer clothing.

They collapsed naked onto the double poster bed, and a shudder of pure carnal demand rippled through him. His inexperience was obvious. He knew nothing of foreplay, and satisfied his animalistic urgency within a very short time.

He rolled over, and for a moment was limp with exhaustion. There was the faint light of dawn coming through the window, and he remembered he had to get back to Earth Base before he and the PVX were missed.

As he dressed, Fifi got to her feet. "I dislike having to remind you about money. The landlord charges us one hundred dollars every time we bring a customer back, and then of course, there is my fee."

Nathan paused in stunned silence. Fifi took matters into her own hands, and pulled several hundred dollar bills from his pocket.

"This should do fine, thank you," she gloated, counting the notes one by one.

Fifi stopped, looked at the money a second time, and ran back to the bed where she pressed a buzzer. Within what seemed like a few seconds three other women came into the room.

Fifi was livid. "This free-loader tried to pay me with counterfeit money."

"I'm sorry. I didn't know – I didn't know." Nathan stammered as he moved towards the door.

The women closed in on him, pushing him backwards. He couldn't escape past them.

One particularly attractive female laughed. "Who's been a naughty boy then? Do you know what we do to naughty boys?"

Nathan tried to get away, but was quickly overpowered. He found himself face down on the bed, with his hands and feet tied to the four posts.

Two of the women undid his belt, pulled down his pants and lifted up his top. Fifi bent over him, with a contemptuous grin, and waved a small curled up whip in her hands.

"You don't get my services for nothing. One way or another you're going to pay!"

Nathan struggled in vain to get free. He had never been flogged before. Corporal punishment was frowned upon by the Terrans. He shuddered at the thought, and realised he had wet himself in fear.

The beating began, and between his yelps and tears, Nathan suffered the additional humiliation of feeling an erection coming on.

"That's enough," said one of his tormentors. "Let's get him out of here."

Back on the Base Aldon was woken by Ebony gently shaking him. "Wake up Boss! A PVX is missing, and I can't find Nathan!"

Aldon jumped up and alerted everybody else. Pletta was beside himself with worry. Had Nathan taken anything else? Was he armed or carrying any secret technology?

Ebony informed them that the only discrepancy was the faulty hundred dollar banknotes, which she had left for Martina the night before.

"Those alone could get him arrested." Aldon groaned. "We must get the PVX back before full daylight sets in, and then try to find Nathan."

While Martina minded the Base, the others set out in a second craft. It was an easy matter to locate the missing PVX, which had an inbuilt tracking device. Andy beamed down and flew it back.

Aldon and Pletta were glad that all Terran cadets had an implant, which enabled them to locate Nathan relatively quickly. They left Ebony at the controls and transported to the surface.

"Better use our invisibility gadgets until we find out what's happened to him." Aldon insisted.

Nathan's transmissions led them to the steps of an impressive house in the seedier part of town. He was face down outside the door, with the hundred dollar bills scattered beside his body.

"A brothel! I should have guessed!" Pletta groaned.

They raced up and got the lad to his feet. Aldon collected the incriminating money, and helped Pletta with his son as they made their way to a park across the road.

Within a couple of minutes Ebony had beamed them onto the craft, and they headed back to Earth Base.

With every move Nathan winced in pain, and seemed unable to sit down. Eventually Aldon and Pletta insisted on examining his injuries. His back and rear end were covered in nasty red welts.

"Maybe that's something I should have done years ago," Pletta thought to himself as he went to get some first aid remedies. He realised his son had serious behavioural problems, and told Aldon and Martina that he would take Nathan back to Mars Base as soon as possible.

"I love my son and realise some of this is partly my fault. I was absorbed in my own career and left his mother to raise him. A boy needs a father's influence in his life. If Zadoc and Xandra agree, I will keep him with me on Mars Base. Perhaps it is not too late for us to bond."

Later that day Aldon overheard a very subdued Nathan break down and pour his heart out to Pletta. Throughout his childhood the lad had clung to his mother, and thought his father had never wanted or loved him. When he was sent to the military academy he was so lonely and miserable the other students called him a 'wimp'. His reaction to the bullying was to become defiant and aggressive.

"Are you going to make a formal report about Nathan?" Martina asked Aldon. "He disobeyed orders and committed several serious offences."

Aldon shook his head. "I don't want to see a stain on his record so early in his career. I think those 'ladies of the night' punished him enough. If the facts were known the he would become a laughing stock. That would not be helpful. Let's see if Pletta can steer him in the right direction."

Xandra and Leandro arrived a couple of days later, and only stayed long enough to change into civilian clothes.

"Catch up with you later. Must go and wish our kids the best of luck for tomorrow night."

They arrived at the bookshop, which was a hive of frantic activity. Fiona and Lucy were making last minute alterations to their new costumes, and Mary was trying to cook dinner in the overcrowded kitchen. Gareth was in the lounge room with Victor, where they were making final revisions to the musical score which would accompany their vocals.

"This time we will be backed by a full orchestra." Victor explained. "They event's producers will be pre-recording it tomorrow morning, and they are only allowing us one hour's rehearsal time in the afternoon.

This is one of Olivia's best compositions and we have to make sure it is just right."

Xandra found a spare corner to sit down. "We aren't staying long. We just came to wish you the best of luck. Tomorrow there will be a lot of publicity. Naturally Leandro and I do not want to appear on television, but we will be in the audience with Tony and Tasha to lend our support."

By midnight Gareth called a halt to the chaos. "We have done everything needed. I'm going home and you all need to get a good night's sleep. It's going to be a big day tomorrow."

The 'Associates' arrived at the venue in the early afternoon, and waited for the other finalists to complete their rehearsal.

"They are very good," Mary commented. "I guess it depends on the voting public who comes out on top! Gareth told me that both the winners and runners-up receive a sizable financial reward in prize money. It will all be worth it, no matter what the result!"

They positioned themselves on stage, and it took several dummy runs before they successfully co-ordinated their vocal and dance routine with the orchestral backing and special lighting effects. Gareth was standing to the side, occasionally giving directions.

He followed them back to their dressing room afterwards. "You all did very well. I want you to rest and meditate, and then change into your costumes. After you ladies finish fiddling with your hair and make-up spend the rest of your time quietly in preparation for the big moment. I will be outside the door to prevent any unwanted visits from the media or any other intruders."

They could hear the sound of other acts which, although not part of the competition, were also participating in the night's program. The crowd was noisy and boisterous, and at times the cheering and applause contributed to their growing stage fright.

When Gareth left the room Lucy slid a small bottle of whiskey out of her bag.

"Hurry! Just one swig each, before he comes back."

Mary hesitated then took a quick mouthful before passing the flask to Victor. When Gareth returned he noticed a slight change in the atmosphere. Lucy was giggling, and looked guilty of something, but he didn't comment.

There was a loud knock on the door. "Five minutes!"

There was no more time to think or succumb to last minute nerves. The applause was deafening as they walked out onto the stage. The three judges were seated in front of them, and television cameras were positioned all around. They looked down at a sea of faces and eager fans, and all took a deep breath as they prepared for the most important five minutes of their lives.

Victor and Leandro watched with pride as the 'Associates' put on a very professional performance indeed! Everything came together -the music, singing, dancing and costumes complemented each other perfectly.

After a thunderous ovation the 'Associates' remained on the stage with the other Grand Finalists. Both groups wished each other the best of luck, and waited anxiously as the voting figures trickled through.

The audience cheered for their favourites as the numbers changed one way and another over the next few minutes. At last the final result was announced. The 'Associates' had been awarded first place by a slim margin.

The judges came on stage and presented them with their cheque and trophy. Reporters were everywhere, all clamouring for interviews and photos. The agent Gareth had engaged took control.

"I know you are all exhausted, but keep smiling. You are to do an immediate television interview for the contest organisers tonight. The rest can wait until tomorrow, when I have arranged five separate appointments during the day. I assume Gareth already told you that the competition organisers have an interest in a record company which is releasing an album of all the performances. Gareth and I will be negotiating a deal on your behalf next week."

Gareth had taken steps to ensure that, to date, the personal details and addresses of the 'Associates' had been kept secret.

"We have to keep it that way for as long as possible," he said. "We must not tell anybody where you work or live. That would attract too much unwanted attention."

Victor was concerned. "A couple of reporters have asked how we met and started performing together. We can't keep avoiding questions forever."

Gareth thought that the wisest course of action was to say that they had all originally belonged to a discussion group which wanted to improve the ecology of the planet.

It was late when they all eventually fought their way through enthusiastic fans, and headed back to the bookshop. Xandra and Leandro were also waiting for them. Congratulations and celebratory drinks were shared all around, before they retired for the night. It had been a big day, and tomorrow would be just as demanding.

The interviews the next day went well, with the Associates avoiding most of the personal questions. Gareth began to realise that it would only be a matter of time before the nosey journalists discovered the existence of the bookshop. Everybody would have to be a lot more careful.

CHAPTER 39

Sarah was behind the reception desk in the vet surgery and Boof was lying at her feet. Through the window she could see Clare lurking around outside. This was not the first time! Ever since Sarah had been given emotions she had felt an intense dislike for this aggressive female.

Unfortunately, although John was not there, the door was open. A couple of clients were coming to pick up their pets and pay the bill. Clare suddenly walked in and demanded to see John.

"He's not here. Go away!" Sarah snapped.

"I don't believe you. He's probably downstairs." Clare barged into the corridor and headed for the basement door.

Sarah experienced a rush of anger and jumped up from the desk. She caught up with Clare, and physically dragged her through the waiting room and back outside.

"Go away and don't come back!"

Clare rushed at Sarah, but stopped when a snarling Boof ran out and confronted her.

Clare paused with a knowing smirk on her face. "Maybe he isn't here, after all. I forgot about the agricultural show down the road. I bet he's there."

As Clare ran off Sarah turned to Boof. "Thanks for that!"

"I'm here to protect you and John. I've been perfecting my 'guard dog' mode."

John was enjoying his role as visiting judge at the local farmers' country event. The animals were the best of their pedigree, and certainly not destined for the abattoir. He hated the slaughter houses so much he couldn't bear to go anywhere near them.

He was deciding which of the horses would be awarded the Blue Ribbon, when one started to rear up in fright. There was noise and shouting coming from behind, and he could see several people running towards him.

"Arthur's bull just broke loose," one shouted.

John grabbed his bag, and pulled out the tranquilliser gun. He could see the distraught animal heading in his direction. That stupid Clare Cuthbert was stumbling along, just ahead of the bull, which was catching up fast.

She called out. "Help me John!"

He was a good shot, and as he ran up he simultaneously got the dart into the beast and pulled Clare out of the way. The bull staggered forward, and although semi-conscious, collapsed in a heap. Before he could secure the poor creature, Clare flung her arms around his neck.

"You saved me! You do love me after all!"

Everybody was watching when John pushed her away. "No I don't, and what's more I want you to stay away from both Sarah and me!"

Clare felt humiliated in front of all those people. If it wasn't for that Sarah, she was sure John would want her. She went back home and found her father's shotgun in the shed. Late that afternoon she made her way across the field towards the surgery.

When John returned he had immediately advised Sarah to be careful of Clare, who was obviously still very disturbed. She was startled when, a short time later, she saw the girl coming up the path carrying a large weapon.

Sarah experienced real fear for the first time since she had been upgraded. She was frightened for her boss, whom she loved in her own android way.

"John - Clare's coming and she has a gun!"

Sarah raced out and confronted her. "Where do you think you are going? I've already told you that you're not welcome here!"

Clare stopped. "You're coming between John and me."

Sarah pushed her back up the path. "He doesn't like you. Why can't you understand that?"

Clare exploded in a fit of temper. "Well, if I can't have him, then nobody can!"

As Sarah tried to wrestle the weapon away from Clare, John ran out of the front door.

He raced towards the pair, calling out for Clare to stop. He was too late. Clare turned and aimed the shotgun at Sarah, squeezing the trigger several times. Sarah fell to the ground. Half her head was blown away, and there was a huge hole in her chest, with wires and electrodes hanging out. There were several diminishing electrical flashes and sparks as her system shut down.

John was momentarily stunned, and stared at the broken body of his beloved Sarah.

Clare gave a startled laugh. "My God – a bloody robot.! Well I can't get into trouble for killing a robot! Wait until everybody hears about this!"

John was consumed with rage and grief, and the mocking smirk on Clare's face caused him to completely lose all self control. Before he realised what he was doing he pulled a ray gun from his pocket and aimed it at Clare's heart.

He had not stopped to check the setting; it was in full 'lethal' mode. As he shot at her, again and again, she dropped like a stone in a contorted, motionless heap.

"Shit! I think she's dead. What have I done?"

Thank goodness there seemed to be no witnesses around. He carried her into the surgery and hid her in the basement. Given the previous problems, once Clare was reported missing, police investigations would surely lead back to him.

John was totally traumatised, and swallowed a couple more morphine tablets. Perhaps they would help his self control. He gathered Sarah's remains in his arms and hurried back to the surgery, locking the doors behind him.

He knew he had to work swiftly; the valuable Terran medical apparatus must be removed and saved before the law arrived. He ordered Max to help him disconnect the equipment and beam it to different agents' locations.

The first to notice an irregularity was Jacquita. She had been in the crypt when a load of medical supplies appeared in the transporter bay.

"I don't understand it," she said to Paul. "These must be meant for our hospital, but Aldon always tells us first before sending anything."

Paul agreed. "I suppose we'd better unpack them. I'm a bit busy at the moment and will check with Earth Base later." In hindsight he wished he had contacted Aldon immediately.

Angela was also confused when she found a large heap of boxes and technology in their shower unit/transporter. She popped Matthew back into his cot, and unloaded the goods onto the bathroom floor. The cubicle had to be clear for Michael's return.

"We'll wait until Daddy gets home. He will know what this is all about."

When John had finished dismantling and transporting everything of importance out of the basement, he turned to Boof and Max.

"The sun has set, and it is getting dark. I want you both to go, as quickly as possible, to Mary's farm. She probably won't be home. You must hide in the tunnel which leads from the cave to the basement under her house. Stay there until someone arrives to collect you."

Boof and Max did not understand what was going on, but obeyed their controller and set off across the field. Max was unsure of himself. It was shadowy and unfamiliar all around. He was having trouble keeping up with Boof, who eventually persuaded the little grey worker to climb on his back for the remainder of the trip.

John was shaking all over, and resorted to an intravenous shot of even more morphine. Perhaps it would calm him down, and help him think straight. Suddenly there was a faint noise from one of the animal holding compartments.

He realised he had forgotten a young cat and dog, both strays he had been caring for until new homes could be found. He put them in carry baskets with an explanatory note for Aldon. After he had beamed them back to Earth Base, he shut down the transporter.

Once he had completed all the tasks, John no longer had to suppress his emotions. He sobbed uncontrollably and sank to the floor with the dismembered android in his arms. The Sarah he loved and treasured was lost to him forever. He lay there, holding her close, and started to drift in and out of a drug induced coma.

The sound of police sirens in the distance wakened him. Were they coming already? He couldn't be sure. He reached over, pressed the 'self destruct' button, and lost consciousness again as the computerised system counted down the seconds to the massive explosion which annihilated the vet surgery and everything in it.

Aldon was mulling over some paperwork at Earth Base when Martina rushed into the room. "Something is wrong at the vet surgery. Ebony found a cat and dog in the transporter. There was a brief note from John attached to one of the cages. It says Clare and Sarah are both dead. Boof and Max are apparently waiting for you in the tunnel under Mary's farm. He said he's sorry for everything, but this is the only way out. I cannot contact him as all his facilities seem to be inoperative."

Aldon jumped up. "I've been a bit worried about John's strange behaviour for some time now. What does he mean 'the only way out'? I'm taking Andy and going there right now, before he does something silly!"

The PVX hovered high over the rural locality, and Aldon realised he was too late. There was a huge black, smoking crater where the vet surgery had once been. Police cars, with flashing lights, were either gathered at the scene, or racing towards the area.

Andy steered the craft away towards Mary's farm, and Aldon beamed down to Bob's home nearby. He knocked on the door to be met by Rebecca and two excited children.

Christie gave him a hug. "Hello Uncle Aldon! Guess what? After we finished feeding the animals we saw one of our little friends from the space ship. He was riding on the back of a big doggie, and they went up the hill behind Mary's place."

Aldon told Rebecca that when Bob got home from work she should tell him there had been an accident at the vet surgery. No-one was to go anywhere near the area. He was about to take Boof and Max back to safety on Earth Base.

Aldon returned to chaos, with multiple arrivals of equipment and medical supplies coming into the transporter area. Once unloaded, they were followed by his Terran agents, who were demanding to know what it was all about.

Boof and Max had provided some information, giving Aldon a limited insight into the sequence of events. He believed that when Clare attacked Sarah she realised she was not human. Perhaps John had killed her and obliterated the surgery to prevent their hidden Terran facility being discovered.

"But why didn't John return to the safety of Earth Base before he destroyed the premises?" Martina asked.

The mood was sombre. Aldon poured drinks all around and proposed a toast to their departed colleague. He would arrange for Zadoc to inform his family, and recommend that John be awarded a posthumous medal for valour.

Victor sat in guilty silence. Now was not the time to tell everybody that he knew John had been hopelessly infatuated with his android, with whom he was having an inappropriate relationship. If he had said something earlier, possibly this dreadful situation could have been avoided. Better to let John be regarded as a hero, rather than suggest he preferred to die alongside Sarah rather than live without her.

The police were at a loss to determine what had caused the massive explosion at the vet surgery. It was only later that Clare's father reported that his daughter and shotgun were missing. The detectives concluded that Clare must have discharged the firearm causing the oxygen tanks and other volatile substances to ignite.

"I guess we can put this one down to yet another case of those 'nutty hillbillies'."

Aldon had arranged a later crisis meeting with Xandra. The Terrans needed a medical facility in the area, and new premises and arrangements had to be made as soon as possible.

They visited Victor and asked about the basement under his bookshop.

"I've got a few things stored down there," he said. "People coming and going during an emergency might create some suspicion. Also, how could I explain the medications, drugs and equipment?"

Mary had been quietly sitting in the corner. "Now John's surgery is gone, there would be no suspicion if another vet moved into the area. Even at the farm we occasionally need one. How about an experienced Terran agent poses as a mobile vet? He or she could have an office and small surgery."

"Good idea." Xandra commented. "But they could hardly operate out of a bookshop/coffee lounge."

There was a short period of thoughtful silence.

"How about the shop next door?" Xandra asked. "Isn't it empty, and up for sale or lease?"

"Yes, and it has a basement bordering on mine," said Victor. "The two could be connected underground, and nobody would be any the wiser."

Xandra was warming to the idea. "Being a mobile vet, the shopfront would only require a small office and surgery. You could expand the bookshop/coffee lounge onto part of the ground floor. The Terran medical facility would be hidden below. Our agent could live upstairs, and would not be as remote and isolated as John had been."

Victor was concerned that this kind of renovation would require purchasing the premises outright. He could not explain suddenly acquiring sufficient money to do so.

Xandra looked at Aldon and grinned. "Remember that company we set up – 'Outer Space Investments'? I think it will be more than willing to loan Victor the money for a mortgage."

"Isn't the name 'Outer Space Investments' a bit of a dead giveaway?" Victor asked.

Xandra chuckled to himself. "Sometimes it's safer to hide things in plain sight!"

As they were finalising their plans, Aldon mentioned that he had persuaded Gareth and Tasha to give the stray cat and dog a temporary home, but they still had Boof at Earth Base. Martina kept complaining that everybody was tripping over him.

"Max is happy with his little 'grey worker' friends, but what are we going to do with this android dog? My entire Base is crammed full with medical equipment, and he keeps getting underfoot."

Victor rather liked the big furry creature. "Let me him stay at the bookshop. Mary can say she found him wandering the countryside after the explosion."

Xandra agreed, with one condition. "Remember he is the product of an important Terran experiment. He is valuable and must be kept safe at all times. Take good care of him. We may need him later, not only to accompany the new vet, but also for espionage activities."

Every so often Boof needed to be plugged into a rejuvenation unit. Victor was unsure how to do this. "Androids have a connection on their backs. Where is Boof's?"

Aldon grinned, and pointed to the dog's rear end. "Where do you think!"

Boof arrived at the bookshop a couple of hours later. He padded around, familiarising himself with the premises. Mishka's fur was standing on end. She arched her back and hissed at this unwelcome intruder.

"Just let her think you are subservient." Victor said, not really knowing if the glorified robot even knew the meaning of the word.

The next few weeks were filled with frenzied activity. Once the adjoining property was purchased, builders were contracted to extend the bookshop/coffee lounge, and modify the remainder of the ground floor into a small office, surgery and storeroom.

"Now for the hidden renovations, which we will have to do ourselves." Aldon said.

Andy and his little grey assistants were put to work. Victor's basement was divided into two, with a secret door leading to the second half of the adjoining building. The proposed vet surgery also had a concealed entry to its underground facility, where another transporter was installed.

The bookshop had been closed during the renovations, and Victor and Mary staged a re-opening party for all their regular patrons and the Friendship Club. The extensions had included a small podium at one end, where they could hold an impromptu concert, or show documentaries on improving the planet.

Boof was an instant success, with everyone making a fuss of the big dog. Nobody guessed that he was observing everything and listening in to their conversations.

The customers all noticed the 'For Lease' sign on the new office next door. Victor told anyone who asked that he needed to rent it out to help pay for his new mortgage. In fact it was all prearranged, but Aldon wanted the new vet's occupancy appear to be a normal landlord/tenant contract.

Edgar, a young Terran agent with extensive medical expertise, arrived soon after. Aldon and Xandra had provided him with a new animal ambulance and false identity papers and qualifications.

Mary and Victor welcomed him at the door. "You must have dinner with us and stay in our spare room tonight. Tomorrow we will take you to buy new furniture and everything you will need for your flat above the surgery."

Although some of John's medical equipment and paraphernalia helped restock the supplies on the island and Earth Base, Martina was delighted when Max and the remainder were sent back to Edgar and their hidden medical centre at its new location.

"I'm glad that's all over," she said. "In one way our hospital is in a much more convenient place, but I wish this whole episode had never happened. John's death was a great loss and tragedy."

CHAPTER 40

After their initial success at the National Singing Contest, the 'Associates' finally had a chance to relax. The subsequent media frenzy had only lasted a short while. Other newsworthy items soon distracted the pushy journalists.

Gareth had been quietly working behind the scenes, and their agent had booked them several Saturday night appearances in the more prestigious local venues and clubs. These did not involve any espionage and were mostly social appearances, which the 'Associates' enjoyed along with the generous fees.

Fiona and Lucy, in particular, were enjoying all the attention - too much so for Tony's liking. There were always a lot of handsome young men showing interest in the twins, who couldn't help but indulge in some harmless flirtations from time to time. Tony felt quite helpless. Although he was in the audience, he had been ordered to stay in the background.

Some of their growing group of fans had discovered the bookshop, and Victor was glad he had agreed to the recent extensions. It was a bit of a worry when they were away for their Saturday night gigs, but they left some lights on and Boof sat guard. Aldon had insisted on installing a low level emergency button which the android dog could reach with his paw or nose. It sounded an alarm on Earth Base and also Edgar's vet surgery next door.

Victor patted him on the head and showed him what to do if anyone broke in. "Not only that. You can call out – 'who's there and what do you want?' – provided nobody actually sees you talking."

A few weeks later, Victor and the group left a bit earlier than normal. That evening they were singing at a snobbish wedding reception, which required evening dress. Tony's heart skipped a beat as Fiona and Lucy went out the door in long pale blue dresses. He had never seen them looking so attractive, and wished he could go with them.

He promised to be there when they got back. Everybody was going on to the farm for the remainder of the weekend.

Sometimes he would go next door and chat to Edgar, but it had been a long day. After watching TV for a while he retired upstairs for a short nap.

He woke with a start. There was darkness all around, and he stumbled for the light switch. Not working! Was it a blackout? He didn't know where Victor kept a torch, and as he fumbled around looking for one he heard the alarm going off in Edgar's surgery.

"Boof – Boof come here," he quietly called. The dog was by his side within a few seconds.

"What's happening?" Tony asked.

Boof explained that all the electricity had suddenly failed, and he heard the sounds of someone trying to force the back door. He had pressed the alarm button, and was about to investigate further when he heard Tony calling him.

Boof was able to see in the dark, and he led Tony into Victor's bedroom, where they met Aldon who was just arriving in the transporter/shower in the en-suite.

"Have you got a torch?" Tony whispered. "Someone's trying to break in. I think they've turned the power off, and I can't see a thing in the dark."

They could hear Edgar stumbling around in the flat next door, and Aldon banged on the wall.

"Hang on in there. We're trying to find a flashlight. Make sure you find a weapon."

They crept down the stairs and could see a dark shape shining a shaft of light around the bookshop.

"Get that torch!" Aldon whispered to Boof.

The dog leapt forward, bit the intruder on the arm, and snatched the light out of his hand. Boof returned to Aldon's side, and gave him the torch.

A male voice shouted out. "Bloody hell! Let's get out of here!"

Aldon and Tony could now see two men trying to reach the back door. One got away, but the second tripped over a chair. Before he could get up Boof, Tony and Aldon pounced on him.

They tied him up and blindfolded him before going outside to repair the power board and restore the electricity. Edgar joined them, and some discussion was held about what to do with their prisoner.

"We don't really want the police snooping around." Aldon muttered. "Let's just find out who they are and what they wanted."

Their prisoner was trembling in sheer terror. He felt a prick in his arm as Edgar jabbed him with a needle. Then he remembered no more until he groggily staggered to his feet in a dark alley.

He caught up with his partner in crime at the local pub.

"We're definitely not going back there again. Why didn't you wait for me?"

"I thought you got away, and were right behind me. What happened?"

The housebreaker didn't rightly know. His mind was a blur. It had been wiped by Edgar after the Terrans had questioned him.

Edgar went back to bed. Aldon and Tony made themselves a nightcap and waited for the 'Associates' to return.

Victor and his colleagues were in a happy mood when they got in. The food and drink at the reception were second to none. Their fee was also quite sizable. Their demeanour soon changed when they heard of the break-in.

"It wasn't what we expected." Aldon said. "Apparently Gareth has nominated you for an international competition. These two men had been hired by a rival music company to try and steal your original compositions before you had a chance to sing them. Don't worry – they won't be back."

The next week Aldon sent Andy to the bookshop to improve security. He helped Victor install an emergency lighting system, and from then onwards everybody had a torch and some kind of weapon next to their beds.

The twins in particular wanted to know more about the international competition that Aldon had mentioned.

"I didn't want to tell you about it until I'd ironed out the details." Gareth said. "It's an annual event and being held in a slightly less than pleasant foreign country this year. You qualified because you won our National Singing Contest. If you do agree to participate, Xandra has a special mission for you."

Despite Lucy's pleading, Gareth couldn't be persuaded to divulge any more information. Instead he advised them that their agent had booked them to perform at the Casino the following Saturday night.

"Oh goody!" Lucy exclaimed. "We love the Casino!"

Gareth eyed her suspiciously. He remembered how the Casino thugs had killed Bart and his cheating colleague.

"You will be there to sing – and only to sing. I forbid any of you to gamble during the night."

Everybody promised to behave themselves, and were eagerly anticipating the coming event. Mary and the twins had bought new matching cocktail dresses, and both Tony and Victor felt very insecure when they saw the amount of cleavage which would be on public display.

They arrived at the Casino, and remained in the bar area until it was time to go on stage. A man and woman were sitting at a table nearby. Mary couldn't help but overhear their conversation.

They sounded distraught. Their young daughter was dangerously ill, and needed an urgent operation. They were never going to be able to raise the money, and were arguing about whether to risk trying to win it on the poker machines or some other form of gambling.

"We can't afford much," said the wife. "Let's think about it, and maybe have a go on the machine with the giant jackpot. The Casino has been advertising it for some time, and so far it hasn't gone off."

Mary looked at the others and winked. They all knew what she was thinking, and each quietly nodded in silent agreement. After the first half of their performance they walked back to the bar for a drink. On the way back they passed the young couple at the special machine.

"All together now. One, two, three!" Mary whispered. They all concentrated in unison, and kept walking.

"Don't look back." Victor murmured as bells started ringing, and a crowd of well wishers started gathering around the lucky winners.

Fiona took a sip from her glass of wine. "I guess their daughter will have that operation after all. Well, we didn't exactly disobey Gareth. We only promised not to gamble ourselves."

Gareth and their agent visited soon after to discuss the forthcoming International Competition.

"It's being held on the other side of the world, in a not so friendly country. I can tell you now that you won't win. The first and second place has already been decided in advance."

Fiona didn't think this was fair. Gareth explained that next year's event would be hosted by the first place getter's country, and in the event of default the country of the runner-up.

"Never mind, perhaps you can come third, which will still be a triumph." Gareth said.

He went on to tell them about how that particular country was in Earth Base Two's area, and how Richard had betrayed all the agents, some of whom were still in hiding.

"This competition requires you to sing the same song during each elimination heat. Olivia has a special composition which contains certain words, frequencies and vibrations which only these agents will recognise.

"I will issue Victor with a communication device which can send and receive encrypted messages. It is in his glasses, and once turned on we will be able to hear and see everything around you. If you are approached by anyone contact me immediately. Xandra will be on standby to issue further instructions."

"Won't you be with us?" Fiona asked.

"No. You will be on your own except for your agent. Xandra and Aldon both think it is too risky for me to enter that country. Even if they are totally unaware of my Terran origin, they are always after the scientists who have expertise in my field."

The 'Associates' couldn't contain their excitement as they packed their costumes and headed for the airport.

Mary was nervous. "Gareth says we have to be extra careful, as the intelligence agencies in this country often place cameras and listening devices in their guests' hotel rooms."

Lucy giggled. "I guess we'll have to behave ourselves. No fleeting affairs with those handsome foreigners!"

They reached their destination, and found their hotel next to the harbour of a large provincial town. As soon as they had unpacked they all went for a walk along the waterfront.

Not many people spoke English, but the locals waved and smiled. One even came up and asked for their autograph.

"Fancy that!" Mary said. "I didn't think they would have even heard of us. They must have watched us on the internet."

"Yes," said their agent. "I have been working hard on publicity. By the way, while you are here, you must never go out alone. Gareth has instructed me to be with you at all times."

The next day was spent at the nearby entertainment centre, where they rehearsed for their performance in the preliminaries that night. This was their first rendition of Olivia's special song. They had to perfect the exact tone and frequency.

They had never performed in front of such a large audience before. Behind the dazzling stage lights were multiple cameras streaming the event to TVs all around the world. Afterwards it was a long wait backstage before they were told they would progress to the semi-finals the following night.

The next afternoon they arrived at the venue early, and were making their way to the dressing rooms when a young woman approached them.

"May I have your autographs please?" As Mary searched her bag for a pen, the woman whispered - "Who wrote the song you are singing in this competition?"

Victor looked directly at her and adjusted his glasses. His communicator was now in direct contact with Gareth and Aldon. Hopefully Xandra was watching also. Only he could positively identify Earth Base Two's agents.

Mary smiled as she went to sign the piece of paper. "Yes, it is a very special song, written by a couple of friends. What's your name?"

"Delia," said the woman. "I think I may also know your friends."

Victor looked squarely into her face so his contacts could get a good view. "Maybe we do. What are their names?"

Delia took a deep breath. "Xandra and Zadoc."

There was a pause, and then Victor heard Aldon's voice in his ear. "Yes – identification confirmed. Can you hide her overnight? We will have someone come in the morning. Just be careful in the meantime!"

Victor moved up beside her. "Sit in the audience during tonight's show, and come to the performers' room afterwards. Pretend you're a fan looking for another autograph."

As the 'Associates' hastened away they wondered how they were going to smuggle Delia out. It was when they were changing into their matching red cocktail dresses that Mary had a sudden thought.

"We have an extra red dress and pair of shoes in case of any wardrobe malfunctions. Perhaps we could dress Delia to look like us. The problem is she has the wrong coloured hair."

Fiona grinned. "Guess what? I have a wig in my bag. I always bring it, just in case my hair is a mess and I don't have time to fix it. If she has the same hair and dress as Lucy and me, nobody should notice the difference!"

Lucy started giggling. "Yes! What a good idea. We've often taken advantage of being identical twins, and done confusing 'double' acts before. This time we'll make it a 'treble', as long as nobody sees the three of us at any one time! "

Delia came around to the performers' private area at the same time the results were being announced. The 'Associates' were included in the five acts which were to progress to the Grand Final the following night. During the confusion of all the excitement Fiona grabbed a bag and led Delia down the corridor to the ladies' room.

"Quick! Go into a cubicle and change into these clothes and wig. Put the ones you are wearing back into the empty bag. We need you to look just like Lucy and me. Wait here until one of us comes to get you."

Mary and the twins went backwards and forwards to the bus which was transporting them back to the hotel. Hopefully the continual movement would confuse their agent and anyone else watching.

Mary then collected Delia. They walked casually towards the coach, and once inside Delia hid below the backseat. They adopted the same routine once they reached the hotel. Soon Delia was smuggled into their room, where they gave her some blankets and hid her under the bed.

Mindful of possible surveillance they turned on the radio before starting a quiet conversation.

Delia wasn't sure if the authorities were aware of her Terran origin.

"I cannot believe that Richard betrayed us, but I have lost contact with the other agents. There is no indication that my cover has been blown, but because I'm a physicist I'm watched all the time. Some of my human scientific colleagues have defected to the freedom and financial gain available in the West. The government here does not want to lose any more."

Victor was anxiously waiting further communication from Aldon or Xandra. They might be able to hide Delia overnight, but then what? They certainly couldn't smuggle her onto their homebound plane.

Xandra realised that they couldn't transport Delia out of her current location. It was swarming with police and security organisations. He had been checking all his contacts, and the nearest was his old friend Sven, a trawler captain who was fishing off the coast. Sven owed him a couple of favours, and agreed to come into port and moor at a wharf near the hotel.

The next morning Fiona and Delia, still wearing their matching red dresses, calmly left the hotel and walked along the waterfront to the jetty.

"Just keep ambling along, as if we're on a morning stroll." Fiona said.

They paused from time to time, pretending to admire their surroundings. When they eventually reached the trawler they both scrambled on board. Fiona hoped that no-one had noticed that she had hurried back to the hotel alone. As soon as she got there Lucy joined her and they made sure everybody saw them in the lobby area together.

"Our agent doesn't seem to have noticed anything amiss. Let's hope the local police were also fooled!"

Sven settled Delia down, out of sight in the cabin, and immediately set off to the open sea. He had cleared the harbour, and was in sight of the international boundary, when he heard the sound of a siren coming up fast behind him.

He panicked, and wondered where to hide his passenger. There was only one place the border/customs patrol wouldn't look. He grabbed Delia's arm and pointed to an open hatch leading to the hold.

"Quick! They won't look down there."

"But it's full of fish!" Delia wailed.

"Exactly!" Sven said. "If you hide down among them they'll never find you."

Delia dropped down into Sven's 'catch of the day', and when she heard the inspectors open the hatch, ducked down under the smelly, slippery cargo. About fifteen minutes later she heard Sven calling to her;

"You can come out now!"

She struggled through the mound of cod and haddock, and Sven pulled her back up onto the deck.

"Oh, my God! Just look at me! I'm soaking wet, with scales and gills in my hair and stuck all over me. I must smell terrible."

Sven laughed. "I'm used to it. Your friends will be here soon. I'm sure they'll find you a change of clothes."

They were well out to sea when Aldon swooped down and teleported Delia up into the PVX.

Andy was at the controls. He could recognise all aromas, and immediately asked Aldon if there were any fish on board. Delia cringed with embarrassment. Aldon told her not to worry. The main thing was that she had successfully escaped. He would soon transfer her to Xandra's shuttle craft.

The Grand Final of the competition was only a few hours away, and the 'Associates' were already emotionally drained after all the excitement and fear of being caught by the local intelligence agency.

They spent the afternoon together, resting and practising the meditation Gareth had taught them.

"I think we all feel a lot better now," said Victor. "Let's get back to the venue to prepare for the biggest night of our lives. We know we're not going to win, so how about we relax, enjoy ourselves and concentrate on entertaining the audience?"

Their final performance went off without a hitch, and just as Gareth predicted they finished in third place. Their agent was in a very happy mood. The prize money, of which he would receive a percentage, was quite considerable. There would also be a reliable stream of income from all the recording contracts and appearances which would result from their success.

The next day the 'Associates' were exhausted after the parties and celebrations which went all night. They wearily dragged their suitcases and equipment to the coach which took them to the airport for their flight home.

The customs officials and border guards scrutinised them suspiciously, but allowed them to board the plane unchallenged.

"I'll be glad when we are out of here." Mary muttered. "I hope Delia got away safely."

They had been back home for over a week when Xandra dropped into the bookshop to thank everyone for their help. He handed an envelope of money to the twins.

"This is to replace the dress, shoes and wig that you loaned to Delia. After being submerged in Sven's hold full of fish they stank to high heaven. My crew complained so much I had to throw them away!"

CHAPTER 41

Aldon and Martina were enjoying a period of relative peace and relaxation. Everything was going to plan, and they were up to date on all their tasks.

Aldon was planning a few social get-togethers with some of his agents, and Martina was going on a shopping trip with Jacquita. They wanted some new clothes and to get out and about like normal people in a vibrant society.

They both groaned when Ebony came into the room with an urgent message from Xandra. There was a 'problem', and he was on his way with Zadoc. They may be staying for a while.

Martina looked across at Aldon. "I don't like the sound of that. What kind of problem?"

"Whatever it is, I bet it's nothing good." Aldon muttered to himself. "We'd better get the guest quarters ready."

Once Zadoc and Xandra arrived and settled in, they held an informal meeting in the operations room.

Zadoc began; "Space Council have asked us to assist in a delicate matter involving the Ibearns."

"Not those pesky interlopers again?" Aldon growled. "I thought we were rid of them."

"Unfortunately not," said Xandra. "It appears that they had a second covert mining operation in Earth Base Two's area – something else Richard failed to discover!

"They were sending a craft to convey the minerals back to their planet, when it crashed in a mountainous part of your own area. The

Ibearns have been forced to ask for our help in saving whatever remains of the crew and equipment."

Aldon was livid. "Why should we risk ourselves for the Ibearns? They weren't supposed to be here in the first place. They well knew that the Guardians had allocated total control of the Solar System to the Terrans. They just couldn't help themselves, and had to trespass and put us all at risk just to pinch some rare mineral deposits."

Zadoc sighed. "You are justifiably angry, and I can sympathise. The Ibearns have always been a nuisance, but we are not at war with them. They have admitted their violation of the agreement, and in return for our help have promised to cease all mining activities here on Earth.

"If we handle the situation appropriately, it may result in better cosmic relations with the Ibearns. At least they have not been in contact with, or assisted the humans in any way. I'm also thankful that the Ibearns are not aware of our role in the destruction of their other mining operation a while ago."

Zadoc said that although there would be one Ibearn diplomat involved with the rescue and evacuation of any of their surviving personnel, he would not be allowed access to, or know the location of, any Terran facility on Earth.

Aldon and Martina both expressed their distrust of the Ibearns.

"Just keep him monitored at all times, and don't let him near your operations or communication areas." Aldon said.

Zadoc agreed, and suggested that the first task was to resolve the issue of the Ibearn's crashed vessel. Once that was sorted they could arrange the closure and evacuation of the remaining illicit mining operation.

They took Xandra's shuttle craft back to Zadoc's main ship, where Aldon met Orvea, the Ibearn representative. He was able to pinpoint the approximate area where their transport ship had crashed.

"Although that's half way up a mountain, it's not too far from a major town." Aldon said. "I would be surprised if the local military haven't discovered it already. I will activate our own surveillance systems over the area before we plan our course of action."

A quick view of the site showed two military helicopters hovering overhead, and a number of army tanks and soldiers already on the road leading to the town. Fortunately the winter weather had slowed their arrival at the wreckage.

Xandra and Orvea managed to transport down through the cloud cover without being detected. The craft was half buried in a snowdrift, and inside were two dead Ibearns and one mangled biological 'grey' android. Its body was a ghoulish sight. The large head was separated from its long skinny body, with the oval black eyes staring upwards from the floor.

Orvea was distressed. "But there should be another Ibearn and three more 'grey' entities! We must find them."

Xandra did not want the local authorities having access to the ship or its advanced technology. He insisted, despite Orvea's protests, in setting the self-destruct mechanism. Just to be sure, he also set two explosive devices of his own to detonate within five minutes of their beaming back to their shuttle craft.

The Ibearns had gone down due to a malfunction in their stabilizer system. When they hit the side of the mountain it took several minutes for the survivors to recover and stagger out into the deep snow.

Their leader realised they could never make it, by conventional means, to the Ibearn mine on the other side of the world. He was sure their comrades would report the transport vessel's failure to arrive. They would have to flee, and seek cover until a search and rescue operation came to their aid.

He ordered his three 'grey' entity assistants to gather some weapons, along with active locator and communication devices. He was seriously injured himself, and needed their help in struggling through the snow and rough terrain as they set off down the mountain.

None of them had any experience with winter conditions, and were constantly slipping and falling as they slowly made their way downhill towards the tourist chalets below.

They heard the massive blast as their craft exploded behind them, and then the sudden sound of the resultant avalanche. A huge wall of snow and ice descended down from the peak, engulfing everything in its path.

The three 'grey' assistants lay motionless for a while, and then managed to free themselves from the blanket of snow, ice and rocks. They dug out their Ibearn leader who had succumbed to his injuries and suffocation.

What to do now? Although their cognition was restricted to artificial intelligence, they followed the last instructions they had received. They must run and hide until rescued by their masters.

The avalanche had caused fear and chaos amongst the winter vacationers in the chalets, and nobody noticed the three strange figures arriving at the outskirts of the village.

The fugitives needed to get away, and looked around for some form of transport. They could hear the sound of an engine running in the car park, and quickly made their way over to the vehicle.

They opened the front door and pulled out the driver, tossing him aside like a rag doll. He got to his feet and ran inside blabbering incoherently about aliens stealing his automobile. In all the confusion nobody took any notice.

As a result the three androids had gained some valuable time. They jumped into the open sports car and skidded off down the road. They swerved all over the narrow mountain pass as the driver gradually learned which pedals were for acceleration and braking, and mastered the art of steering on the icy road.

They soon reached the connecting highway leading to the nearby town. Although the snow cover was much lighter than up the mountain, they stopped in the middle of the road to decide where to go to from there. They were telepathically debating what to do. Where could they hide?

The emergency services were preparing to check on the avalanche and the escapees could see multiple vehicles approaching from the urban area. Before they could turn around, and head in the opposite direction, a police car came speeding up and blocked them from behind.

Two officers got out and approached the car. "What do you morons think you are doing? Get off the road!"

There was a horrified pause. The policemen stared at the large grey heads and skinny bodies visible in the driver and passenger seats. Three pairs of enormous black eyes were gazing back at them.

"My God! I don't believe it! Do you see what I see?"

All the androids knew was that they had to flee and hide. Before the stunned constables had time to react the sports car sped off down the highway towards the town. It accelerated past the emergency services convey, and entered a side street in one of the outer suburbs. They stopped the vehicle, and scanned the nearby buildings for suitable concealment.

The Terrans were monitoring the situation from above. They had tuned into the police and military radio channels, and could hear the excited chatter about aliens causing an avalanche and later stealing a sports car.

Aldon was concerned, and turned to Orvea. "We're going to have to beam them out as soon as we can get a lock on their locators. Can you contact them on one of your communication gadgets?"

Orvea successfully ordered the three to stay where they were, ready to be transported out to safety. Aldon transported the first one on board, and was just latching onto the second when a military jeep raced around the corner. Several soldiers, with automatic weapons, jumped out.

The lieutenant called out to his men. "They really are aliens! Try to take them alive."

Everyone was on edge, and the troops started shooting prematurely. The two remaining 'greys' returned fire with their superior weapons. Aldon was able to retrieve the second fugitive relatively intact, but by the time he beamed up the third remaining android it was totally destroyed by enemy bullets.

Before departing in great haste, he looked down at the carnage below. Incidents like this always had repercussions. At least his human allies knew that the 'tall greys', who were the only aliens sighted, were not associated with the Terrans.

The next day, despite the government's attempts to suppress any publicity, there were eyewitness reports of 'aliens' driving a car into town and having a gun battle with the military.

Luckily news of the avalanche took precedence, and most newspaper editors were sceptical of gossip blaming it on some 'non-existent' flying saucer crash. Aldon could see the humorous side, and souvenired a cartoon showing a crashed disc, with gun toting 'greys' hanging out of a sports coupé and waving.

Orvea was not happy about the loss of his crashed ship and most of the crew. The Terrans didn't really care. Everybody's attention was now focused on the more difficult task of decommissioning the Ibearn's mine in Earth Base Two's sector.

Aldon was relieved that he was not involved in the recovery of personnel and technology. That operation was being conducted by Orvea, Zadoc and Xandra

Zadoc held several planning meetings aboard his ship. Their course of action required a strategy of close co-ordination. Orvea contacted his officers in the mine and instructed them to start shutting down the facility.

The two shuttle saucers, attached to the underground base, would evacuate the entire workforce along with as much as possible of their valuable technology. Zadoc had agreed to transport what was left of their equipment onto his larger transport ship.

"I can only extract items which are small and lightweight," he stressed. "That craft can only hover in Earth's atmosphere for a very short time. The success of this entire mission is dependent upon everyone adhering to our planned tactics and schedule."

A few hours later Xandra took a PVX and hovered low over the mine. Orvea quickly transported down to the ground, and banged on the entry.

"Let me in, you idiots. Didn't you get my message?"

Some of the personnel had not taken his orders seriously. There must have been a mistake. Surely the Ibearn High Command would not abandon a valuable enterprise into which it had invested so much time, effort and deception?

Orvea was dismayed at the lack of preparation, and asked Xandra and Zadoc for more time.

Zadoc was irate. "Not possible! You only have ten minutes. This county's air force is quick to detect and respond to any intrusions"

The Ibearn officers and their robotic assistants quickly raced around turning off as much technology as possible. They placed some equipment in a pile in the middle of the floor and gathered the rest in their arms as Orvea hustled them onto the shuttle saucers.

He followed them aboard, and closed the hatch behind him. All personnel were accounted for, but the decommissioning process had not been fully completed.

He thought he should not mention this to his Terran accomplices. Perhaps the Ibearns could come back one day, and continue their covert mining operations.

The two saucers shot up into the sky, and met up with Zadoc's vessel which had just finished taking the extra technology on board. As soon as Orvea and the Ibearn craft were safely in the shuttle bay they accelerated high into the atmosphere, and watched as the local air force flew into view.

Xandra was hovering down below, and knew he had to move swiftly. The Terrans had no intention of leaving the Ibearn mine intact, for their possible later return. He saw that Orvea had been in such a panic he had forgotten to close the external door to their saucer bay.

That was actually a lucky break for Xandra and his team. The enemy planes were closing in fast; they only had seconds to spare. He beamed down a very large explosive device through the opening, and followed up with a sophisticated projectile which detonated upon impact.

The subsequent blast shook the terrain all around, and caused the incoming fighter planes to momentarily veer away.

"Quick – get us out of here!" Xandra yelled to his crew.

The Terran craft shot straight up into the sky with the air force planes following in hot pursuit. They had started firing rockets, forcing Xandra to deploy some anti-weapon shields and increase his speed and evasive manoeuvres.

Zadoc was reassured when Xandra was out of range, and joined him on board his transport vessel.

"Good job on decimating their underground base and mining operation. You should have seen the dismay on Orvea's face when he saw it blasted into oblivion!"

Xandra chuckled. "Surely he didn't think we were naive enough to give them any chance of coming back?"

They joined Orvea who was looking very despondent. They could hardly contain their grins when they asked him if anything was wrong. His answer was unexpected.

"I promised to bring everyone home, but two of my Ibearn officers are missing. The others told me that they ventured out into the countryside a few months ago and haven't been seen since.

"They are very different in appearance to humans, and it is feared they may have been captured. Our technicians picked up some military chatter which mentioned an alien internment camp. Do you know anything about that?"

It wasn't the first anybody had heard of it, and the possibility of such a place could not be dismissed. Before sending Orvea and the Ibearns back to their planet, the Space Council asked Zadoc and Xandra to investigate whether an 'internment camp' actually existed.

CHAPTER 42

Xandra and Leandro had dropped into the bookshop for a quick visit. Xandra was sitting very quietly with a slight frown on his face. It was only after Mary asked what was bothering him, that he spoke.

"There was good reason you felt compelled to move to the farm, on a higher elevation, and develop the ability to become self sufficient. We are disturbed that a great many of Earth's population have become so dependent upon modern technology they will be unable to survive without it. In fact, if there was a worldwide disaster, it will be the planet's poorer indigenous inhabitants who will stand a better chance of a continued, but primitive existence.

"Until recently, all your knowledge was contained in books and manuscripts. We are concerned at the ever-increasing tendency for your scientists and other intellectuals to electronically store their information and discoveries. Even many government sponsored libraries have digitally converted some of their book repositories.

"Most large libraries are located in major cities, which are often adjacent to the ocean, and also the primary target in any conflict. Accumulated knowledge and wisdom is the life blood of a civilisation. If hostilities or a severe cataclysm occurred, this could be lost forever."

Xandra went on to explain that over fifty years ago, the Guardians had initiated a project to preserve all of the planet's important scientific and other literature. They had 'taken' many brilliant young university students when they were out on field trips in remote areas. Although these young academics were left with a period of 'missing time', and little memory of the actual encounter, they all felt compelled to collect as many scientific and technological books as they could.

"This group of involuntary 'recruits' are now entering their retirement years, and have amassed many hundreds of thousands written works. Although we implanted instructions in their subconscious minds, as to where all these books should be stored, very few have followed these directives."

Aldon told them that, on behalf of the Guardians, he had been tracking down these intellectuals' private libraries, and was dismayed to discover the books had been stored in damp basements, decrepit warehouses, shipping containers, country barns and galvanised sheds. One had even left thousands of books in his back paddock. They were packed in pallets, with only a few tarpaulins to protect them from the elements.

"All their work and effort will have been in vain once deterioration sets in. There is an additional problem with some of the relatives, who consider the books to be the result of an irrational, often psychotic compulsion, and want to get rid of them. We have already needed to remove these extensive collections, sometimes without permission, to a safe location.

"The entire project is still ongoing, and Zadoc, Xandra and I were hoping that all of you here tonight would be willing to assist in what could be one of the more difficult operations."

Everybody was in agreement that it was a worthwhile project, and they would assist wherever possible.

The Terrans had already located another suitable storage spot. It was sturdy and weather proof, well above sea level, and whilst isolated, not too far from civilisation.

It comprised a large unknown cave system, situated in a mountain range about two hundred kilometres inland from a major city. The entry was sealed with camouflaged doors, and after a few days work by their robots the facility was ready.

A few nights later, Jervis Thompkins went out to check on a couple of his sheep. He wended his way between the multiple pallets of books, and thought back to the recent argument with his wife. She had been demanding he get rid of them, but that was something he couldn't do.

He never really understood why, but he just had to buy every new technical book he came across – not just in the bookstores but at fetes and charity shops as well. For a long time he had the urge to excavate a type of secure bunker, to store them in. His wife wouldn't agree to him digging up part of the property, and somehow it all seemed too much trouble.

It had all started after that field trip into the country, when he was just a young student. He and his mates were travelling back to a local town for dinner. They had noticed what looked like headlights coming up fast behind them, and pulled over to the side of the road. They all felt a little dazed, and when they drove on, the town was in darkness. It was four in the morning.

His memories of that night were vague, although he and his colleagues had occasional flashbacks and dreams of a spacecraft and beings 'not of this world'.

He was returning from the paddock when his trusty border collie let out a yelp and bolted for the house. A bright light suddenly surrounded him, and he could vaguely see two figures approaching.

The next thing Jervis knew it was morning, and he woke up in bed, with no further memory of the previous few hours. He felt groggy, and after he went to the bathroom, staggered to the back door. Jervis stared out in disbelief at his empty paddock.

"My books! My books! Where are my books?"

His wife came running out of the bedroom, still in her nightdress and hair curlers. "What are you carrying on about? Don't be silly, how can your books be gone? They were there last night, and it would take several trucks, making a lot of noise, to move them."

She felt a sense of great relief when she saw the empty space. They really had disappeared, presumably into thin air.

"It was those aliens! Phone the police! Those aliens stole my books!" Jervis yelled.

Mrs Thompkins was hesitant, and didn't want to report the theft. She had visions of the authorities taking her husband away for psychiatric treatment. Just as he was about to make the phone call himself, she noticed a thick envelope on the hall table.

"Wait a minute, Jervis. Look – there is a lot of money in here – tens of thousands of dollars. At least your alien friends have more than reimbursed you."

The operation went to plan on several occasions, but they ran into difficulties with Professor Davis, now a crusty old bachelor, whose library was stored in a damp basement under his inner city home. Xandra could not use a larger, more noticeable, heavy lifting vessel. The books would have to be carried out, late at night, into his tiny back garden, and quietly transported away in smaller loads.

Mary infiltrated his university class, pretending to be a student, and after a couple of days was able to place a tracking device under his car. She also lifted his private mobile phone for a few minutes, which enabled Earth Base to further monitor his movements and telephone conversations.

Ebony had been recording all the information, and had detailed what appeared to be the professor's regular schedule. She noted that he often ate dinner at a local restaurant, and was normally home by 8pm.

Mary also examined the university calendar, and saw there was an awards dinner and presentation scheduled the next week. Not only was

Professor Davis listed as a guest of honour, Gareth and Tony's company was one of the major donors to that particular university faculty.

"I have an idea," Gareth said. "We have to keep Davis away from home until at least three in the morning. I can arrange to attend the dinner, as the company's representative, and take Tasha with me. Tony can take Lucy. After the function we will invite the professor and a couple of his colleagues to the casino for a late night drink and a little flutter. I know the Dean likes gambling. Lucy will be with us at all times, giving Fiona an alibi if the professor leaves early, and she has to prevent him going home."

The twins, being identical, had played tricks since they were small children, and considered this plan to be enormous fun. They were also thrilled to be able to purchase very fancy matching evening dresses at Terran expense.

On the night of the dinner, Lucy was in her element at the prestigious event. Fiona was not so happy sitting outside in the cold with Victor. Never mind, Tony had promised he would make it up to her.

Towards the end of the evening, when it looked like he might leave early, Lucy purposefully made a fuss of Professor Davis. Although he was rather flattered that this attractive young woman, who was actually Tony's companion, was paying him so much attention, he declined the offer to join her and the others at the Casino.

It took him a few minutes to walk to the parking lot, only to find that his car would not start. He was considering calling a 'Roadside Assist' mechanic, when a car pulled up beside him.

Fiona looked out of her driver's window. "Would you like a lift?"

Professor Davis hesitated, and then got into the passenger seat beside her. This was the same young woman who was flirting with him earlier! Maybe he was going to 'get lucky' tonight. As they drove off into the city traffic, he felt a slight prick through the arm of his jacket, and everything went black.

Fiona looked over her shoulder at Victor who was in the back seat. "What now? Perhaps we should take him somewhere more secluded until we get the 'all clear'."

About three hours later, Aldon contacted Victor. "Xandra has collected all the books. It's safe to take the professor home. Although he may not realise his library has gone, tell Fiona to play it safe, and not to go in."

Professor Davis woke with a start. The young lady said, "Wake up! Here we are – got you back home safe and sound." He was a little confused, thinking he must have fallen asleep. He got out, but before he could invite Fiona in for a nightcap she had driven away.

As he opened the front door he thought it odd that the light was on in the hallway. He looked at his watch – something was wrong – it couldn't be 4am! Why was his basement door ajar? His heart sank as he peered into the empty space below. Where were his books? He'd been robbed! If only he had got home earlier!

The next day he asked about the attractive young woman who had been with Gareth. "Oh," said the Dean. "She was the life of the party. We didn't leave the Casino until after 5am! You should have come with us."

Back on Earth Base Martina was asking Aldon about the progress of the book repository. "Why has it suddenly become so important?"

"I think, in Zadoc's mind, it's a case of planning for the worst, but hoping for the best. Although nearly all the Xvars and Katons have left, there's no telling if they may come back in force. Also humans themselves could start a dangerous war. It will be too late to start these beneficial preservation projects after any hostilities commence."

CHAPTER 43

Tony, Michael and Tasha were busy in the laboratory when Gareth came in and took them quietly to the side.

"I know our computers are all closed circuit, so nobody can hack in or launch a cyber attack from the outside. It seems that we may have a threat from within the corporation. Some scientific data and research from other departments appears to have found its way into the hands of opposition organisations.

"We all know that whilst the information we are sharing with humanity is meant for beneficial purposes, it can also be misused in the most unethical ways."

Gareth insisted upon tighter security measures from now on. He knew that they already changed their passwords on a daily basis. In future, unless one of them was in the room, all electronic gear should be closed down.

He explained that he suspected there may be a traitor within the company, who was probably selling the information. It was possible that it involved organised criminal conspirators who would be well paid for the latest technology.

Nobody had been approached or offered a bribe, so it was difficult to identify any possible suspects who may be guilty of the espionage. Gareth met with Aldon, who gave the matter some thought.

"Perhaps we should enlist Camellia's help. Her paranormal and mind reading abilities may be of assistance. How do we get her into the building? She can hardly just walk in and wander around."

Gareth sat in silence for a while. "I have an idea. One of the canteen assistants is going on holiday for a fortnight. I can get the boss to hire

Camellia as a temporary replacement. Not only can she mix with the staff at lunchtime, she will be able to take the tea trolley around every morning and afternoon."

Arrangements were made for Camellia to tell the circus people she was going to visit a sick relative in the city. She arrived a couple of days later, and stayed with Fiona and Lucy in their apartment.

The twins were excited that a real live Terran was staying with them. Every night she would regale them with tales of her life, not only at the circus, but also out in the cosmos. She liked the girls, and really enjoyed her stay in town. She was also able to catch up with Tony, Michael and Gareth, and it was a well needed a break from the confines of the fairground and her caravan.

Camellia was well versed in social skills. Within a few days of working in the cafeteria she had become quite popular. She was careful not to ask any leading questions. That may have caused suspicion. Instead she quietly concentrated her telepathic and mind reading skills.

At the end of the first week she was able to provide Gareth and Aldon with the names of two suspicious employees. She had surreptitiously placed monitoring devices on both.

Aldon tracked them both back to their partners in crime.

"It's just a small group of unsavoury characters, who use extortion and intimidation to steal and sell the latest technology. We need to take out their informers. After that we'll deal with the major players. They're based on a large motor cruiser, anchored in the harbour. We've already got their phones and computers under surveillance."

By the time Camellia returned to the circus, the two offenders were no longer with the company. One had been involved in a fatal accident, and the other was sacked after stolen goods were found in his home.

Gareth had been told that they should all still be on their guard. Aldon had discovered that these criminals were still considering how to infiltrate the corporation and gain further scientific secrets.

The following Saturday was the company's social club's special 'men's only' night out. Michael wanted to opt out, as he always went back to the island with Angela and Matthew. Angela thought it would be good for Michael to have a night out with his friends, and Gareth, Tony and Victor persuaded him to accompany them. They thought it might be a bit of fun, and a diversion from the sometimes monotonous day to day routine.

Tasha was a little miffed, and had arranged a similar outing for Mary and the twins. There was a 'ladies' night at the local music hall.

"What's good for the goose is good for the gander!" Lucy giggled.

Gareth ushered several of his male colleagues into the 'strip club', and was surprised to see Chantelle was also in the audience.

"It's okay," she said. "Aldon asked me to keep an eye on things. He is still certain those crooks are up to something, possibly tonight, as this outing has been promoted for some time."

There were about twelve men in the party, and Gareth admitted that he had some reservations about all of the corporations' scientists being in the same place at the same time.

They settled down with some drinks, and were soon cheering and calling out along with everybody else. Chantelle suddenly moved up behind Gareth and whispered in his ear.

"Aldon says to get out of here quickly. There is a team of three thugs on their way to kidnap whichever scientist or technician they can grab. He and Andy are going to waylay them. In the meantime, you four are all to make your way over to the venue where the girls are."

Gareth motioned to his three colleagues that they were leaving. Once they were back in the street, they decided to walk the few blocks to the 'Palladium' where Mary, Tasha and the twins were enjoying the variety show.

They had nearly reached their destination when they heard the sound of shooting and a high powered vehicle coming down the road. Tony pushed the others into a side entry of the music hall.

"Quick! In here!"

They found themselves in a narrow corridor leading to what appeared to be dressing rooms.

"That must have been the backstage entrance." Gareth said. "Aldon is taking care of those crooks right now. Let's find somewhere to hide until it's all over."

They were still debating where to go when one of the stage managers rushed up and pushed them into an empty room.

"You guys are late. You're one of the highlighted acts, and due on in a few minutes. Hurry up and change into your costumes."

As he shut the door behind them, Tony picked up a pair of underpants, check shirt, tie and denim jeans. There were several wild-west hats and gun belts piled on the chair.

"I assume we're supposed to be cowboys," Tony said. "I know lots of country and western songs, so I guess we'll get by."

Victor noticed that all the seams were made of Velcro. "I don't think singing is what the organisers had in mind."

His heart sank when he realised what the act they were impersonating exactly was. They could still hear the sound of some form of altercation going on outside. No matter what, they would have to carry on with the deception, and they quickly undressed and donned the costumes.

"I'm not leaving my weapon behind." Tony said. "I'll put it in the holster."

The others followed his example, and soon they were being ushered up onto the stage. The music started up, with the audience singing along to the catchphrase – *'You Can Leave Your Hat On.'*

They stood in a line and nervously looked across at each other.

"Just watch me and follow what I do." Victor whispered. He took off his tie, waved it around in the air, and threw it into the audience.

They started to grind and bump along to the music, with the female audience shouting enthusiasm and approval.

"Get it off! Get it off!"

They didn't know where to look as one by one they removed their clothes and threw them into the crowd below.

Tasha, Mary and the twins were staring in a mixture of merriment and disbelief. When it came to the 'Full Monte', they hoped the guys knew where to place their hats at the crucial moment.

When they were left wearing nothing but their gun belts, several pairs of lace panties and a fancy bra landed at their feet on the stage. They fled to thunderous applause, and a few minutes later their dressing-room door was surrounded by new female admirers.

Tasha looked at her companions. "We all know our guys are good looking hunks, but they belong to us. Let's get 'round there before one of those oversexed bimbos leads them astray!"

Mary and the twins followed her into the corridor, and pushed through the crowd. Tasha opened the door and looked back at the eager fans.

"Push off you lot – before I make you!"

"Are we ever glad to see you?" Michael said. "I don't know what's scarier – a band of Xvar warriors or that mob of horny human females."

Gareth and the others quickly changed back into their own clothes; - better get out of there before the original act arrived.

Everybody gathered later at the bookshop for a nightcap before heading their separate ways. Although the predicted kidnap attempt of one of the scientists was disturbing, they were laughing about the evening's events and impromptu performance.

Gareth and Tasha had just got home when they received a message from Aldon. The carload of thugs had somehow become stuck on a level crossing, and was hit by a freight train. The motor cruiser in the harbour had experienced a mysterious explosion, and the occupants had gone down with their boat.

"When did this happen?" Gareth asked.

"Just after you entered the 'Palladium." Aldon replied.

Gareth groaned. Maybe he had better not tell the others that their 'show all' embarrassing performance may not have been necessary after all.

He looked at Tasha, who was getting ready for bed. "I can't believe you girls were jealous of the attention we were getting. I guess you must really love me."

Tasha smiled. "Of course I do. Whatever made you think otherwise?"

Gareth hesitated. "Sometimes I wondered if I was the only way off that science spacecraft."

Tasha walked over and put her arms around him. "Don't be silly. You're my handsome prince! Although I must admit that there were times when I thought I might have just been a convenient escape from your controlling parents and the future bride they had chosen for you."

Gareth took her in his arms and carried her into the bedroom, kicking the door shut behind him.

"I'll soon put your mind to rest about that!"

Mary and the twins couldn't help involving Victor and Tony with a bit of friendly banter about their recent striptease performance at the 'Palladium'.

"You two could really spice up our 'Associates' act." Lucy giggled.

Gareth had arrived, and announced that their agent had received a request for a much more informal engagement.

"But you can forget about any male strippers," he added.

This was to be a charitable performance for a war veterans' home, situated in the countryside. The old servicemen were fairly isolated, and there was no money or opportunity for much entertainment.

The manager and care workers wanted to hold a birthday party and concert for an old fellow who was turning one hundred.

"Oh let's do it," the twins enthused. "Tony – here's your chance to sing with us. Nobody will recognise you out there."

Lucy giggled and suggested they wear their sexiest costumes. "Let's make it exciting for them. Perhaps Chantelle can come also - in one of her flimsy outfits."

Gareth admired their enthusiasm, and thought that might be too much excitement for the old geezers. Somehow or other Lucy had her way, and Chantelle agreed to add a bit of glamour to the entertainment.

They all set off one Saturday, ready to give the old-timers a memorable afternoon. Victor and Mary had spent the morning baking cakes and pastries in the kitchen. They were sure the tasty treats wouldn't go astray. Victor had also purchased a huge birthday cake and decorated it with candles and a motif saying '100'.

"Call it my Birthday present to the centenarian," he said.

They were saddened by the state of the care home and facilities. The old men, many on walking frames and crutches were wandering aimlessly about. Many others, confined to wheelchairs, were sitting motionless and staring into space.

There was a depressing aura all around. The lounge room had an ancient television in the corner, and several lumpy sofas. The rest of the sparse furniture was worn and aging.

The staff welcomed them with open arms. The 'Associates' could see that they cared about the residents, but had few resources to work with. There were some goodies on the table, and a large punch bowl and cups.

"How can humans treat their old soldiers like this?" Tony muttered. "Terran war heroes are given the best of everything."

They unpacked all the extra food, and as the table became fully laden, the old men reacted with enthusiasm.

"All for us? I can't believe it," said one as he reached for a cream cake.

They started setting up for the show, and more of the elderly patients came into the room. Most headed straight for the pastries before taking their places for the concert.

The 'Associates' played a lot of songs from bygone eras, and encouraged everybody to sing along. Tony was really enjoying his time being part of a live performance. He felt a lump in his throat when he saw the smiles and joy on the previously gloomy faces of their audience.

When Chantelle did her 'Dance of the Seven Veils' the applause was deafening. She had stripped down to a g-string and strategically placed sequins. Before she went to get dressed, she walked over to the birthday boy and gave him a kiss on the cheek. The previously lethargic residents all started whistling and cheering.

Next came the cutting of the birthday cake, and everyone tried to mix with the party guests and talk to as many as possible.

Tony noticed that one old guy on a walking frame was staring at him from the corner of the room. He walked up and started a friendly conversation. The man's name was Terry, and after a few minutes Tony noticed an unusual ring on Terry's finger.

Tony was startled. The veteran was wearing a Terran signet ring, the kind only given to senior officers and diplomats. It was made of heavy silver, and the gemstone in the middle was glowing. He beckoned to Gareth and they both asked Terry where he had got it.

He smiled knowingly. "You're Terrans and you recognise it, don't you? It will only glow when it senses Terran vibrations and frequencies. I've been waiting a long time to pass a message onto you. Please come with me; I have something to give you."

They followed him to his tiny bedroom, and he pulled a small case from under the bed. In it was a large crystal rock, which was wrapped in a soft protective cloth.

"Many years ago, during the war, my men and I were stationed on a tropical island. We were combating the enemy in thick jungle when we entered a clearing. We were taken aback to find a strange silver craft sitting in the middle of a circle of 'standing stones'. They looked similar to that 'Stonehenge' place, but maybe not quite so big.

"We crept around the object, wondering what it was and where it had come from. It didn't seem to pose any threat. The rest of the platoon moved on, but I stayed back and gently placed my hands on the smooth exterior. I was intrigued, and thought that maybe it was something from outer space.

"Suddenly a flap opened and extended to the ground. I crept up the gang-way into the thing, and was surprised to see multiple screens and lights all around the interior walls."

Terry went on to explain that, when he pressed a couple of knobs, a voice suddenly spoke to him.

"It told me that I was inside a time machine which would soon disappear. The occupant, who had met with misadventure, had been sent to relay an important message. While he was still able, he had recorded the information for someone to find at a later date.

"I was asked to take the ring and the crystal out of a compartment. The ring would glow when I met the persons to whom the crystal and information must be given."

"But what are we supposed to do with the crystal?" Gareth asked.

Terry explained that they must go back to the island, and find the 'standing stones' in the middle of the jungle. At exactly midnight on summer solstice they must place the crystal in the middle of the circle of stones, and join hands around it. The more Terran participants there were, and the stronger their frequencies and vibrations, the clearer message would be.

"Only the frequencies and vibrations that Terrans' possess, along with the crystal, will activate the inter-dimensional entity which has been left to finish the time traveller's mission.

"The voice told me that the future is not set in stone. It can have several alternatives, dependent upon our own actions in the here and now. I was instructed to press another button and look out of the window. The lush green vegetation had changed to dry, dusty desert, with no sign of life in sight. The voice told me that this is what the future would look like if the wrong decisions were made in the here and now.

"Apparently the message waiting for you is of great importance to the future, not only of the Earth but the Terrans themselves."

Gareth carefully took the old man's crystal, and tried to clarify the details of exactly where this mythical island was located. As they walked away to join the others, who were starting to pack the van, Tony asked Gareth if he thought this was 'for real'.

"I really don't know," he said. "His ring appears to be genuine. Although this is a little far-fetched, we cannot ignore it. I have heard of time travellers before, and am going to play it safe and refer the whole matter to Xandra and Zadoc."

CHAPTER 44

Gareth and Tasha joined Tony who was having lunch in the company cafeteria.

"Are you going to the International Science Convention?" Tony asked them. "It's on all this week."

Gareth didn't look very enthusiastic. "Yes – we're going this afternoon. I've seen it all before, but I promised Tasha. She wants to familiarise herself with Earth's progress and possibilities. Also both Aldon and our own boss want me to report on what everybody else is up to."

They arrived at the large convention hall, which was filled with various booths and technological displays. They started mingling with the crowd and were soon engaged in conversation with fellow scientists.

Tasha introduced herself as Gareth's wife, and left the talking to him. He had told her not to reveal any details about herself to strangers.

Many of the large corporations, along with their latest inventions, were represented. Tasha was quietly standing at Gareth's side when she felt a piece of folded paper being slipped into her hand. She turned around to see an unknown man quickly walking away.

During her time in the Terran military Tasha had been trained in espionage techniques. She quietly made her way to the ladies room and opened the note.

My name is Alain. I have been implanted with a tracking device, and whilst in your country I am being watched at all times by intelligence agents. My corporation has sold its soul to the devil. It is devising new weapons, and conducting horrendous experiments on innocent people who are being held captive. Any scientist or employee who tries to leave or escape to the West is murdered or dies a suspicious death. Please help me to defect to your country. I am leaving the number of a 'burn' telephone which I secretly purchased when I arrived here.

Tasha returned to Gareth's side, and insisted he take her for a cup of coffee in the nearby restaurant. His mood changed as he read the letter.

"We must not arouse any suspicion, and will wander around for the next half an hour. Then it's straight back home, where I will contact Aldon immediately. This may be a trap, but it is too important to ignore."

Aldon soon arrived in Gareth and Tasha's apartment. "This bloke comes from a remote district which was in Earth Base Two's area. Richard never reported anything suspicious whilst he was in charge, but he was obviously too busy with his love life to perform his own duties adequately.

"We need to talk to him without being identified or apprehended by either his minders or this region's surveillance. Ring him from an untraceable source, and arrange a meeting on the roof of his hotel."

The next day Chantelle walked into the lobby and entered the lift, as if visiting one of the delegates from the Convention. She got out at the middle floor, and once away from the security camera's view, activated her invisibility device.

From there she walked up several flights of stairs to the entrance to the roof, being sure to deactivate the automatic alarm on the door. She hid behind a water cooling structure,

Alain came out and looked nervously around. No-one in sight! He hesitated and was about to leave when he heard a quiet voice behind him.

"Don't be afraid or turn around. We're here to help."

Chantelle could hear agitated voices coming from the stairway, and immediately messaged the PVX hovering high above.

"Now Aldon! Now!"

She threw her arms around Alain and they beamed aboard the craft together. Andy was monitoring the area, and reported that two men, with guns drawn, were frantically searching the top of the hotel.

Aldon was sure these agents would check the hotel's security cameras. Once Chantelle was assured that Alain was safe, she beamed back into the hotel's corridor. She switched off her invisibility unit, and pretended to be leaving a client's room. After reaching the foyer, she mingled with the crowds before slowly departing.

Alain was startled to find himself aboard some kind of craft and asked what had happened.

Aldon reassured him. "Don't worry. We're the good guys. First we need to remove your tracking device, before we go anywhere."

Alain felt something cold pressing against his neck before he descended into nothingness.

Aldon and Andy removed and destroyed the implant. They knew they still had to be especially careful as to what Alain could see or know. He was somewhat of an unknown quantity. Who knew where his allegiances lay? Zadoc was on his way, but where to keep this scientist in the meantime? They had to avoid Earth Base or any of their agents' premises.

Aldon remembered his trawler captain who had already helped him out once before. A ship at sea seemed an ideal hiding place. He zoomed down over the waves, and hovered next to the boat.

"Sven! Can Andy come aboard with a fugitive who needs safe refuge?"

The burly seaman was pleased to see his old friend, and welcomed Andy and the drowsy scientist into the cabin. Aldon advised that he would be back soon, and whispered to Andy to keep Alain insensible until he returned.

Zadoc arrived a few hours later, and they revived Alain, who was totally confused as to where he was and how he got there.

"The most important thing is that, for the moment you are safe. Nobody will find you here. We need to know all about what happened back in your own country, and why those men were chasing you?"

Sven brought in some refreshments and left them alone to hold their meeting in the privacy of his quarters.

Alain explained that he lived under a very tyrannical regime. They had sent him to work in an experimental facility, which was situated in a very remote area. Although it was classified as a private company, Alain soon realised that it was really a military subsidiary developing some unspeakable weapons.

"There were always special government armed forces at the gates and patrolling the perimeter. There was no escape, and this trip to the Science Convention in the West was my only chance to get away."

He described what appeared to be scalar and electromagnetic devices, which he did not want to be involved with. They were holding innocent people captive, and using them as test subjects.

Alain hesitated. "You may not believe me, but at one stage I saw ugly alien looking beings in part of the underground facility. They had some metallic robots working alongside of them."

Alain became emotional and stumbled over his next words. "That was not the only crime. There is even worse. Another building housed some biologists and computer geeks. I was not allowed in there, but had to deliver a piece of equipment one day.

"I peeked into a couple of laboratories to see artificial figures – sort of a mixture between robots and clones. There were real humans – men, women and even little children, in glass tanks with tubes coming out. I think they were using them to make some form of phony people. I couldn't bear to ever go in there again. All I could think of was how to get away.

"One day, a long time ago, we saw a strange craft, just like those pictures of 'flying saucers', come out of a hidden building. It shot off into the sky and out of sight. I haven't seen any of those ugly aliens since. The metallic robots are still there, and seem to be in charge."

Zadoc and Aldon soon realised that the beings Alain was describing were the Xvars. It seemed that they had disappeared before their colleagues in Earth Base One's area fled the planet. But why?

Zadoc was feeling gloomy. "I thought we were rid of them when we demolished their other bases. Obviously there may be more we'll have to deal with."

Zadoc and Aldon realised that Alain would never be safe, no matter where he went. He told them that he had no family. His parents had been killed in an uprising, and he had never married.

Zadoc asked him if he would like to leave planet Earth, and work as an ethical scientist in another part of the galaxy. Alain didn't understand at first. Zadoc explained about their Terran integration.

"You have a choice. You can come away with us, or we can erase your memory of this meeting, and leave you in a place or country of your choosing."

Alain sat with his head in his hands, trying to absorb what he had just been told. Eventually he looked up.

"This is a future I could never have imagined in my wildest dreams. If I stay on Earth, my own people will hunt me down, no matter where I go. I must be mad, but accept your offer. Just promise me you will do something to put an end to the evil I have escaped."

Zadoc thought that the Xvars kept coming back like a bad dream. He felt uneasy about this situation. Something wasn't right. He needed to glean as much information as possible before deciding on a course of action. Prior to taking Alain back to Space Base, he activated his covert spy network to find out what was going on in this facility.

When he received the reports he was stunned. The situation was worse than he anticipated. He and Xandra visited Aldon and advised they were facing a potentially devastating threat.

"The Xvars were, as Alain told us, covertly working with that country's military doing illegal experiments and developing dangerous technology. They were careful, just like us, not to impart any knowledge to humans which would present a danger to themselves.

"The authoritarian government wanted more, and persuaded the aliens' very advanced robots to rebel against their masters. This foreign government imprisoned several Xvars, including the families of two who were stationed there. During the confusion one Xvar escaped in a craft to seek help, but unfortunately his ship crashed.

"Since then the robots seem to have taken charge, and have assisted in more serious technological advances. These mechanical morons are close to perfecting a new human/android clone, which will enable them to infiltrate the local population.

"The Xvar captives are being held at an internment camp, but we don't know where it is. It is only a matter of time before they are also sacrificed in further experiments to produce Xvar/android clones."

Aldon was flabbergasted. "Everybody knows that robots and androids must be designed with an artificial intelligence that obeys its controllers, and cannot be hijacked by anyone or anything else. What were the Xvars thinking when they built these ones? Did they inadvertently give them the extra cyber abilities to upgrade themselves, or was there a flaw in the manufacturing process?"

Zadoc didn't know the answers. His main concern was to destroy their opponent's facility, and the doubtful technology the human administrators were acquiring. An even more formidable danger was the possibility that the robots had learned to have power over their own creators.

Zadoc took Alain back to Space Base and then on to an urgent meeting with the Guardians. While any remaining Xvar presence on Earth was problematic, that was not the greatest concern. It was intergalactic consensus that no robot or android should be totally autonomous. If the intelligence was accurate these rogue machines must be totally annihilated before they left the confines of their current location.

The Space Council decided that they would conduct the operation themselves. Their elite special forces soon arrived at Solar Base to liaise with Zadoc and Xandra. Although the attack needed to be made without delay, it required careful planning.

Xandra was pessimistic. "That particular part of the Earth is very militaristic and has powerful defence systems. They have too many eyes in the sky for my liking. Penetrating their air space without being discovered will be no easy matter.

"We then have to access and destroy the entire base before they can raise the alarm. It will take split second co-ordination to corrupt their satellites and communication systems. Once we are on the ground we must simultaneously immobilize all the military in the facility and surrounding area. This operation is not going to be as easy as when we rescued our Terrans from that prison, which was not so secure or heavily guarded. This time, for various reasons, we cannot deploy our own robotic warriors and weapons."

Zadoc agreed, and insisted that regardless of the danger, every last piece of Xvar technology, including blueprints and digital records, must be destroyed.

"What about the robots?" Xandra asked.

Zadoc gave a disparaging snort. "If it were up to me I'd turn them into scrap metal. The Guardians want us to dismember at least two of them, so they pose no threat, and if possible bring the pieces back. They need to determine how they reached the stage of becoming rogue."

The raid was scheduled for the early hours of the morning, when very few personnel were on duty. The Space Force troops successfully evaded all warning systems and left the guards and employees immobile.

They entered the base, and were met by a large silver robot which was heavily armed. Several Space Force soldiers fell under its onslaught, and the remainder retreated behind the nearest corner.

"Nothing I've got seems to disrupt its circuits," one whispered, "and my weapons don't penetrate its outer casing. We have to think of something else. Perhaps we can reason with it?"

His colleague uttered a few choice expletives. "You must be joking!"

The officer in charge had a sudden inspiration. "What if we trip it up? No – don't look at me like that. It's not such a silly idea. I saw a huge axe and laser shears in a laboratory back there. We would have to work as a team, and hold it down just long enough to chop off its head. That should totally disable it!"

They ran back and grabbed the axe and shears. They could hear the robot pounding down the corridor as they strung a nearly invisible cable across the entry to the room.

The robot charged though the door, and temporarily lost its balance as its foot caught on the rope. The soldiers pounced, and struggled to restrain the powerful automation. Their commander, who was a giant of a man himself, needed all his strength to cut its head from the body.

He suffered several mild electric shocks as sparks flew from the severed wires and connections. As he sat back, trying to recover, he was startled to see the headless remains still moving, and emitting a squeaky metallic cry.

"Malfunction – malfunction!"

Its arms and legs were flailing as it tried to rise back up on its feet. The commander jumped up.

"Bloody hell! Do something quick!"

His men raced forward and started hacking off the arms and legs.

"Better secure all the parts away from each other," he advised. "I can't believe it. This machine seems to be trying to reconnect itself."

A second military unit joined them, and received instructions on how to disable the enemy. Before they could set off to find any remaining robots, they heard the sounds of a second one running up the corridor.

Had it been pre-warned? The commander realised that these machines may be in contact with each other, and ordered his men to hide behind a set of freestanding shelves which were heavily laden with equipment.

The metallic giant strode into the room, and as it bent over its companion the troops threw their combined weight behind the shelves which toppled onto it. The battle to render this second robot inoperative was just as difficult as the first.

They found the laboratory Alain had told them about, and confirmed his reports of captive humans, and experimental androids. Zadoc's orders were quite explicit. Everything, including the scientists, prisoners and records, had to be destroyed. Not a trace could be left for later redevelopment.

Time was of the essence before the local military realised something was amiss. They loaded the dismembered robots on board their craft and set the fuses.

They had just enough time to make a hurried departure. The terrifying explosion decimated the entire complex. It had all the devastating power of a nuclear detonation without the radiation.

Zadoc was pleased when Terran intelligence later reported that several governments in the world had accused the foreign power of testing some form of new weapon in contravention of an arms treaty agreement.

Robots which could go rogue were a danger to the entire galaxy. The Guardians were examining the remains of the captured machines to determine how they had acquired autonomy.

Humans were only at the beginning of developing artificial intelligence. Originally each computer was developed to excel in a particular narrowly defined area. Later computers, and then robots, were built to combine multiple skills in one unit.

More and more artificial intelligence was surpassing that of their human creators. It was strict policy throughout the galaxy that the advanced ethical and cognitive abilities of robots and androids must always be restricted. They must never be given free will or the ability to prevent themselves being decommissioned.

Of secondary importance was Alain's report of the internment camp holding Xvars and their families hostage. Xandra was charged with locating it, and taking the prisoners into custody. It was an important assignment which was going to take some time. He wondered about the missing Ibearns and his own Terran agents that he couldn't locate. Could they also be in that same internment camp?

CHAPTER 45

Chantelle's shower transporter contained several safety features, and it would not activate unless all her recognition factors were satisfied. Her assignment was a dangerous one, and Xandra was concerned, not only for her safety, but also that of Earth Base where she took her unwitting victims.

He arranged to meet with her to voice his concerns. "I've already told Aldon and Martina we suspect that before the Xvars and Katons left Earth, they implanted tracking and other devices in some of their human collaborators. While we can disrupt the signal from the carrier wave frequency, we cannot risk Earth Base being located, or your mission and wellbeing compromised by any transmissions.

"I've arranged for you to return to Solar Base with me for a few days. Zadoc and the Guardians need to meet with you and discuss your future assignments. While you are away our boffins will modify your transporter to prevent activation, and warn you if it recognises any alien signals. This will also tell us who, among your clients, is either an enemy associate or their unsuspecting pawn.

"You are very vulnerable, alone in that apartment, so we are also going to install an emergency alarm, which will connect with Earth Base."

Chantelle gave Xandra a mischievous grin. "Are you checking up on me? I didn't know you cared."

Before Chantelle left with Xandra for Solar Base, Martina took her to the side. "I think Xandra does care about you, but is hesitant to say something due to your distrust of all males."

Chantelle tried to shrug it off. "I like him too. He's different to other men. Be realistic, he wouldn't want any serious relationship with a glorified hooker."

Martina grabbed Chantelle's arm. "Don't run off! Xandra is a really nice guy. He doesn't look upon you as a high class escort. In all the conversations we've had he refers to you with the utmost respect – a fellow Terran military officer doing her duty.

"You've been demeaning yourself far too long. Just because, in the past, a couple of men treated you badly, that doesn't make you worthless. It reflects on their lack of moral character – not yours! If Xandra does try to start a relationship, promise me you will at least give him a chance."

"We'll see," Chantelle muttered as she left.

The trip back to Solar Base was relatively uneventful. Chantelle started to relax and enjoyed the one-on-one conversations with Xandra and the crew. She found herself slipping back into her military officer persona. Perhaps she had been on Earth a little too long.

They stopped over on Mars Base for a short interlude, and she was impressed with the additional modifications which had occurred since her last visit.

"Now is the time to take precautions. Better safe than sorry! It would be unwise to wait and see if the Xvars decide to invade." Pletta commented.

Zadoc was waiting for Chantelle at Solar Base, and once she had settled into her temporary quarters, she was ushered into a meeting with two representatives from the Galactic Council.

Their welcome was warm and respectful. They expressed their gratitude for the difficult, but essential assignment she had been performing on Earth. It had been central to the detection of Xvar and Katon facilities.

Chantelle was slightly overwhelmed when they presented her with a medal for service above and beyond the call of duty, and advised they were promoting her to a higher rank. She could not admit she had rather enjoyed her incognito position and the material benefits which came with the profession.

"We now wish to 'chop the head off' the enemy's support base," Zadoc said. "That requires concentrating on individual politicians, corporate executives and military officers. Are you up for that?"

"The male species can be unpredictable, but I'll do my best," Chantelle assured them.

During her short stay at Solar Base, Chantelle spent many hours with Xandra, and realised she had become rather fond of him. He had confided his love for his son Victor, and even though Tony and Gareth were in constant contact, asked her to keep an extra eye on him.

When Chantelle returned to Earth and her apartment, she confided in Martina. "I feel torn between her two separate identities – one as a Terran officer – the other as a 'for sale' high class escort."

Her new targets required cultivating various contacts and attending diverse functions and locations. Some military officers and corporate bosses did not appear to have any Xvar connection. These were transported to Earth Base for the regular Terran implant and dissolution of recent memory. When other customers triggered the Xvar sensor she merely treated them as a normal client, and notified Aldon as soon as they left.

Xandra had told her not to concern herself any further than that. They would deal with the traitors. She often felt guilty when she heard that some of these men had met with unfortunate ill-health or accidents. Others had been jailed on trumped-up charges.

Xandra was correct when he considered that her role came with a certain degree of vulnerability and danger. She always refused any clients with a predilection to bondage, violence or other similar perverted sexual activities.

The Terrans desperately wanted to negate the influence of one Xvar sponsored politician. He held a couple of influential positions on Defence Committees, and was always authorising huge amounts of government funds to be diverted to the Xvar infiltrated corporations.

Chantelle had managed to seduce him at a drunken party, and took him back to her apartment. He activated her Xvar sensor, so she concentrated on his weaknesses – there had to be one! Sure enough, in his drunken stupor he asked her to dress in a schoolgirl uniform. She felt disgusted when she reported it to Aldon.

"Some explicit photographs would discredit him, and wreck his political career," he told Martina, "but we can't risk Chantelle being identified."

A few nights later, the politician was drinking alone in his electorate headquarters. Martina and Ebony had raised their invisibility shields before entering the building. When they opened his office door, Ebony suddenly materialised. Her hair was in pigtails, and she was wearing a very short school uniform.

He became quite disorientated – torn between desire and commonsense. Ebony moved towards him and with a swift movement spread a small amount of aphrodisiac cream on his hand. He became consumed with erotic craving, and soon Martina had photographs of Ebony sitting on his knee, in his embrace, and worse.

As quickly as she had appeared, Ebony vanished into thin air, and joined the unseen Martina. The politician jumped up in astonishment. Where had she gone? He looked out of the door, but there was no-one to be seen in the corridor. He heaved a sigh of relief - it couldn't have been a set-up, that pretty little girl was totally alone.

A few days later the incriminating pictures were all over the digital media. Even though no-body was able to trace their origin, his political career and influence came to a crashing end.

Chantelle always knew that, no matter how careful she was, sooner or later she would encounter a dangerous and violent client.

She had entertained a company executive Raymond Soocha, and her sensors identified him as an Xvar underling. His sexual tastes bordered on domination. It wasn't a pleasant experience, and she was glad when he left.

"I wish we could have transported him to our base," Aldon told Chantelle later. "Don't have anything to do with him again! Xandra is looking forward to dealing with Raymond. He's a vicious bastard – one of the individuals responsible for those horrific human experiments below the facility Karine destroyed."

Chantelle certainly didn't want to see Raymond again, but one night her front door flew open, and he came barging in.

"Surprise – surprise!" he said leering at her. "My company can disable any security system. You and I have a little more business to attend to!"

Chantelle took a step backwards. "Go home, Raymond. You're drunk."

"I haven't got a home to go to. My wife threw me out. It's all the fault of whores like you!" He took a swing at Chantelle, and as she raised her arm to deflect the blow, kicked her in the abdomen, knocking her to the floor. She got to her feet, and ran for the hidden emergency button. He kept hitting out at her, trying to drag her back into his grasp.

As soon as the alarm sounded, Martina grabbed a weapon and jumped into the transporter. When she stepped out of Chantelle's shower recess, she could hear the fracas in the next room. Martina opened the door, and aimed at Raymond's chest with a full blast of her stun gun. He crumpled into a lifeless heap on the floor.

"Thanks, friend! Just in the nick of time." Chantelle said, pulling herself together and staring down at Raymond's limp form. "What now?"

Martina thought for a moment. "He's still alive. First we have to erase his memory. Because of his Xvar tracking implants, we have to make it look as if he left your apartment under his own steam.

"You are hurt, and need medical attention. Transport up to Earth Base, and I'll get Ebony down here to give me a hand." Chantelle was soon in Aldon's care and Ebony down in the apartment.

Martina had a plan. "Get him to his feet," she told Ebony, "and we'll walk him out of the building to his own car down the street. The normal security cameras cannot detect us if we use our invisibility shields."

Once they had placed the senseless Raymond into the driving seat, and closed the door, Aldon messaged them to let him take it from there. He was pleased the car was one of the new automatic pilot models, and could be operated by remote control.

As Ebony and Martina re-entered the building, they heard Raymond's car roar into life, and speed away up the road. Aldon steered it through the streets, and up a steep rise on the outskirts of town. When a traffic policeman gave chase on his motorbike, Aldon accelerated even more, and sent Raymond and his car hurtling over the edge.

Martina questioned the wisdom of Aldon's virtual execution of a defenceless Raymond. "Xandra won't be happy!"

Aldon wasn't in the least repentant. "This is war, and we have, as soldiers, both killed many of the enemy. He attacked Chantelle – that was excuse enough for me! Anyway, I really enjoyed doing that. The man was a monster, and Xandra was only keeping him alive to gather further intelligence."

Xandra wasn't happy, because Karine and some of his intelligence agents were still tracking Raymond. He said no more about it when he learned of the attack on Chantelle.

Earth Base tended to her bruises, and mended two broken ribs. Despite her assurances that she would be okay, Xandra insisted that she stay with Paul and Jacquita to recuperate.

There was a funeral for Raymond, and his wife shed the obligatory false tears. While his body was badly mangled from the accident, the company was still suspicious and quietly investigated his death. They traced his movements on that last night, and discovered, to their satisfaction, that he had been drinking heavily.

They checked the security cameras in Chantelle's apartment building, and could see he had entered and left of his own accord. While it was most probable that their boss had merely been driving drunk, and nobody else was involved, they decided to keep an eye on Chantelle and her activities. Something didn't seem 'quite right' about the high class callgirl.

Xandra visited the island a few days later. Chantelle was relaxing in the sun when he suddenly appeared carrying a large bunch of roses. She went to get up but he put his arms around her.

"No – you stay right there," he whispered and kissed her on the cheek. "You have gone beyond the call of duty in the Terran cause. No more! I never realised how much I cared for you until now."

Chantelle was momentarily lost for words. Her eyes met Xandra's and she found herself blushing as her own emotions started to surface.

She looked away and murmured, "What would you have me do?"

He knelt down in front of her. "I'm not speaking as your commanding officer, but as a man in love with a beautiful woman. Return to Solar Base and stay with me there as my wife."

Paul and Jacquita came out to invite Xandra to lunch, and stopped dead when they saw him holding a smiling Chantelle in his arms.

"Oh my goodness! I didn't expect that!" Paul exclaimed.

Xandra looked up. "Congratulate us — we're getting married. And I want you to perform the ceremony before she changes her mind!"

Chantelle had only one condition. She would sell her apartment, and buy a small holiday cottage on the island. Nobody would find her there, and it would be a good getaway for her and Xandra when they needed a break from the enclosed atmosphere of Solar Base.

Mary and Martina went with Chantelle to buy a wedding dress. She announced that she was also getting bridesmaids outfits for both of them. When they arrived back at the bookshop Victor couldn't help teasing Chantelle.

"I'm going to have a stepmother younger than I!"

Paul had the church ready within three days. It was filled with flowers, and the native children sang as the bride walked up the aisle.

It was all very sudden and unexpected. Victor was best man, and a stunned Gareth, Tasha, Tony, Michael and Angela were in the front pew. Aldon was obliged to stay in control at Earth Base, and had arranged an informal wedding reception in the lounge room later.

They were toasting the newly married couple when Zadoc and Pletta arrived with wedding gifts and their best wishes. They were both pleased to see two lonely colleagues find happiness with each other.

"What will you do when Xandra's tour of duty ends?" Pletta asked Chantelle.

"We're going back to Excelsior, his home planet. It might not be for a long time, at least not as long as we're fighting the Xvars."

Xandra put his arm around Victor's shoulder. "You know son, if ever you decide to marry your Mary, you can both come and stay with us on Excelsior. I have a big estate there, with plenty of room for us all – and who knows, maybe some little ones!"

CHAPTER 46

Zadoc and Xandra messaged Aldon that they were on the way to liaise with them regarding the crystal stone that the elderly veteran, Terry, had given to Gareth and Tony.

As Martina prepared for their arrival, she asked Aldon if he really believed the elderly man's story.

"I'm not sure," he said. "We are close to achieving time travel ourselves. It stands to reason that it will become a reality one day. If the old guy did meet someone from the future then we cannot brush the whole thing off as demented imaginings."

Zadoc told them that the Guardians and the Space Council also shared Aldon's opinion. This was not a matter they could afford to ignore.

"I am going to form an expeditionary party to visit the island and these 'standing stones'. There will be a couple of Terran soldiers along with Tony, Jacquita and Aldon. This could be dangerous, and I don't want to take anyone with a family. I will be in command, and Xandra's PVX and my ship will be standing guard and monitoring from above.

"Before we can do this we must determine their exact location. I'm afraid that old soldier was getting on a bit, and his memory and directions were a little vague."

Small surveillance drones spent several days searching, to no avail, above the dense tropical rain forest. They were starting to run out of options when Gareth suggested they try probing for residual Terran emanations.

"Surely there must be some traces present. It is the very same frequencies and vibrations which will supposedly activate the Time Traveller's message."

"Good idea!" Zadoc mumbled. He was a little miffed that he hadn't thought of that himself, especially when Gareth's suggestion proved successful, and the drones pinpointed a small area deep within the most impenetrable part of the jungle.

Zadoc gathered his party of five together, and the shuttle ship set off for the location where they beamed down into the thick undergrowth below. The whole area was covered with underbrush and vines, and they were just about to give up when Aldon noticed a lone man emerge from the jungle. He was obviously very old and dressed in shabby peasant type clothes. He smiled and pointed to the one side of the dense vegetation.

Aldon thought he must be one of the local villagers, and made his way over to speak to him. Suddenly he was 'gone', like he had vanished into thin air. He looked around and noticed a rock protruding from the bushes. It was one of the 'standing stones.'

"They're here....they're here," he called out.

Jacquita looked tentatively into the shrubbery. "There are always snakes in this kind of environment. I don't like snakes!"

They messaged Xandra to send down a robot and some mechanised gear to clear away all the vegetation. Snakes, which were easy enough to frighten away, were not their only obstacle. Several chimpanzees were watching from the trees, and chattering amongst themselves.

Suddenly one leapt upon the robot's head and peered into its visor. The android came to a dead halt, totally confused and devoid of vision. Three others bounded across, with one latching itself onto Tony's back.

Before he had time to react, it snatched his laser gun and jumped back onto the ground. There was a frantic scramble to grab hold of the mischievous creature before it could escape into the trees. It kept slipping from their grasp and was waving the weapon around, shrieking loudly to its comrades. Suddenly the firearm discharged, narrowly missing one of the soldiers. The chimp' dropped it in fright and fled into the bushes.

"Oh shit!" Zadoc yelled. "These little creatures are a total nuisance. Hold your ears everyone. I'll use a 'sound wave' to frighten them off. I just hope it doesn't attract anybody else in that village down the hill."

It took some time to complete the job, and the site was now as Terry had described; a clearing surrounded by several large blocks of stone.

One of the soldiers asked Zadoc what was so special about the stones, and how they worked. He explained that the stones were often located on the convergence of Earth's energy leylines. Each stone amplified and reacted to a certain frequency or vibration.

Zadoc and his five companions sat in a circle with the crystal in the middle. They held hands and concentrated, but nothing happened.

"Damn!" said Tony. "Well, the old geezer did say that it had to be at exactly midnight on Summer Solstice. That's a couple of days off. I suppose we'll have to come back."

On the night of the Solstice they returned, and quietly beamed back down into the jungle clearing. Darkness surrounded them, and as they stood together, holding hands, their small lights cast eerie shadows onto the crystal resting in the middle of the stone circle.

An unusual mist, accompanied by a gentle breeze, descended over them. One of the soldiers was looking over his shoulder. Disturbing noises were coming from the undergrowth.

"No distractions." Zadoc counselled. "Everybody concentrate, and sing our special Terran frequency song. Project your psychic abilities onto the crystal."

The mist and air began to circle around and above them, and the crystal started to glow and vibrate. They could sense a presence starting to evolve.

The crystal became brighter and brighter until a dazzling white beam shot out, high into the air. A holographic type figure seemed to manifest within the light. The Terrans shielded their eyes, and gazed in astonishment.

"I am no longer with you," the apparition said. "I have travelled through time, in the hope of changing an unfortunate future, which was originally caused by your existing civilizations, who are living in what is now our past.

"When I arrived there was a war being fought by humans, and I was unable to pass my message on to the right people due to suffering an injury which will prove fatal. I have recorded this in the hope you will hear my words before it is too late.

"My current cosmic society is fraught by war and violence, with many planets destroyed and billions of beings slaughtered. I am forbidden from altering the past by divulging specifics. You can help generate a different, more peaceful future. You need to put thoughts of revenge to the side, and show compassion, forgiveness and reconciliation to your enemies.

"If you heed my words, you will save later generations from a life of continual misery and hostilities, and my sacrifice will have been worthwhile."

Zadoc and Aldon desperately wanted more details, but the column of light and hazy figure quickly faded. The crystal had stopped glowing, reverting to an inanimate piece of rock.

Jacquita heard a movement in the bushes nearby, and the elderly man they had seen before stepped out. He smiled, and told them when he was a child he had come across the 'visitor', who was badly injured, and lying under a tree in the jungle. Before he died the man told him that he had left a message in his silver craft, which was in the clearing.

The peasant was too scared to enter the contraption, but had later seen a young soldier go inside. Not long after both the metallic ship and the body of its occupant had seemed to dematerialise, and just vanish into thin air. He was glad someone had received the message the stranger had given his life to deliver.

After they returned to Earth Base, Zadoc and Xandra discussed the significance of the message with Aldon.

Zadoc felt frustrated. "The information was both explicit and confusing. The Time Traveller didn't give any indication of when and where the particular events will occur. I have to brief Space Council soon.

"What do I tell them? Next time the Xvars and Katons attack we should just smile and invite them to dinner?"

Space Council listened carefully to the message, and agreed that it could not be dismissed. Everyone had to be mindful of the disastrous consequences of war and other hostilities. For the moment, they had to concentrate on one of their immediate priorities, which was to locate this alleged 'internment camp', holding extra-terrestrial prisoners, and located somewhere within Earth Base Two's area.

Zadoc brought Carol back. Since she had been second-in-charge of Earth Base Two it was hoped she may have a better idea of where the camp may be located. She was also familiar with the various governments, their languages and covert activities.

Carol didn't think such valuable, high profile detainees would be housed within the normal population of criminal and political prisoners.

She started with a process of elimination, and soon narrowed her search down to three possible locations. One in particular was situated in the middle of an isolated area, with more accommodation for guards and staff than inmates. Not only was it surrounded by a vast array of electronic shields and defences, there was no mention of its existence in any official government or military records.

"This certainly looks to be the most likely." Zadoc commented. "It's also going to be the most difficult to break into, and we don't even know if that's where our cosmic colleagues are being held."

He organised a secret meeting, under much more security than usual. They could not risk anyone even suspecting their plans, as this operation depended upon the element of surprise. It must be unexpected. There were several obstacles to overcome if they were to successfully rescue the alien captives.

Carol was tasked with launching a cyber attack on the local military, and also creating a false diversion in another part of the country. Zadoc, commanding the operation from his craft above, would initially immobilize all the facility's electronics before Xandra, Aldon, Karine and his troops disabled the guards and released the prisoners.

They were glad there was a heavy mist obscuring their presence when they quietly entered the internment compound. A couple of sentries were silently taken out. The rest of the guards and staff were asleep, and a harmless anaesthetic ensured they would not wake for several hours.

"So far – so good." Karine whispered. "Now to find the prisoners and whatever else is kept at this desolate place."

They accessed what appeared to be the detention centre, and entered a large central room which resembled a communal recreation area. There were several corridors and doors leading off, which they assumed must be the sleeping quarters.

The first contained three Ibearns, who were gently woken. They started up, obviously frightened. Xandra motioned to them to quietly accompany him into the larger room, from where they were quickly transported up to Zadoc's special 'containment' ship.

A Terran male, David, along with his wife, Beryl, and two children were located a bit further down the corridor. Carol confirmed that he was one of their missing agents, as were another man and woman in the next two rooms.

Xandra took them to the communal area and quietly questioned them about the facility. He learned that they had been captured several weeks before, and subject to intense and often brutal interrogation. David took Xandra outside and over to the centre's operations block, where they found their two main inquisitors still affected by the anaesthetic.

Xandra messaged Zadoc; "Beam these two up, and keep them under strict confinement. You can give them a taste of their own medicine when you get them back to Space Base!"

With David's help they destroyed all the records in the operations centre, and then headed back to the accommodation building.

Beryl indicated that she and the children also wanted to leave Earth and go away with David. They were a family, and there was no life or safety for them anywhere on the planet.

Xandra was about to make preparations for them all to leave when David asked, "What about the Xvars and Katons down the other corridor? We can't leave them behind."

"What Xvars and Katons?" Aldon growled. "Just leave them to me!"

He ran down the corridor with his gun on the ready. "They killed my family! Now it's payback time!"

Aldon burst through the first door, and turned on the light. An Xvar man and woman were cowering in the corner, trying to shield their three somewhat bedraggled children.

He aimed his weapon and then paused. One small boy, anticipating the worst, had his hands over his eyes. The entire family seemed to be petrified with fear. Aldon realised this was how his own wife and children must have felt before they were so cruelly slaughtered. How could he do the same to beings who probably had no part of it?

As he recalled the painful, suppressed memories, his whole body was racked with loud sobs and he lowered his weapon. The little Xvar girl, no more than three or four years old, ran over and hugged his leg. She looked up at him.

"Please don't cry. It makes me sad to see you cry!"

A concerned Xandra had raced up behind him. "I know how you feel, but don't do anything you may later regret. Remember the Time Traveller's words about compassion."

"No – no! I'm okay now," said Aldon, wiping the tears away from his eyes.

They ushered the family, along with a Katon and another two wild eyed and dishevelled Xvars into the common area. All the children greeted each other, and seemed to be on the best of terms.

"We are not enemies here." David said. "The wars our governments fight do not concern us. We have learned to get on together, and become friends."

Zadoc transported their enemies' people back to the 'containment' ship. Whilst they would be treated well, and were not essentially 'captives', he could not take any risks until they were all delivered safely to the Space Council.

Aldon was relaxing and enjoying a glass of wine and 'nibbles' with Martina. He had confided his reaction to the Xvar family and personnel in the internment camp, and she realised that the confrontation with his own memories and emotions had enabled him to find some peace at last.

She saw him reading a report, which had just been received, and asked; "What's the latest news from Solar Base and the Space Council?"

He smiled. "It's all good. The war with the Xvars and Katons is over! When everyone, including the Terrans, whom we rescued from the internment camp, arrived at Space Base they demanded to speak to the Guardians.

"They were very persuasive in their submission that we are all sentient, feeling beings who experience the same emotions and desire for happy, peaceful lives. In fact we have more in common than our differences. If they could co-exist harmoniously during their imprisonment, why couldn't the rest of us?

"An Xvar delegation arrived to conduct a prisoner swap, and soon engaged in peace talks. Concessions made by both sides eventuated in a permanent truce. These things happen when least expected!"

Aldon recalled the Time Traveller's words and wondered if that was what he meant. This new and welcome peace would not have occurred if he had succumbed to his vengeful impulses and killed the Xvar family.

Martina took another sip of her wine. "I guess we'll never know, only time will tell."

www.ingramcontent.com/pod-product-compliance
Lightning Source LLC
Chambersburg PA
CBHW070151120726
47909CB00001B/61